I.

Just step up to the bar and order, my friend! He's not going to bite. You might not think he'll understand, but believe me, he's not who he seems. His English is perfect, probably better than yours. You won't detect even the slightest accent. In fact, he speaks many languages like a native, though I happen to know he's self-taught. Yes, Spanish was his first language, but English was his second, and I know for a fact that he can speak Portuguese, French, Italian, German, and even Dutch, I think. He'll be able to communicate with just about anyone who walks in.

I'd suggest a fine, sipping tequila, or, if you prefer, a Mezcal, its less-noble cousin. But please don't order a frozen margarita. I know it's tempting, but we're not at the beach, after all. Any standard tequila blanco will do. Would you mind a suggestion? Yes, that's a perfectly good one. He has quite a variety, some of the very best. But I don't want to get too deep into the details, frankly. Believe me, he could go on for hours about it. Let's spare ourselves that kind of agony. See? There you go! Quick service. And with a smile. The consummate professional. Oh, really? By all means, sit. Join me at my table. Perhaps a toast is in order?

Isn't this place great? So open and airy. So well lit. Don't you just love atriums? With all the glass, and the geodesic design? These palm trees are just extraordinary. And the orchids. Have you ever seen anything like them? Stunning! Not a bad place to work. And not a bad place to hang out. Look at all the people. From all over the country, and the world. Whether they're here on vacation, or at a convention, or getting married, or just letting loose, we're all here in this bar together—which, for some reason or another, though we're in Las Vegas, the proprietor named Casablanca. I guess both are in the desert. It's not Rick's Café, but there is a theme, a certain vibe. And he's not Rick. But, like him, he's supremely comfortable in his environment. He's not from here originally, but by now, nobody'd be the wiser. He's just as comfortable here in America as he is in Mexico. He was born in Mexico City, but he can code-switch seamlessly. More bicultural than assimilated. He seems the same no matter where he is. He's very flexible. It's just the details that differ. I like people like that. I've worked with some pretty troublesome people, in the past. In difficult circumstances. So it's nice when what you see is what you get.

But I wouldn't necessarily assume his attentiveness and superior communication skills mean that he's not wary of strangers. Surely you must know that most bartenders have seen and heard a lot, and much of it isn't pretty. While you might want to volunteer some tidbit about yourself, or your life, or what you've experienced, you might notice he may be a little reticent to take the bait. A little suspiciousness is not a bad quality.

See that display case over there? Those items under the glass? I don't know if you can make it out, but there's an obvious void there. Something's missing. There used to be another object in there besides the champagne glasses, the bow tie, the brooch, and the cufflinks. Well, I happened to arrive here just after he set that up, and shortly before the missing piece disappeared. He sure

GIOVANNI MAC ÍOMHAIR

Descent of Man

Contents

Chapter I.	1
Chapter II.	14
Chapter III.	58
Chapter IV.	119
Chapter V.	193
Chapter VI.	227

seemed nervous about it. That's when you might've noticed that there's more to our bartender than meets the eye.

I mean, you can't blame the guy. I think we all need to be a little suspicious at times—including myself—despite my obvious sociability. I love to talk, and seem to attract people. I'll engage with anyone, but keep a respectful distance. When I lived in New York—New York City—if I stumbled upon an intriguing person, you'd be sure I'd start to dig. Whether I found dirt or not, I wouldn't necessarily hold it against them. Same now. Oh, yes. By all means. Let's have another. Now we're even. Isn't tequila wonderful? Doesn't it just make everything glow?

Will you be in Las Vegas long? Interesting town, don't you think? Intriguing! I left New York some time ago, but I certainly remember the electric atmosphere. The skyscrapers, and the hustle and bustle. A real piece of theatre. Where all the world's a stage. All the people straight from central casting. Millions of extras. I think every other person there is an actor—characters in their own personal drama—in search of either fame, fortune, or gossip, or some kind of glamor-filled life. I guess we shouldn't be too judgmental. It's not as if many of us aren't after the same thing. But when you look back on it, was it worth it?

People here are interesting in their own right. Not a lot of glamor, but plenty of glitz. But at a slower pace. What's everybody doing? You see those women over there? Each having a drink with a guy? What do you notice about those couples? They don't seem to match up, do they? Well, for each of those couples over there, there's another guy you don't see, waiting in the shadows. The guys who are making the real money. They live off these women like bloodsuckers. The couples at the table, in and of themselves, are actually having an honest transaction. They might be very needy, or in a little bit of denial, but they keep it clean otherwise. The bloodsuckers, however, might need to work a little harder, and do a bit of not-so-subtle persuading. Might need

3

to hire an enforcer, every once in a while, when the commissions fall short. Of course, they would never lower themselves and bloody their own hands unless they absolutely had to. But you have to acknowledge what they do, when they do it. You can't claim that the rest of us don't do our own type of dirty work. Not at all. But we do it more subtly and tastefully. Almost unconsciously, and imperceptibly. It's easy here, and very much encouraged. Just drag a body out to the desert and watch as the vultures slowly circle and finally descend. If they don't pick the bones clean, don't worry, the ants will. It'll get done, eventually. Another clean transaction, and so thoroughly satisfying.

Ah, here they are. Cheers! They'll just keep coming until we tell him to stop. Yes, he calls me 'Doctor'. No, I'm not a plastic surgeon, though there are tons of them around here. He likes to show a little respect, naturally, because I'm a good customer. I'm here almost every day. It's like an office. I was a psychiatrist at one time. But I left that all behind. Now, I act more like a witness. Or a confidant. Maybe even a guardian angel, if the occasion calls for it. Of course, on a small scale. Wouldn't want to be too much of a martyr, after all.

Let me introduce myself—I go by Clemens, that's all. No need for a first name. We're not going to get to know each other *that* well. But I'm glad to meet you, and even more delighted to serve you. Let me guess. You're here for a conference? Am I right? It's okay, you don't have to get into specifics. No one's going to hold it against you. You're just one out of the millions that come in and out of this city every year. But it might be wise, nevertheless, to hold your cards close to your chest. Let me guess again. Let's see. You seem almost as old as I am, just enough in the way of wrinkles and gray hair to prove that you've lived a little, experienced some things. I'd guess that's a tailored suit, too, and maybe even a manicure. Upper middle class? Yes, there's something more sophisticated about you, and you would acknowledge that, if only to yourself, because admitting it publicly might make you blush. But I feel as if you're already inclined to understand me, and that you're open to discourse. So I guess... Ah, never mind, it's not important. I'd guess that you're more or less the kind of person I'd like to talk to. That's even more important to me. That we're more or less the same sort of animal.

Let me ask you a question, if you don't mind. If you don't think it's too personal. Do you make a decent salary? A fairly decent amount? I mean, it's pretty obvious that you do. I'm guessing you make more money than you can spend. I imagine you give some of it away, or at least your company does. There's no problem giving money away here. No, in fact, people come from all over the world to squander it away. Gladly part with it, without the slightest illusion that they'll be getting anything back. Everyone knows the odds are entirely *not* in your favor. Everyone knows they'll *never* be. Yet that doesn't stop people from coming and giving tons of it away. Yes, they might have a nice meal and a drink before they part with their money, or see a good show afterwards. And the more adventurous types might indulge in a few lines of coke, and/or a quick romp with a hooker. But that's usually the only trade-off that happens. For most people, it seems well worth it. It has to be, or else it wouldn't happen in the first place. And keep happening. Are you game for that?

As far as I go, as far as my profession is concerned, your guess is as good as anyone else's. Had the bartender not already given you a not-so-subtle clue, you might have taken me for someone entirely different. With my physique and look, you might have guessed something more active. I wanted to be a baseball player when I was young, but that was just a childhood fantasy. Thank god I didn't go down that route. It's really a miserable business, even if you make it to the most elite level. You're nothing more than a glorified performing monkey. Always at the beck and call of an audience. But you can tell, in contrast to your average

5

gladiator, that I have a certain way with words, and a certain flair. Not to mention manners.

Did you drive here? Did you come from a nearby state? Did you notice any of the mountain ranges along the way? Some of the more temperate of them have alpaca. Not roaming free, but on ranges set into the foothills. They shear the animals for their fleece and make fabric from it. As you can see, my jacket is made from alpaca. It's not your run-of-the-mill, off-the-rack kind of garment. No! No prêt à porter for me. Custom fit is the only way to go, especially around here—subjected to this relentless and uncompromising air conditioning, in this icebox of a room. It's not bad to have a silk lining, either. Imagine, in the middle of the desert. In a place called Casablanca. Yet you can see with your own eyes, I'm a little stylish. But also well prepared and appropriately casual.

I think I finally know what I'm doing here, and I'm quite sure I know how to do it, yet I'm still not certain about you. I'm confiding in you, based mostly on your appearance. That might be a risky proposition, but don't let that fool you. I can do equally well in the trashiest of places, the most obvious of dives, and still be perfectly comfortable in the environment. But I prefer Casablanca, with its charming ersatz veneer. I like that ambiguity, the double nature of it. That's how I am. And how *everyone* is. Part spectator, part participant. These days, it's not a job, it's a vocation. People don't owe me anything, and I don't owe them. I don't need to earn any money, and I don't need to give any away. So, you see, we're all even in my eyes... Ah! Did you hear that? I think someone just won a jackpot. Certainly not the last one tonight. But just the right number of them, intermittently reinforced, to keep the slot machines cranking all night long.

Oh, is it time to go? Okay, then, time to settle up. It's been great to get to know you, however briefly. I hope you felt welcome here. You know, I'm here at Casablanca every night.

Any time you want to drop by is fine by me. Where are you headed? Well, actually, it might be time for me to call it a night, too. I'll tell you what, I happen to be headed the same way. My place is past yours. If you walk up the Strip with me, I'll just continue on from there. Better yet, let's just wind our way inside as far as we can. It's awfully hot out there today. We can just thread ourselves through the corridors inside the casinos to avoid all of the chaos out on the street. The sidewalks outside aren't good, at least around here. Unless you want to get tripped up and knock shoulders with everybody and their cousin, be harassed by hundreds of street vendors, or asphyxiated by the exhaust of a fleet of idling tour busses. In Paris, you might inadvertently step in dog shit. Here, it's melted ice cream and chewing gum. Nothing like scraping those off the sole of your shoe.

We have to walk north, through the passageways that bisect all the buildings. They're all lined up perfectly. You can walk for miles like this. Just every now and again, you might have to go outside to cross a street, or hop onto a skywalk. But don't worry. You'll be thoroughly entertained along the way. There'll be so many opportunities for impulse buying that your head'll spin. It's like a mall within a mall, with all the stores lined up on top of each other. Too bad they don't have moving sidewalks, like at the airport, so your feet don't get sore. Come, follow me! I know the way. It's awfully confusing for the average tourist, but the trail starts over there, in that corner. You'd never know it, would you? Every corner seems isolated, and almost identical. I think they do it on purpose. It's so easy to get lost and turned around here.

We'll go north toward Old Vegas. You know, the old Rat Pack Vegas of the fifties. What Vegas used to be before they built this magic kingdom. It was a simpler place and a simpler time. Sure, there was the same glitz, and the same neon, but on a much more modest scale. It held a certain charm and innocence. Much less of the crass commercialism you see here today. Then again, the mob

7

had a little more influence back then. It was a little more in-your-face and obvious. You'd've had to keep your nose clean, that's for sure, or you might've found yourself in heaps of trouble. Not so much today. They've pretty much gone full-on legit. You can tell by the easy-going attitude of the people—like our friend, the barkeep.

You know, in Old Vegas, there used to be mobsters everywhere. I've heard stories about them from my landlord. They used to have hangouts where the condominiums are now. Back then, if you crossed the mob, they'd take care of you. There were lots of guys who owed them money, and were late with the payments. Guess what the bosses did? Just like in the movies, they'd give you the option of which finger you'd want chopped off. In the end, though, it didn't matter—because if the loan wasn't squared up when it came due, you'd be summarily chopped to pieces! They weren't playing back then. Even now, when I walk the streets of my neighborhood, I tread lightly. Where your hotel is, in the new part of town, there's really no need to resort to any kind of violence. The bosses today are merely dubious businessmen, whose main occupation is to reel in more chips, and stack them ever higher. The only weapons they sling are the power of money and corruption, and eminent domain. But there are some who still view them as latter-day heroes. It's all about getting the job done, no matter what the personal price or level of humiliation. Just doll it up with some bells and whistles, and impress the people with your shameless swagger. Everyone loves a winner!

No! No, thank you! Leave us alone! We don't need any of your junk today. Neither does anyone else! These hustlers are like swarms of bees, aren't they? You'd think by this time of night they'd be tired of peddling their garbage. But thank god for the tequila, the only light in this sordid darkness. Isn't it wonderful to weave your way through here as if you're shielded from everyone by a thick blue alcoholic haze?

Then again, wouldn't it be preferable to finally go outside and walk on empty sidewalks mile after mile? Perhaps light up a fine cigar. Like on a cool, clear winter evening? Musing about this or that. Ah, never mind. Fat chance. There goes my imagination again. It just runs on and on. I don't want to overwhelm you with it. Let's just refocus, get back to square one, and simply be in the moment. Despite everything, there's still something intriguing about this place. With the hotels, the casinos, the nightlife—and, of course, the gambling. All churning along smoothly in this desolate, desert plain. The sun beating down through the rarefied air. The pavement like a frying pan. An utter contradiction!

Yet we're making good progress along our little corridor—passing all the fabulous stalls selling such useless things, such dead things, as if we're glancing at the dusty dioramas of an old, dilapidated museum. They make these trinkets for pennies on the dollar—and just as quickly as we buy them, we discard them. It's like we're marching in place, trudging along in a dream that might not end, while everything useless passes us by. Imagine how these peddlers enrich themselves penny by penny. Thousands of us walk by each day. And you can be sure that, like moths to a flame, their knickknacks are impossible to resist: T-shirts of every stripe and color, key chains, refrigerator magnets, shot glasses, playing cards, poker chips, dice. No need for carnival barkers here. We're more than happy to throw gobs of good money their way, just to remind ourselves later, when we're back home, how good life really is. Note how every swipe of the credit card and every ring of the cash register adds up, and contributes to a sizable down payment for them on a McMansion in the suburbs.

Ever notice how easy it is to spend money when you have a few drinks under your belt? How deep your pockets can be when the opportunity presents itself? It's fortunate for you that we've made it through without stopping, even once, despite the lure of the neon signs... Just step out those double doors in front of you.

9

This is the end of the line. A quick left down the alley outside, followed by an immediate right, and we'll soon be right on the Strip.

It kind of hits you like a hammer, but try not to wake up quite yet. Even if it feels like a nightmare. There are even more people out here—in lockstep, like an invading army. Look at all the stores! And all these talented street performers funneling you toward them. It's really high-end, high-class stuff. We're talking platinum and diamonds. With this kind of profit margin, you'll easily afford that McMansion, but with a really swank in-ground pool in the backyard. Maybe even own a private jet!

It's funny how Las Vegas, as a whole, always reminds me of a giant airport. You've got the runway right here, straight down the Strip, and the glow from the storefronts acting as approach lights. The hotels and casinos are like the terminals. And the beacon, the one sitting atop the control tower, the lure that pulls everyone in from all over the world, is the fantasy of winning that big prize— one that will make you so rich that you'll never have to work another day. Everything else you see here wouldn't exist if it weren't for that.

Remember the old Dutch East India Company? That good old-fashioned colonial goose that laid all of those golden eggs? People still look back on those days with a certain amount of nostalgia. It seemed so romantic. The grand schemes of the capitols of Europe. Watching their treasuries grow with no bound. Dispatching merchant ships and navies to the four corners of the world: Java, Japan, Taiwan, Malaysia, Ceylon, Mauritius. Any place where vast amounts of natural resources could be harvested, processed, packaged and exported with deadly efficiency and ease. Stolen wealth appearing as if out of thin air. It was literally like money growing on trees. But set in exotic locations and tropical paradises. You had 'The Silk Road' and 'The Spice Routes'. Doesn't that sound nice? One if by land, two if by sea! I can almost imagine the thieves wearing expensive robes, sprawled on chaise lounges, sipping tea. The truth was, they felt it was their god-given right to steal; that they were entitled to take whatever they wanted with impunity; and they had the unmitigated gall to simply seize it, from right under the noses of the natives, at the barrel of a gun. An honest trade, they'd say, with fringe benefits, for whoever wanted it. We'll take everything they have, destroy their habitat, and leave them hungry and starving, dying of foreign diseases and plagues. And they'll thank us for it.

Did you notice the same here? Oh, I'm sorry, did I step on your foot? Please excuse my clumsiness. Are you seeing it now, through the haze of the tequila? I know it's hard to concentrate with the dazzle of the neon lights and the distraction of the entertainers. It's enough to make you dizzy. But it's all a dream, too. Except, in this case, we're exploiting and colonizing ourselves. All night and day. Accepting it voluntarily, even wholeheartedly. There's no end to the river of people entering our modern-day holy sites. The casinos'll suck you in. Pull on you, like the Sirens, toward the rocks. Pilgrims come from all over the country. And the world. Have you ever noticed how there's a direct flight to Vegas from just about any locale in the United States, no matter how small? Including charters. Through all the great airport hubs, it's only slightly more difficult to get here from just about anywhere else in the world. Have you ever noticed how precisely McCarran's runways are lined up with the Strip? Just a few degrees difference. It's almost as if they could just deploy your plane's emergency chutes and dump you straight into the casinos. Like a colossal off-ramp.

Yet, nobody's *forcing* you to come... They do want you to feel at home, though. Give you something familiar to hold on to. Just look at the names of the establishments: there's New York-New York, Paris, Rio. Fun places to be, but also great places to visit. Still others that remind you of more fabulous settings: Bellagio and

Tuscany; Luxor, Sahara, and Mandalay Bay. So romantic and exotic. But all in one place. A self-inflicted brand of colonialism —but inverted, you see. That's exactly what's going on here in Las Vegas. People come from all over the world to part with their money, yet you can't quite seriously claim that they've been flat-out exploited. They're coming here—whether they realize it or not —by their own free-will. That's the beauty of the system. Those who are the most desperate to win the big jackpot, but who are also among the most economically vulnerable. With the greatest hopes, they try so desperately to succeed. They just can't help failing, though, in the end. It's literally built into the system. They can't avoid shooting themselves in the foot every single time.

Well, maybe I'm getting a little carried away. But what you *can't* deny is that Las Vegas has become the template and prototype for the rest of the world. It has replicated itself an untold number of times, like a virus. Did you notice—at one time—that there were casinos popping up just about everywhere? In every state, city, and small town? Even on the Indian reservations. There's a certain poetic justice to that though, I admit. Like Montezuma's revenge. But a winner's a winner! It's like there are little fiendish hives buzzing everywhere. Scattered across the globe. But Vegas is the queen, the greatest colony of them all. It might be a little tacky and distasteful, and in the middle of nowhere, but it's still hard to resist. Just about anyone who's anybody will find themselves here, eventually. They might not understand why, but that's the mystery of it. It's obscure by nature. Ah, but you knew that! You're a sensitive man. There's really no competition, no other place or strategy to aspire to. We don't want to get caught up in that old-style, authoritarian brand of exploitation. That dark, sticky, Orwellian kind of muck. We prefer the clean, anaesthetized, pleasure-seeking, Brave New World aesthetic, the kind Huxley warned us about. They'll gently persuade and seduce you. The world will come freely, to the very heart of the machine. And like you, some will wander into Casablanca, this dear old watering hole! My little slice of paradise. Where I await.

Well, this is where we part ways, my friend. No, I can't continue on with you. If you just continue down that way, you'll find your hotel. I need to get off the Strip now. This is where it thins out a bit, and there are these wide-open, empty spaces that give me the creeps. I never cross through them. I walk around them. They make me feel so vulnerable and exposed. You can never be sure what might happen. I guess I could just sprint through them, but I'm afraid I might freeze halfway. Who knows, I might even catch a draft. But I've still got to get home somehow, despite my superstitions, no matter how much it nags at me and makes me feel uncomfortable and ridiculous. I'll make my way right through the canyon of buildings over there, as usual. Thank god for them. Anyway, good night, Sir.

Oh, those women over there? Strolling toward your hotel? Who do you *think* they are? Don't be shy. They might just treat you to a wonderful fantasy, if the price is right. Imagine yourself in Bali, among the beaches, the batik, the gamelan, and the shadow play. Immerse yourself in that fantasy. Smell the sweet aroma of the grass and the sea. It'll be worth the trip.

II.

Ah, so you're back! You've decided to have another session with me. To sit here with me and continue to bear witness. You never know what might come of it. From day to day, *I* don't even know what might happen, but that's precisely why I'm here. To find out. Maybe I should explain to you what I mean by that.

You see, many years ago, I was a psychiatrist in New York City with a fairly high profile and a thriving practice. You know I didn't give you my real name, right? I *can't* tell you who I really am. And everything I say here should be taken in absolute confidence. Strictly speaking, I really shouldn't be telling you any of this. But it's okay, because I'm very good at disguising the facts, so that you'll never figure out who I am or who any of my patients were.

I specialized in the most hopeless and complex cases. A real do-gooder. In contrast to most of my colleagues, I wasn't the type of psychiatrist who spent most of their hours writing prescriptions. You know the type: a patient every fifteen minutes, a few key questions, sending them out the door with a handful of scripts, and

14

that'll be four hundred bucks please.   No, perhaps some very targeted pharmaceutical intervention—but mostly talk therapy, believe it or not.   Good, old-fashioned psychotherapy, at reasonable rates. Often, at no charge at all. Except to the taxpayer. I don't mean that as a disparagement. The system can actually work pretty well for some, despite what you might have heard. It *can* be efficient, given the immense nature of the challenge.

My meat and potatoes were the sickest of the sick—people with schizophrenia, psychosis, bipolar disorder, major depression, borderline personality disorder—the deep end of the spectrum. Many of my patients had multiple diagnoses, and often had substance abuse issues layered on top.   Can you imagine what that's like?   It's like one of those Whack-A-Mole games.   Once you manage to knock one out right in front of you, another one of those little rascals pops up five feet away. Just barely out of reach. But that's alright, because I had other people to help out with everything other than the therapy. They'd take care of all of that— the more mechanical or mundane parts—and leave the heart of the matter for me.

There's a certain art to the practice of psychotherapy. I say that because there's a misconception amongst the general public that effective therapy is primarily a consequence of good technique, or other components that are based on objective scientific knowledge. But the truth of the matter is that the most effective means of helping a patient is by simply building rapport. Rapport accounts for the vast majority of positive results, believe it or not. All of the research very clearly supports that. As a counterexample, I had a mentor who was from the 'tough love' school of therapy. He had a bipolar patient whose hygiene was highly questionable. There was no doubt that he hadn't bothered to bathe or wash his clothes for some time.   But instead of inquiring about it and gently encouraging him to change his hygienic practices, if only for selfish reasons, my mentor felt the necessity to shame and humiliate him. His only intervention was to walk straight up to him, take a few exaggerated sniffs of the air, screw up his face, and exclaim, 'You stink!' Not the best approach. Not the best results either, as you can imagine.

On the other hand, I had a patient who was *floridly* psychotic, who was suffering from severe postpartum depression. She had just had her second child, and was bathing her children when she suddenly felt the compulsion to drown both of them in the bathtub. Luckily, her husband had just come home from work and caught her in the act before it was too late. She was immediately committed to the psych unit and placed in lockdown, where she began to stare at the walls and talk to them as if they were people. She ran her fingernails violently down the walls—screeching like chalkboards—wearing her fingertips down to the point of bleeding. When she had to use the bathroom, she didn't use the toilet. She preferred shitting in the wastebasket. I mean, this woman was *completely* gone. More like an animal than a human, despite the fact that she happened to be a very striking and beautiful young woman. She was originally from Africa, and spoke very little English. She spoke a language that was so obscure that I don't even recall its name. We couldn't even find a translator to help us out. Of course, the first line of attack, predictably, when she was admitted, was to try to medicate her out of her psychosis, which only made it worse. By the time I got to her, the only thing I attempted to do, at first, was to sit with her for a while. To try to act as a stabilizing presence, to start to get a feeling for what might work. I didn't have any good ideas, admittedly. I couldn't even communicate with her. But what I did notice, eventually, was that when her husband or other relatives came to visit, there would be a marked improvement in her behavior. As soon as they arrived, and started speaking with her in their native language, and eating their native food together, she began to act almost normally. You would've never known otherwise. So ultimately, that was the preferred treatment.   Lock, stock, and barrel!   Within a mere couple of weeks, she was discharged as if nothing unusual had happened.   When she left, her behavior was completely normal and remained that way.   No different than you or me.   The whole incident taught me something very valuable, and forced me to feel a certain amount of healthy contempt for my profession.   I can tell you so many stories just like these, but you get the idea.   I really began to wonder if we, the professional staff, were even necessary, or helpful.   But a job's a job, after all!

There was something deeply satisfying about working with people who society has decided to discard.   Let's face it—just about anything I did helped.   Therefore, in a sense, my patients could only get better.   That was more than enough to keep me going.   On the other hand, years later, there was a time when I worked solely in private practice.   Mostly soothing the superficial wounds of the highly neurotic, although we've been told not to use that term anymore.   For example, I used to do some couples counseling.   Unsurprisingly, most couples come to therapy hoping to save their relationship, or what is left of it.   By definition.   But what they don't realize is that by the time they ask me for help, nine out of ten times it's already over.   Too late.   If they're straight couples, it was usually the woman who had to beg the man to attend therapy, and he'd typically come kicking and screaming into the first session.   Then you almost always find out that the man, predictably, lies at the root of most of the problems.   Almost without exception.   If he's not a complete jerk, he's been beating on her for years, either literally or by some other means of abuse. The better she's treated him, the worse he treats her.   It's like a battle to the death between the male ego and the female nurturer. In my opinion—after those kinds of experiences with couples counseling—the earlier women put an end to it, the better.   My job was mostly to accelerate the process.   When it's finally time to leave, do so decisively.   Keep the sword safely tucked away in the scabbard. Pull the gun straight out of the holster and aim for the heart.

I didn't last very long in the couples therapy business, as you can imagine. People usually terminated before I could really get started anyway. They never seemed to truly want to work on it. They just wanted to get credit for appearing as if they did, and then bail at an opportune time. No, give me back my hopeless cases. They really seemed to appreciate what I had to offer. And, they were so much more interesting than the others. And often talented individuals, on top of it. They have a certain way of looking at things. From interesting angles. As if they can get to the bottom of things, to the truth of things, with fewer distractions, and more perceptively than the rest of us. At the very least, you knew you'd never be bored.

The trickiest part of working in the mental healthcare field is to avoid the pitfalls of whatever institution you happen to be working in. You need to work around a lot of people, but also keep a low profile, particularly if your results stand out. Too much of a good thing, in this domain, is *not* a good thing. If you get your patients out the door with the least amount of damage, I'd call it a resounding victory and success. At the same time, despite assurances of advancement and upward mobility, job promotions are to be avoided at all costs. Once, they even wanted to present me with an award. But I, wisely, wanted nothing to do with it. They were going to honor me in the company of my colleagues, but I purposely called in sick that day. I did find a lovely plaque, framed in a beautiful hardwood, commemorating the event, in my mailbox a few weeks later. But after I retrieved it, and recognized what it was, I quickly tossed it into the nearest trash can. It wasn't smart to keep that kind of incriminating evidence around. The only reward that really gave me any kind of gratification was providing excellent services at reasonable prices. The lower the better. Better yet, free! But I made a good salary. I didn't need much, after that. It was good enough.

If I've given you the impression that I didn't like my work, that would be misleading. I actually got a deep sense of satisfaction from it. I just didn't like my bosses, typically, or the overall system. I would routinely go well beyond the call of duty for my patients, however. Do things that other practitioners wouldn't do. But that's not to say I was a martyr. I worked a pretty standard schedule. Five days a week, eight hours a day. Nothing more, nothing less. I think my patients liked me and trusted me. I think they felt satisfied with the services I rendered. But there was a limit to how far I'd go in terms of work/life balance. If it was a Sunday, you could be sure I'd be out on my boat fishing. Happily taking in the ambiance and scenery. I needed to have a part of my life that was only for me—because without that, my work and sanity would've surely suffered. I also wouldn't go out of my way to help people in the course of my personal life, or volunteer within the greater community, unless it was absolutely necessary. But, if a chance presented itself and the reward was high—and the price not too dear—I'd be happy to oblige, although I might hesitate to be the first in line. For example, if someone became lost and asked for directions, it was a matter of pride for me not only to provide directions, but to be rather detailed and precise in their presentation. If someone was begging for spare change, and I couldn't avoid the unpleasant feeling of passing them by, I might just go all out and invite them for a meal, rather than plunking some spare change down in their paper cup. I wasn't likely to be judgmental, either way. If they wanted to use what I gave them to go grab a fifth of cheap whiskey, I figured they knew what was best for them, better than me.

I'd say I take a rather neutral position as a civilian. I try not to feel superior to anyone. I try to imagine myself as the sort of character that blends into one's surroundings, like a doorman, or a

19

maître d'. Discretion is the key. Although I have manners and tact, I wouldn't say that I utilize them quite like a diplomat, or an ambassador. Sure, I'm friendly, even chivalrous to a degree, but my main goal is to be useful and of service. The only exception to that rule is women. I'll go out of my way for an attractive woman, gladly opening doors or giving up a seat. Don't you? I'd be lying if I didn't admit that I get a lot of pleasure from that.

I also get a lot of pleasure from being generous, but not in the way that you might think. There are many ways of giving—so many opportunities to pitch in—it makes your head spin. Just look at all the philanthropists out there, and all the do-gooder organizations that are constantly hounding you for money. And the corporations that set up foundations and give money away like candy. You would think that we live in some sort of utopia, where people can stop working for a living and just pick freely from these money trees whenever they feel the need to. But unfortunately, for every dollar that's collected and given away, it's pennies on the dollar for the people who really need it. Meanwhile, the executives and managers who run these so-called nonprofits, or their more disguised stepchildren, not-for-profits, live very well off the welfare and fat of their donors. Corporations give only a pittance of their wealth away—mostly as cover for their wide-ranging malfeasance. And leverage their charitable foundations mostly for the purpose of generating self-serving, favorable spin. With such sophisticated and subliminal campaigns that they fool even the most cynical of their opponents, who otherwise would naturally advocate against them. You know the types, the venerable names from the past—the Rockefellers, the Carnegies, the Vanderbilts—the old robber barons from the turn of the century, and all their descendants. Winners are winners, they say! We've got the same types today, only with less recognizable names or titles. The titans of tech. Just give them a little time to catch up. They have vast technological resources at their disposal, and monopolize the colossal bandwidth with which they disseminate their propaganda. You ain't seen nothing yet! Everyone just *loves* a good brand name.

I never give any amount of money to any of these folks. I know it won't do any kind of good, even remotely. In fact, I sort of assume it will actually do more harm than you can even imagine. If I ever do donate money, I do it directly. Literally right into the pocket of whoever needs it, whether it's a small or larger amount. As I said, I figure if they need it so badly, they're as competent as anyone to know how best to use it. But that attitude even seems to fall short for me. It seems a little too easy to just throw money at a problem. What people really need, what's most precious, is your time and energy; direct action, whether that amounts to real physical action, or just being present for moral support. That alone makes a real difference. Don't let anyone tell you otherwise. The rewards are intrinsic, and the benefits manifest and undeniable.

I can't tell you how satisfying it is to perform these sorts of acts of kindness, even if they happen to present themselves completely randomly. And the more anonymously I can carry them out, the better. I can recall a patient who was in the most desperate situation at the psychiatric hospital I mentioned previously. He was a young man who had had a serious drug habit. It appeared that as soon as he got himself hooked on heroin, his life, predictably, went to shambles. I wasn't completely sure if he was suffering from any other concurrent mental health issues, and he wasn't even assigned to the ward that I was responsible for. But I just happened to be walking through his ward when he approached me with his tale of woe. He was quite clearly in the throes of withdrawal, in an unbearable amount of pain and discomfort. You could literally see the desperation in his eyes. He pleaded with me for help. He told me that he had been in the ward for several days and had still not been seen by any professional who could offer him some real relief. He would approach the doctors, the social workers, and the substance abuse counselors for assistance, but was blatantly ignored. They would just pretend they didn't hear him and walk by without so much as a hesitation in their step.

When he approached me, he did so respectfully, despite the prior maltreatment. He stated his problem very clearly and succinctly with very little in the way of bitter commentary, or self-pity. He told me about his circumstances and how he was rapidly approaching the point where he couldn't take it anymore. If he couldn't get relief somehow, some way, right away, he would be forced to take extreme action, either through grievous self-harm, or worse, to put an end to the suffering by suicide. It wouldn't have been the first time someone attempted suicide there, so it wasn't an empty threat, by any means.

And his situation was not unique. It turned out that almost every patient on the ward felt the same way, for the same reason. They all needed to be given an opioid antagonist, and there were only two psychiatrists on staff who had the necessary credentials to prescribe it. One was the head of psychiatry, who was sufficiently competent and always at the hospital, but never available because he was too busy attending meetings called by the administration. The other was a real sadist: her excuse was always predicated on the principle that the patient was invariably 'drug-seeking'. That they wanted the drug in a manipulative way to feed their own addiction, rather than for therapeutic purposes. Notice that they don't call it 'medication-seeking'—that would make too much sense. Because that, in all honesty, is what it seemed like to me. If they needed a medicine that could help, by all means, prescribe it. But I couldn't. I didn't have the clearance to. The Feds decided that only a certain number of doctors were to be trusted with this drug, and in order to pass muster, you had to go through ridiculous extremes to prove you were worthy of this privilege. So, my only option to help this young man, in a timely manner, was to somehow compel my resistant female colleague to write the prescription.

Unfortunately, she and I had had some very unpleasant history between us, in the not-too-distant past. To make a long story short, one of my supervisees came to me one day and told me that this same psychiatrist had falsified clinical notes in a patient's chart to make it seem as if she had had the required consultations with her patient, when she hadn't. The supervisee reported it to me and wanted some guidance on how to handle it. Of course, as a mentor, I reflected the question back to her, and she wondered what kind of mechanism was in place to deal with it, and who was responsible for follow through. I told her that I was ultimately responsible for it because I was her supervisor, but that it wouldn't be unreasonable for her to take action herself, if she chose to. That it might be an excellent learning experience for her. Without much hesitation, and because she was such a gifted, principled physician already, she decided to report it herself to the aforementioned head of psychiatry. The good news for my supervisee was that, as a student, she was not technically considered an employee of the hospital, so the likelihood that there could be any repercussion for her was seemingly quite low. On the other hand, it didn't take a genius for my delinquent colleague to figure out that I had probably had a hand in her eventual reprimand. So, asking for a favor from her wasn't really in the cards. But, luckily for me, I knew a way around it. I had a very powerful ally in the substance abuse clinic who, I had no doubt, could provide the leverage to get this young man the medicine he was entitled to.

For whatever reason, when I first started at the hospital, this substance abuse counselor, Bob, I think, conducted the orientation for all new employees of the hospital, regardless of their rank. He was very charismatic and skilled at what he did. But, during the course of the orientation, when he got to the part where ethical standards were discussed, the part of the program that guided us on

23

how we were to conduct ourselves in this new environment, he used some of his own life experience, as a case-in-point, to drive home the lessons. It turned out that Bob himself had had a previous history with drug abuse, years past. He was raised in extremely poor economic conditions with few resources, with little support, and found himself, like many others do, operating within an alternate economy to survive, which ultimately led to his own drug addiction and fateful, downward spiral. When he hit rock bottom, instead of admitting that he had a problem and needed help, he and a buddy decided a better plan would be to rob an armored car instead. They thought having a lot of money would suddenly fix everything. And they were *almost* right. They pulled it off!

They held an armored vehicle up at gunpoint, stole millions of dollars in cold, hard cash, and moved to Montana without having to fire a shot. It was done seamlessly. They left no clues and the police had nothing to work with. Once they fled to Montana, they invested some of the money into a hotel, a fancy resort that quickly grew into an empire. From the outside, their operation looked legit. They made even more money, on top of the money they had already had, because the resort was actually operating as a de facto casino, on the sly. They generated riches that they could have never imagined. Because they were on the run, their success could've attracted a little too much attention. So they laundered a good amount of their proceeds, and actually buried some of the rest of it, in cash, in the middle of the desert somewhere.

But the dream didn't last forever. Eventually the IRS caught up with them—Al Capone style—and they were eventually linked back to the original robbery back home. It didn't take too much arm-twisting to connect the dots, and after a quick prosecution and trial, Bob found himself in the slammer—potentially for a good long time. But, being the resourceful man that he was, he did manage to strike a good plea bargain with the prosecutors, which meant that a whole bunch of other bigger fish also went to jail, while his sentence was ultimately reduced. I think after about five years in jail, he was released and determined to repent for his sins. He wanted to start a new life that was legit and based on new, sound, moral principles.

And what better profession to get into than the one that was associated with what got him into so much trouble! Except flipped. Now, *he'd* be helping others with *their* drug problems, before they even had the remotest possibility of getting into anywhere near the sort of trouble he got into. There was a certain beauty to it, and grace—a delectable kind of sublimation going on. The absurdity of it seemed to have motivated him to succeed, to thrive as a substance abuse counselor.

So, on that day, with that young man presenting the conundrum he was in, it only made sense for me to reach out to Bob, to gently persuade—read, force by intimidation—my psychiatrist colleague to do the right thing. Write that prescription, or else! She had been to that same orientation as the rest of us, and had heard the same scary Bob story. I think Bob even insinuated that he had had to 'sideline' more than a few people along the way, to ensure the integrity of his operation. Not to mention the biker image he projected, with the handlebar mustache, leather jacket, tattoos, and piercings all over his body. In the end, by his mere presence, the intimidation factor alone, the script was written and dispensed within a matter of minutes.

It was very gratifying to see the dramatic emotional transition that this desperate young man made—in a matter of hours—from utter desperation to relative calm and composure. It was like he was a different person altogether. He must have felt like the luckiest person alive. He must have wondered how things had changed so quickly. After some investigation into it, he managed to put two and two together, and realized that I had had some hand in it. So the next time I entered the ward, a few hours later, he ran right up to me and thanked me profusely for getting him through the crisis. I told him it was nothing. Anyone would have done such a thing, or at least should've. It wasn't necessary to overemphasize what I had done, or to make a big deal out of it. That, in my opinion, would have been playing into the dysfunction. I accepted his thanks as humbly as I could and moved on, somewhat embarrassed by the acknowledgement.

But then I remembered later that the whole ward was full of patients that were in the exact same position as he had been in, and they were all just as desperate. The young man had actually drafted a letter, addressed to the C.E.O. of the institution, meant to protest the appalling conditions that the patients were subjected to, in the hopes that their suffering would be alleviated; and furthermore, mentioned the role that I had played with him previously, in particular. His praise was effusive, arguing that I was the rare exception to the rule, that I was one of the few practitioners in the whole hospital who genuinely seemed to care about the welfare of the patients. But if that wasn't enough, he circulated the letter to every patient in the ward and had them sign the document as well. He sent one copy to the C.E.O. and gave another to me, which I still have in my possession. What was I going to do? Throw it out? I have to admit, in retrospect, that it is one of my most prized possessions, honestly, in contrast to the official award I'd received from the hospital, which, as I said, I threw in the garbage. I held onto it not so much to stroke my ego with, but to remind myself how such seemingly inconsequential acts can have such profound repercussions, and how institutions can become so inured to their own failings. That was the prize, in and of itself. While I appreciated the heartfelt sentiment, it flew in the face of my desire to fly under the radar. But what was done was done, and I reluctantly accepted his gift.

It appears as if, when given the choice, I often find myself allying with those at ground level, with the people in the thick of things, so to speak. Striving for the lofty peaks never seemed that appealing to me. No matter how consequential the goal might seem, I have always had an aversion to scaling the heights, to reach down from above to try to affect change. Even here, sitting with you, in this environment, that doesn't feel quite natural to me, it takes quite a bit of personal fortitude to be able to stomach it. I'd rather be sitting within the safe confines of my cozy little condo. But I'm here because it's important to be amongst the people, especially the ones who frequent Casablanca, or any other venue along the Strip. How else could I build a good caseload? Where else? This is the place to be, as far as I'm concerned. I wouldn't have settled here if I didn't truly believe it.

I didn't really have a choice. Do you really think I would've wanted to get a job as a bartender, or a croupier? Or, worse, a concierge? No, never! First of all, I'm terrible with numbers. Secondly, I'm not a very good multi-tasker. Despite what you or I might think of these professions, it simply wasn't in me. And while the setting might not be ideal, it's perfect for what I need to do. And what I need to do can't be entirely clear to you yet, or to any of our tablemates or neighbors around us. It's serious business, believe me. I'm not here to pal around or to get drunk, or to do aimless things, like most people. I'm almost constitutionally incapable of wasting time like that, anymore. It seems almost criminal to me.

But I don't want to give you the wrong impression. I do cherish my little condo, even though it has just a small balcony and a dreadful view. They built the building about ten years ago. I have to say the mortgage is fairly reasonable, on the grand scale of things. But it doesn't help that half the units are empty and there's never anyone in the hallways. Most of the condos are owned outright by very wealthy people who only spend a few weeks here each year. I'm one of the few year-rounders.

Can you imagine how much it must cost to own a place in *this* building, right above the casino and Casablanca? I'm sure it's astronomical! That's why I'm so happy I can just set up shop here and *act* as if I live here, as if I have an office here, when I don't. I've managed to make a comfortable arrangement with my friend over there, who I introduced you to, the first day we met. As I said, this is where the action is, and this is where I like to spend my time. There really isn't any other option, just like there wasn't any other option when I eventually had to admit to myself that I'd have to settle in Las Vegas in the first place...

While I was a practicing psychiatrist, while I worked at the psychiatric hospital I mentioned before, I also maintained an office and private practice in midtown Manhattan, not too far from the Chrysler Building. Isn't it a magnificent structure? One of the tallest and most conspicuous buildings in New York City. In fact, the tallest for some time. Yet, despite its oversized dimension, it's still very beautiful, tastefully adorned in spectacular art deco splendor. Style counts for something, in my book. But even in my wildest dreams, I could've never afforded an office in the Chrysler Building. Nor in its successor—only as far as size is concerned— that ugly box-like structure that stands so grotesquely several blocks away, with its disproportionally-sized antenna. Naturally, the one that a deranged, oversized ape would choose to climb up and terrorize people on. No, the Chrysler Building's architects had some tact. It would have been lovely to have an office there, but all that costly ornamentation and attention to detail meant I could've never afforded it as a tenant. But at least I had a good view of it from my office, though—facing south.

My office, naturally, was in one of those cookie-cutter type buildings that are a dime a dozen in Manhattan. Not too tall, and nothing to distinguish itself from any other building. But, like this makeshift office here in Casablanca, there was no end to the foot traffic. All I had to do was put a shingle up, and the city itself provided an ample clientele. I had to turn people away. Imagine all the poor, neurotic citizens of New York wandering around on their lunch hour, in dire need of an empathetic ear, someone who'd be willing to patiently listen to all of their First World problems. Oh, don't be offended! New Yorkers would be the first to admit it. Come on, you know everyone and their uncle has a therapist in New York. Think of it logically—shit only happens where there are people. And where there are lots of people, really shitty things can happen, and often do. That's half the reason I ended up in New York. Other than the restaurants and the theatres and the art museums. If you want to make a difference, you have to put yourself in the middle of it. I relished it, for a time. Just like I relish being here with you. I like people, and people seem to take to me, too, even if I have to make some minor adjustments. It's the interaction with people that makes it feel so right.

Unfortunately, although the view outside my office had great charm, it was utterly ruined one fine September morning, some twenty years ago, when a handful of desperate madmen decided to take things into their own hands and perpetrate murderous retribution on thousands of my fellow New Yorkers. I had an unobstructed view of the twin metal boxes downtown, through the crystal-clear blue sky, with which to see the second plane plunge into the second tower, the one without the antenna, I think. It was the kind of day that you wished you had a lousy view. It was certainly not something you wanted to see, under any circumstances. Yet, at the same time, though I had seen the destruction with my own eyes, in real time, it felt unreal, like a nightmare.

What I knew for certain, though, when I began to process it over the next few weeks and months, was that I was eventually going to feel compelled to leave the City for good. I just felt it in my bones. And the sooner, the better. It didn't end up turning out that way, but the seed of that idea had been firmly planted. It would take another decade, and another set of circumstances, before I was shaken like that again. Before I actually followed through with it. But I had been shaken to the core that day. I suddenly woke up from a deep slumber. That old feeling of relative safety and security was replaced by a new feeling of profound restlessness and nervous agitation. It was as if a wide curtain had been drawn back, and I could see more clearly than I had ever been able to see before. I wasn't sure what the future held, but I knew it was going to be played out in a different place, on a different plane.

I must admit, there was a certain cold, calculated logic to the way the terrorists carried out their slaughter of the innocents. It concerned me that I could, even to a certain extent, begin to understand the abominable nature of it. It isn't surprising to me how people can find themselves in such difficult positions, in true dilemmas, where they feel like they have no real alternatives other than inciting chaos and death. When they feel like they, themselves, have been surrounded and inundated by dark forces, either literally, or through the lens of their own interpretation—no matter how convoluted it might be—and feel compelled to act, and act decisively, as some kind of payback or restitution. Act irrevocably, with overwhelming force and extreme consequences. The more drama the better—like their actions are at least equal to, and opposite, to their adversary's. Whether they're an aggrieved terrorist, foreign or domestic, or some other kind of homicidal individual, like a mass shooter, their motivations are drawn from the same well. There's only so much bullying and bombing that you can take before you react instinctually. And it's so easy to become indoctrinated, to lose your sense of self when you have next to nothing left. Better to go out in a blaze of glory, or infamy, than wither away in obscurity. It's almost as if 'I am somebody, and I deserve respect' is written on each bullet and bomb.

Ironically, whatever the effect, it really only continues to affirm the cycle of violence and disempowerment, as a whole, and people will forget you just as quickly as they were forced to acknowledge you. Sometimes, I feel like with many of the sickest of the sick, the majority of my usual caseload, the same is true. But supporting them provides me great satisfaction, no matter the outcome. They might thrive or implode, but as long as I know I threw everything I had at it, I would feel good about it, especially if damage could be minimized. In short, I tried my best to lessen their pain. Life happens. People try to adjust, and I try to work with it from the inside, on a level beyond the simplicity of good and evil. I'm free to act, and feel liberated, bound only by the limitations of reality.

On the other hand, something fundamental *did* change inside of me on that day. I had the impulse to run but was also too afraid to follow through with it. There were going to have to be some adjustments made, admittedly, if I wanted to keep my sanity. Regrettably, and somewhat subconsciously, I began taking on a different kind of patient. In fact, I started referring to them as 'clients', and fewer and fewer of them necessitated bold intervention. Before long, most of my clientele consisted of people who had never been hospitalized, let alone suffered any kind of decompensation in their histories.

My practice became the quintessential private practice, run out of the same office, but with a much lighter footprint. It felt like I had returned to some sort of prior state of innocence, in comparison. A great weight had been lifted, surely enough. My mood even improved. I could still assert myself vigorously when necessary, but most of the time I felt more casual about things, and more in tune with the rest of the world. In the past, my patients were my mission. I swept down on them like an eagle from the sky. After that day, it became more like approaching them from below, and meeting them where they were. Suddenly, I wasn't taking things quite as seriously, and even started taking time off to socialize. I think my friends noticed, and wondered where all this newfound attitude and charm came from. I might say they genuinely started to like me, in a conventional kind of way. Who would have thunk it? A complete catastrophe downtown at ground zero, but a bit of a makeover uptown, at least for me. I know! I still can't quite explain it. It doesn't add up. And I've given up trying to figure it out.

I guess what happened was that I brought more balance into my life. My new practice felt far more sustainable. Like a better fit, certainly. There was a small part of me that felt like I wanted to soar above it all, see it from a wider perspective, yet still be able to reach into the dark corners and deal with it gracefully. At the same time, on a personal level, I tried to get out of my own head and embrace my holistic self, which had been sorely neglected for many, many years. I wanted to feel alive and vibrant again, from within, like I assumed other people did. To reconnect with some sense of joy—or at least satisfaction, if not harmony. I wanted to feel comfortable in my own skin, and attract others who felt the same way. For the first time in a long time, it felt like the universe was finally smiling at me.

Did I mention to you that my father was a doctor? He was a brilliant surgeon who practiced at one time, like me, in New York. His reputation was so supreme and unquestioned that even laypeople knew about him. He was a masterful neurosurgeon, the type who could literally be the difference between life and death for a patient. An extreme form of one-man triage. Like St. Peter at the pearly gates. Thumbs up, you go to heaven; thumbs down, straight to hell. His intelligence was keen, but it was his unrelenting focus that distinguished him from everyone else. There are plenty of intelligent and talented people out there, but perhaps few who feel compelled to follow through with it, to its natural consequence. I saw my father as a role model, and wished to follow in his footsteps—but very quickly learned, honestly, that

I wasn't cut from the same cloth. I didn't have the same singlemindedness that was essential to being a surgeon, but did manage to sail through medical school with what seemed like a minimal amount of stress. Psychiatry seemed well-suited to me. Although to this day, I feel somewhat resentful toward people who presume that psychiatrists are somehow inferior to other types of physicians. It seems to me that most people will be fortunate enough to float through life without suffering any major or chronic medical issues until they're near the end of their lives. Yet, no matter one's age or station in life, people are confronted with some variation of a mental health issue, even if it's just a minor complaint. Mental health is challenged each and every day, whether you're aware of it or not. Yet, it's almost as if it's routinely dismissed or denied as something that's not real, or worse, a problem of one's own making. In some ways, it's what distinguishes psychiatrists from other doctors, what makes me actually feel privileged to be one. Maybe people don't see it that way, but it made me feel like I had special powers—that I was, to a certain extent, chosen for the profession.

Of course, I don't mean that in a traditional, religious way. I mean it more spiritually. In the sense that I have faith in myself and in my training, even if I might not have much faith in the system. I might've even underestimated myself, because I understood that I was simply fulfilling a necessary role, filling a void that society itself creates. Yet that void has produced an army of us, whose sole mission is to help heal those very same societal wounds. And there's a ton of work out there. I could throw myself into the work and feel good about it at the same time. Without expecting any rewards from on high. I wouldn't go so far as to say it was elation, but it was certainly the opposite of drudgery, until the evening when... Don't worry, I'm going to get to it. To what I alluded to before. But for now, I'm enjoying these rapturous thoughts for what they are. There were periods in my life when I felt a great sense of fulfillment—though, perhaps, of an imperfect kind.

In my personal life, on the other hand, I was living high on the hog. Once I had established my livelihood and a robust salary, I took full advantage of it during my downtime. I loved being around people and socializing. Although I couldn't share much about my work—because, of course, it's confidential, by definition. So, I just indulged in the moment. Having loads of fun: drinking and cavorting, flirting with any and all women who seemed receptive to it, dancing my heart away with full abandon, to the degree that I felt both blissful and spent. It almost felt as if I had found the key to life until, obviously, on more than one occasion, I woke up the next morning with a raging hangover and regrets. But the next night I would be out doing exactly the same types of things. For a time, like a perpetual motion machine. Continually operating, but never knowing how it was possible to keep up. Hoping it would never end, until... But I don't want to get too dramatic. Before I go on, let's have a toast to life! And to our outstanding bartender over there. Remember, order in any language whatsoever, any language at all.

Life's funny, you know? All sorts of things can happen. You never know what's coming down the pike, and even if you do, you might not know how you're going to deal with it. Some people seem to be able to roll with the punches better than others. It seems like if you're dealing with something and you don't have to do it alone, you're that much better off. It's good to have a solid support system. But if you don't have one, that's where the challenge is. I feel like you need to find some way to resonate with others.

Look at us, perfect strangers, just sitting here sharing a drink. But more importantly, a moment together, an exchange. It might've happened rather randomly, at first, but you have to admit, while I come here every day for a reason, *you* came back, too. Yes,

I definitely felt some kind of sympathetic vibration between us from the very get-go. It's a good feeling to have. I think we all crave that. I'm not sure how you feel about it, but I know, from my perspective, even the simplest expression of any kind of sympathy often comes in short supply. Receiving any expression of empathy is an even more remote possibility.

In my case, as a psychiatrist, and in the mental health profession in general, we've come to professionalize empathy. It's a step up from sympathy, certainly a more holistic experience. A personalized variety of it, as if you're stepping into your client's shoes and experiencing it firsthand, using your own life experience as a guide. Every shrewd mental health professional knows, and is warned, that good practice means maintaining good boundaries, and when one crosses over the threshold from empathy to something deeper, something that makes you more vulnerable, you can find yourself in a heap of trouble. There's a good possibility that you might even fuse with your patient, or, alternatively, begin to suffer from burn out. In other words, the pathology might spread more generally and make matters worse. Not only will you *not* be serving your patient well, you'll be feeling the negative effects, too. Yet, I've found that an occasional, well-timed self-disclosure—or a specific, targeted use of compassion—can lead to very fruitful results, despite what your colleagues or your profession might claim. Oftentimes, patients just want to see that you're just as human, and as vulnerable, as anyone else. The purest form of empathy can sometimes feel terribly impersonal and unsatisfying, especially to a patient in the throes of the deepest kind of pain. Patients want to get the sense that you've felt that kind of pain in your own life, or that you at least understand it on some kind of visceral level.

As a corollary, it always amazes me how many therapists have never gone to therapy themselves. If you're not capable of—or haven't tried to wrestle with—that kind of deep, soulful search and the feelings that inevitably come with it, how do you expect others to use your services to their full advantage? If there's no resonance on that level, you might as well both be banging your heads against the wall. In other words, sympathy is cheap and comes easily. Empathy comes with a price. But in those very rare moments—when you go beyond what is typically expected from the average practitioner—that's when the payoff is most exceptional. If your patients get the sense that you've been able to handle things capably in the past, they might begin to feel inspired that they can handle it, too. You need to open up once in a while, in my opinion, to keep it real, and you'll be amazed at how effective it can be. Your patients can make incredible progress, by leaps and bounds, if you only have the courage to show just a tiny bit of yourself every now and again. Just be careful not to abuse those privileges.

On the other hand, though, when you're a therapist, people often assume you must be more or less healthy and well-balanced. After all, you have some tools to work with, presumably, to help you cope. But many of us have actually become therapists precisely because we've been in the same position as our patients previously, at least to some degree and for some time. Or we might very well *still* be grappling with the same types of personal challenges. There is some truth to the sentiment 'it takes one, to know one', my friend. But that doesn't mean that your friends or family members, or even your colleagues, will check in on you, or inquire about your mental health, on a regular basis. You could be right on the brink of suicide and nobody would ever know. If you do have a caring person in your life, or are very self-aware about your own state of mind, you're lucky. When things are going well, you have nothing to worry about. But when things are awful, that's typically when you're the least self-aware and *precisely* when nobody's going to be calling to check up on you. The moment you're slipping, that brief stretch of time outside the usual and ordinary, always comes out of nowhere, like a flash of lightning. It strikes all at once and unpredictably. That's why it's so important to have some really good flaws. Just to make people aware of your existence. If you don't happen to have any serious flaws, by all means develop some quickly... But beware the martyrs out there. They'll have you convinced that they don't need to care for themselves *and* don't have any issues whatsoever. But they're always the first ones to do the real damage. And, if they're not careful, risk destroying themselves in the process. Like the courageous soldier ordered to charge the enemy against impossible odds, only to be cut down as cannon fodder.

Yes, yes, I know. I still haven't gotten to the story that I was going to tell you about. You have to be patient. There are other things that I have to tell you about, now that we've gotten onto the subject of mental health. As I said before, when you've got a purely medical issue, you kind of know what to do, and hopefully do something about it. With mental health, it's a little trickier. It's not so simple. First of all, you've got to recognize that there is a problem. Then, once you're aware of it, you've got to consider it serious enough to take action. *Then* you can finally act on it. But most people never get past the second stage. There are armies of people out there walking around with a multitude of invisible wounds. Have you ever noticed? Probably not. The only time we really notice is when it's just about too late. It's either gotten to a very acute stage, or regrettably, has already crossed over into the realm of the self-destructive or suicidal. Just the thought of suicide, alone, makes everyone uncomfortable. Except, ironically, for the person who is actually considering it. We tend to want to run away from anyone who feels so dreadfully awful that the only viable option left to them appears to be the instinct to annihilate themselves, rather than address the problem. That includes therapists. I understand why.

For example, I had a patient whose only daughter died in a car accident. She was out of her mind with grief. It just so happened that grief was one of my specialties. But even I had to pause and collect myself before attempting to help her, because her daughter died very violently, under unusual circumstances. The daughter had risen in the early morning, as she was accustomed to, to leave the house to arrive for her shift on time, in order to avoid rush hour traffic. She was a nurse at a hospital in town. At that same moment, a young man who had been out on the town the previous night, had gotten into his car to drive back home. They met at the edge of the town somewhere, where their cars collided and ignited into a giant fireball, both vehicles exploding upon impact. I mean, what is the likelihood of that? It just doesn't happen that way, ordinarily. They were both killed instantly and burned beyond recognition. Can you imagine what it must have felt like for the parents to have to go identify their children in that state? Devastating. As if that wasn't bad enough, there was an article published about the incident in the local newspaper. And it was reported that my patient's daughter had likely fallen asleep at the wheel, had veered into the opposite lane, and struck the young man's car head-on. So naturally, while my patient was devastated over the loss of her daughter, she was also feeling a deep sense of guilt by association. Especially because it seemed so out of character for her daughter.

There was some finger-pointing going on in the community, including within the young man's extended family, who felt that the daughter was undoubtedly to blame for what had happened. Despite this uncomfortable tension, after the funerals, someone from the young man's family decided that it might be a good idea to get the surviving family members together, in order to diffuse the bad blood. Despite her instincts, and her guilt, my patient agreed that it might be a helpful thing to do. They met, they commiserated, and they felt a deep, common, communal kind of distress. And cried, and consoled, and danced cautiously around each other to find some kind of meeting of the minds, despite their pain and suffering. There were no outward expressions of regret, or remorse, or bitterness, but there were also no easy answers, or any kind of greater understanding, or even the beginning of any kind of closure. Just a time and a place to be together, in search of some kind of relief—or at least the possibility that things could evolve or move on, even if just barely.

My patient left, not knowing if any of it had made any difference, perhaps not even being able to tell one way or the other, because she was still feeling so much internal shock and numbness. But then, weeks later, after a thorough and painstaking official investigation had been concluded, it appeared that her daughter had had absolutely nothing to do with the 'accident'. It turned out that the young man had been drinking heavily the night before, and that his friends were concerned about him driving back home. That on his way home, he had been texting with one of them as *he* veered into the oncoming lane. And that was how it happened. Despite what the paper reported, the reality was that the daughter had done absolutely nothing wrong; that, in fact, not only was the young man at fault, he was irrefutably negligent, and it could've all been avoided entirely, had the young man and his friends been thinking just a little more clearly, carefully, and persuasively.

The truth threw my patient into a deep and dark chasm. After all those weeks of feeling unnecessary shame, it morphed and nosedived into a blinding rage. There was no acknowledgement after the fact, there was no opportunity to process what she had suddenly been confronted with. The funerals and memorial services, or any other kind of contact between the families, had already passed—they were already beginning to fade from memory, if not actively pushed away. There was no follow-up in the newspaper, no updating of the record. The official story was still what had been reported shortly after the incident, before the investigation had been completed. My patient even wondered if there was some kind of conspiracy going on, because the young man's family was well-connected in the community, had powerful and influential friends, and it seemed as if the investigation kept dragging on and on, despite its lack of any kind of real complexity. Why did it take so long to discover the truth?

By the time she was referred to me, a couple weeks after the results of the investigation had been released, she was suffering so much pain, grief, and distress, she could barely function, even in the most minimal of ways. I learned a little more about her prior history, including the fact that she was a nurse, just like her daughter, and a recent cancer survivor. She told me about how she had stopped taking her medications, which included a drug that is taken to prevent recurrences. In fact, she felt there was no point in doing anything. She stopped going to work and eventually quit her job; she lost her health insurance because it was tied to her job, but didn't bother trying to replace it with anything. She didn't even want to come to therapy, but her colleagues convinced her to give it a try. She had had some therapy in the past, but felt ambivalent about it because her prior experiences had been disappointing at best. She wondered aloud how therapy could help. She said it would be like putting a Band-Aid on a shotgun blast. I had to admit, that if you looked at it from an outside perspective, a lot of people would've agreed. There was a palpable sense of hopelessness, but I wondered if I could at least help her cope in some way.

But before we got the chance to explore that, before we even had a second session, she terminated with me, unfortunately. I thought I had come up with some ways to bridge the gap, and if those happened to fall short, I believed that just being with her and listening would've been helpful, bare minimum. It felt that way during our first session. I felt like we had already established some solid rapport. But perhaps the timing was off. Perhaps it was too early to dive in. Nonetheless, I tried to persuade her to come back for just one more session to see if there could be any way forward, or if it might be more advantageous to connect sometime in the future. But she declined, claiming that she would only be a waste of my time, that it would be more productive for me to use my time on other patients. By then, despite my reluctance to let her go, I felt like I had to accept her perspective, and respect it, even though I didn't necessarily agree with it wholeheartedly. Perhaps it was too much even to think about it yet, let alone talk about it. She asked me if it was wrong to feel the way she did. She said that she hated the young man and that she hated his parents. When she first heard the findings of the investigation, she had the impulse to go over to their house and kill them. She assured me that she wasn't ever going to do that, but she also told me that if the parents died, not only wouldn't she care, she might even be happy if they did. But after that discussion, I never heard from her again. Ever. I didn't necessarily want to know, or find out, what happened to her after that.

After years of experience in cases like these, I had decided that I would only offer one chance for a patient to reconsider and reconnect after they decided they wanted to terminate. I just knew from experience that they almost never came back. It seemed to me that if someone is going to turn things around, they need to take that step on their own, under their own power, so to speak. That if they can't convince themselves that it's worth it, I won't be able to convince them of that, either. That principle has served me well over the years, and I stand by it because, by and large, the evidence almost always supports it. But what struck me most, and what was most regrettable, was that I knew that she had already started to adapt, to some extent. The very fact that she didn't want to think about it, to ruminate on it endlessly, convinced me that she was, in fact, coping with it as best she could, at the time. And if she did start to process it, to a certain degree, that meant she might fear that the very memory of her daughter might start to slip away, and she would be gone forever. Not to mention what to do with the rage: because even if she didn't go gun down the parents, just the thought of feeling homicidal was bad enough.

That's not to say that if she had continued with me, I would've felt completely competent and confident regarding how I would've approached her. I have to admit that I, too, felt vulnerable and insecure, and that there was a small, but not insignificant, sliver of me that didn't know what to do, even a feeling of wanting to avoid the situation. If she felt hopeless and helpless, it naturally made me feel more powerless, too. I might even have felt a little bit of resentment that I wasn't given an opportunity to help her cope. But, after some reflection, I reminded myself that she was, in fact, coping to some degree, and that even if she didn't seem to be coping well, at least there was a good dose of healthy denial. And denial, after all, is a defense mechanism, as long as it doesn't outlive its usefulness. So, somehow, I had to come to terms and be comfortable with that paradox. That absurdity.

I realized that she had come to the same conclusion, though she was probably not quite conscious of it yet. She told me how she had been spending her days ever since her daughter's death. I'm not sure how she was getting by practically speaking, but most of the day involved waking up early and getting on her bike, riding around like a maniac for hours on end, into the evening, until she was utterly spent and exhausted. I can understand that. I can understand how she wanted to numb herself, both physically and mentally, but I also wondered if she was purposefully making herself vulnerable, hoping that if she was just careless enough, she might get run over by a car and put out of her misery. There *was* a certain logic to it. It made a certain amount of sense.

Despite what people might want you to think, there are times when suicide does seem like a reasonable solution to one's problems. Otherwise, why would there be so many of them? It's just a normal part of the collective life experience—statistically speaking—as far as I'm concerned. Can you deny that when the only thing left is misery, just unbearable pain or nausea, that it wouldn't be a good time to put an end to it? Yet, even then, people will resist the notion. I think it's a crime that people are often denied the option, and hypocritical that it's done routinely, within the medical community, as long as it's not recognized as an assisted suicide. It's so taboo that even alluding to suicide is enough to cause controversy. Nobody wants to be reminded of their own mortality, particularly if they feel culpable, in some way, for their own demise. But they're even more resistant, actually terrified by, the possibility that they might be capable of carrying it out themselves. On the other hand, it seems to me, that if you haven't considered suicide at some point in your life, there must be something amiss. That you've lived your life very timidly. That you've avoided any sort of conflict indiscriminately. And, therefore, any of its repercussions—either positive or negative. It's a more fundamental variety of denial that places you into a very distinct class of people.

That was certainly not the case with my patient, and I think she sensed that I wasn't one of those people, either. I think it was pretty clear to both of us that I wasn't in the business of trying to force her away from the danger zone; and in other circumstances, I might not even try to dissuade someone, if it made sense. But I got the distinct feeling that even though she sensed this about me, she still felt that if you hadn't experienced anything like she had, what she had experienced specifically, then you wouldn't be able to help. I couldn't really argue with that, because in the end, she was, in fact, the only one who could truly save herself. The best I can do is assist. I've had a whole range of patients with a stunningly diverse set of challenges across the spectrum of life, most of whom have an innate instinct and inborn ability to overcome even the most extreme of circumstances. Then there's the few who simply *cannot* cope, and furthermore, have no more hope left in their reservoirs. The irony is, the closer they are to that point, the less you have to offer, by definition. That's the paradox...

The worst part of it is if they actually end up killing themselves: that's when the judgement sets in. Not only my own self-doubt as a psychiatrist, but the collective judgement of the departed's family, friends, and even other caregivers, believe it or not. Sometimes judgements by professionals are the most ruthless and damning of all. But there's no one left standing for the counter-argument. If you're going to commit suicide, you'd better realize that the survivors can frame it any way they want, often in a self-serving manner, and that's going to be the final word on the subject. Just imagine the chatter at the memorial service, and how many times you'll overhear the expression, 'Isn't it a shame?' But as soon as it's over, I assure you, not a single additional thought about you or your legacy. They'll wash their hands of it and move on. Bygones will be bygones.

But there was a back story to all of this drama that my patient also shared with me. It turned out there was another young person, a blood relative, also relevant to this extended web of pain. The daughter had had a half-brother who lived somewhere in Europe, the son of my patient's ex-husband, by a previous marriage—in other words, my patient's stepson. He wasn't too much older than the daughter, no more than about five years her senior. But the daughter looked up to him, and they had had a warm and loving relationship despite the geographical distance between them. They visited as children but also after they had both become adults. He had always been a talented child, and had made some inroads into the world of the fine arts after he graduated from college. He seemed to have a dedicated following, a fanbase for his art, and was verging on the precipice of fame and fortune before his star began to dim and burn out. Whether it was because he had had a troubled life growing up amongst the chaos of his parents' failing marriage, or because he found himself running with the wrong crowd, he made the mistake of turning to drugs to ease his pain, and got addicted to heroin at an early age. He struggled valiantly to kick the habit, but its grip was just too strong.

Nobody knew about his troubles, but my patient's daughter sensed something was wrong and reached out to him, to see if she could help him straighten out his life, when he confided in her. I don't think it was accidental that he chose to tell her. She had always been a very sensitive and observant girl, and had chosen to devote her life to a caregiving profession, after all. They maintained regular contact and even visited each other when they could. But her main role in his life, besides the blessing of having a sibling in the world, was to help him keep his head screwed on straight, so that he could thrive despite the circumstances. She devoted a lot of time and energy to it, and there were long stretches of time in his life when he seemed focused in the right direction and on the brink of finally vanquishing his demons for good.

But, as is often the case, quite a few ultimately slip through the cracks, and he was no exception. She received a fateful phone call from her father one day and learned that her half-brother had taken his own life the day before. No warning, no note. No explanation or apology for his actions. Just there one day and gone the next. Of course, she was devastated by the loss. There was a deep connection between them. But she tried not to be upset with him. She just tried to accept it and withheld judgment. It would be a long road to recovery for her, but her mother expressed to me how proud she was of her, how maturely she handled the grief. On the other hand, my patient had had a fairly tenuous relationship with her step-son. She had tried to bond with him, but he was never particularly accepting of her. He held her at a distance, and that was how it ended. Thus, she had never been very invested in his life and told me she didn't feel much of anything when she learned about his death. But after her daughter died, she admitted she was thankful for her connection to him, and one of the few things that

45

gave her any sense of comfort was imagining her daughter and stepson together somewhere—at least if they both had to die, they would be in each other's company. It helped her with her grief and gave her some measure of relief.

Now you would think that losing two children within a few years of each other would've been devastating to the father, my patient's ex-husband. I'm sure it affected him deeply. How couldn't it? But he seemed to be able to cope with it more easily. My patient was disadvantaged in the sense that she had nothing to resort to, to find compelling answers. She, unlike her ex, didn't practice any faith or embrace any kind of formal spiritual tradition. The only way for her to deal with it was to tough it out, use whatever she had or could find that would help. Her ex, on the other hand, was a deeply religious man. Religious to the point of dogmatic. He looked to God to supply the answers. And his answers were predictable, yet exasperating, to her. He trotted out the usual platitude about how God works in mysterious ways—that just because we don't understand him, doesn't mean that there's no plan in mind, presumably a higher purpose for those in his flock; that, by nature, the motives lie on an elevated plane, that defies our comprehension. It always amazes me how many people can pivot so deftly like that, yet not succumb to the seduction of doubt, or even the ruthlessness of cognitive dissonance. How is that tenable? In his case, it appeared more than possible—indeed, likely. My patient confided to me that, from her perspective, her ex always maintained emotional distance no matter how close he is to someone, including her and his children. That there was a coldness to their marriage and to his style of parenting. That was partly why she left him. She told me he had always had a very casual approach toward relationships in general, yet despite that, he always had the need to have someone in his life, presumably to take care of him and his interests. The kind of guy who cycles rapidly through wives and children. So it didn't surprise her that immediately after their divorce, he found a new companion within weeks. And then another child within a year. She imagined that he had been grooming this new flame for years, and that perhaps they had even had an affair.

But what irked her most was how other people perceived him. She remembered the memorial service, in particular. How he seemed to attract all the attention. How people seemed to focus their condolences on him. It was true, she said, that he had a certain amount of charm and charisma, and that his style of mourning appealed to people at the memorial service. Just like he was able to rationalize the awful tragedy of his daughter's death and convince himself that there was a reason for it, or some sort of logic to it, he had little trouble encouraging and convincing his guests to feel the same way. In the meantime, she told me that she felt ostracized, like people were actively trying to avoid her. Most likely because they could sense her raw, intense pain, and didn't know how to deal with it. With her, they felt helpless. With him, they could focus their attention on his more palatable form of grieving, and be comforted, despite what he might be suffering, because at least he had a new family and newborn to soften the blow.

My patient really resented what she had experienced. She began to feel pitied. That her grief was being stifled by it. Instead of attempting to support her, uncomfortable though it may have been, she felt like most of the guests at the service were more interested in relieving their own discomfort than anything else. Just seeing her ex with his new wife and their baby, and what they represented, made her seethe with anger. She resented the fact that she felt angry, and was disgusted by her guilt. She resented the fact that she would probably never have another child again, too. She even resented that her daughter had been so nurturing to her half-brother, and to the newborn as well. She seemed to resent just about everything. Yet, all I could feel for her was love. The kind of love you feel for someone who has been wronged. For someone who has suffered an injustice. The kind of love that you reserve for your heroes. I felt her alienation. Her pain. And I wanted to affirm it. I wished I had witnessed it alongside her. I wished I had been there to protect her. And to comfort her. But those wishes would have to remain unfulfilled.

It's so strange. You never really know what goes on inside the minds of people when they're attending a funeral. You see the evasion. You hear the rationalizations, the attempts to reconcile and have closure. But you also notice that there are essentially two different camps on hand: the aforementioned, and the rest. Those who think about it a little bit differently. But let's face it—funerals are no fun. At the very least, underneath it all, they're an obligation, a necessary ritual. Just as soon as everyone arrives, many people's first impulse is to wonder how long it's going to go on for, and what you have to look forward to when it's over. There are some people who haven't a clue, and others who seem to get it. They almost seem practiced at it. They take on just the right tone and attitude. They hit the sweet spot. It's good enough for them to just be there and say something that truly resonates, a choice word or two when the inspiration strikes.

Then there's that very tiny minority of folks who almost seem to shine in the moment. They wouldn't miss a funeral for the world! They don't see them the same way as the rest of us. They understand that they're moments of great drama. Respites from the mundane and banal. They know that death is only a starting point. While I'm sure that most people attend funerals with the best of intentions, I think there are few who will follow through afterwards, in an open-ended manner, the way you hoped or envisioned people might after one's own death. Let's say, for example, that my patient did end up killing herself. Would any of the people who went to her daughter's funeral come to hers? I doubt it. They might've imagined why she did it. They might've accepted it. But they probably would've reacted in the very same manner that they did during her daughter's service. They would've turned their attention elsewhere, away from the inconvenient truth. They would've done anything to find an excuse to skip it. And bury the whole thing for good. Never think about it again. Like a period at the end of a sentence. I had hoped to be there for her for the next chapter, so to speak. How I had wished that I had been contacted prior to her daughter's funeral. To witness all of it. To be there with her as her daughter's casket was lowered into the ground. It wouldn't have been likely to happen, in this case. But perhaps that's my own vanity speaking to me. The futility of it! It might not have made any real difference, but at least I could have sat with her. And would've tried not to judge her.

What nobody knew about my patient, and that she had only told me, was that she had actually gone to the funeral of the young man who was responsible for her daughter's death. Up to that point, the investigation had still not been completed, so the assumption remained that her daughter was to blame. Yet she still went, partly to pay her respects, but also, she admitted, out of guilt. She had every excuse not to go. She feared that she would not be welcome. She had to take unpaid time off of work. Even the weather was terrible, but she pressed through all of it because she felt it was the right thing to do. Out of respect for the family, and in order to avoid stirring up controversy, she sat by herself in the back of the church where the memorial service was being held. She hardly spoke a word to anyone. Although nobody quite knew who she was, nobody inquired, either. Can you imagine how that must have felt? Can you imagine how alone and conflicted she was?

No, I imagine it would be hard for anyone to put themselves in that situation. It was for me. I know I keep going on and on about this, and I haven't even gotten to the other story that I promised you, that you've been waiting so patiently for. But bear with me. I haven't quite finished this story yet.

Did I mention that no one from the young man's family came to my patient's daughter's funeral? Not a single person, that we know of. I wouldn't say that they were conspicuously absent. But there might have been some small expectation that they would've somehow made their presence felt, whether at the funeral or in some other way. But neither the mother nor the father came, nor anyone else, as far as we knew. Maybe that was for the better— there was the suspicion that the other family didn't consider what had happened an accident.

Even when the meeting between the families did eventually occur, the other family didn't seem to understand who my patient was at first, even though she had been to the young man's funeral just a couple of weeks before, and had shared her condolences with the parents face to face. Yes, it was just a fleeting moment, no questions asked. You can imagine that the parents were not in a state of mind to be very sensitive or observant—that they were in the thick of it, feeling distracted by their sorrow, and focused on their inner grief. You might've imagined that someone might've noticed or inquired about my patient. Not so. You really can't blame anyone for any of it. But the families, tragically, were like two ships passing in the night, further enshrouded in a layer of dense fog. It wasn't their fault. But to my patient, it certainly felt that way. Especially when she thought about it later, after the facts of the investigation were released, and it was determined unequivocally that the young man was solely at fault. It was like insult upon injury. She became enraged, as I've told you. But there was nobody to run to, no one who knew about this other aspect of her private suffering.

That's when she came to me. She had no one else to tell. It was the only thing that we alone shared, and I thought it could be an essential element that would bond us. That would make it possible for us to work through it together, to process it, and then begin to process everything else. But, sadly, it wasn't enough. She let it out and left it hanging—but also left *me* hanging. That's when she wrote the note telling me not to waste my time on her. Which was really just another way of her saying, in an externalized and depersonalized manner, that she was intent on giving up. She ignored my reply, and I didn't attempt to contact her again. I just dropped it. I never heard anything about her again, and I never went searching.

But I thought of her often. It wasn't easy to forget someone like her, someone who dissolved right through your fingers. I had had only one other patient, in my whole career, who haunted me like her, in terms of the feeling of hopelessness. That patient had a chronic medical condition, making her life very difficult on a day-to-day basis. She felt ill most of the time, either uncomfortably nauseous or in significant pain, due to a rare disease that the medical community hadn't yet fully acknowledged. Which meant that not only did the diagnosis come late and reluctantly, it was often challenged by some of her very own doctors. Not to mention that none of the treatment, whatever it was that they could patch together for her, was covered by insurance. Her prognosis was poor, death was inevitable within five to ten years, and she had already had quite enough by the time she came to see me. She was tired of trying to cope with it and also felt, after one session, that therapy wasn't going to be helpful, either. In fact, when she told me how she felt, she used the very same phrase I heard from my other patient: 'I don't want you to waste your time on me.' She added that 'I'd just be taking time away from other patients who could really benefit from your help.' And just like that, she disappeared. That time, however, I didn't try to convince her to come back. I just told her that I respected her decision and that if she ever felt the inclination to re-engage, I'd be willing.

But enough of these kinds of stories. Let's get back to what I was going to tell you about in the first place, before I got off on another tangent. Despite the difficult and frustrating moments I've told you about, my private practice was thriving. I had had a particularly busy schedule one day, seeing patients, one after the other, from dawn to dusk. That same evening, I was looking forward to a little time to myself when I finally did manage to get off work. I was hoping I wouldn't be interrupted. And yet...

It was a fine winter evening, a bit chilly, but with calm winds, and as clear and dry as a sky could be. I had decided to take a walk along the East River, not too far from my office, just as night was falling. As I looked back over my shoulder down the corridor carved out by 57th Street, I remember seeing the sun just about to set, its rose-colored hues streaking the amber sky, before descending into my favorite park. The street lamps were already lit, but struggling against the encroaching darkness. The park is a small green space nestled against the river, cut off from the rest of the city by a long, winding staircase covered in vines. There are a few benches along the water adorned by a minimum of ornamentation, including only some statuary and some small flower beds. Other than that, the park is a well-kept secret and it's surprising how few people it attracts, even in the daytime. In the winter, however, you'd be lucky to see anyone around, even the heartiest of souls. But I found a comfortable spot to sit, shuffled my feet through some leaves, and spent my first minutes there staring out into the calm, glassy water, watching it shimmer against whatever marine traffic happened to come by.

The East River is actually, technically, an estuary, connecting Long Island Sound to New York Harbor and the open ocean waters beyond it. It's a very convenient passageway for commerce, but also for the wildlife that finds its home on it. It's a joy to watch the jumble of birds and waterfowl navigate their way through it, and adapt themselves, so cleverly and cunningly, to it. While I imagined many of my fellow city dwellers packed into the bustling restaurants along First Avenue north of the U.N., enveloped by the warmth of the room and the din of clinking dishes and glasses, I was thankful I was embedded, instead, in this quiet little sanctuary below them, with only the modest, almost comforting, hum of cars passing by in the distance. When I looked up to my left, I saw the great arc of the 59th Street Bridge spanning the river, straddling Roosevelt Island, its lights twinkling along its profile. Yes, Christmas Eve was only ten days away, and the sky seemed full of ornaments, no matter which direction I gazed. There was a blanket of stars above my head, and I felt satisfied. I had had a very busy and tiring day, but it was finally over. I had managed to help a few people out, gotten a few thanks, and felt like I had done everything within my power to get as many obstacles out of my patients' ways as humanly possible, and still have time left over for myself.

I had spent nearly an hour soaking in this imperfect bliss. I had nodded off a few times toward the end of that hour, then suddenly found myself abruptly shaken from a deeper slumber. I often found that just dropping off to sleep for a few minutes was enough to get me through the rest of the day, as if I had gotten in a good, long nap. So, I roused myself from the bench I was sitting on and somehow felt inspired to take a brisk, spontaneous walk. I'm not sure what got into me, but after threading my way through the East Side and mounting the steps onto the bridge that I had been looking at, I found myself directly above the river peering down on the very same scene I had just alighted from. I imagined myself still sitting there, and felt a peculiar surge of altered consciousness come over me, like I was seeing more clearly, more objectively— the way people talk about 'perceiving with a third eye'. I couldn't quite make out what was going on in the river below, though, as it had taken on a darkened, almost black, hue from above. Nevertheless, I drew several, consecutive deep breaths into my lungs, and watched as the streams of condensation coming from my mouth trailed away chaotically and unpredictably, carried by the breezier conditions up high.

But that was exactly when I noticed an annoying and entirely vexatious buzzing in my pocket, which could only come from the ring of a cellphone. I couldn't actually hear the ring. My first instinct was to reach into my pocket and immediately mute it. But, given my profession, there was a countervailing pressure to answer. I spun around, as if that would've forced the ring to go away. The longer it kept buzzing, the more the tension rose. I could feel my heart pounding inside my chest. It's not like this didn't happen all the time. You would've thought that I would've become used to it. But, no! After all these years, and particularly after such a long day, I still resisted, with all my might and fortitude, to answer the call. I finally muted it. But my spell was broken, and I decided that my little reverie was over and it was high time to return home for the night.

Besides, I was getting hungry by then, and when I finally hastened to the doorstep of my apartment building, I felt faint and a little out of breath. Once inside my home, I ran directly to the fridge to grab a snack and then settled onto the couch in the living room. I tried to collect myself, after the flush of hunger left me. I had broken into a bit of sweat on my way home, so I went into the bathroom to freshen my face with cool water. Just as I was done drying myself with a towel, the phone rang again. I stood frozen before the mirror, wondering which part of my temperament would answer—the responsible side of me, or the side that just wanted to pitch myself into bed. I opted for the former. I grabbed the phone quickly from my pocket and realized straight away that I had several messages on my phone, mostly texts I assumed were of little importance or significance. But someone had texted repeatedly from out-of-state, and that same number was calling again. I seemed to recognize the number vaguely, but wasn't quite sure who it was.

When I finally answered, I realized immediately that it was a former patient, one I had worked with many years before but who had moved out of New York, and he was in grave distress. At first, I didn't understand what he was talking about because he was speaking a mile a minute in a disjointed manner—but not incoherently, or disorganized, in any way. He told me that there had been a shooting, a school shooting, and that it was very likely that his son had been amongst the victims. I wasn't aware of what had happened yet, and I didn't doubt what he was saying, because he had never had any serious psychological breaks, as far as I remembered. But he was reaching out to me because he was very distraught and didn't know what to do. He was in the midst of a complete emotional breakdown, yet he seemed to be holding it together. He said that the authorities were still in the process of identifying victims, and that he should know by the end of the night whether his son was amongst those who perished that day. Can you imagine? Just hearing about it put me into shock. Then he told me that he didn't have much time to talk, and he wanted to know if he could call me back when he had a chance. Of course, I told him he could contact me at any time, day or night, no conditions. After getting some additional facts from him, I advised him that the best thing he could probably do right then was exactly what he was already doing—the other members of his family had been accounted for, they were all gathered together at a nearby facility, with all of the other families that had been affected. I added that, at least at that moment, nothing could be more helpful than to be around others caught in the same position, as long as they were being supported by a team of crisis workers. He told me that they had already been in touch with them, and with that, he had to go. He told me he'd call back. I wished him luck as he abruptly hung up, and I stood in front of that mirror a very long time before I could move again.

I no longer saw that duplicitous face I had seen just a few minutes before. You know those masks from Ancient Greece? The ones that the members of the Chorus wear, while performing a tragedy? That was what my face looked like. Grotesque. A mix of shock, horror, and disgust. Followed by helplessness. All I could do was bury my face in my hands and sob.

But enough of that, for now. I just got distracted by that man over there. You're curious about the rest of it? Of course, you are! That's why I'll expect you back here tomorrow evening. No, I can't stay much longer. You see that man over there? The guy who looks like a cop? No, he's not a cop, that's just what the security guards look like around here. I need to go talk to him. He's a good guy. Well, he might be a *little* shady, but people are constantly harassing him, for whatever reason, including the cops. He might look very intimidating, but it's not like he's ever murdered anyone or anything like that.

You might be surprised to learn that he used to be an actor. He spent many years in L.A. in that grind. But then he got sick of it and started working behind the camera, so to speak. He began working for a prop master, and before he knew it, he became one of the most successful prop masters in the entire industry. It seemed like every other film being made, his name was in the credits. Not so much anymore, of course. He spends most of his time here in Vegas, doing whatever security guards do.

But see that glass case over there? You might've noticed it before. That was his idea, originally. And you remember the barkeep who's usually here? I might not have told you before, but he actually owns this place, and he also owns an estate back in Mexico where he produces the tequila he's been serving you. You see, almost everybody around here has a double life. You might think that you know who they are, and believe only what you've seen, but there's so much more to it than that. Just because he looks like a security guard doesn't mean he's not a thief, too. You remember that old movie *Casablanca*, right? What do you see in that case? Yes, there's a black bowtie, and a diamond brooch, and a couple of champagne glasses. You might recognize them from the movie, but there's actually one item that used to be with them that's been missing for some time now. Well, never mind, I'll fill you in on the full story some other time, if you're fortunate. But for now, I need to consult with my associates over there. I'm sort of their guardian angel. That's part of my mission, if you recall. I'm here to serve all these people, whether they're aware of it or not. It's not like there's a credential for that. But I do seem to attract people. Maybe it's my odd sense of humor, or my sober earnestness. Those help. But I don't shy away from anyone these days. I can't afford to! Whether you're an angel or a devil, you're going to intrigue me, at the very least. But what I know for sure, is that nobody's completely innocent. Okay! Okay! I'm coming! If anyone tells you otherwise, and truly believes it—don't trust them, my friend! Never trust them!

III.

You *have* been listening, haven't you? I could tell you're the curious type. You didn't forget about what I told you last night. To tell you the truth, it's still hard to think about. But it's all safely tucked away in my head. I have a tendency to get ahead of myself.

You're probably still curious about what happened to the man who called me that tragic winter night. My former patient in distress. You've probably guessed. It was all over the news. You couldn't've missed it. Then again, there are so many mass shootings these days that you might mistake one for another. I purposely didn't watch the news until the following morning. I probably should've. Just in case my former client called me back. But you can't necessarily trust what you see on the news. I wanted to have an unclouded mind and hear it directly from the source.

But because I didn't hear from him until the following evening, late into the night, I caved in and flipped on the television and got the whole story, more or less. Absolute mayhem. A bloodbath. Many, many deaths. Much, much misery. More trauma and unbearable grief to come. But, as is often the case, a multitude of heroic acts, too. Supposedly, no motive. In all, 20 six-and-seven-year-old children dead. Including, unfortunately, my former client's son. He told me right away over the phone. I could tell the bad news was coming. His voice sounded half-dead already, with just the first few words out of his mouth. Then he started sobbing uncontrollably—the kind that makes it hard to breathe, that feels like it's going to choke you. He gagged and wailed, and continued for some time. All I could do was listen, and tell him how sorry I was to hear the news. So very sorry. What else is there to say in a moment like that? If I had been next to him, I would've embraced him with all the love and tenderness I could've mustered. I would've held him in my arms like he was my own son, to try to ease his pain. But it wasn't possible, and wouldn't have been possible. I just knew that I had to be present in that moment, that I had to assure him that I was there with him in spirit, and we'd take it from there. You can imagine the rest. I don't want to get into excruciating details, but can you imagine what it must be like not to know whether your child was dead or alive, for hours? Then to have to go to the morgue to identify your deceased son? Then to have to say goodbye forever, never to have another word with him again? Totally devastating. And totally senseless and pointless. Let's hope that there are very few people on Earth who'll have to experience anything even remotely like that.

A few days later, he called back again, and wanted some advice on what to do next. He was already doing what I would've suggested, but I think because we had already established a good working relationship from before, he was naturally hoping to engage with me again, in some form. I couldn't refuse, but I had to take on more of a consulting role, at best, because he lived out of state, beyond my practice jurisdiction, and wasn't going to be coming into the city on a regular basis. He understood my limitations. But I suggested that he would probably benefit more from working with a psychiatrist out where he was anyway: first, because I was sure he could find someone who was qualified; second, because someone from the community, and familiar with the lay of the land, would be much better positioned to deal with it organically; and third, but most importantly, he was already connected with all the other families from the school who suffered the same fate, and the greater support network that had already been mobilized for their benefit. Even through the fog of his torment, he saw my line of reasoning. He would call me back on occasion, when he had a specific question; but other than offering a little more support, I didn't have much more to contribute.

But I did think about him often, especially when I was anywhere near where I was when he initially tried to contact me: either at that same park, or within view of the bridge. I was also reminded of him when I saw anything in the news that had something to do with the shooting, or any other mass shooting. It appeared that he had become very involved and active on the political stage, joining forces with some of the other surviving family members, in an effort to change the laws governing the possession of firearms. Whether or not he was coming to terms with his son's death on a personal level, I was happy to see that all signs seemed to indicate that he was able to function well enough to follow through with his new role as an advocate. You would've thought that if there was any type of mass shooting that would've finally been the tipping point to usher in a new era of sensible and pragmatic gun control, exceptions would've made for the welfare of children, and in honor of these children's lives. But despite the greater coordinated effort, it failed, nonetheless. What would it take, ultimately? Just a few years later there was another school shooting that killed a similar number of people, but this time high school students. Their peers, the surviving students, however, were old enough and determined enough to continue the fight, in the political arena. They formed a coalition to take down their greatest enemies any way they can—and are wholly committed, for as long as it might take. Although the gun laws haven't changed yet significantly, they were able to make some minor inroads and are on the brink of hobbling some of their greatest enemies. They might not have won the war yet, but they are winning some battles and chipping away at the edifice. It may seem hopelessly futile, but they're tenacious, and it's unlikely that they'll ever give up. It really made an impression on me.

It made me really angry though, too. About how some people can be in such denial, even when children die en masse. On the other hand, there were some notable exceptions. For example, I remember I had one patient who was a military veteran—in fact, he was one of those guys who was all gung-ho when the war in Afghanistan began. He had already been in the Navy previously, but had rejoined the services right away, this time with the Marines, and ended up being shipped out within months. His main role once he got to Afghanistan was to go in ahead of the rest of the troops and clear the rooftops and surrounding area of any opposition that might be in the way before a major offensive. He was an expert marksman, and had had a lot of experience as a sniper, but never in an active combat zone. This was his opportunity to put his skills into action.

He had a lot of success, with an increasing number of kills under his belt. He received high marks for his service, and official recognition. But when he was deployed the second time, disaster struck. He and his fellow soldiers fell victim to a roadside bomb on the way to their next mission, and my patient, unfortunately, was severely injured. He'd suffered a traumatic brain injury, and had to be sent home for treatment. It was a very difficult time for him, as you can imagine, and he didn't seem to be getting the help that he needed. He wasn't going to be discharged yet, but on the other hand, he wasn't healthy enough to be sent back, either. He spent many months in a state of limbo before it was determined that he was no longer able to contribute, even in a supporting or administrative role. In addition to the brain injury, he was suffering from Post-Traumatic Stress Disorder, and it was manifesting in ways that made it difficult for him to get along, even in the civilian world. He was frustrated and angry a lot of the time, and he began drinking to excess. His marriage began to deteriorate and he had trouble holding down a job. It was right about the time that he began to feel seriously suicidal that he came to me.

I had worked with quite a few veterans in the past, and although many of them had had severe mental health issues, very few of them seemed to ever get adequate treatment. What I learned, very early on, was that treatment within the purview of the military world was woefully inadequate, for the most part. The main focus of concern within the system was to do whatever you had to do to get the soldiers well and prepared to go right back in, wherever they'd left off. The primary concern wasn't about their overall mental health. It was to achieve a level of functioning that their superiors could sign off on, so that the next deployment could go ahead. They had a real shortage of manpower after just a few years into the wars. They needed to deploy and redeploy and keep the cycle going, or else the wars would screech to a halt, or be curtailed in some way. And it's even worse, from the military's point of view, when they end up getting discharged, because then vets really serve no purpose at all. The government provides the most minimal of services that they can get away with, and then it's up to the veteran to fill in the rather obvious and substantial gaps.

Don't you find it strange that a man can go kill another man, go to therapy, and never even broach the subject? There are many soldiers out there who have been so brainwashed by their training that they don't even make the connection between taking someone's life and their own mental health. And then there are some who seem to be perfectly fine with what they've done. But don't tell me that a human being can kill another human being and not even have it faze him, on any level. In the case of my vet, it had everything to do with his suffering. The truth of the matter is, he killed many people, complete strangers, whom he almost certainly held no personal animus or grudge toward. For all we know, under normal circumstances, during peacetime, he might have had something in common with his victims, even been friendly toward them, or had some other kind of other meaningful connection to them. Yet, until he came to me and expressed guilt about it, it had never previously come up.

Well, I worked with him for a number of years, trying to parse out the different elements of his distress, and he had gotten to a place that was much more psychologically tenable for him. He started to piece his life back together again—he saved his marriage and even went back to school to become a social worker. I was so very proud of him that he had transformed his life so profoundly and successfully. But what struck me most was what he told me shortly before I discharged him.

During the course of our work together, I was aware that he had had suicidal thoughts, and that he often felt so frustrated with other people in his life that he feared he might hurt someone. He never admitted to having a plan to carry it out, or to follow through on it in any way. But just before I discharged him, he told me that he had come precariously close to killing himself on one occasion. That on one night, a couple of years prior, everything just seemed to be closing in on him, and he suddenly felt desperate enough to put an end to all of it. He certainly had the means to follow through with it, as he was still an avid gun enthusiast. One of the ways he managed stress and found pleasure in his life was to go to the shooting range for target practice. I was a little concerned that he had access to guns in his house, access to lethal weapons—but, overall, after considering it carefully, it seemed like the benefits of continuing to use firearms far outweighed the risk to himself or others. Honestly, without a plan or another clear indication that he would use them inappropriately, let alone to kill, there was little I could do, or wanted to do, to discourage him. If I had had any concerns, of course, I would've been inclined to discuss it with him. To ask him to give the guns up voluntarily.

He had a whole stockpile of them. You can imagine the types of weapons he was accustomed to handling. He finally admitted to me one day that he had come very close, indeed, to putting a bullet through his head. He told me it was only one time, and that since then, he had never considered, and would never consider it, again. But what was most astounding to me was when he told me that he had just gotten rid of all of his guns a few days before his confession to me. I was truly staggered! Of course, I didn't let on to it. But he also added that he had done it because he had seen the massive carnage at the elementary school, had felt the anguish over the deaths of those little children, and was so affected by it that he knew he had to do something specific about it, something personal. And the first thing he thought of doing was to give up his arsenal, his precious gun collection, that had served him so well over the years. I was so impressed by his gesture, that I couldn't resist embracing him when we finished our last session together, while he was readying himself to leave the office for the last time. I felt so much love for this man. I had seen him go through such an enormous struggle; I had accompanied him down such a treacherous path. Witnessed the transformation month by month, over the years, from such an intimate and privileged vantage point. I was so gratified to see him come out on top. To see the strides he'd made, and how far he had evolved as a human being. I was truly touched, and he began to cry when I took him into my arms. I teared up, too. And that image of us holding each other was burned indelibly into my consciousness.

I became almost obsessed with thoughts about this man, as well as my other patient who had lost his son due to that very same mass shooting—the one that had spurred them both on, and that became a vehicle for transforming their grief into real, palpable action. It was like I suddenly had this smoldering flame inside of me that constantly nagged at me, that wouldn't let me go, from that moment on. But not in the way you might think. It didn't seem to inspire me to follow their lead, at least at the time. It felt like it had to be dealt with, somehow. But yet, I didn't have the ability or means to make that happen. I began to feel more and more depressed as time went on. I started having dark thoughts and feelings, though they were rather amorphous at first. I even considered putting myself on antidepressants, but I realized that that was not the solution to this new problem of mine. All the drugs in the world wouldn't have cured what I was dealing with. I needed to figure it out, to do something different, to do something dramatic. To find a new mission and make a greater difference. To reinvent myself. And that's exactly what I did! I eventually closed up my practice, bought a car, and drove all the way across the country. And what better place for a new beginning, than Vegas? But I'm getting way ahead of myself.

I don't know about you, but talking about all this stuff is starting to exhaust me. Maybe it's the weather. I feel like we're going to have a change at any moment. I can always tell when the air starts to feel heavier. It gets softer. Less sharp on the lungs. Even indoors. My friend, what do you say about getting up and getting ourselves outside and having a bit of a stroll? Let's stretch our legs and have a walk. That ought to get me out of any kind of rut, or malaise.

Yes, indeed, a walk never fails to stimulate again. How couldn't it? Just take a look at all the neon and glitter around us. How it dazzles the senses! How this penetrating desert air lends an exceptional crispness and lucidity. After all those horrid winters I experienced in the Northeast, it was a real pleasure to immerse oneself in this oversized sauna. Then again, the heat can be utterly oppressive, especially during the summers. One has to get used to it—and to the fact that mostly everything you do here will have to be done at night or indoors, in the deep freeze of unrelenting air conditioning.

Do you know what 'Las Vegas' means in Spanish? 'The Meadows,' my friend. Isn't that endearing? Not a speck of green for miles! Well, that's not exactly true. Before all this was built up, this valley did have some life to it, apparently. And water—there were springs here before they dried up. There may've even been an actual meadow here. At least part of the year. But don't let that fool you! There are still flash floods on occasion, and if they don't manage to sweep you away and end up killing you, once they wash over the terrain, you'll see a sudden, but short-lived, bloom arise. A momentary blush, just a few bits of vegetation, a stray wildflower or two, scattered haphazardly through the cracks in the streets and sidewalks. Only to wither away and be reclaimed by the harshness of the next stretch of uninterrupted sun. Everything else you see here is artifice. Artificially brought in and cultivated by the businesses that dominate the man-made cityscape. Besides the floods, and the torrents of rain that spawn them, this patch of desert has very little water to speak of that's innate, that isn't imported from somewhere else. You couldn't grow any food around here naturally. You'd have to get some good greenhouses, I imagine.

It's odd to think how fertile the land is just a few hundred miles away from here. California's Central Valley lies due west of here, past Death Valley and over the Sierra Nevada Mountains. It is one of the richest agricultural regions in the world. Fruits and vegetables and grain as far as the eye can see! And then there are the grapes and wine up north, and the vast and fecund ocean beyond that. A virtual paradise compared to here. I can only think of a few places to rival it: perhaps Provence, in France, with its undulating hills, blanketed with sunflowers and lavender; or some far off Hawaiian island, where tropical fruit abounds and the scent of coffee permeates the air. All that water and sun, producing such an abundance. Not here. Barely a puddle to dip your foot in. Thoroughly landlocked. Unless you include Lake Mead. And you probably know how that came about.

Yes, all this neon! As far as the eye can see! It makes you a little dizzy, no? It has a way of mesmerizing you, like a moth to a flame. It's almost as if you can't turn away, like you're utterly transfixed by its power. All the color and motion. Every marquee tells a story, has a theme, or, at the very least, an appealing motif that beguiles you. Just like the thousands of slot machines inside. They're summoning us like the Sirens, seducing us with their flashing lights and bells, with whatever fantasy has enough personal appeal to encourage you to gladly part with your last few dollars, or at least suck a few shekels from your vulnerable soul.

What do you get in return for your sacrifice? Hope? No, surely you can't be that naïve. If there were any other industry that treated you the way the casinos do, anywhere else, people would be outraged. It would be a major scandal. Taking your money and giving nothing in return? It's a glorified pyramid scheme. Artificially propped up. There's no trickle down. You think the average worker here, the casino and restaurant workers, the venue workers, all the people who are here to serve you, get anything of significance from any of this? No, they're treated like minions, like slaves. They don't have unions to back them up anymore. They don't get any respect. The whores don't even get paid enough. They get pennies on the dollar. Crumbs off the table. Anywhere else, there'd be picket lines and righteous demonstrations everywhere you turn, and riots in the streets! The casinos would be run out of town, and their bosses would be lucky to escape with their lives. In the past, just stealing one head of cattle would've gotten you shot or hanged. Not here. They distract you with a wealth of other delights to make sure you don't notice, or think about it. Free hotel rooms, free drinks, free entertainment, whatever your heart desires. But don't let them fool you. Don't let the lure of false hope turn you into a victim.

There aren't any virtues here, my friend. No *real* hope, or temperance or charity. Just vices: greed, gluttony, and lust, more or less. Just a lot of hidden misery, and addictions of all shapes and sizes. All in the service of a very select group of people making billions for doing nothing. They doll everything up to make it look entirely acceptable and palatable. Remember the old Times Square in New York City? At least there was some honesty there. They didn't try to pretend that it wasn't sleazy. What you saw is what you got. Now, it looks like a Disney theme park. Same thing here. All this luxury!

Yet, if you drive just barely out of town, you'll find the most abject poverty you can imagine, in its shadow. There are other types of reservations not too far from this one, just a few hours away, where things certainly aren't very pretty. There are casinos there, too, but at least there's some kind of poetic justice to what they're doing. Providing a means of sustenance for their people. Yes, at the expense of their historical enemies, their oppressors, but what's more fitting than a little economic payback and revenge? How do you say 'touché' in Navajo? Well, whatever it is, we know Montezuma lives another day.

But don't try to convince anyone of these facts. It's useless. The people in charge have been spreading propaganda for a long time, claiming the opposite is true. Just try to convince someone, anyone, that this place is a complete wreck and is profiting off your gullibility and weakness. I challenge you to stop someone right here on the street, and repeat what I've just said to you. They'll laugh at you. In fact, they'll ridicule you, to your face! The same way an addict does who's in denial. But then they'll go home and take it out on their wife or kids, because they know it's true. Or, at the very least, they'll kick the dog…

The key to understanding Vegas is to realize that the fundamental principle at work here is sadism. No, I'm not kidding. There's nothing more appealing to the forces in power than keeping the population and its visitors in bondage and servitude. To make them submit, and to dominate them. If you resist, you'll be punished. It might be hard to see out here on the streets. But in the back alleys, the privacy of the hotel room, and other more obscure places, there's an abundance of masochists for every sadist, and the more unaware they are of their own exploitation, the better.

In fact, there's no need to force people to submit. They eagerly conform of their own accord. Or they'll finally be converted by applying unrelenting pleasure—the type that's so intoxicating that it's like getting force-fed foie gras, to the point of gagging. Pleasure to the extreme. Pleasure that transforms itself into a peculiar type of pain. A sickliness that requires more and more reinforcement for the same effect. That's never satisfied or satiated. Everyone's in on it here! From the casino owners, all the way down to the humblest service provider. Everyone wants a piece of the action, and they convince themselves, and each other, that it's all good, that it all makes sense. It's a self-fulfilling prophecy, of sorts. Even the janitors and maids get theirs. No matter how much puke they clean out of the toilets, or how much cum they remove from the bedcovers, they'll always have an outlet downstream. Someone to dump on. To look down their noses at. There's no end to the number of people on the streets, homeless or otherwise, who've come to a desperate place in their lives—the gamblers who've lost it all, and then some; the escorts and other garden-variety prostitutes who proudly proclaim that they're somehow empowered, only to lose all self-respect; the alcoholics and junkies, who have no good answers other than giving up. Few of them are capable of having even the most minimal amount of energy to protest, let alone the ability to answer with some meaningful pushback.

But, again, don't try to convince anyone that Vegas is in the undertaking business. No, sir! They'll call you uptight. They'll say 'If you don't like it, don't come here in the first place!' They wholeheartedly embrace the dysfunction. They flaunt it and tease you with it. Even though it's vacant and empty, with nothing substantial or satisfying to back it up, they'd rather die than own up to the fact that most of the time they're doing their dirty little things, they're actually ashamed of it. Behind closed doors, in secretive spaces and the recesses of their minds. The 'do-gooders', whether genuine or fake, are the enemy, according to them. But do-gooders will also have a very hard time here, despite what they imagine they can accomplish, because of their own twisted little fantasies. Sometimes they're just as twisted as their counterparts. They've got that 'holier than thou' attitude. They might think they're here to save people from their suffering and degradation. But they don't realize that they're profoundly impotent—because they don't understand or speak the language. Nobody wants to be saved if the cure is worse than the disease, right? So, it's like you've got all sorts of cult leaders here with their flocks, and none of them want to be taken to task or contradicted. Either you're with us, or you're against us, amigo. And if you're against us, you'd better get the hell out of town!

Ever notice how people are always smiling around here? And, god forbid, you're not. They're going to do anything within their power to make you happy, whether you want to be or not. Just imagine, one day, when you return to your hotel room after breakfast, and you've forgotten to put the 'Do Not Disturb' sign on the doorknob, and the housekeeper is still servicing your room. How you get that sour, sinking feeling in the pit of your stomach, just because you might need to use the bathroom urgently, or because you just want to get back into bed and kick your heels up

70

for a while. You just can't get them out of there fast enough! Yet, you both force a smile for propriety's sake. If you were to catch a glimpse of yourself in the mirror, or glance quickly over, when her guard is down, you might notice a momentary, fleeting grimace. A subtle indication that all is not well in paradise. The only way to make things right, to put an end to the discomfort, or at least your own guilt, with a minimum of effort and pain, is to awkwardly drop a disproportionately oversized tip on her just before she runs for the door. That'll bring a smile back!

See, I'm not immune to it, either. I've also noticed, if you want to keep up appearances, and maintain the peace, don't go too far afield for anything. Stick to the places in town. Don't go looking for anything too authentic, because then you'll have to go to where the real people live, on the outskirts of town. They don't necessarily want to see you, or any other tourists, in their downtime, because it's just going to subconsciously remind them of their parasitic connection to the industry, and to you. There's no point sticking people's noses in it. Not even for a fabulous meal.

It's not just that there's abuse from the top down. There's also abuse from side to side. Economic exploitation is leveled in every direction—but its final resting stop, obviously, is at the bottom. It *has* to be that way, or else it wouldn't work. No matter where you are in the hierarchy, though, those in the levels above don't really want to hear any complaints from below. They'll despise you for reminding them of how they're blatantly oppressing you. So, if you're unlucky enough to sink toward the bottom, and there're no more dogs left to kick, they'll just suck in more victims, from the rest of the world.

Short a few positions? No problem! It's not that hard to convince people to come here to earn barely minimum wage, if that, plus tips, when they're making pennies on the dollar per hour, in some awful overseas sweatshop hell. We'll even arrange for the visas. Vegas is the top of the line, friends. No other venue can even come close to competing. You'll be able to indulge in everything it has to offer, and still be able to send a good amount of cash back to your relatives in the old country.

Or, if you're one of the lucky ones, and it's not imperative to relieve your family members of their despair and misery, you might even save up for something special. Perhaps a Hermès handbag, or a shiny new Rolex! If you're really ambitious, you might even save up enough to embark on a good college education. But for most people, they'll only be trading one compromised position for another.

The important thing, though, is to keep on working, and smiling! Don't think about it too much, and don't let those doubts or negative feelings trip you up. Your supervisors won't approve of that. They'll do anything within their power to keep encouraging you. They're not in the business of offending you, my friend. Have you noticed how nice and tidy everything is around here? How clean it is? How appealing everything is? There's a reason for that. It's not just for the visitors. You don't really have truth in advertising here. Can you imagine the signs you'd see? Can you imagine how embarrassing it'd be if they publicly acknowledged what they're actually doing? *'Feel like a loser, and about to give up on life? C'mon in! Get shit-faced drunk and forget all about it!'* Or, *'Need to pump yourself up? Check out this magnificent treasure! Buy a Rolex with your kid's college fund —and they'll thank you for it!'* Or, *'Tired of your nagging wife? Our girls will screw you so hard that you'll be begging for more!'* Just imagine the scandal and moral outrage…

I know why *I'm* in Vegas. But do you think most people understand why *they're* here? What do you think? I always wonder what people are trying to get away with here. Or, is it more simple than that? Am I reading too much into it? Don't be shy. You can tell me what you think. I want to learn. You do understand that everything you say in my presence will be treated confidentially? Your words, the thoughts you share, will never be traceable back to you. After all, I don't even know your name, do I?

If I were to be a hundred percent honest, I'd say I get away with everything and nothing here. Simultaneously. If I were wearing a mask, it'd be two-faced. Half tragic, half comic. The sign above my door would say, '*Trust me! At the core, I'm an honest broker.*' My business card would read, 'Clemens, Witness/Confidant'...

You know, when all those children were killed—slaughtered, in fact—it *really* affected me. I think it affected everyone. But, regrettably, it didn't seem to change much in terms of the bigger picture. You would've thought that if there were anything that could have changed minds, that should've done it. It's so sad to think that even then, after that bloodbath, there still wasn't enough will in this country to make a difference. What could be easier to form a consensus on? To act on? It should have been a slam dunk, but it began to feel downright hopeless. It began to feel as if all the pleas and attempts to stop the madness were just a waste of time, lost in a tangle of words. It's like we're trapped in some kind of Tower of Babel. Moving our lips, but not being understood.

Not to mention that those tragic losses, rather than being leveraged for change, were instead deliberately negated and forgotten about, if not exploited, by officials who could've used their influence to make a difference. Opportunities were squandered and lost, time after time. Left in limbo and to die in the ether. Honestly, most of the time, they occupied themselves with meaningless and irrelevant activity, only pretending to care... But how can we be sure that *anyone* is listening, including the people I speak with? Truly listening with an open heart and an open mind. Whatever the case, I guess I'm committed to the notion that I'm going to say what I have to say whether we end up connecting or not. If any of it manages to reach someone, if anyone finds any meaning in it in any way, it's worth it, even if it gets interpreted in ways that I didn't intend. At the very least, it might stimulate further thought on the subject. If it hits the mark —like I said—it's fine. I'm happy to take a bow. If not, then at least it's off my chest. Even *that* counts for something.

You might accuse me of extreme vanity, having these kinds of thoughts ricocheting around inside my head. Believing that I have something to say that—on its face—might be meaningful or worthwhile to my partners across the table at Casablanca. But I'd say I'm actually quite modest, at least as far as my approach is concerned. The most important thing for me to remember is to just continue on with it, no matter the outcome. I've gotten comfortable with that, and I encourage you to join me in that spirit, too.

Because it's not about me, frankly. It's about the people I engage with, and what they do once they leave the safety of this environment. I try to be as straightforward as possible, to get to the point as soon as possible, as efficiently as I can. Because if it seems like you're just blabbering on and on, forever, you'll lose them, for sure. I think I've always been very generous with my time, and have received just as freely. But it's also important for me to feel as if I'm being met halfway, so to speak. To feel as if, once I've engaged with someone, we're going to establish some sort of kinship—or at the very least, some kind of peer relationship. That we're actively collaborating toward a greater, more elevated goal. I have to say, I'm proud of myself for having the skill to talk with just about anyone. I'm a jack-of-all-trades, in that regard. That's what my father used to say about me, in general. He meant it as a covert criticism, a put-down, I think—in the sense of having mastery of nothing. That's how he felt about it. It wasn't surprising coming from him, as brilliant as he was. But I might argue that, taking a more expansive view of things, despite my modest abilities, that being above average at a handful of things can be used to my advantage. I'm like a modern-day, bush-league Renaissance man, if I may say so myself.

You can laugh. But I think we've gotten so exceedingly specialized that it's undoubtedly had a very negative effect on the world. Gotten us into a lot of trouble here on Earth. I'd like to think that I've developed the ability, with time and practice, to be more flexible than your average person. I was lucky to be born a sensitive soul, to have the instinct to adapt when necessary, and am therefore willing to cast a wider net. I wanted to excel at everything, even if I didn't like it, didn't want to hear about it, or didn't seem to be well suited to it. For example, when I was young, I was a very good piano player, despite never having the drive to put forth the effort and discipline to practice. Nonetheless, I could've had a future in classical music, in some minor capacity. But ultimately I had to admit to myself that the constant repetition and rigid perfectionism that I had to be a slave to, in order to be successful, wasn't a good fit, given the personality I had. I had to allow myself not to be so single-minded about it. To have a more relaxed attitude, a more workable approach, and more balance in my life. The exactitude itself didn't seem to sit well with me. The extreme, even in the abstract, seemed to scare me off. But after I had distanced myself from that world, and had had other, more satisfying life experiences under my belt, I discovered that I could still channel that previously uncomfortable and anxious disposition that I applied to playing the piano, into something more constructive and benevolent, as long as I could manage it appropriately. That even though I had resisted committing fully to any kind of specific, highly specialized discipline in the past, I *had* learned something valuable. That I could tolerate a more extreme attitude when necessary, as long as it was channeled into a cause or mission that seemed worth it. It became more or less natural to utilize this more complex and sometimes contradictory plasticity of mind in the service of others, for example; in practice, I became comfortable and satisfied by any amount of progress that was made, no matter how small. If I didn't feel totally satisfied, it just motivated me to do better.

After those fateful days, and in particular, the day the children died, there was a creeping feeling inside of me that was gaining steam and wouldn't go away. An awareness that continuing along as if nothing had or could change would not be sustainable. Their little faces kept popping up in my mind's eye. Sometimes at the most unexpected moments. There was something bigger urging me on, and each day brought more clarity, through the veil of my own denial. I wasn't exactly sure what I was in denial about, but it was there and it was undeniable. I had to acknowledge it and take the time to literally pick my brain apart—to look back on the arc of my life and figure out why I was suddenly feeling so uneasy and dissatisfied; to take time to listen to myself better, to these pangs of conscience. I thought I had already been doing a good job listening to, and through, my patients, but I discovered that I had to tap into something deeper, across a wider spectrum; that there was something tugging at me more forcefully, that was greater than just the microcosm of the psychiatric world, and the internal machinations of people's minds. There was so much more going on in the greater world to pay attention to—and not acknowledging it, as a therapist, was a serious oversight. A serious mistake. There are man-made disasters, but natural ones too: wars going on, epidemics, famine, forced migration, poverty. I started donating more time and money to a whole slate of charities and causes, but mostly from a distance, at arm's length. I had to eventually admit to myself that other people were doing the real work, not me. In short, despite my natural inclinations, I started to understand in a different way, and felt the first stirrings of an emerging, political awakening.

Then again, having your head in the sand has its upside. If you stay away from politics, people are willing to disclose just about anything. They're thrilled that you're even making the effort to listen. It's easy enough to lure in even the most cynical of people, particularly if you maintain a more or less neutral position. It's not hard to form an immediate intimacy, but it may be limited in nature. On the other hand, just throw around even the most innocent of political commentary, the slightest whiff of controversy, and people will scatter like cockroaches. Except, of course, for the people who are legitimately engaged in figuring out what it's all about.

The people who don't want to engage, the people who aren't comfortable enough to toss ideas around, whether or not they have a strong opinion on the subject, run as if their lives depended on it! And they'll abandon you with such theatricality that they might just as well kick you on the way out. Sometimes, I think drama is the whole point with some people. Some people's lives are so uninteresting and empty that it's the only thing that makes them feel alive. So, for that reason, when in the realm of politics, I rarely take on more than one person at a time. I can't afford to lose anyone. You know, keeping to the 'two's company, three's a crowd' philosophy. It's astonishing how quickly two people can turn on each other, and want to destroy one another, if you so innocently engage a threesome. They'll be at each other's necks in no time flat, and there's not much you can do once the cat's out of the bag. Just try to wrangle them back in. Just about impossible. Believe me, I've tried. On one too many occasions. It's a waste of time, at a certain point. They might even start blaming you for starting the whole thing. Leaves a bad taste in everyone's mouth. I've discovered that, in essence, you really only have a couple of chances to do it right.

Whatever the case, I go to Casablanca every day with no expectations. I just let it happen. I'm not necessarily going to come at you with the hard sell, if you know what I mean. Just let the people come! It's up to me to figure out how to be clever—

how to proceed given the personality at hand in front of me. I do have a bit of an advantage after all, given my former profession. Yes, I *used* to be a full-time psychiatrist. Now I'm...

I really do prefer talking with women. They're so much more open-minded and invested. It seems to come naturally to them. Men, on the other hand, as a whole, play all sorts of games to ensure themselves that they'll get the upper hand in the end. It's that macho thing. They're much harder to reach, and there's an arrogance built in. Not at all surprising, since men are mostly responsible for the mess we find ourselves in today. Let's face it! Or, do you think that's too much of an exaggeration? In my experience, more often than not, men almost always come with some sort of chip on their shoulder, and want to get into a pissing match. You seem to be an exception to that rule, my friend. And I thank you for that.

You might ask, if I feel so pessimistic, why bother? Why bother engaging at Casablanca at all? After all, my only weapons are words. It's just talk. While that might be true, I guess words are the only weapons I've ever had. It's the only way I feel empowered and competent. No, don't laugh! I guess for a certain time, it just wasn't in me to dive into the world of direct action, the world of actual political activism. I can't tell you how many picket lines I've been in, only to be spat on for asking for the most modest improvements. Or how many hours I've wasted begging resistant people to join the union, for their own benefit. I've done that before and can only claim that my excuse is that if I spend too much time in that world again, my heart might rot, and then I'll be of no use to anyone. To some degree, it's too late for me. I've been contaminated. I'm too bitter, too impatient. There's too much resistance. I'm afraid it will defeat me. To be perfectly honest, I'm just damn tired. No, really. I'm just trying to be realistic.

Besides, there seems to be an excess, these days, of overly energetic young people and their allies who seem to be more than willing and able to engage, to eat and drink the frontlines. They seem to thrive off it, thank god. More power to them! Just look at all the young people taking the reins. I truly admire them! They seem to have an unlimited and irrepressible amount of energy to take down the opposition, and usher in progress. And then there're the people who come here, and find motivation. It does happen, you know! I do have some minor influence, even if it may be ephemeral. I can be quite stubborn, actually. I'm a little like the turtle to the hare. There are folks who get results, who get a lot of attention up front, but my strength lies in the long game. Down the stretch. You might say Apollo is my god. A bit cool and detached. But effective. We already have plenty of Dionysian energy out there doing its thing. The more in-your-face approach. I prefer a bit of stealth. Besides, it works better with the more difficult cases. Perhaps that's the best analogy to illustrate how I'm trying to accomplish things.

But let me share an experience with you that I had shortly after I arrived here in Vegas. It's a perfect example of what I'm talking about, about how things can go terribly wrong, with respect to what we've just been talking about. Of course, from my point of view.

One of the first things I did after I arrived here, even before I decided to settle here, was to visit one of the casinos, just to see what they were like. I don't remember exactly which one, but I'd never spent any time in a casino, even outside of Vegas, surprisingly. In fact, on this first encounter, keeping with the spontaneity of the mood I was in, I decided to duck in and take a look around, with, admittedly, a rather devil-may-care attitude. My first impression, as I weaved my way through the thousands of automated slot machines that filled the room, that were all firing off in a fanatical cacophony of light and sound, was how people could manage to concentrate at all in such a dizzying environment. But people weren't having any trouble at all. In fact, they were engaged to such an extent that you would've had a very hard time distracting them from all the fun they were having. Despite that, I couldn't help think that it seemed sad that there were literally hundreds of people sitting in front of these machines, drinks in hand, pressing down on those flashing buttons in near unison, mindlessly and mechanically squandering away nickels and dimes, dollars and cents—lunch money, or mortgage payments, even small fortunes—in the hope that they'd be lucky enough to strike it rich, against all odds. It was like a scene out of the movie *Metropolis*—so many people going through the motions, but without so much as getting the slightest satisfaction of pulling down on an actual lever. Not very interesting or inspiring, as I saw it. Quite the opposite.

What I imagined and expected was something more akin to what you'd see in a different kind of movie. A more glamorous Hollywood-style production. Elegant people dressed in tuxedos and gowns, actively engaged against their competition, hovering over a beguiling assortment of games of chance. In the casino, the card games seemed most interesting—at least they required a certain amount of skill to be successful at. But I, like most people, seemed more attracted to the games that offered the most emotional feedback, the most dramatic of responses, understandably. The Craps table seemed interesting, but I was so confused and baffled by the intricacies of the game, I just didn't have the patience to try to wrap my head around it. Roulette seemed more my speed, a little more comprehensible, but just as exciting—so I decided to observe for a while, close by, to take it all in.

There was a thick crowd of people surrounding the table, of all stripes and varieties, some of whom were actively engaged in the game, others who were just about to jump in or out, and still others who were merely observers. The majority were dressed in regular street clothes, but there was a rather elegant-looking couple standing across from me who immediately attracted my attention. I assumed they had just attended a wedding, or something of that nature, because the man was decked out in a well-tailored three-piece suit, and his female companion, dressed to the nines in an elegant, backless, celandine green gown, highlighted with shimmering, iridescent sequins. It would've been hard *not* to notice them. They seemed to be enjoying the game, acting and reacting like everyone else, but with perhaps a little more relish. They seemed to be a little more invested in choosing which number, of all the numbers, they were going to place their pile of chips on. I was curious about their approach, and tried to make sense of it in my head because any number that was chosen at random would be equally likely to pay off, in a completely random fashion, presumably.

But then I noticed, before one spin of the wheel, they shifted their chips after the ball had been thrown into the wheel well. It took me by surprise, and I'd wondered if anyone else had seen the same. To add to my astonishment, they ended up landing on the winning number. I was shocked! It seemed to me that they had just cheated, technically speaking. Before I knew it, my mouth seemed to take over, and I blurted out, 'Hey, they moved their chips! Did you see that?' I was wondering if anyone else had noticed. I was standing next to a guy who looked over at me and shrugged, while the rest of the people surrounding the roulette table erupted into wild cheers. After the celebration died down, I repeated myself, but more vociferously, in the direction of the croupier. He smiled feebly, but only ignored me, preparing himself for the next spin. He certainly didn't seem to care either way, nor did he make the slightest fuss about it. All the chips on the table were collected before he nudged a hefty stack back in front of the winning couple. They appeared to be thrilled with what had

81

happened, but I had the distinct feeling that something suspicious was going on—I swear I detected a slight indication on their faces and in their demeanor—that somehow there was a minor conspiracy going on, right under our noses. I got the feeling that they hoped nobody had noticed what had happened, or heard what I had blurted out.

Then, all of a sudden, a guy who was standing next to me started shifting his feet around restlessly, mumbling muffled words to himself. He was a middle-aged man, with a great shock of platinum gray hair under his trucker's hat, balanced like a bird's nest on the dome of his head. An angry red sunburn radiated from his cheeks and forearms. He wore a cheap pair of shorts and a T-shirt, held together by the obligatory fanny pack that accentuated the paunch of his flabby stomach. The moment I reiterated my point, he seemed to become mortally offended, as if he were being accused of cheating himself. Even though everyone else around the table had already moved on, turning their attention away from the potential controversy, not feeling obliged to meet my dangling words with any kind of rejoinder, this agitated man, of all people, insisted on engaging with me, meeting my words with a challenge of his own. He said something along the lines of, 'Hey, Bud. What's your problem? Mind your own business.' To which I didn't reply.

It seemed sort of pointless for me to press on in any way, but this guy didn't want to drop it. It seemed like he wanted to have it out with me. Then he added, 'What the fuck is your problem? What—you think you know how to run this place better than they do? You're a real jerk! What a loser!' Again, my intent was to continue to ignore him, until the situation diffused itself. But then the guy gave me a rather forceful shove, pressing his open hand against my breastbone, getting into my personal space, throwing me back a bit from the table. With that, my reflexes instinctively kicked in, and I responded by swinging my arm in his direction, catching his ear, unfortunately, with an open palm. It was purely reflexive. I didn't even have time to think about it. It certainly wasn't in my character to start a fight, but that's sort of what happened, at least how it appeared from the perspective of a random observer. It seemed my hand landed on a very vulnerable spot, and the blow, though nominal, forced him to collapse into a heap on the floor. He did, in all honestly, seem to be in quite a bit of pain, even though I hadn't intended it to be quite so violent. It was simply automatic. But it might not have appeared that way, especially with my adversary's pathetic attempt to embellish. As you can imagine, with all of the sudden commotion, in-house security was called immediately, and they had the unenviable task of trying to figure out what had just occurred. By all appearances, it did appear as if I were the aggressor—and the man, as pitiful as he was, certainly did not discourage that interpretation. All at once, it looked like I was the bad guy, and everyone who had witnessed the event, to the person, seemed happy to pile on. It just goes to show how people love to bully, and like to feel superior. Yes, real winners—all of them!

It wasn't long before the police showed up, of course. I don't want to get into too much detail about what happened after that, but I really began to wonder if the whole thing was some sort of setup, planned from the beginning. Whether the guy was making a commotion on purpose. Whether he had been planted there, expressly, to cause a stink to distract people—the casino personnel, in particular. Was it possible that the man and the couple were secretly working together? I don't think that was ever considered, or resolved. But I knew, whatever the case, I was angry that I had been assaulted in that way, and felt really vexed by how I was treated. Even though I had gotten some semblance of revenge, there was something left inside me that felt as if a great injustice had taken place, and that I should've applied a more conscious and extreme response than I did.

In fact, the incident seemed to provoke murderous fantasies inside my head, and I was surprised by how violent they were. For the next few days, in my daydreams, I concocted another scenario in my head—one in which this same man, who had merely shoved me, was then a clear and present danger, a more obvious and violent perpetrator—and that it would've been absolutely essential for me to meet the threat in a much more aggressive and forceful way. At the same time there was a fear inside of me, because I wondered if he might be armed, and whether he had the right to 'stand his ground', as the law allows in some states that have strong 'Second Amendment rights' sentiments. Nevertheless, in my fantasy, I was the one who took out a handgun, fired at him, and cut him down to size. Honestly, I really had to think about that for a while.

Oh, look over there! You see those little rivulets starting to build up along the curb? It must be raining, somewhere. Let's just hope it passes quickly, that it's just a temporary thing and we don't get a serious flash flood here. We should probably take a seat for now—let's grab this bench before someone else does. Let's keep an eye on the water to make sure it'll still be safe to be out here.

Anyway, after the police came—there's a whole other part to the story that I'll tell you about, at some point. But I think the reason I had had these violent fantasies is because, in the end, I felt that justice hadn't been served. In other words, what had appeared to happen was not the actual story, the real story. I mean, my only sin was that I noticed people were breaking the rules, and I just reacted reflexively to it. My mouth just blurted out those words. Technically they *were* cheating, and not only did they get away with it, somehow I ended up paying the price for it. If I were going to have to play it out again, knowing what I know now, it seems to me that the moment the guy shoved me, I would've been more than justified to lash out at him much more aggressively. A punch, square in the face, would have been better, in hindsight. At the very least, it would have felt more satisfying—and made more sense if the punishment I received had been more commensurate with what occurred.

Having said that, I couldn't deny that there was a part of me that demanded a kind of vigilante justice, the kind that was clear, decisive, and revengeful; in short, where I would've been seen, by all involved, as the incontestable, unequivocal 'winner'. But as soon as I caught on to the stupidity of my gut reaction, I realized that it would've been better had I handled it more maturely. There's a lot of truth to the idea that violence only begets more violence—even though it might feel cathartic in the moment, it will only backfire against you in the end. But there was still a lingering desire to want to 'win', if not through direct action, then certainly in the private space of my own mind, where I continued to process what happened.

I had more fantasies of how that might've looked. Instead of hashing it out with clenched fists, I imagined the cerebral equivalent: persuading with words, with wit, with cutting humor— the kind that would disarm your opponent nonviolently. Attacking stealthily, but with the power of your intellect. I remember when my father first asked me what the most dangerous weapon on Earth was, and how inadequate my answer was, because I answered so naïvely, so literally. I mumbled something about the H-Bomb. His only response was to point to his head. He was right! Besides, what the hell did I care if anyone'd cheated? Why should I even want to get into it with them? They sure did cast out a line and hook me in. I can just imagine them getting a good laugh at my expense. So the moral of the story is 'choose your battles wisely'; and if you decide to engage, don't necessarily shout from the rooftops about it in advance. Because it's more than likely to trigger an automatic response and instant resistance, equal and opposite, that works at cross purposes to your interests.

The main point, though, was that I felt hypocritical, whether or not I swung reflexively. The fact was the repercussions of my actions were not in line with my principles. And whether or not anyone cheated, while the impulse might've been to defend the principles of integrity and honor, I should've been smarter than that. The point was to 'win' by *not* playing the game, and not allowing them to gain a misplaced sympathy by victimizing them. Easier said than done. But I certainly learned something about myself.

Oh, the rain has finally arrived! I wasn't sure if it was going to get to us, but here it is. Let's move up under that awning over there. There's another bench we can grab, as long as we reach it first. If and when the water should come over the curb, we might just opt for going into a casino again. But for now, this isn't a bad perch. I've got a whole bunch of other stories to tell you. So, indulge me, if you will.

Other things happened after that notorious scene around the roulette table. They're a little more complex, naturally, because they involve women. I haven't yet gotten into my love life with you. Not exactly. But you should know that I love women. And always have. There are so many attractive women here in Vegas. Have you noticed? I'm not just talking about their looks. I'm talking about intriguing women. I probably don't have to point that out to you, my friend. It's pretty obvious. You might not imagine I've had much success with women, given my personality and what you know about me so far. But I've actually done quite well in that arena. I'm not an unattractive guy. I have my charms. I have to put some effort into it, but, then again, it hasn't been too hard, either. So, you can understand, at a bare minimum, that I've had some interesting experiences that I can share with you. No matter what your experiences have been with women, I'd bet that every man has at least a few good stories.

One thing men have to realize is that you don't need that much of a strategy to be successful with women. That's not meant to be a slight against women. You just don't need to come up with any kind of elaborate scheme to attract them to you. Just be yourself, but—here's the essential part—be a very good listener. That's *the* most important thing. Whether or not you turn out to be a good match, that's something you can decide when the time comes. But it's the listening that's essential—your presence and focused attention alone account for so much. You've already gotten halfway there, with that alone.

But you can imagine how my profession and personality played to my advantage. From a very young age, I realized that I resonated much more strongly with girls and women than with boys and men. There was a natural fit. Why wouldn't there be? After all, whether you're male or female, we all come from the womb and are nurtured by women as soon as we're born. Most boys and men have that natural caregiving capacity beaten out of us at a very young age. In my case, however, it never seemed to get entirely extinguished. In fact, once I had more control over my own destiny, I reclaimed my deep love and admiration for women and the qualities that distinguish them from men, from mere brutes.

Yet, the misogyny persists, overall. It's absolutely vulgar, if you ask me. How *can't* you prefer the company of women, when you're faced with the alternative? Just look around you! Look at all the crowds of creepy men crawling around Las Vegas. It's not too high a standard to surpass, no? At least that's what I think. But I'd go further. I believe, sincerely, that women are superior to men, *especially* here. You know what the men are looking for, right? The other woman, more or less. It really doesn't matter if they're currently in a relationship or not. They're looking for what they *really* want, or, should I say, what they *think* they want. Which is mostly driven by the desire for sex. Let's face it.

Why do you think there're so many conventions here? Think about it. I knew a guy who was absolutely outraged that his industry association's convention wasn't going to be held in Las Vegas anymore. The powers that be thought it might be a good idea to mix things up and have a convention in some other city, for once. Just once. But the opposition was so universal and vociferous that they were forced to return to Vegas the very next year, and they never even thought about going anywhere else after that. Right back here in Vegas every single year since then. Why? Because it gives men an opportunity to get away from their usual lives—meaning, their wives, or significant others, or whoever—to have the freedom to hire hookers and strippers out in the open. For their indulgence, without the inconvenience of having to feel guilty about it. That's the truth.

It's completely normalized here—and even if most of their partners should find out about it, more often than not, they've been groomed to tacitly accept it, rationalizing it away as if it's just the normal price to be paid for maintaining a relationship with a man. Even industries that are a majority of women come here for their conventions. That's how deeply warped and ingrained it is. Some women even wholeheartedly embrace the aesthetic that has been established by men, and act on it, in their own way.

But imagine, if you will, what it must feel like for a woman to come here and discover a man who isn't like all of the rest. Who reminds them of what it feels like to be respected and treated like a whole human being, not just a piece of meat. Yes, that's a very powerful thing. Never underestimate the effect this has. Yet, almost everyone will buy into the denial, in the most predictable ways. I, personally, consider most women to be superior to me, as I said, so it's only natural for women to be well-positioned to take advantage of me. Don't laugh! I'm not kidding. Yes, it might not come naturally for women to notice how malleable I am, or for them to take advantage of it, once they're aware of it. But I'm the *biggest* pushover. Very easy. Very loose. Any woman who wants to have her way with me will not find the slightest resistance from me. I'm more than happy to oblige, free of charge. I bet you didn't suspect that about me, did you? C'mon, admit it. Don't be surprised! I've had my share of successes, but not in the way men would normally comprehend. It would make them feel very, very uncomfortable, to even imagine themselves conducting themselves that way.

But, just imagine, for argument's sake, that I had met someone who I was *truly* interested in? Not that the odds are naturally stacked that way. I think the probability of finding someone in the 'soulmate' category is next to nothing here. In some ways, that's a good thing. It fits with the overall program. Even with all of the opportunities I had. I certainly wasn't bored, nor was there any lack of congratulating myself. It may seem like I'm a pretty dull guy. But, even if it's true, I always enjoy the company of women —and sex, in particular. Why mince words? Sex has always been very important to me. I enjoyed it from a young age and will continue to enjoy it. As long as it's clean and uncomplicated. I do connect emotionally, but I've come to the conclusion that there will probably be only one true love amongst all the relationships I've had or could have. And that true love was in the very distant past. So, perhaps, it's no mistake that, most recently, I spend more time focused on the more superficial aspects of relationships. At least it appears that way. But I'm no hypocrite, like most of the men around here.

During this period of my life, I look for every and all opportunities to engage with women, for my own needs, but also for theirs. We've had a lot of fun along the way, and I've tried to keep focused, despite the fact that it could've easily distracted me. There are so many women out there who are desperate just to be treated well. Of those who still want to have anything to do with men anymore. I have plenty of resources, I can indulge them in any way their fantasies lead them. I guess I could've spent money on prostitutes, but what would've been the point of that? That's just a simple base transaction. Nothing more comes of it. Besides, there are plenty of wayward husbands who can fulfill that need, and their own needs, too. They're perfectly matched and suited to each other. Lost sheep in a lost world—but lost together. I have a greater mission, so by definition, it's more of a challenge. I need a lot of turnover, or else there's no point to it. I'm so lucky—there are so many different kinds of women from all over the world here. It really is a kind of paradise. They know what they need and want, and I gladly give it to them. The only thing I want in return is a dialogue. I get the sense early on who would be on board with that. I think most women would be receptive to my point of view, even if I just come out and say it directly, in undisguised form. But I don't insist on anything. I think that's why they love me. I'm not your typical man. I'm not nearly as selfish.

In fact, I'm seen as 'one of the good guys' by many of the women I've interacted with. The type they've been looking for, one they hoped to find all their lives, but with none of the attributes that make a relationship boring. Most 'good guys' are exceedingly tedious and dull. Not me! Spend a little time with me and I'll show you a good time, while I'm doing my work in the background. It'll be a win-win situation! I promise you. Women, in general, never have a hard time having a good time. It seems to be part of their nature. Yes, I admit, there might be a little bit of playacting going on on my part, but generally speaking, the relationship will hinge on its inherent nature, its essential innocence. There you go, again! Laugh all you will. But I'm serious...

I haven't told you yet about my past, about my marriage many years ago. I had actually found my great love in the past. I had found 'the one'. You didn't suspect that, did you? Admit it! Men don't pick up on those things. Yes, it's true. She was everything to me. But I lost her to chance. To pure, dumb chance. Only women seem to be able to pick up on that. They can see it in my eyes. In fact, I've told some of the women who I've met about this love. You might think that it stirs up a certain kind of jealousy. But it only enhances things—the effect it has on them. It encourages them to know that I'd had that history. When I speak of a former love of that kind, I can see their hearts melt. It spurs them on. To reach for more. To reach for the heights.

Yes, when women know you're capable of having a mature, loving relationship, they get seduced by the very notion of it. I admit I played that to my advantage. Why wouldn't I? But then you also have to be constantly aware of it, and discourage them from thinking that if anything happens between us while they're here in Las Vegas it could go any further once they've left. If they claimed they loved me, I'd tell them that I'm not capable of love anymore. If they pushed harder, I'd tell them that going any further down that path would inevitably end poorly. If they somehow became infatuated, I'd make light of it, and tell them how foolish they'd feel as soon as they returned home. If they still didn't get the hint to drop it, I'd just insist that I was still in love with my deceased wife, and that there was nothing they could do about that. That usually put an end to it, even if they contended that more than one love is possible in a lifetime. I'd finish with 'not for me.' I truly did think that it'd be next to impossible for any woman to live up to my wife's standard. I truly felt that way. But to avoid getting into too many arguments of that nature, I'd sprinkle most of my conversations with some vague pessimisms, like 'I don't know *what* to feel anymore' or 'I'm so tired'. In other words, even if the magic could happen, I'd be incapable of recognizing it, or having enough energy to follow through.

The absolute truth of the matter was that I wasn't on the market, that I was focused on other things that were more important to me, that superseded any personal relationship. On the other hand, if I felt that they were starting to slip away from my grasp, I'd go back to the other end of the spectrum again. I had to keep them in my clutches long enough so that a dialogue could be had, and see where it led us after a few days' time. It's so much harder to hold on when you don't have as many tools to work with. That's why it's so much harder to keep men engaged—there's just less to leverage—your only currencies are values, language, and the power of persuasion. You only have so much time to work—if you can utilize any kind of shortcut, by all means do so. In the case of women—a little flirting, a little manipulation, even. Yes, I'd let them all know how little time I had available so that they'd be certain to fit some in, on their end of things. I also tried to play off the dynamic of their relationship to their male partners, often arranging time together when I knew their husbands wouldn't be unavailable. I had them make up questionable excuses for their absence, hoping to rub it in their partners' noses. I knew their schedules, when their vacations were coming to an end, and exactly when they'd be going home. All this detailed knowledge worked very well for me, of course, but, if I was too careless about how I used it, they'd be begging me to help them leave their husbands. While that would've been counterproductive for me in the moment, and uncomfortably awkward, I actually thought how great it would be if they did, as long as it didn't affect me, as long as they wouldn't try to circle back to me romantically. That wasn't the main point of our relationship, our interchange. At least from my point of view. It was never the point.

Even so, there was always a small minority of women who were much more difficult targets. Who were much more difficult to persuade with the standard approaches. And ones who didn't think I was necessarily the best looking or attractive man available. For whatever reason. Let's be honest, I'm just one man who can't possibly appeal to all women. Well, there are some men who think that *every* woman will be receptive or accommodating to them, no matter what. I'm certainly not that man. So, admittedly, in the early days, I confess that I was much more manipulative than I should've allowed myself to be. I did lay it on way too thick sometimes. Telling them how absolutely horrible their partners were. How they did themselves a grave disservice by staying with them. That I had an 'inexplicable feeling' about them that couldn't be accounted for on any rational plane. That there was a great mystery to it all.

If I drank a little too much, it would be helpful in accentuating how deeply I was supposedly suffering. I'd be a little more melodramatic, pretending I was a bit of a loose cannon or on the verge of falling into a deep depression. Or I'd suddenly become a little more unpredictable, or feign indifference. I'd even start to shift around and pretend to be on the verge of getting up and leaving if it got too far out of reach. There were limits, though. I wouldn't resort to absolute lies, like 'if you don't love me, I might have to kill myself.' No, that was even too much for me. That would've been absolutely shameless. Honestly, what I was doing wasn't necessarily consistent with my values or with what I was trying to accomplish. But I didn't ask for absolute loyalty. Even so, I would sometimes go a smidge too far. Even if I didn't convince them to engage with me, eventually, they would certainly remember me and recall our time together. Not to say that many women, especially the ones who had their shit solidly together, didn't just dismiss me out of hand. Can't say I blamed them.

On very rare occasions, there'd be a woman who'd come along who was a real romantic. By that, I mean someone who had clearly bought into all the usual tropes regarding how relationships should work, from the perspective of what is ingrained by society. The type who buys wholesale into the idea that a woman's main role in society is to be supportive and subservient to men and all their needs. Who 'falls in love,' despite glaringly obvious shortcomings evident in the object of their affection. While that made my job easy, it also made it almost impossible for me to separate myself from her when the work was done. When the time came for her to return home, a woman predisposed to this inclination often dove into a deep depression and anxious jumble of nerves upon separation. She could become downright suicidal. In all honesty, my conscience truly suffered when this happened. Once things had turned in that direction, it was obvious to me that I'd led my subject into very dangerous territory, that the damage had already been done and would continue to happen. And that that kind of abuse—yes, abuse, although not premeditated, not entirely predictable—could not be permitted or tolerated, in the future. You have to make sure you don't fall into bad habits; and realize that every contact made should be evaluated on a case-by-case basis. It wasn't good enough to act by instinct alone, even if one had to pass on the most luscious of carnal delights, that were, at first blush, almost impossible to resist.

Unfortunately, the lesson I should've learned from that experience didn't sink in entirely. I had to wait until a few months later until I finally got the comeuppance I deserved. There was a woman I'd met, who was unique in her own way, in that she appeared to be a prime example of what an empowered woman is. There didn't appear to be anything I could provide for her that she didn't already have, as is the case with most women. We first met by pure chance—casually, up at the bar, in Casablanca—despite the cunning nature of my operation. Although I'm not sure what brought her there, before you knew it, we hit it off and became fast and furious compatriots, if only for a brief time. She was in Vegas with a group of her friends, and I assumed they were having a great time together on their own, in their own space, doing what groups of women do when they're in Vegas. For whatever reason, she made her way to Casablanca alone one night, and found me. It wasn't long before we were ordering each other drinks and starting to feel really loose. There was no question that I was attracted to

94

her. She even reminded me a little of my late wife: not only in attitude, but physically. And it certainly seemed like she was attracted to me. There was a lot of flirting going on. There appeared to be absolutely no reason not to dive right in.

The nature of our conversation lacked focus, but it was free-flowing. It's not like I was intensely focused on it after we'd broken the ice, but we'd gone a good distance toward getting to know one another. Then, suddenly and abruptly, after no more than an hour or so of interchange, she came right out and invited herself to my place! It was a bit cheeky, but then again, I wasn't sure whether she had a place to herself or not. So I acquiesced. I don't ordinarily like to have people in my apartment, but for this woman, on this occasion, I was more than happy to make an exception. I was a little taken aback by the directness of the proposition, the lack of finesse and subtlety, but then again, it seemed well within the bounds of her effervescent personality.

There had been no physical contact at all during the cab ride to my apartment, but as soon as we entered, she let loose. She was very aggressive and intentional. She unbuckled my belt, and then demanded that I remove all my clothes at once. I felt a little vulnerable standing there in front of her completely naked, while she was still fully dressed. Naturally, when she approached me, I assumed the next step would involve removing her clothes. But, when I reached for the top button of her blouse, she immediately swept my hand away. She directed me straight to the bed, and laid me out on my back, before crouching over me. Then it was just a matter of doing what she pleased, when she pleased, and how she pleased. I didn't really have a problem with that, but it did seem a bit odd and disconnected. I couldn't have complained, though, because she was very skilled in her way, and she brought a lot of pleasure. It seemed like her approach to sex was what you might expect from a man. While none of it was out of the ordinary, she was very dominant, yet adventurous.

95

But the thing that was lacking was even a scintilla of any kind of deeper emotional connection, other than the passion in the moment. I'll give her credit for staying and engaging wholeheartedly for an hour or so, but just as quickly as it began, it ended, and in reverse order. When she was done, she got off of me and turned onto her back next to me for just a little while, while she recovered. It wasn't much more than about five minutes when she abruptly got up to use the bathroom. As soon as she returned to the bedroom, she got dressed quickly and prepared herself to leave. And that was it. No exchange of information. No further plan. No hug or kiss. Just the crack of a smile while grabbing her purse, and out the door. No attempt to part politely or fondly, other than exchanging a few empty, perfunctory words. It wasn't like I was going to get up suddenly and throw on a bathrobe to run after her, out the door and down the hallway. I was just left there, a bit stunned, yet somehow grateful for the encounter. Then when I started thinking about it, I realized that it was not the kind of experience that felt right to me. There didn't seem to be a lot of generosity of spirit involved. There didn't seem to be much attention to what I wanted. And although I knew very well what I might be getting myself into, it left me feeling very cold. And cheapened. Very much like I was an object.

There was no point returning to Casablanca that night after that. Because by then, it was too late to get anything done anyway. So I just ended up turning over and falling off to sleep. The next day I woke and went about my morning the usual way. Then just before I was about to leave my apartment for a long walk, I noticed an envelope sitting on my dining room table. There were no markings on it, no indication of its origin. But it was the type of envelope that had the character of fine stationery. A thick gauge and palpable surface texture. Not the ordinary type of business envelope. There was only one way it could've gotten there. It could've only been left there by my companion from the night before. That was the only possibility. I wondered if it was meant for me, or if it had been accidentally left behind. Perhaps it dropped out of her purse on the way out. It seemed to be holding a thick wad of papers inside, as if they were important documents of some kind. I held the envelope up to the light, but because of its heft, I couldn't discern any clue as to what lay inside. All I knew was that I would somehow have to get the envelope back to its rightful owner. Unfortunately, as I said, I didn't know where to find her, unless I just ran into her randomly, or perhaps again at Casablanca. For all I knew, she might've gone back home the very same evening I saw her. Well, as it happened, after my walk, and a late afternoon lunch, I prepared to return to Casablanca for the following day's work. As soon as I arrived at my usual table, guess who was sitting across the room, with a gaggle of her girlfriends? Yes, of course, it was her and about seven or eight of her friends who were getting an early supper. They looked like they were about to descend onto Las Vegas with a vengeance. I have to admit that they all looked stunning, and were a very attractive and enviable group of female diversity. I almost couldn't look away.

After a few minutes had passed and I was settled in, wondering how I should approach the subject of the mystery envelope, I noticed that the group at the table seemed to be alive with activity and chatter, seemingly connected to my presence. My companion from the previous night was facing me from a banquette against the wall—the unofficial ringleader, it appeared— with her friends arrayed around her, like she was holding court. I could see her glance over at me several times, and then more glances from her companions. Followed by some smiles and nervous tittering and a short exchange of words. Some of her friends who had their backs to me even turned around to take a quick gander, before continuing on with the interchange at the table. I really couldn't tell if they were having a good laugh at my expense, or if I were the object of

97

their focus in a more jocular or playful way. What was clear, however, was that the others had been briefed in detail about our encounter, and that there was a bit of boasting going on—that she had apparently been proud of her conquest, and wasn't shy about sharing her experience with others. It actually didn't bother me much whatever the reality, because how could I be offended, given the circumstances? I tried to be a good sport about it, and accepted it as a reasonable price to be paid when one gets involved in that manner.

Then suddenly, there was a quick shift at the table, and my companion seemed to be getting up from her position, scattering her friends in her wake as she headed out with that same purse from the night before, clutched tightly to her hip. I realized that it might be my only chance to engage with her, so I chased after her before she could disappear from sight. When I caught up to her, I reached for her arm before she turned around to face me near the lobby of the casino. She asked me what I wanted and I told her that I had found an envelope in my apartment in the morning, and that I'd wanted to return it to her since I might not have another chance to see her again. She replied that she was in a hurry, and that if I wanted to return it, she would be available later that evening around eleven o'clock or so, and if I would be kind enough to bring it to her room, it would be appreciated. So, right off the bat, a confirmation that she was somehow attached to the envelope in question. As it so happened, even though I had had the envelope with me at that moment, she refused to accept it and insisted that I agree to follow through later in the evening as planned. She did seem to be in an awful hurry. She insisted that I not just slip it under her door, as she had concerns that it might be lost in the transfer. That someone else might find it and keep it for themselves. It seemed a little odd, but because I wasn't sure what was inside of it, it seemed like a reasonable enough request.

Anyway, when I returned to my table, some of the aforementioned gaggle of women were still engaged at their table, having fun and enjoying themselves. I sat back down, a little ruffled at the edges, but nonetheless no worse for wear. I could sense that there was still a little energy directed my way, but overall, things settled down before most of the women at the table got up and readied themselves for the excitement of the night ahead. Only two women remained huddled behind—they seemed very locked into their conversation, which seemed hushed and confidential in nature. Eventually, they parted ways; one following step, like the other women, out the door, the other grabbing the remainder of her drink and heading directly toward me. She seemed a little shy about approaching me, but, nonetheless, she did. And she was lovely. In every way. After the initial awkwardness, we seemed to ease into a nice groove. Both conversationally, and in the way that we delicately danced around each other's cues. In addition to her obvious charms, I got the feeling that she felt a little sorry for me. That she understood what had come to pass the previous night with her friend, and that there was a trace of empathy being projected my way, as if to communicate that she, and possibly some of her friends, were slightly embarrassed by the association with their unhinged friend. She didn't need to get into the details about it. I made it clear to her that I felt no resentment. But I also tried to delicately acknowledge the gist and graciousness of her stance. We spent such a very brief moment on it before we quickly turned the page on to other things.

From that moment on, it turned exclusively to us. I was still a little wary from the previous night, but I sensed something very genuine about my new companion that gave me permission to relax my attitude and just go with the flow. And the flow turned out to be absolutely lovely and enchanting. We spent the next few hours in the evening with each other, before she invited me back to her room for a quick nightcap. That turned into a rather surprising, lengthy, languorous spell of intimacy. Sort of the opposite of the night before. Tenderness, with some amount of hesitation. Some tentative gestures of heartfelt sensuousness. Followed by deeper, drawn-out expressions of physical and emotional connectivity. Not to say it wasn't casual. But it felt truly authentic, I think, on both our parts. There was a glow and expansiveness between us that lingered on, far beyond the experience itself. Unfortunately, our time was limited.

By the time I left her room, I was truly in a blissful state. I didn't push it any further, because I wanted to honor her lead. And it didn't seem as if we would be going any further, either. I didn't ask for any personal details, or what her status was, in terms of what her life was like back home. I didn't want to ruin the moment, so I accepted it on her terms. It wasn't as if I was going to be able to pursue anything further, even if it had presented itself. I was past that point of wishing for anything more, with anyone. I had decided to commit myself to my freedom, as I think you can understand, from what I've told you before. And I think she felt the same. But I will certainly cherish the time I had with her, and the memory of it. I had enormous respect for her because she maintained boundaries well, and also didn't seem to care whether any of her friends knew about what had happened between us, including the friend I had spent the previous night with.

As it happened, though, when I finally forced myself to leave her room, guess what? Yes, my friend, I guess it's obvious—it was inevitable. As soon as I heard the door latch behind me, my previous companion was just returning to the room right next door. When I noticed her, I attempted to engage, only to be dismissed by another antagonistic swipe of the hand, leaving me standing outside alone. I hadn't noticed the room numbers until then. That the room she had just entered was the room I was supposed to return to later that night. I wasn't going to even attempt to do anything more at that moment, so I just returned to my post at Casablanca, for the interim. I needed a break, honestly.

Later that night, after I had rested, I returned to the room she directed me to, at the appointed time. I took the elevator directly to her floor and rang the bell, slightly out of breath. She came to the door immediately, wearing only a slinky gold kimono, adorned with crimson figures and highlights along the edges. She seemed composed, but somewhat impatient. I walked into the room prepared to give her the envelope. But she didn't seem to want to accept it. She deposited herself on a couch near the balcony of her room, mostly ignoring my presence. When I approached her to give her the envelope, she still seemed disinterested in receiving it. I had to verbalize my intentions—but her only reply was 'that was meant for you.' At first, I wasn't quite aware of what she was trying to imply. My impression was that she had accidentally left it in my apartment. Then she simply directed me to open it. Inside was a bundle of fifty-dollar bills, totaling around a thousand dollars. Did she win a big jackpot the day before? Was she on the way to the bank to make a deposit? Was it cash that she wanted on hand, to use while in Vegas? Apparently not. She made it abundantly clear that she meant it for me, to leave it for me. That she left it quite consciously and purposefully. I asked why. She didn't respond. She only laughed, and added in a quick staccato, 'What? You can't accept a gift from a woman? Use it any way you'd like. No strings attached. Go buy yourself a nice watch or something. Treat yourself to something special.' I told her I couldn't accept it, no matter the intention. It just didn't seem might to me. I put the money and the empty envelope down on the glass table in front of her.

Then she laughed more scornfully, in such a manner that it made me suspect that there was more to the story than I was aware of. I began to wonder whether she'd considered what had happened between us only a cold, disconnected kind of transaction.

If it hadn't been so comically ridiculous to believe that she mistook me for some sort of gigolo, or at least someone who was used to receiving money for sex, I might have gone there. But that seemed pretty absurd. I don't think I was going to be getting to the bottom of it, whatever the case. I noticed, though, that after I'd refused to take the money unambiguously, she became even more irritable and agitated than before. She became much more aggressive, angry and cutting. Then another ridiculous thought occurred to me. Was she jealous? Was she angry with her friend for engaging with me? I don't think I was going to get to the bottom of that either, but it sure did seem as if her attitude toward me had changed radically, at that point.

Then, just as abruptly, her mood seemed to change again. Now it seemed she was trying to pretend as if her feelings hadn't been hurt. And since I had returned as requested, she guessed she might as well make the best of an imperfect situation. She asked me not to be so uptight about it. She said she was sorry if there was some sort of misunderstanding. And that we could start fresh, if I wanted. Then she suggested that if I wanted to return the money to her, we could make a fun game out of it. To even things out. She started to tell me about a fantasy that she always wished she could act out with someone. I wasn't sure what she was getting at, but I was starting to think that this new experience might not end well. I stammered out a few words about how I might've misunderstood things, that perhaps I didn't understand her intentions, that maybe it wasn't a great thing that we didn't get to know each other a little more before we indulged. That I felt bad because it seemed like we had had a good time until... She laughed again, this time with a heavy dose of condescension and contempt. She began to tell me how silly I acted, how stupid and naïve I was. I don't remember if she used those exact words, but that was definitely the gist of it. At that point, she really wasn't mincing words anymore.

Then she asked point-blank if I'd be willing to start over *again*. Reiterated her willingness to bridge the gap. She had an idea that she thought might appeal to me. She said that, if I was willing, we could pretend that she was a prostitute and I was a john. We'd pretend we were other people, people who hadn't met before. And that once I 'paid' her, with the money still lying on the table, I could do as I pleased with her. That was her fantasy. I thought about it for a little while. I can't say that it didn't turn me on at that moment. But it didn't stop there. She elaborated on her idea, and told me she wanted to be dominated and manhandled, and wanted to know if I'd be up to the task. She began to encourage me to take on the role, and made a first move to encourage me. She asked me what I wanted. Then left it up to me to decide how we would proceed. I'm sorry to say I didn't have the backbone to resist entirely. I ended up giving into my lust, initially. But I should've known better. Because once I started, committing to a sort of vanilla version of her fantasy, she not only wanted to be treated like a prostitute, according to her original narrative, but she wanted to be shamed and abused. To be humiliated. She wanted me to insist how horrible she was. How worthless she was. How disgusting she was. And to continue on in that vein and be utterly convincing, or else, she said, it wouldn't be worth the time and energy to continue.

It reminded me of a similar circumstance that a former patient related to me, years before. Of course, I couldn't process it at that moment, but when I reflected on it later, I understood, firsthand, how my former patient had felt, through the immediate experience I was having with this disturbed and unstable woman. It was uncannily similar, in essence. My patient was a solid, dependable man who had had a girlfriend who, by all outward appearances, seemed the very epitome of perfection. It appeared, by all accounts, that she had everything going for her. She was an educated woman, a professional, with an advanced degree, and had a responsible, well-paying job. Her boyfriend, my patient, was being groomed as a potential husband. The woman's parents were very proud of her, but also very controlling and demanding. They could, with a minimal amount of effort and ease, pull her strings quite effectively, when they wished to. It was clear that they still had a very strong grip on her, even though she had already launched from their household and become an adult, for all intents and purposes. She had, in fact, conformed, very neatly, to every vision they had of her in their minds—the embodiment of the ideal daughter, from their perspective. She did everything right and seemed like the perfect woman, to everyone who was watching.

What people didn't know about her was that she had some very, very deep issues that went well beyond the usual norms—not so innocent fantasies. There was a very, deep, dark streak inside of her that was very much textbook Freudian: that all that perfection and good behavior, expressed and lived to the extreme, led to very unhealthy adaptations within her. And secrets. Her personality was literally split—if there was going to be a perfect part of her, there was also going to have to be a very imperfect part of her, too, that balanced out the 'angel' in her. There would have to be some kind of devil inside her that kept her sane—yes, sane—that made her human again, in some way.

It turned out that she took this posture to the extreme, and internalized it, and the only way she could express her sexuality as a woman was to take on an extreme stereotype that contradicted the perfection everyone saw on the outside. My patient eventually confided these facts to me, in far fewer words, and confessed that he was very unhappy with the relationship, and deeply unsatisfied with their sex life. He also didn't see a way out, regrettably, despite his genuine love for her. He told me that the only way his partner could have sex with him is if he was willing to humiliate her. Not just some of the time. Not just to a certain degree. But to an extreme degree, that was positively repulsive to him. At first, he was willing to play the game. But then it began to feel real to him, as time passed. It wasn't role-playing anymore. It got to the point that he, at least, couldn't tell the difference. To the point that he was losing himself in it. He told me he was willing and able to participate for the sake of saving his relationship, but that he couldn't continue anymore. And that any kind of sex, under those conditions, had become repulsive to him. Which meant that, eventually, there was no more sex between them.

Well, that's the kind of headspace that came to mind when I tried to carry on with my companion. I mean, I'm no prude, but I soon felt exactly like my patient had. It wasn't exactly clear what was going on inside the head of my companion, but it didn't matter, because I wasn't feeling comfortable with what we were doing. It could've been a one-off kind of fantasy for her, or perhaps something deeper or more ingrained. But it became clear to me that I could've been dealing with someone who was, at the very least, challenged by some pretty significant mental health issues, whether she knew it or not. Truth be told, upon further reflection, she probably met the diagnostic criteria for bipolar and/ or borderline, at a minimum. While it might be true that many healthy people utilize all sorts of alternative sexual practices to enhance their experience and pleasure, that's not what was going on, in this case. The more experience I'd gained as a psychiatrist in this domain, the more I considered the possibility of maladaptation amongst those who've chosen to push the envelope sexually. So even though I was no longer in the business of psychiatry, strictly speaking, and didn't need to adhere to the ethical principles of the profession, I had to stop cold and hard, for what were essentially moral reasons. There's a very good reason that mental health professionals need to guard against dual relationships—and in this new endeavor of mine, at Casablanca, it became even more obvious to me that I would have to have the personal fortitude and backbone to build pretty strict firewalls between myself and those I encountered, especially ones I became more engaged with. Fundamentally. Across the board. With no exceptions.

Anyway, with this very willful and aggressive companion, I realized much too late that I wasn't going to be able to continue on with the appalling scenario and twisted little fantasy we found ourselves engaged in. I flat out apologized to her when I told her that I couldn't continue. I simply stopped and exclaimed 'I can't do this, I'm sorry.' With that, she flew into an extreme rage and started to hurl more invective and demeaning insults at me. Can't say I blamed her, really. Then she grabbed the money off the table and flung it at me, literally in my face. She yelled at me, demanding that I get out of her room instantly, threatening to call security if I didn't move quickly enough. I can tell you that I scrambled out of there as fast as I could, half-clothed, as I gathered what I could, and finished dressing myself out in the hallway. I walked away as quickly as I could and went home to lick my pathetic wounds. Yes, my friend, I certainly learned my lesson! And to tell you the god's honest truth, I was practically thankful to her for what had happened. It was a pity. I had had some very lovely and exciting experiences with many, very lovely women. But from that point on, everything was going to have to be strictly platonic moving forward, with few exceptions, my friend.

I have to thank you for your indulgence, because I can sense that you have made an effort to maintain a polite silence, even if your sensibility has been injured after relating this tawdry tale to you in some detail. Is it possible that you've experienced something similar to this in your own life? When I recall the story, I certainly have regrets, but I'm also reminded how absurd the whole affair was. I mean, can you imagine a former psychiatrist falling for that song and dance? Kind of ridiculous! But then again, I'm only human, too, after all. We psychiatrists have the exact same human failings and vulnerabilities as everyone else. I have to say there are times when I feel a nostalgia for how simple it was to perceive other people's foibles, from the distance that a professional relationship permits. It can be frustrating to have to maintain a distance with women, but it does keep things uncomplicated, for the most part. I had to re-evaluate what I was trying to accomplish at Casablanca, as a Witness/Confidant. I have to keep my eye on the prize, so to speak. Vigilantly. I can allow myself to enjoy my interactions, but I have to be careful about keeping it on the up and up. I have to avoid the complication of having any kind of dual relationship—it only muddies the water. And I have to remain continually in touch with my moral compass. Or else it's not going to work. A generous spirit's a good thing, but not when the ego and vanity get involved.

Once I started down the slippery slope of relaxing standards, indulging in physical relationships with the women I was interacting with, it was difficult to turn back. My basest instincts started to kick in. I was blinded by them, and couldn't see how detrimental it had become. I'm quite determined never to go down that path again. I don't, however, think it's necessary to go to the opposite extreme. I think some mild expressions of interest is okay, like anything that would be socially acceptable in public, as long as it's clear that it's done in the spirit of friendship, not romance. As soon as I feel the urge to push beyond that, it's imperative I stop. A hard stop. No matter what my counterpart's reaction might be. It always seems to work better that way anyway, because if there's still an urge on their part, driven by their own fertile imagination, I can bend with it—but I don't necessarily need to take responsibility for it. It seems reasonable to strike a good balance between encouraging interchange, while also honoring the absolute right of my female counterparts to preserve the freedom, integrity, and self-determination of their own mental health. To encourage otherwise would be another violation in its own right. It's not to say that I don't suffer from a serious loss—

the lack of physical contact and emotional intimacy has had a detrimental effect on me. But for the sake of the mission, it's something that I'll have to live without, because it seems difficult for me to decouple the two worlds, honestly, no matter how hard I try. I try to take on the attitude of a monk, or a Buddhist—despite what I've lost, I can be satisfied that I've attained a more sustainable self-respect. I felt much better about myself once I committed to this new approach, and in the bargain, I'm able to get a lot more work done. It's clean living, as far as I'm concerned. And as far as my counterparts go, even if they're disappointed by this new attitude, this frame of mind, at least they, too, can go home with a clean conscience. Who knows what'll happen when they get back home? At least their minds won't be adulterated, in that respect, by my influence.

I have to say that when I reflect back on this time in my life, I'm a little disappointed and embarrassed by my behavior. For not being able to clearly see the consequences of my actions beforehand. I was acting out of weakness and using women for my own selfish purposes. I was being disingenuous and inauthentic—and for me, that's a kind of death. I wouldn't want to repeat that sort of thing in the future if I can help it. The sacrifices I made worked out very well. What it means is that I can now focus better on what I can do for others, and for their well-being. Emotional entanglements should be avoided. In that respect, the ends certainly *did not* justify the means.

Believe me when I tell you, I'm a much happier person now. I feel so much more satisfied. At the same time, I enjoy a peace of mind and freedom that I've never felt before to this extent. I'm so grateful to women, and what they've taught me—whether it's by example, or on occasion by counterexample, as was the case with the woman who served up my ultimate lesson, the well-deserved comeuppance. I mean that in all seriousness. For their willingness to be open-minded, and to have the confidence to throw themselves raw into the experiment of living. And to act with courage and discipline, for the most part. To ground their wisdom with emotional intelligence. The problem with men is that we tend to wield whatever powers we have like a cudgel. It's not good enough to be merely clever. It has to be tempered with something more subtle, or substantial. Unfortunately, most of the time, with men, it's leveraged in the service of flexing muscle. To project power. Violently, more often than not. That much is obvious. What can't men do without? Guns and women. I've never felt the need to own a gun, personally. And even though I have a weakness for women, after the farcical experience I had, I think I'm going to swear off sex for a good long time. Suddenly, I feel a new sense of chastity within. A cool, comfortable purity. I never thought, in my wildest dreams, that I'd be so willing and able to commit myself to a life of celibacy!

I imagine you find it hard to believe that I've ended up in this state, but that's a price I'm willing to pay. You might think I feel kind of castrated. But when it's voluntary, it makes all the difference. There's no shame in that. In fact, I feel like there's been a vast improvement. Everything I do feels more honorable, more charitable. I feel like I've risen above the fray. That I've become a little more dispassionate, in the best sense of the word. I hope you can acknowledge my progress, in this respect. I think it's evolved to the point that it's become internalized. It's not like I have to think about it that much anymore. What a relief! Just imagine what that feels like, my friend.

Uh oh. Looks to me like the water's building up, like it might start breaching the curb. It might be a good idea to get home before it's too late. The rain's probably ended, but it doesn't look like hailing a cab's going to be easy. I'd better get going. I'm getting tired and it might be best if I turn in for the night. I'm going to have to cut straight through there. I don't usually go that way. But would you mind just walking me through, at least as far as where you are? We might have to hop our way over some puddles, but I think we can manage it. I guess I never told you why I always avoid this area. You see that open square over there? Are you aware of its history? It's hard for me to even look over there. I feel very uncomfortable and vulnerable just standing *near* it. Just get me to the other side, and I'll tell you more. It wasn't so long ago, you probably heard about what happened in the news. There was a mass shooting there. Do you remember? It was in October...

Yes, that's what I'm talking about. I probably don't need to go over the numbers with you. You probably recall the kind of carnage that occurred. He was shooting from high up, from that hotel over there, down into that area, picking people off at will. It just so happened that I had just left for home when all hell suddenly broke loose. It was just after ten o'clock at night. I had been with a woman, was just leaving her room above Casablanca, and was on my way home. It was a typical night, other than the fact that there was a big music festival going on next door. It was dark outside, but the sky was clear, with mild temperatures, around the mid-seventies by that time of day.

I felt good—my body was drained, but relaxed. I was feeling happy and satiated. It felt good to be going home and into bed. I was looking forward to a pleasant, leisurely walk back to my apartment. But as soon as I neared the square we just skirted, I began hearing a series of pops in the air. Just a rapid series of them echoing through the air haphazardly. But then, shortly after that, the clamor came in a series of rapid bursts. People said it sounded as if firecrackers were going off. Well, it wasn't more than a few seconds later, maybe a minute tops, that it was absolutely undeniable what was happening—people were running for their lives, scattering any which way they could to avoid being shot by automatic gunfire. A stampede was forming. People were streaming from the festival grounds and were trying to pour into

110

the surrounding open spaces to get away. Some were hopping over fences. Others were pushing through them. Whatever was necessary for the safety of shelter. Unfortunately, there weren't a good number of places to go to get out of the way. Most of us didn't even know where the bullets were coming from, at first. It was mass chaos and confusion. Piercing screams began penetrating the air. There were bodies falling everywhere in front of me. In various states of distress. There were people who were simply in shock, and others who were shot, either already dead or dying, or actively bleeding out, I couldn't exactly tell. I stood there, frozen for a moment, with a jumble of thoughts cascading through my mind for what seemed like an eternity.

I thought of running, but I couldn't move. I was literally trembling. I felt flushed with cold and in complete shock. The kind of shock you get when you can't believe what you're seeing before your eyes. I guess I had a few choices. You know, the fight or flight thing. Well, there was nothing within my reach to fight and my legs were not exactly cooperating. I guess I could've tried to save my own hide. I mean, why not? But it was like my mind took over and convinced me that if I was going to die anyway, I might as well die trying to do something before the end came, anything at all that could make some sort of difference in that type of situation. Of course, if there was anyone there who could've made a difference, it was me! I thought of my father. I thought of what he would've done. And there was no question what he would've done. We were both physicians, first and foremost. And as soon as that wash of thoughts solidified in my head, my legs suddenly sprang into action as if they had a mind of their own, and I dove right into the chaos. I can't say I spent another millisecond thinking about my own welfare after that. I forgot all about it. I jumped in with surgical precision. I felt invincible, actually. I could make a big difference. And I did make a difference.

I ended up treating a good number of people at the scene. I had to make some very difficult decisions, like I was on the battlefield, but, all and all, I think I did what I could've with the abilities I had, in the moment. Did I make some mistakes? Not really sure. But the point was that I was compelled to do what I did. It was like an out-of-body experience. It was like there was a force compelling me to do it. No, I'm not kidding at all, my friend. I don't know if you've ever experienced anything like that, but that was exactly how it felt. I was running from one victim to the next, trying to stop the blood from spilling, mostly. The street was covered in it. But there were others there helping, too, whether they were professionals or not—they were ripping their shirts off to use as bandages, or using belts as tourniquets for cutting off blood flow, or attending to those with more minor injuries. I was there for almost an hour before more professionals had finally arrived in numbers, and gotten the scene under reasonable control. But by the time I left, I was soaked, head to toe, in blood. Both literally and figuratively. You can imagine what it looked like. But, strangely enough, it was like I was newly baptized in that blood. The blood of hundreds of people. A few first responders wanted to attend to me, but I replied that I was a doctor and that I lived nearby and that they shouldn't waste their limited resources, just then, on me. I just turned away, when there was nothing further left to do, and walked home under my own power.

You can imagine the blank and horrified stares I got on the way home. Some of the people on the street still didn't even know what'd happened yet. When I finally reached the lobby of my building, the doorman looked at me like he had seen a ghost. He had already heard about the carnage and inquired if I was okay. I filled him in, and told him I was fine, before I quickly hopped on to the elevator. I'll never forget the look on his face: it was frozen midway between horror and concern. It acknowledged both, but wasn't able to settle on either. I slipped my shoes off, of course, before I entered my apartment, and headed straight for the shower, clothes and all. I had been careful to make sure I sealed myself in properly before I turned on the water. I didn't want the blood to splatter into the rest of the bathroom. I got the water temperature as hot as possible, as hot as I could bear, before I tucked my head under. I removed each piece of clothing, from top to bottom. I rinsed each item thoroughly, wrung them out, and piled them in the corner before I started cleaning my body, from crown to heel. I watched the water run off—transitioning from clear, to rust-colored, to brick red, and back again. Over and over again. I washed my body as I would've had I been preparing for surgery. Scrubbing each surface and crevice with conscious attention. At the same time, the images from the scene of the crime, just played out an hour or so before, flashed through my imagination in a continuous loop. It would've been nice to have been able to wash those images out with everything else, but...

As soon as I emerged from the shower and dried off, I immediately became very thirsty and hungry and frigid again. I wrapped myself tightly in my bathrobe before I headed to the kitchen to gulp down buckets of water. I was in no mood to eat despite my hunger, so I opted to grab a beer instead. It would calm me down, take the edge off. I sat on my couch for a very long time before I could contemplate moving again. Once I was warm enough, and then dressed, the only thought I had was to go back into the fridge again to get another beer, and sit out the night on the balcony. I could still hear a continuous din off in the distance, the whirl of helicopters in the air, punctuated by the sirens of the emergency vehicles that were still arriving and leaving the scene, one after the other. Oddly enough, it didn't seem to upset me, knowing that every resource in the area had been called in to tend to the massacre. But I was also taking in the ordinary scene below me, which, if you hadn't been aware of what had just occurred just a few miles away, you could've assumed was just another typical

113

Sunday night. People in their apartment buildings doing the usual things. I sat there until my body became flushed with alcohol, numb enough to nudge me toward sleep and bed.

My mind was still very restless, as I'm sure you can imagine. I struggled to control my racing thoughts, turning my attention away from the chaos of the day's events toward more abstract meditations on the greater implications it gave rise to. Of course, I expected to hear all about the gunman the following day. 'Gunman', of course, because women almost never commit this kind of violence. He would probably fit the usual profile: a disgruntled white male, most likely of the white supremacist variety. Then the usual blaming of the mentally ill, instead of those who typically perpetrate this sort of violence. Then more attention turned to another round of gun control legislation, only to have it end in political stalemate. What was the point of thinking those tired old thoughts again? Spending time mulling them over could only result in a hopeless, masochistic exercise. Of course, I couldn't avoid thinking about all the previous mass shootings I knew about, and how they affected the victims, including my former patient. Remember him? His pain. His family's pain. The community's pain. The pain everyone involved would suffer from, from that day onward. It seems like only a matter of time before everyone will find themselves confronted by that type of bloodbath. It turned out that one of the survivors from that terrifying night in Vegas, died the following year—the victim, again, of a different mass shooting! I can't say I was surprised. Given the statistics. It's like you can't avoid it anymore, no matter what you do.

But my mind began wandering onto other topics, too, on a bigger scale. It seemed to me that if we haven't put an end to gun violence after all these years, how are we going to be able to deal with the larger, more intransigent issues that require our attention even more urgently? We will surely need a fundamental change in attitude and approach, a monumental paradigm shift, or else we're going to end up destroying ourselves. Do you understand what I mean? We don't have the luxury of doing things incrementally anymore, the way things were done in the past. Bit by tiny bit. And we need to stop wasting so much time thinking about it, studying it, treading water, squandering resources; and spend more time and focus acting for the benefit of the immediate, collective interest. Which should be, essentially, identical to the sum of our higher self-interests. If we continue to act the way we do now, and if there is a sizable portion of the population that doesn't want to conform to new approaches, we're in for it! Don't you think? Maybe it's time to start working around the naysayers, the selfish people; or, better yet, just ignore them if they choose not to cooperate, leave them to their own devices. Literally, leave them behind. Don't even engage with them anymore. There's no point continuing to argue with them, while everything, meantime, goes to hell. That's what some of them want, and that's what fuels their sense of relevance and power. It's true! If they can't get theirs, they'll hope you can't get yours, either. We'll all end up going down together, while Rome burns. They'd rather die, than lose even one battle. Think how extreme that is! It's not funny anymore. It's not the slightest bit amusing. When are we going to finally wake up to reality? When will enough be enough?

We've got so much to do! Everywhere you look, there's lies, fraud, and corruption. And plagues and phonies everywhere. We don't have much more time left to deal with it effectively. The world is literally closing in on us. We don't have the luxury, anymore, of people discovering it for themselves. We need to get out there and sound the alarm and start demanding change. We need radical change. Our lives depend on it! But hopefully, we won't have to perpetrate any more violence on anyone to get there. No more war. No more famine. We need to convince people across the globe, to the very depth of their souls, that each and every individual has to buy into the new game plan, and make the necessary sacrifices, if we're going to survive in a world that we still recognize and wish to live in. It has to become a *moral* imperative. To explain to people that there is a better path to a better world.

Even if it seems absurd and hopeless, we have to have the absolute drive and discipline to forge ahead. Even if progress seems incremental. Because all of those modest improvements can add up quickly. Faster than you think. Let's at least give it a shot. If we continue to be in denial, if we continue to try to evade and avoid, chaos will eventually come home to roost. I'm absolutely sure of that. And if you think it's bad now, just imagine...

I'm sorry. I've been ranting away like a teenager. It's not like people don't know what's coming down the pike. I'd better stop now. It's just getting me upset again, and making myself sound like a lunatic. But thanks for walking alongside me. Thank you for your assistance. Your kindness and care. I can manage the rest of the way on my own...

Anyway, when I woke up the next morning, I guess reality set back in. I couldn't avoid thinking about what had just happened. That goes without saying. But I also remember being in a bit of a post-traumatic fog for the next few weeks. I felt very irritable and angry for quite some time after that. Nevertheless, I do recall that next morning, after the bloodbath, with extraordinary clarity, having no choice but to collect myself and focus on moving on. First, getting the bloodied and soiled clothes out of the shower. That couldn't wait. I gathered them up and sealed them tightly into a large, black plastic lawn bag. I can still smell the scent of the remains of the blood, to this day. You know how you can *smell* blood when there's been a lot of it around? All of the plasma and iron left in there. I chucked the bag into the garbage chute on my way out, before I left for Casablanca for the day. That macabre, yet simple, action seemed to ground me, for whatever reason. It seemed to free me for a moment, just long enough to get started with the day.   I continued on as best I could, given the circumstances...

My friend, thank you for accompanying me all the way home. You didn't have to, but you did anyway, and that means a lot to me. My home is my sanctuary. I don't think I would've been able to make it on my own, in all honesty. After telling you that story. There's still a part of me that gets flashbacks, now and again. That's why I usually avoid that square...

Yes, I'll see you tomorrow, if you're still up for it? I can fill you in on the rest of it, if you want. But why don't we clear our minds and take a ride out to the country, instead of meeting at Casablanca? Would you like that? Yes, I'll take you out to one of my favorite places. To Hoover Dam. And environs. Have you ever seen it? Okay then, I'll pick you up at Casablanca at around eleven? Is that okay?

Believe it or not, I still have a car. I don't use it much, but it's good to have around, to get out of town every once in a while. That's really the only reason I've held onto it. I drove it cross-country after I finally bailed on New York. Anyway, I imagine you might still have a few questions about what happened that night. You wouldn't be alone. But I'm not inclined to talk about it much. Because it's not really the point, anymore.   At least from my perspective.   I seem to have found a new sense of purpose following the shooting.

As it happened, the following morning, it appeared as if the news media was looking for me, to follow up on various aspects of the story. To ask a few questions. I think they'd heard that I'd been in the thick of it. That I was on the scene, and that I was a physician who had attended to some of the victims. But I didn't want to say anything more about it, publicly. I didn't want to become a focus of attention. For any reason. You know how they cover these things. Same old story. Same old questions. Same old

117

profiles in courage and the never-ending, sorrowful biographies of the victims. What does that ever accomplish, really? Tell me, what difference does that ever make?

IV.

That's quite the technical achievement, huh? Quite an engineering marvel. Can you believe people are capable of building such things? Don't bother heading to the gift shop. You're not going to find anything there that tops this. Just sit back and take it all in, while you can. You know, the Hoover Dam was built in just five years, during the Great Depression. A year and a half ahead of schedule. Imagine thousands of workers swarming over this whole area to get it done on time. Yes, over a hundred workers died in the process, and the habitat downstream suffered a serious amount of devastation because of it. But on the other hand, think of all the renewable energy these plants produce. About forty percent of the total goes to Nevada and Arizona. Naturally. That's Nevada over there. And there's Arizona. Guess where the rest of it goes? Yes, my friend, I'm not surprised you knew the answer. Yes, California gets around fifty percent of it. Southern California and Los Angeles in particular. But the greatest percentage of the total energy produced actually goes toward providing drinking water for those same areas in California. Drinking water for all the people who live in places that have next to no natural water resources. Oh, the irony!

Well, I guess that's better than going nuclear, wouldn't you say? We weren't around in the good old days when you used to be able to see and feel the rumble of the nuclear detonations coming from the Nevada Proving Grounds near Las Vegas. You could see the mushroom clouds from downtown, from a hundred miles away. In the fifties, they carried out around a hundred above-ground tests. They spewed radioactivity all over the area, and the country. Utah, oddly enough, got hit worst, in terms of the adverse health effects on the population, with spiking rates of all sorts of cancers. But it could be detected all over the country and beyond, including significant readings as far away as Idaho and Montana, Wisconsin and Illinois, Arkansas and Oklahoma, even the northern reaches of New York State and Vermont. Did you know that? Not to mention that certain parts of the Nevada testing grounds will be contaminated with excessive levels of spent plutonium and uranium for tens of thousands of years. So, I guess the price of the collateral damage from the construction of the Hoover Dam seems small, in comparison.

But just take a look around here. Why aren't we making an effort to exploit the sun and the wind that's so abundant out here? There's really no need to build dams anymore, to have nuclear power plants, even to burn any more fossil fuels. No need to destroy our rivers, to continue to stockpile spent nuclear fuel, to pollute the air and water. All we need to do is put up a bunch of solar panels and windmills, for god's sake. Seriously! There's nothing stopping us, technically speaking. The sun itself is the mother of all nuclear reactors. Without any of the mess. One hundred percent clean energy. And it'll never run out. Life on Earth will be long gone by then. Do you know that we would only have to cover a tiny section of the Sahara Desert with solar panels to meet the entire energy needs of all the countries on Earth combined? Why haven't we done it? Once the basic infrastructure's built, it's unlimited free power, forever. Imagine! It's not like we *can't* do it. When there's a will, there's a way! Just look at the Manhattan Project, as an example. How did we get that done? We got a bunch of geniuses together, funded and empowered them, and they managed to build the bomb. A heroic effort. Another colossal technological achievement. But, oh, the tragic irony! We built the bomb and dropped two on Japan, killing hundreds of thousands of people in a flash. Okay, maybe it did bring an end to the war. But surely we can do better in the service of peace and humanity, and for the benefit of ourselves and the environment. We're capable of doing great things—but why in the service of our basest instincts, more often than not?

Nevertheless, you have to admit that the dam is pretty impressive. But when they first built it, the area downstream went dry for years. The estuary south of here, near the mouth of the river, was adversely affected. Whole species were wiped out and never recovered. On the upstream side of the dam, however, north of here, Lake Mead was born. Water built up in front of the dam and created a whole new body of water that replaced the historic contours of the Colorado River. It helped control the natural flooding, but also served as a new playground for people to enjoy —or exploit, depending on your point of view. Inevitably, the waterway became overcrowded with throngs of people and pleasure craft, and, combined with receding waters later on, its use was restricted. These days, most of the time, water levels are much too low to sustain an overall healthy ecosystem, let alone to be counted on for recreational purposes. So, although the dam still generates a lot of energy, the natural environment has suffered greatly. If you situate yourself in the middle of the lake, you'll be surrounded by cliffs that have been exposed since the waters have receded. You can make out the various geological layers that have been formed over the centuries. When I see them, I can't help but be reminded of the depths of hell, with its concentric rings, that symbolize the degree to which each of its inhabitants have sinned. Even the colors of the rock formations look like fire, or blood. On occasion, the water below can take on an unnatural, cobalt blue sheen, matching the brilliance of the usually wide, endless sky. When they align just right from above and below, the world seems all but empty of life. Everything becomes quiet and still, yet dazzlingly crisp and clear. You might spot a random contrail in the upper atmosphere, or detect its ghostly hum. But if you're really fortunate, a kettle of vultures might suddenly appear from nowhere, to break the uncomfortable and eerie silence. Just circling above, riding the thermals, hoping for a chance to descend on some poor, dead creature below. Ripe for the picking, they'll surely pluck those bones dry.

It can be so exceedingly stark and lonesome out here. Then again, even at Casablanca, I can feel a little lonely and alienated, at least in my own head. But I wasn't always such a loner. I used to have lots of friends, if you can believe that. Even though I have a lot of contact with a diversity of people at Casablanca, it's not the same, to be honest. Not at all. Do you know how I lost all my friends and became so lonely? All at once? It was simple. I lost my friends when I lost my wife. Oh, I guess I haven't told you about that yet. Yes, I'm actually a widower, believe it or not. My wife died of cancer many years ago now. She was everything to me, especially as human relations were concerned. We had a great marriage, and a great life—perhaps one that many might be envious of. Once we settled into our relationship, after we had attended to the customary necessities and accomplished the usual goals of young adulthood—launching our careers, and buying our first home—it seemed as if things were moving along very smoothly for a period of about ten years. We were living in L.A. I was working in the movie business as a producer. Yes, believe it or not! Can you imagine me as a hustler in Hollywood? It was a great job, but it was also kind of pointless, honestly. Most of the films I produced were not the kind I would've wanted to see. But compared with your average job, it definitely had its charms. A lot more fun than usual and, generally speaking, a nice bunch of people to work with. My job was simple—to raise the money to make films. Not the most glamorous of positions in that world, but I did get a certain amount of respect and even a little notoriety because of it, not to mention excellent compensation. My wife, meanwhile, was an attorney. She was a partner at one of the most prestigious corporate law firms in the country—with an impeccable pedigree, and held in the highest regard—who were generally in the business of protecting their corporate clients from any kind of civil or criminal complaints that were headed their way. You can imagine what *that* involves. But we both made very handsome incomes, so we certainly weren't hurting in that respect. We had more than enough resources to live the good life in L.A., and then some. But my wife balanced it out with a good deal of pro bono work—mostly related to representing women in domestic violence proceedings. She had a growing reputation that began to supersede the strictly legal—she was seen as an individual with an unshakable moral backbone, who could be trusted to be eminently fair, independent, and assess, as much as humanly possible, without bias. All bundled in a very attractive woman with a charming personality, who wasn't quite conscious of exactly how beautiful and truly special she was. Everyone adored her, without the faintest taint of jealousy or envy.

She established a loyal and robust clientele, whom she advised as an attorney, but also as a consultant to help enforce the in-house ethical rules they had established for themselves. Then, within just a few years' time, she had had numerous opportunities to conduct formal internal investigations—not only for private institutions, but within government. Ultimately, she became an inspector general for a very fine and well-regarded quasi-governmental institution. The entire job was to self-police the institution. It was work that she very much enjoyed, albeit at a lower, but decent, salary and, more importantly, with more or less nine-to-five hours. We had made a conscious decision, at a certain point, to scale back our lives, so that we could spend less time working and more time actually enjoying our lives. Imagine that!

But that's, tragically, when my wife first discovered the lump in her breast that turned out to be malignant. She was only in her early thirties when she was diagnosed. That's pretty rare. But by all accounts, because it had been caught so early, there was almost complete consensus amongst her practitioners that she would have no trouble beating the cancer—and would soon be back to enjoying a normal life. But it didn't turn out that way.

After a few months of remission, following three years of treatment, it came back and metastasized. It was only another two years before she died. It seemed like no matter how good her chances were at any one time—at any moment in her treatment— she would inevitably be amongst those with unfortunate outcomes. Almost every time, with very few exceptions. It didn't make any sense at all, from a medical perspective. So, despite the favorable prognosis, she lasted just shy of five years before she died. Five years of sheer bravery and determination on her part. She barely missed a day of work, if you can believe that. She was the very picture of graciousness under mortal pressure. Our usual, daily lives suffered very little, believe it or not. Until the very last two months or so, we pretty much continued on as if things were normal, whenever and wherever we could. Then when it looked like there was no hope left, her body just shut down all at once and that was the end of it. She died peacefully in her sleep, with me at her side. I had been sleeping by her side every night—then one night, in the wee hours of the morning, I noticed, rather haphazardly and belatedly, that she had stopped breathing. I didn't notice it at first, because of the din of the fan that was constantly trained on her, to ease with the overheating she experienced. That's sort of how these things work, in real life. It's not like it's portrayed in the movies. It's usually much sloppier and less dramatic. No final loving words, then rising joyously up to heaven.

Then, when I was certain she had passed away—which is not always necessarily clear or obvious to the untrained eye—I suddenly felt a tightness in my chest and had trouble catching my breath. I had a bit of a panic attack, standing there in silent disbelief, even though I had been more than prepared for it. After the shock of that, I have to admit that I felt a brief tinge of relief, knowing that it was all over. After her body was taken away and cremated, I entered into a period of depression that I had never experienced before. I was devastated, understandably, but I wasn't even capable of emoting anymore. I had already done a lot of that, secretly, before she died. The numbness just set in. I just wanted to sleep forever, and forget about everything that had happened. I felt increasingly alone and untethered. I had had counseling all along the way, which surely helped alleviate the load I was carrying. But then I realized that soon things would change dramatically for me, that I had little to no control over it, and that I was going to have to mourn that, too.

Many people attended my wife's memorial service, and it was truly humbling to hear how much they sincerely valued and adored her. I felt very supported by our extended family and friends throughout the struggle leading up to her death, and during the immediate aftermath, with few exceptions. But then as I emerged from my self-imposed isolation, and resumed ordinary life, about two months later, I began to notice that many of the very same people I had once relied on during my long ordeal had moved on, and seemed to want to leave the whole miserable mess behind them. I can't say I blamed them, but there were times when I wondered if they still remembered what had happened, or if they still remembered me. I understood that they were anxious to get back to normal life, but I was still suffering and needed attention. I still needed human contact. I still needed to be loved. But nobody seemed willing to check on me. I had to initiate everything. I began to feel more and more like an exile. Like I didn't fit in anymore. When I was in their company, it felt very awkward. It felt like they'd rather be somewhere else, with anyone else. That I was a burden, and a reminder of what they had lost. I guess I began to slowly realize that the friends I thought we had were really, in essence, only my wife's friends, and that they, in effect, died along with her. I became more and more depressed and then began to stubbornly embrace my isolation, which only made me feel worse, if not suicidal. I was never afraid of those feelings, because I knew I would never act on them. But they did force me to confront my new dilemma, to begin to figure out how I was going to move forward in this new life that was forced upon me.

Ultimately, I concluded that I would have to start all over again. So, I did. What did I have to lose? I made some rather radical changes in my life, I have to say. I had the means to, partly because my wife and I had set ourselves up pretty well in advance —we already had retirement accounts, a good amount of savings in the bank, that was further augmented by a rather sizeable life insurance death benefit when she died. I knew I had to keep myself busy, to stay engaged, to be constructive. But I had to figure out something that made more sense to me, on a variety of levels. Going back into the movie business felt like a dead end. It had already been feeling suspect to me for a long time. I felt like I had to find a passion, or at least a mission, that would fulfill me on a deeper level. I literally sat down one day and flipped through a book that exhaustively listed every profession on Earth, wondering what direction I might take. Wondering what the sum total of my experience could lead me to. Then, all of a sudden, out of nowhere, it was like my father's presence appeared before me like a ghost. As if to point me in the right direction. What he was suggesting seemed like utter madness, complete folly for a person my age, in my position. But the more I mulled it over, the more I pondered it, the more perfect it seemed. I was finally going to do what my father had always wanted me to do. I was going to go to medical school, after all!

No, I wouldn't be following in his footsteps, setting my sights on becoming a surgeon. I was quite sure of that. I wasn't quite smart enough for that, honestly, nor was I interested in such excruciating specialization. I had the sudden urge to become a psychiatrist instead, of all things. Why? Well, I guess all the therapy I engaged in over the years convinced me that it was a worthwhile endeavor. I had become quite the expert on anxiety, depression, and grief, as you can imagine. And what better way to use what I had learned through experience than to become a psychotherapist myself. There was something attractive about taking the pain of that experience and converting it into something that could benefit others. The poetic justice of it very much appealed to me. I figured if I had to go through all of that, the pain and loss associated with losing my wife, I shouldn't fritter the experience away so thoughtlessly. So, even though I was really much too old to consider going to medical school, at such a late stage of life, I went ahead with it anyway. It was all rather rash and impulsive, but I figured I could always drop out if I had second thoughts.

I certainly had some catching up to do, that's for sure. I hadn't been in school for quite some time. But I had taken a number of premed courses as an undergraduate, and I only needed to complete a handful more to be able to apply for medical school. After I had taken close to six months off to care for my wife during her final days, I never did return to my work in the film business. I never really considered it, to be honest. It just felt so empty to me, after the intense experience that I had had with life and death. I felt completely uninspired to dive back in. People were very understanding about that. But I got the distinct sense that people thought my new plan was completely unhinged and crazy. Yet, when I was ready to start all over again, about a year after my wife passed away, it was really exciting to enter into a whole new world, inhabited by a completely different set of people in a totally new environment. My father was certainly very proud of me. I appreciated his very keen enthusiasm and encouragement. It didn't take me too much longer to start medical school, and once I was in, I really just buckled down and got it done, with surprising ease. My residency went fairly smoothly and I even managed to get a paid fellowship after that. But the best thing about those years was that it kept me very focused and busy. I was still in a world of anguish and pain, but staying active helped enormously. I really didn't have much time to be miserable.

But then, once I did settle into my new career and began feeling comfortable with my practice, I began to feel my depression sneak up on me again. It was no surprise that after all those years of intense concentration—and ignoring my emotions— I would have to pick up where I left off, so to speak. I realized that I hadn't processed as much as I should've years before, and felt the strong pull to go back into therapy before it got too far out of hand. I was suddenly reminded of all I had lost—and despite my most genuine efforts to stave it off, I fell into an even deeper depression. I began to feel desperately lonely again. I felt disoriented, because I hadn't managed to keep up an adequate support network while I was so busy and determined to become a physician. I realized I was still grieving, and I had to pause a little to take care of it. I wasn't feeling suicidal, but I was feeling a kind of spiritual exhaustion, or spiritual malaise. Nevertheless, with help, I was able to come to terms with my sorrow and to exert enough discipline to carry on.

My new work was very satisfying. I started work in a local clinic and felt like I was making a small but significant difference in the community. I continued to feel disconnected in other ways, though, especially in terms of my personal life. I had let my social life slip for such a long time—and even when I had the opportunity to engage with a valued colleague or acquaintance, who I could engage with in a fully satisfying manner, I didn't make a lot of effort to reach out. A lot of it was on me, to be perfectly frank. I felt zealously protective and guarded, with respect to the details of my personal life. I didn't share much about how I was feeling, and next to nothing about the history of my old life, when I was happy with the life my wife and I were living, the one we had so skillfully carved out for ourselves. I wasn't investing much in other people, and I didn't blame others if they didn't care to invest much in me, either. Honestly, I was pretty sure I could've killed myself and nobody would've noticed.

Maybe it was better that way. It would've been hard to recreate what I had had anyway, because it would've been almost impossible to find someone who could've lived up to my wife's standard; and because finding good, solid friends can be just as difficult. I felt caught between a rock and a hard place, and it put me in a perpetually crabby mood. There were times when I felt a creeping resentment stirring beneath the surface. Most of the time I resisted acknowledging it. But occasionally, I was seduced by its beguiling power. My wife's death, though brutal, was a completely random act of nature. There was nobody to blame for it. Nobody to be held accountable. But I realized that it was all too easy for me to go looking for something or someone to pin it on, to displace my anger and sorrow on. I admit that I began to resent many people from my past life. For being insensitive to how a life is affected when you lose a spouse, the way that I did, in the very prime of life. For forgetting how much I cared about my wife, and not feeling fully recognized for all the love and support and care I gave to her for so many years. With hardly a complaint the whole time. I knew people who had abandoned their friends, spouses, and other precious family members when the shit hit the fan. Not me. No, sir. It just wasn't in me. I often wondered who, among those I knew, would end up being that kind of person. If not that, then who would be constitutionally incapable of rising to the occasion, of upping their game, over the long run. I admit I almost wished ill on others. To suffer the same fate as me. Just so that they'd begin to understand how I felt.

But, of course, I wouldn't truly wish that fate on anyone. I gave the people who understood how it felt, without having to actually experience it, a hell of a lot of credit for their deep sense of empathy. But they're a rare breed indeed, my friend. A rare breed. No, many people are more than happy to just forget all about it, to just wipe it clean from their memories. It was true in my case. I had been forgotten about long before, and I had, truthfully, returned the favor. But I also imagined they couldn't forget me entirely. Every once in a while, I'm sure they felt guilty. Had an occasional pang of conscience. Yet, instead of embracing those feelings and leveraging them to bridge the gap, I'm convinced that, more often than not, it was easier for them to make up excuses as to why it wasn't necessary to follow through on their instincts. I can hear all the rationalizations, that were once spoken aloud, in my head right now: 'It's too bad, but we're busy', 'He doesn't need our support anymore', 'I wouldn't know what to do', 'It's so awkward', 'It's too late', 'He's fine, he always has been', 'He doesn't want to see us', 'It'll only remind him of his misery', 'He's a therapist now, for god's sake, he should know how to take care of himself', 'He's living a new life, with new people', 'Let's not upset the apple cart', probably even a 'I never liked him in the first place, honestly.' So many narratives to choose from. So many reasons to avoid the whole thing entirely. A lot of people are just not good with death and dying, and/or grief.

I admit I found myself falling for the same reasoning, at times. But the ones who are the worst are the ones who go out of their way to pity you, to stick your nose in it. You have to give them credit for wanting to engage, but the only reason they do is to feel good about themselves and sorry for you. To enjoy feeling superior to you. To pretend as if, with a peculiar kind of magical thinking, something like what happened to you can never happen to them. That mawkish, paternalistic attitude that feels downright insulting. Just imagine if I had been seriously suicidal, and weren't too cowardly to follow through with it. That attitude alone, when faced with it, might very well push someone right over the edge. The more I thought about all of it, the more I weighed the pros and cons of living my life at the time, the more I began to think that having another fresh start, in another way, was exceedingly overdue. And it quickly occurred to me that finding a new and novel environment might just be the solution I was looking for. To have a clean break, as it were. To move away. There was nothing left to lose, really, only things to gain, as I saw it. So, that's when I devised a plan to leave town. I left for New York City about a year after I had that first inkling.

Why New York? I was actually born in New York, but only lived there a very short time, until I was a toddler. I have absolutely no recollection of it at all. I grew up in California, after my father was offered a plum position there, early on in his career, accepting a position at a prestigious research hospital that he could hardly refuse. When I was a young man and just on the verge of launching from my parents' household, the idea of moving to New York was much too intimidating to me. I felt like I would've been overwhelmed. I had visited a few times and had good experiences, but I couldn't yet imagine living there. Southern California still seemed more appealing to me, especially with the better weather and easygoing lifestyle. But after being in L.A. for such a long time, and intent on a new start elsewhere, I guess I was determined to force myself to have a radically new kind of experience. I knew I wanted to continue living in a large city, so New York became the obvious choice as it was the epitome of the quintessential urban experience. A very different environment than Los Angeles. Built up instead of out. And no more need for a car. Almost too much to do, but I guess that's what I wanted. I wanted to throw myself into an environment that would challenge me. Yes, I'd have to be careful not to get too distracted by all the enticements. But even with all the hustle and bustle, there was a simplicity to living there. I had my apartment, my workplace, the streets below, and the neighborhood around me. Everything I needed or wanted was within walking distance. There would be an occasional outing to a theatre or a museum, and the necessity of leaving town on occasion, to cleanse your mind and breathe some fresh air. But other than that, it was all just there in front of me, in plain sight.

I had a temporary job lined up from the get-go, in a hospital psychiatry ward, and settled into it quickly. Professionally, not much had changed. The real difference was in how I conducted my personal life. When I got to New York, I began to feel better. There was a new sense of freedom, a new sense of engagement that had been missing in L.A. I felt stimulated, and my mood, generally speaking, matched it—it definitely went up a notch and stayed there for an extended period of time. New York is the kind of place you can thrive in if you maintain a certain amount of flexibility, and that seemed to affect me internally, in terms of the way I was thinking, and how it was reflected in my overall state of mind. It was also an environment that made it easier for me to spend more time alone, to reconnect with my inner core. To spend time in meaningful solitude, as opposed to aimless loneliness. That was something that I had neglected to consciously do for a very long time. I began to feel much more relaxed, and much less resentful, than at any time in recent history. To the extent that I felt like I had regained a sense of abundance and generosity that made it easy for me to let go of my anger and any grudges I still harbored. There was a part of me that was ready to forgive and forget anyone who I had felt slighted by, in any way. I might even say I began to enjoy life again, and felt happy and ready to love again. I certainly did not feel pitied anymore. I had begun to forget the sting of that, and those who projected it onto me. I didn't have to force it, it just faded away naturally. In short, I called a truce, of sorts.

On the other hand, there was considerable culture shock moving from L.A. to New York. I was used to a much more laissez-faire attitude, and tried to wrap my head around the brash intensity of the new environment and its people. People were far more competitive, far more decisive and assertive, even aggressive, simply driven to get things done efficiently, with scant attention paid to the cost or any collateral damage done in the process. It seemed to me that, in the greater universe outside my profession, there was a lot of back-stabbing going on in a world where 'dog eat dog' is acceptable. There were certainly plenty of self-absorbed and arrogant men walking around, convinced they were god's gift to the world. Looking for conquests in every aspect of their lives. And an extreme cliquishness amongst the powerful—a country club mentality—the kind that judges whether you're 'in' or 'out'. The stakes seemed to be much higher, in general, and people acted accordingly.

But I didn't shy away from the game entirely. In that kind of environment, it was wise to proceed with caution—not to stick my neck too far out, or to fall prey to the powers of seduction. There were far too many pitfalls to step into. I didn't feel adequately prepared, at first, to expose myself to that level of vulnerability. I kept everything close to the hip. It was one thing to put out some feelers, nurture some acquaintances, take random stabs at new friendships, or even have an occasional date or two. But quite another to go much further. I noticed that I started holding people who I was interacting with to an impossible standard, well beyond even what I expected from those I had once been close with, who I held in the highest regard, in my past life. It just seemed like everyone was going to come up short in my view, one way or another. I wasn't exactly sure why I was persisting so stubbornly with that attitude. And I didn't really have a great explanation for it. But good enough didn't seem to be good enough for me anymore, for whatever reason. I guess it made some sort of vague sense, given the extremes of what I had experienced before committing to the move.

It was hard adjusting to New York, over the long run. And alienating, to a degree that I hadn't anticipated. It was difficult to establish solid new relationships, given the playing field. But I can't deny that I was partly culpable, too, due to the psychological baggage I brought to the table. I'm willing to admit, wearing thick psychic armor certainly didn't help. But I also felt sure that people wouldn't be aware enough to grasp where I was coming from. How could they have been? I hadn't given them much to work with, after all. If I seemed a little suspect to them, I couldn't blame them for those feelings. I probably seemed a bit cold—or at the very least, a tad too aloof—if not detached or apathetic. They knew for certain that I wasn't even close to being like one of them, and I had to agree they were right. So it was just a matter of tolerating the differences, the contrasting mentalities.

I tried my best to live by the principle of focusing on the things I had some control over, rather than wasting my time on things beyond my grasp. That meant focusing on my work. But of course, even there, there were challenges. Psychiatry is a sticky subject and, by its very nature, it doesn't happen in a vacuum. I was working mostly with individuals, but those individuals have families, and they interact with other people, and institutions—that often work at cross-purposes to their interests—whether we're talking about a legitimate conflict that needs to be hashed out on a

134

micro scale, or because the very structure of our society creates opposition on the macro level. There are quite a few institutions that are significantly compromised and dysfunctional—including the healthcare system—that have been corrupted to such an extent that their primary mission, these days, is to perpetuate their own interests and goals over those of their clients, including the ultimate objective of institutional self-preservation, no matter the cost. In short, they've become bureaucratic monsters, with their own peculiar, internal logic, and that's very difficult for the average citizen to comprehend. Unless you somehow discover unequivocal evidence that they're actively plotting against you. The propaganda is so strong that oftentimes clients will truly believe that *they* work for *them*, even though they don't compensate them. And even if *they* pay *them* for a service, they still want to act like the boss. Surely you know what I'm talking about? And that's where the trouble usually lies. Because not only can I not tolerate that personally, I have even less tolerance when it comes to my patients. And that's what got me into trouble one time.

I had a patient, with a moderately autistic son, who sought my services primarily to help her cope with the demands of parenting a child with significant behavioral challenges, in a world that otherwise only views these special needs children as problems that need to be managed or controlled. The mother was actually doing a very fine job raising her son, and was only having trouble coping because of the institutional incompetency that she faced on a nearly daily basis. She owned a thriving business, and had been divorced from an abusive and narcissistic spouse for many years. She had to raise her son on her own, for all intents and purposes, because not only was the father of the child abusive toward his own son—often verbally abusing him, calling him fat or stupid— he seemed to have endless excuses as to why he couldn't support the child, including financially. It certainly wasn't because he had any real financial hardships to speak of. But, nonetheless, the mother and child carried on, doing the best they could under very challenging circumstances. The child was getting into trouble at school several times a week, from relatively minor offenses— which the school seemed to be able to handle—to more violent episodes, when the child would verbally and/or physically threaten other children, destroy property, out of sheer frustration. Or, as I already implied, because of the incompetence of the professionals who attempted to intervene during these episodes.

By the time I arrived on the scene, the school had shown its incompetence quite thoroughly, and that it was incapable of dealing constructively with the situation. When a conflict occurred, the only action they seemed to take was to call the school strongman in to restrain the child. This strongman was actually doing a reasonable job of intervening, despite the fact that he should've never been restraining a child in the first place, was not properly trained, nor was he the type of professional who was appropriate for the job. When the strongman wasn't available, the next course of action was to call the mother in to do the work the school should've done. She would have to take whole days off, or whole segments of days off, each and every week, to go into the school to either remove the child from the environment, or deal with it as best she could so that the child could continue on with his day. Again, it's important to note how she, despite her considerable skills to lovingly redirect her child, was not formally trained to do the job, either. That's where I came in.

I had been trained to deal with these types of situations, although I admit that I had been hesitant to work with an autistic child. Not because I didn't think I could be helpful, but because I didn't have a lot of experience working with people with autism, let alone a tween, and assumed there must be someone else more willing or qualified to work with her son. But unfortunately, that wasn't the case. The mother pleaded with me to take her son on as a client, so, as a courtesy to her, I did. It was absolutely clear that the status quo could not be maintained, in the interest of the child.

The first order of business was to evaluate what was going on that was leading to undesirable outcomes. One way of doing that was to go into the school during a moment of crisis and experience firsthand what was going on. The very first time that happened and I was called in to assist, I discovered what the problem was. As soon as I entered the classroom, the most striking thing wasn't the behavior of the child, but rather the behavior of the teacher, who was, by the way, specifically hired for and trained in special education. While the child was acting out—launching staplers randomly around the classroom, putting other children at risk—the teacher seemed mostly concerned about her own well-being, standing safely in a corner, out of the way, frozen with fear, like a 'deer in headlights'. It would've been comical, if it wasn't so alarming. She seemed completely helpless: either not knowing what to do, or refusing to jump in. I appreciated the fact that she made the decision to call me rather than the strongman, but I didn't realize that that meant her not attempting to do anything at all. There seemed to be no effort to deescalate—although to her credit, she did have the instinct to start ushering the other students out of the classroom.

The young man had clearly had enough. Even though we had already formed an excellent therapeutic bond from our previous work together, I had never intervened physically before—so, naturally, I became 'one of them' by my very presence in the classroom, equivalent to the enemy, from his perspective. That was understandable. So he continued to throw objects around, and some were probably even purposefully thrown in my direction. I remember I got grazed with the tip of a pencil, causing a superficial scratch on my arm. But what I understood, fairly immediately, was that he was way past the point where any kind of rationally-based de-escalation technique could've proved effective.

I quickly realized that the best, and probably the only, course of action available to me was to model physical self-control. I opted to simply sit down at a desk and clasp my hands together, maintaining the calmest demeanor possible, only moving if necessary, while objects kept flying in my direction. He continued to toss things around for what seemed like hours. But then after a few minutes, not only was he choosing less intimidating and damaging projectiles, he seemed to be throwing them mostly at the classroom walls. In the next few minutes, he stopped throwing things entirely, and began to dart around furiously in the open space near me. Given a few minutes more, he was pacing right next to me, and began to communicate a little more normally. As you might predict, it only took a few more minutes for him to abruptly park himself down right next to me. I had already focused on drawing some pictures at the table some time before, and his natural curiosity turned his attention my way. He was still heightened, yes, but he was finally beginning to throw in the towel. He didn't join in with the drawing immediately, so that's when I asked him if he knew whether there was a deck of cards in the room. As it turned out, there was. After he quickly retrieved them and sat back down, I took them out, shuffled them, and dealt out a hand.

A good fifteen minutes had already gone by since I arrived, and although he was still fuming, and agitated, he was able to begin to participate with some very direct coaching on my part. Before long, it was as if he forgot all about what had just happened, and not only were we having a rousing game of cards, he began to act like himself again, even beginning to smile and laugh a bit. You can imagine how the rest of it went. We started talking about what had just transpired, just briefly. But rather than getting into it too deeply at that moment, I thought we'd save the details for our next session. It was more important to get back to the business at hand in front of us. When he was ready to turn that corner, and I was ready to turn the classroom back over to the teacher, I rose and put my arm around him, before giving him a good, long hug. And that was it. It really was that simple. When the teacher saw that, I think she was shocked to see a totally different kind of person in her classroom. The other children filed in shortly afterwards. And that was my cue to leave.

Later that day, when I reflected on what had happened, I had a few thoughts that kept running like a reel in my head. The first was related to technique, and how people feel compelled to have to do something drastic during these types of crisis situations, as opposed to just being present and cashing in on the rapport that has been previously established. The second was related to time, and how everyone seems to need to have a crisis resolved immediately, rather than just letting events take their natural course. What was the hurry? It was pretty clear to me, that with the right attitude, and enough time, and the right people, almost every crisis can be resolved with very little effort. Yes, a few things might have to be sacrificed for the greater good—there might be some property damage—but even that unfortunate occurrence can be utilized to teach a lesson. For example, after the young man had thrown the stuff around, I asked him to help me return everything to its rightful place. And if things were broken, I suggested that he make recompense—which he happily did, the following week. The fact was, this child, despite his condition, and the usual assumptions about people with autism, had an extraordinary capacity for emotional intelligence, I might presume well beyond even some of his very own family members, and certainly superior to many of the professionals that were charged with caring for him. Tapping into his positive attributes and reinforcing them was much more consequential—certainly more effective than trying to punish him, which is essentially what the school was doing, whether they realized it or not.

So, with that in mind, hoping to improve things with an eye toward the future, we set up a meeting with the officials at the school. We collectively agreed that the child should receive more services, including, but not limited to, psychological testing for learning disorders, and a weekly session with the school social worker. To work with the child preemptively, so that the cycle of acting-out and externalizing behavior could be cut off earlier on, before it escalated to a heightened, more disruptive level. We left the meeting very pleased with the plan and continued to monitor the situation as necessary. At first, there seemed to be some improvement in the child's behavior, and he began to thrive both academically and socially.

Then, over the course of months, it seemed like whatever support was in place was no longer helping. Even though he had had a whole network of school professionals assigned to him who were in place and dedicated to his service—including a special education teacher, a school psychologist, a social worker and a dedicated one-on-one personal aide—we found out that he wasn't continuing to receive what the school had promised on an ongoing basis. They weren't following through, it turned out, in any serious way, with the educational plan that had the implicit imprimatur of the state and federal government. They were knowingly breaking federal regulations freely, and, it turned out, with impunity. So, as the mother had to spend increasingly more lengthy and disruptive periods of time away from work to deal with the new crises that were developing, to the detriment of her work life, we asked to have another meeting with school personnel, to hash it out.

This time, however, as soon as we sat down at the table, it was clear that the formerly inviting atmosphere had changed dramatically. Instead of convening with the usual suspects, the people who were currently working with the child on the front line, we were joined by a whole additional committee of administrative professionals whom I had never seen before. Now the principal of the school was involved, and a representative from the school district, ostensibly an expert on autism, brusquely took the lead. It was clear from the get-go that this was going to be an entirely different kind of experience. First, the child wasn't invited to participate. Then, the so-called autism expert began with her discourse on the subject. It amounted to an entirely facile lecture on autism, as it were. The materials she presented were completely inappropriate for his age, as a pre-teen; they were associated with protocols that were applicable to very young children, that he had already been familiarized with as a kindergartner. No, I kid you not!

As the mother became more and more agitated by the tone of the presentation, I had no choice but to butt in. I tried my best to intervene in a friendly way, to point out how the materials were inappropriate without attacking the professional reputation of the district representative. Then I tried to steer the conversation toward what the presenting problem was, inquiring about which professionals were involved, and in what manner. To be helpful, I even brought up a specific example from a few days earlier, when the child had had an incident on the playground during recess. Well, you would've thought that I had called them all idiots, and that I had yelled at them and hurled personal insults their way! When I started asking the frontline personnel about how they handled that recent incident, it was clear that just replying to my questions would be controversial. The fact-finding questions themselves seemed to be a threat. The principal very quickly put the kibosh on it: not only did she censor and redirect the conversation, she had the gall to accuse me of being hostile! It was becoming very clear that all her employees were instructed to keep their mouths shut, and that the whole meeting was really a setup, of sorts. There would be no more collaboration, apparently. Then the district representative chimed in, concurring that I had been hostile to her, and that she wasn't going to continue tolerating being abused. I'll tell you, my friend, I had never experienced such a lack of professionalism in my whole career, up to that point. The district rep stormed out of the room, and added that because I had had such a bad attitude, she wasn't going to leave the materials that she had prepared for my clients, as punishment. Can you imagine? Penalizing the clients because of her own egotism and incompetence. And the obvious projection onto me!

Well, by then, it was clear that nothing positive was going to come from this second meeting. As the district rep stomped out, I shook my head in disbelief, and sent her off with an abrupt and sarcastic 'Bye!', with a wave of the hand. After that, the principal took over and continued to dissemble and obfuscate further. She claimed that she didn't have to answer to me, that the services that we had asked for, and the professionals associated with them, were somehow suddenly not available to the children at the middle school level anymore, et cetera, et cetera, even though I knew that was unequivocally false. They had certainly agreed to the terms of service, but then it was as if they had never had the previous meeting. She was straight-out lying to me, right to my face. I could see that the other subordinated professionals in the room were starting to squirm. Not only couldn't they say anything, but I could also tell that they felt implicated and soiled by the experience. They couldn't stop shifting in their chairs, knowing that a professional peer from the outside was witnessing their utter humiliation. By then, I was really surprised that they hadn't arranged for a school district attorney to be present to help with those kinds of strong-arm tactics. But then it occurred to me that having an attorney present might actually backfire on them, exposing the principal and staff to potential legal liability, because they were not adhering to the guidelines that superseded their own small universe. But it was a complete ambush, that's for sure!

After it became glaringly obvious to me that we were wasting our time, and immediately after the meeting was adjourned by the principal, we didn't spend any time or effort withdrawing with the usual social graces. All I could think of was how sad it was that my patient's child was forced to attend this school, and I wasn't going to be nice about it anymore. Unfortunately, sending him to another school was all but impossible, because the mother couldn't afford the tuition. Although we left the meeting aggrieved, my client and I agreed to follow up on it at our next session, to figure out where to go from there.

The mother agreed that the meeting had been a complete hoax, and was now fully convinced that we would have to work around them in the future. In fact, they would probably go out of their way *not* to help. It turned out that the father, who had also been present at the meeting, who had only sat there like a helpless lump, had since then objected to my participation, and requested that I no longer be included in future meetings. Of course, that was completely self-serving, because he had shown time and time again that his motives had nothing to do with the welfare of his child. He was also very clearly conflict-adverse, in the worst way, and it was apparent his development as a person ended sometime around late adolescence. So I had no alternative but to accept that.

He couldn't interfere with his son's therapy, though, because both parents' consent was not legally necessary. So while I continued with his son's services, which he wasn't paying for, he decided to rupture the already tenuous relationship we had had. From that point on, he distanced himself even further from his responsibility as a father. Meanwhile, the mother was still on board and continued to value what I could offer. We spoke about the meeting afterward, debriefed it in fine detail, in the son's presence, and had to devise a new strategy. The most obvious option was to get lawyers involved. Understandably, the mother was not inclined to go in that direction. She had already consulted with some previously, and even they admitted that the investment in time and money would not produce a satisfying outcome, given their past experience, and the inherent politics of going up against a school district that had so thoroughly proven it was acting in bad faith. So then we were left in the unenviable position of doing the best we could with few resources. I had to be careful not to enable the school district by continuing to intervene every time the boy had an incident. I refused to do it, on principle. Particularly because they would've had no problem taking advantage of my unpaid labor. I tried my best to empower the child, and continued to support the parents, although I knew it would be asking too much of them to solve everything on their own. But what options were there? Not many.

But the good news was that we learned something valuable from these interactions. We learned that they were only going to do the bare minimum, if that, and that all the services they claimed to have for their students, that were prominently displayed on their website and across all platforms, were a hoax. It was nothing but self-serving propaganda. It was clear that they only wanted to project the *image* of a benevolent, community institution, and get credit for it without doing much to justify it. Think of all the money and effort wasted on researching and implementing a mental health behavioral program that never existed! Maybe that was the whole point of it—to leech off the taxpayers' dollars. But at least after that, we knew where the school stood. We could only try to work through it or around it, using any means that could get real results. Eventually, though, after another year of suffering and little progress, the mother, fortunately, managed to strike a deal that made it possible for her son to be transferred to a private school. And what a difference it made! Not only was he getting a better education, he had a full range of services that were provided free of charge. It was like night and day. A total contrast to the previous experience. And instead of being a pariah to them, I was accepted—and fully embraced—as a member of the boy's educational team. They couldn't have been happier to see me and get my input, which, of course, I gladly provided.

The funny thing, though, was that after the boy's transfer to the new school, I happened to run into the principal of the old school again, by happenstance. I tried to pretend I didn't see her, but she seemed determined to corner me, face-to-face. Once she forced my attention, she acted as if nothing unpleasant or contentious had transpired between us. She just smiled at me and wanted to chat, like it was just another typical day, in the same old universe. A complete and thorough gaslighting, no doubt. Can you imagine the gall? What nerve! She explained that she was retiring after a decades-long career in education. Literally prompting me to pat her on the back for a job well done. To the uncritical public eye, her retirement might've appeared to be the icing on the cake for her, after a long, successful, self-sacrificing career. But she couldn't have left any faster, as far as I was concerned. Any more lasting damage to even *one* more student would've been tragic.

When I look back on it, the thing that bothers me the most about it is that I took a far too naïve and trusting approach toward people who didn't earn it from the get-go. I thought if I tried to help people, and others were presumably trying to do the same thing, we'd be natural allies, on the exact same page. But no! The truth of the matter is that there are always people who are determined to get in the way, are determined to sabotage whatever you try to do, no matter how noble the cause. It appeared their primary position was to put me in my place, to make me do things their way, to further their agenda—otherwise they wouldn't have anything to do with me. These days, if anything remotely reminiscent of that experience presents itself, I *begin* by trying to work around it, because, after all, the whole focus of my existence is to benefit the people who come my way. That's always the guiding light, the guiding principle. I guess that's why I enjoy private practice so much. Regrettably, though, that means most of the burden of dealing with the greater forces and powers of the world, especially the ones who are erecting barriers all along the way, sits squarely with the patient. But in the end—to some degree —that's a good thing. It's essential that clients learn these types of crucial skills, how to navigate through the system. I'm more than happy to continue to support them with that, to a degree. But even given those limitations, I discovered, to my delight, that my practice continued to flourish. Even though I'd admitted defeat on the broader scale, at least temporarily. In short, there's nothing that can be leveraged against me. I'm beholden to no one. Truly a free agent! That's why I get so many clients. And also why there's resentment from my adversaries, because I hold a mirror up to the very people who lack integrity, and I'm not afraid to call them out.

That was just one example of the kind of negative energy one finds oneself up against in any caregiving field, and in society in general. Everyone has experienced that kind of resistance, and it seems like it just keeps getting thicker as the years go by. If you end up spending too much time battling those forces, you're going to end up wasting a lot of time. You shouldn't be forced to share your success with those kinds of people. If you can manage to shape your own world and have power over it, you'll be better off, ultimately. I found an enormous amount of satisfaction in my own little world of private practice. I was the king of my domain, and nobody was pressed to comply, if they didn't do so voluntarily. If they didn't like the results they were getting, they were certainly free to find a better fit with someone else. But if one chose to work with me, one knew, beyond a doubt, that you'd get my full attention, in a dedicated manner. The ulterior motives, if there were any, were down to an absolute minimum. We could concentrate our full resources—which I guarded tenaciously—on the welfare of each and every patient. Better satisfied, free, with possibly limited success, then frustrated, beholden, and dependent on a warped system, feeling confused and wondering what the benefits actually amounted to. The choice couldn't be any clearer!

And that was another reason that these types of institutions despised me: they knew I was having great success with patients, and had a loyal clientele that appreciated my efforts. I think my patients built a level of trust with me and rewarded my efforts by engaging with enthusiasm and sending more clients my way. I didn't even need to advertise! It was all word of mouth, most of the time. Of course, there was a limit to how many patients I could take on at once. Even so, I sensed that many of these institutions hoped I'd go out of business and clear out of town. They'd be happy if I were expunged from the public consciousness. Why? I certainly wasn't a threat to them as far as the bottom line went, in terms of profit. They just couldn't tolerate being reminded of their own incompetence and hypocrisy. They didn't want *their* clients to discover just how paltry their services were, dispensed at a much higher price, both financially and psychologically. They, like the principal, often tried to paint me as a loose cannon—or some other kind of rabble-rouser—and my practice as less worthy and rigorous than theirs. I guess their voices outnumbered me. But nobody bought it! And it just fueled my determination to excel even more, and be that much more successful. So the joke was on them! It amused me, really tickled me and I proudly wore their disapprobation as a badge of honor.

No, their kind of energy was something I just couldn't countenance after a while. There was a certain amount of spitefulness that was being continually projected my way. When institutions are critical of you, it's akin to being bullied on the playground. Their 'strength' is grounded in numbers—once one bully starts, the rest of them naturally join in. Like some kind of twisted survival instinct. To kill, or be killed. That's what they're afraid of, essentially. All they have to do is agree on the same narrative, float some nonsense about you and make sure they stick

147

to the story. Pretty soon, even the casual, disinterested bystander can be swayed. Just attack a person's reputation, imply that one is not a good-faith actor, and it's amazing how quickly one can fall. While your voice might be powerful, it's still only one in a sea of antipathy. It's only your word against all of theirs. Institutions count on that. There's an inviolate logic at work from within the belly of the beast. And it spills over into the greater community. There's a defensiveness because there's a belief that institutions have inherent value by their mere existence. Like they've always been a part of the greater plan over the course of time, in the best of all possible worlds. They don't go so far as to try to convince people that they're perfect. Even for them, that would be stretching it. But, just the same, they're not inclined to stomach anything that will contradict the vision they have for themselves. Every effort is made to steer clear of even the mildest criticisms. Especially if it stings, when the truth is self-evident. But if exposure is unavoidable, and everything else is even, as a rule your average person will be more likely to take their side, if for no other reason than to break an intolerable tension. It's the easiest way out. Surely no single individual, no matter how empowered, can be that exceptional?

I mean, I don't mean to brag, but sometimes I think I do more good from within my own little fiefdom than entire agencies do throughout the vastness of the domains they oversee. Certainly, in terms of the old Hippocratic doctrine of 'first do no harm'. To be effective, in the sphere of human affairs, at the core, I believe it begins and ends with three very simple principles: treating clients with kindness, decency and respect. The problem with most bureaucracies is that they spend far too much of their resources maintaining power for power's sake. If there's a single trait that personifies what this kind of bureaucracy embodies, I'd suggest 'vanity'. No matter who the client is, or what their status is in society, they're forced to prove once and again that they're *worthy* of the services they're seeking to receive. That inclination often bleeds over to other aligned professionals from outside the organization who might be contributing. Although not entirely analogous, the attitude of the autistic boy's father is a perfect case in point. Even though I represented and acted in the best interest of his child, he chose, instead, to align with the very people who refused to do even the least due diligence for the welfare of his son. Then, rather than let it drop, he took the additional step of deliberately freezing me out of the dialogue. I wouldn't've been surprised to hear that the school had decided to ban me permanently after that. I never found out if that was the case, because the feeling was mutual—and I didn't need or want to have any further access, anyway. I really didn't care one way or the other. None of it bothered me, except for the fact that the father, who'd sabotaged me, got wholehearted and enthusiastic validation. The school patted him on the head for being such a good boy.

Meanwhile, if I had been the least vengeful, I could've leveraged what I knew very powerfully against the school. Even though it didn't seem worthwhile to pursue the matter through legal channels, it would've been very easy to report them to the supervising authorities, concerning the egregious violations of the child's educational support plan. Discriminating against a disabled child not only looks bad, it can have serious consequences for the transgressor, far beyond the immediate issue at hand. Regrettably, however, even the mother didn't want to press the school to that degree. I understood her hesitance, and had to honor her decision. Because even if you end up absolutely nailing them with it, with irrefutable proof—and there's absolutely no doubt about the record or any of the evidence—they'll plead innocent. They'll claim it was just a momentary oversight. An exception to the general rule. They'll be thoroughly defensive about it. 'How *dare* you challenge us! How *dare* you go over our heads! Who are *you* to question our motives?' And more. They'll say: 'We educate all the children in the community, and *this* is the thanks we get? Shame on you!' I have to admit; they know they've got the odds in their favor. Because the fact is, public opinion is often on their side out of sheer laziness and apathy, and the bureaucracy overseeing *them* can often be an even bigger, more deeply entrenched one, with an even richer shortsightedness and narcissism, and it's *more* than likely that they'll let the offenders get away with what they've been doing all along. Perhaps a light reprimand, at best. Even if it's systemic and self-evident. Oh, they'll ask who's responsible. They'll poke around. But in the end, they'll conveniently pretend that they can't pin it on anyone in particular. They'll claim it's just the nature of the beast. Or, alternatively, they'll pull the 'we just don't have the resources to investigate' excuse. They'll try to convince you that it's all 'very unfortunate' on the one hand, then ask for your support with the other. They'll say something like 'if only people invested their time in the system', or 'Why don't you come to the fundraiser we're having in a few weeks. One of the other parents organized it!' Remember the 'thousand points of light' campaign? I don't buy into any of that volunteer business for one minute, the temptation of it. They're always playing the victim. Always claiming to be in the poorhouse.

Yeah, I understand that there are a lot of good organizations out there doing the real work, the good work. I have no problem with that. But I have to say I get immediately suspicious when I'm asked to volunteer. Automatically. Reflexively. In most cases, volunteering is akin to being taken advantage of. And you're probably only enabling dysfunctional institutions by doing their work for them. You're absolving them of their responsibility to ask *their* higher-ups for an adequate budget, of advocating for the community they serve. Or, alternatively, it's just a great opportunity for people in the community to get the heavy burden of guilt that's been mercilessly nagging at them for far too long off *their* chests—because they almost never do anything even remotely generous by their own initiative.

Take my sister-in-law, for example. She volunteers at her local public school all the time. Why? Ostensibly to help out. Mostly because everyone on the inside is too spineless to demand the proper fiscal support. Because god forbid anyone speak up—or raise taxes—even for the most obvious and politically neutral of purposes. But what my sister-in-law's neighbors don't realize is that her *personal* motives for volunteering at the school have so much more to do with her own psychological needs than it does with the perceived benefits. People want to make up for their worst deficiencies in the easiest, most convenient manner possible. Even if it has no connection to the problem at hand. The truth is she's there to absolve herself for the mortal sins from her past, and to avoid taking responsibility for the choices she made. Did I tell you how she abandoned her sister in her hour of greatest need? Yes, it's true, she completely disappeared for the whole five-year span my wife was fighting off the cancer that eventually took her life. They were extremely close for most of their lives, until the challenges of middle adulthood took hold. In short, my wife rose to the occasion and did everything right. Her sister, however, buckled under the pressure. She made all the wrong decisions, and ended up a mess, more or less. But rather than trying to rally and recover, to make corrections and chart a better course for herself, she doubled down on the path to misery. She was in a deeply unhappy marriage, gave up her career, had no focus except her own martyrdom. She was so self-centered that she actually got angry with my wife for getting sick, for needing help and attention. Can you believe that? I know it's hard to comprehend, but it happens more often than you think. It's crazy, but it destroys families. In the end, she did condescend to visit two weeks before her sister died. To say goodbye. But even her goodbye became an appeal for sympathy: the main focus of her interchange was to complain about their mother, who, by the way, *was* one of the heroes amongst all the misery. For example, when I was having trouble coping with the demands of the situation, she was the *only* one who was able to hold me high. The gist of my sister-in-law's bitterness was that my wife was being favored, and had always been favored. Can you imagine how narcissistic you have to be to take on that attitude, during those very sensitive moments? Well, I can't say that she was wrong, exactly. But not for the right reasons. The way she framed it was completely wrong—but if that's the way she honestly saw it, it *must've* been excruciatingly difficult for their mother to resist favoring the daughter who did everything right, over the one who fucks everything up! And my wife was the one who perished! There truly is no justice.

Anyway, you get my point. The original point being that if you're going to devote time and energy to an institution that's asking for help, make sure you know what purpose it serves, and why you're doing it. Otherwise, you'll be enabling, and completely off the mark. Entirely unaware of the consequences and long terms effects on yourself and the institution. You have to examine the overall calculus before you pledge to commit. Most of the time, volunteering will only benefit the institution's hidden agenda, and you'll get nothing in return. It almost doesn't matter what your intentions are.

In fact, I'd go even further. I'd advise you to think very carefully about whether you'd be willing to volunteer or collaborate in any way, at least in the traditional sense. You might also want to examine if you're comfortable disclosing certain types of information, or highly-sensitive data, to these institutions, even if it's mandatory. Ever notice how much data entry you do for all sorts of organizations, free of charge? There's a potential price to be paid. It can make you extremely vulnerable without you ever realizing it. I try to remind my patients of that routinely—they typically think they'll receive more, the *more* they cooperate and disclose about themselves. But often, it's exactly the opposite. It's a little counterintuitive, but if you're not aware of that from the beginning, you'll learn that lesson sooner or later, probably the hard way. It'll continue to backfire on you unless you exercise some sort of discipline and begin to understand how institutions work. Confide in your closest associates, by all means, and even some professionals—the ones that you know you can trust, who have earned your respect—but don't go much further beyond that. Up to and until it's absolute necessary. Just like in personal relationships—let's face it, we judge, and are judged—information is continually gathered and recorded, and you're constantly being reevaluated based on the data gathered. But unlike a friendship or intimate relationship, an institution is much more likely to be stubborn to the extreme, and ruthlessly unforgiving. It's taking very careful notes, and processing on multiple levels, most likely to deny you what you're asking for. They aren't inclined to provide you with what you're entitled to, from the very get-go. You might say that's cynical, but why does it take an average of three applications and a slick, smooth-talking attorney to finally get the disability one deserves? The facts mostly stay the same.

I remember when my wife died, I automatically qualified for death benefits, as a recently widowed individual. Do you know what the clerk tried to suggest to me, from the instant the meeting started, which was convened explicitly to educate me about my rights? She all but insinuated that it was my god given and dutiful responsibility to get married again as soon as humanly possible so that they could cease the payments I hadn't even begun to receive yet. No, I'm not joking. That kind of not-so-subtle manipulation goes on all the time, in various guises and incarnations. I've witnessed it over and over again, especially with regard to my patients. Some of them have very serious conditions and require intensive services, which, at inflated rates, can add up exceedingly quickly. That's when the bureaucracies try everything they can to

153

get in the way. Now, if you're a supposedly hopeless case, a person who can *only* survive by being completely dependent on the good will of the state, *and* it would be utterly ridiculous for them to deny the claim, *and,* mostly critically, it would trigger a flood of enormously negative publicity and outrage if they ended up denying you, they will begrudgingly take you on, as long as you comply to the n'th degree. You will have to do exactly what they tell you to do, and agree implicitly with how they want it done. They know you can't answer back, because of your absolute dependence. In fact, you'd *better* appreciate it! Or you'll end up on the street. That's not an exaggeration.

Have you seen all the homeless people out there? How do you think they get there? They literally get dumped on the curb by a whole host of institutions conspiring together, if you don't comply *precisely* with the plan. In a just and caring society, there'd be no such thing as homeless people. 'Don't these underserved people realize how few resources are available? If you don't want them, move to the side! The next guy'll take them.' If you have too much of an attitude, you'll be marked as a troublemaker for life. Seriously. That's why homeless people move around a lot. Ever notice? Because most of the bridges have been burned a long time ago. Most people think the *homeless* people burn them. No, sir. That's not how it goes. The institutions can't burn them fast enough. The more fortunate among the victimized are actually lucky if they happen to stumble into the system of revolving door care—in and out of disreputable institutions, in a never-ending cycle. But the underlying ethic undergirding it all—again, I'm not really exaggerating—is 'that's how things are, unfortunately', with the added implication that that's how it's always been, and there's nothing anyone can do about it. They want to pretend that there are no good guys or bad guys. If you should conclude otherwise, they'll label you as either profoundly naïve or not competent enough to judge. They frame it as analogous to picking fruit from the tree of knowledge—in the Garden of Eden, if you're arrogant enough to even attempt to reach for it, you'll risk the very real possibility of being expelled from their perverted paradise forever.

The essential thing to remember is that, on the most fundamental level, there is a war of attrition going on, and that time is on the institution's side. They'll promise you something, but then they'll ask you to have what amounts to eternal patience with them before they finally try to justify how they might squeeze it out of the system. Even then, they probably won't give you what you want. If it's not the revolving door treatment, you might get the impression, with the passage of time, that they've forgotten about you altogether, the mental equivalent of dumping you on the street. A 'reverse mortgage' theory of healthcare. It might just be in your best interest to forget about them *before* they forget about you, so that they can't run the clock down and leave you hanging. No, I'm serious, it's gotten that bad.

At least with my practice, I had a legitimate, functional operation and made an honest dollar. A solid hour of therapy for a reasonable rate. A direct transaction, with no middle men—no insurance companies, no managed care—in fact, no grifters of any kind, who enjoy getting rich off of other people's pain. The system tried everything they could to ridicule my enterprise, to marginalize me, and to have a laugh at my expense. What I did seemed like insanity to them. But for me, it was the only path forward, which ultimately led to getting out of that business altogether, and reinventing myself as a Witness/Confidant. I'm fortunate enough to be in the position where I don't have to charge for my services anymore. I just sit at Casablanca and accept what comes. These days, from my perspective, the only sane course of action is to continue to chisel away at things, one chip at a time, until we get the desired outcome. There's no problem too big or too complicated that can't be overcome with a coordinated and persistent attack. If we're going to ultimately prevail and survive, and have any kind of quality of life along the way, we need to coordinate more like a colony of ants—putting the welfare of all over the interest of the few. Whether you work within the system or not, your allegiance should align with those who are reaching for a higher plane, for a loftier goal. Let's just hope we don't get there too late, when the game's over, and the problem itself has vanished. Once you've seen the light, been baptized, like me, with the blood of initiation, there's no turning back. We all need to get there, no matter how painful it might be. It's not easy, but it's a necessary evil. They'll be many who try to discourage, distract, and/or demean you, but no matter how hard they try to twist it around, use whatever tools you have to carry on. It's not hopeless. The right answers *must* come in the end. That's when we'll finally be on the road to saving ourselves, and we'll discover our true and authentic selves for the very first time.

That's not to say that people aren't constantly in conflict with themselves. Just look at me. I've already told you about some of my shortcomings. I'm not exactly the most modest, or humble, person in the world. No, it's okay. I can see that subtle smile forming in the corner of your mouth. Have a good laugh at my expense! And yours, too, frankly. Yes, I assume you understand what I mean. It's good not to take ourselves *too* seriously. *None* of us are exempt from contradicting ourselves. Just let your memory drift over your past. It's chock-full of questionable moments, right? It's ridiculous not to admit it. I guess we're all equally prejudiced to assume that our own best attributes are the ones that shine through most brilliantly to others. Yet we seldom acknowledge our failures, even if they lead us, indirectly, toward beneficial outcomes. It's frightening how difficult it can be to tell the difference between a worm that's eating the apple innocently for a wholesome meal; or one that might, with sufficient time and cunning, core the heart out of you. I can't deny there's a little bitterness inside me, and that sometimes I feel lonely and even a little sorry for myself. But when I give, I try to give freely. I don't expect anything in return. Anything I do comes with no strings attached, as much as that's possible. Conversely, though, if you try to return the favor with or without any kind of acknowledgement, I'll just pretend I didn't have anything to do with it. That's just the way I operate... Nothing personal.

You might be interested to learn that if I do have any decent qualities, they came late to me. Let's just say my parents weren't the best role models, and the environment I grew up in left much to be desired. As a surgeon, my father was rarely home. He was very intelligent, obviously, but he was essentially half a man. Not a lot of warmth inside, not a lot of time to devote to other things. My mother, cursed by beauty, was exceedingly vain. She spent most of her time either bored, or tending to herself and the home, which she decorated with great care and impeccable style. In some ways, my parents were perfect for each other. But they weren't what you might call nurturing. Good traits didn't come naturally, let us say. I had to learn and earn them. As a child—given that type of upbringing—I was too self-absorbed to notice what I was missing. Like the familiar story about the goldfish in a bowl who wonders what water is when asked about it. But as soon as I was on my own—which I would trace back to about the age of fifteen, when I became more independent, due to a job and a car—I was forced to do a little soul searching and have a reckoning. I think I knew who I was, and who I wanted to be, but a vast gulf lay in between. I knew I had to try to transform some of my flaws into strengths, and the only way I could succeed... How does it go? 'Fake it 'til you make it'. Or something like 'How's that working for you?' When you conclude that it isn't, the next most logical step is to try to do the complete opposite of what you've been doing for so long. According to that rule, I very rapidly turned my faults into virtues: my deviance was what helped me engage; my indifference gave rise to fortitude; my selfishness became generosity. All of a

157

sudden, I had a vision; whether or not it caused controversy, at least I had a point of view and an opinion. I may even have become a bit of a martyr for a time—self-sacrificing to the extreme —to make up for all those years of narcissism. But then later, I also learned how to temper that—to let loose, to have some fun, like I'd never done before. In short, I had to make up for a lot of lost time and learn a lot of new things very quickly.

I rarely refused any sort of novel experience. I rarely turned down a drink, a woman, or any other pleasurable experience. I tried to stay true to myself while also respecting others. And I think I succeeded at that, in spirit. I was growing and evolving, and because I persisted, I eventually found my calling: a mission I'm still pursuing. It took decades to arrive where I am. Once I got there, there was no turning back. This mission *had* to take precedence over everything else. Everything else had to conform to *it*. I'm always trying to stay on course, trying to contribute, but given the enormity of the ultimate goal, there's no question that I often fall short. There's no denying that. But it's okay, because I get a genuinely deep sense of satisfaction from just following through. I wouldn't call it happiness—that's too much to ask for. Satisfaction is good enough. It's a reasonable goal. There will always be forces that are hell-bent on cutting you down to size, that will want to push you back on your heels, that will try to make you less than happy. Even sad and angry. And there are moments when you will want to give up. But don't fall for it! Don't slip up! Just get outside for a while, take a good walk, a deep breath—clear your lungs and your mind—and get right back in the saddle again.

If there's any lingering self-doubt, I guess there's always the question of whether anything you do has any real consequence, ultimately. Or even makes a dent of any kind. As individuals, perhaps the effect we have is much too feeble. We're just one element in a vast universe that's often indifferent to our interests. It can be overwhelming. I remember when I was younger, it was hard enough just to focus. Finding motivation seemed practically impossible. When I observed what other people were doing, I often wondered how they managed to become so committed, how they bought so deeply and unequivocally into what they were trying to accomplish. I mean, I understood it on the surface—the obvious, tangible rewards. But I'm not so sure I understood the motivations that came from deeper down, from the core of their being. Just when you think you understand, when it's within your grasp, whether you're scrutinizing others, or yourself, the moment you clasp your hands, it inevitably dissolves between your fingers. I wondered if people could even feel it, or detect it intuitively. Did they know it when they saw it? I still wonder about that sometimes. Are the rewards they seek going to be of any real value? Or is it all just cold and empty? Like going through the motions? Just the trappings of a successful life? Is there any authenticity to it? I wanted to know what that meant. When I was having trouble wrapping my head around these questions, getting increasingly frustrated by what seemed ineffable in the end, my mind, understandably, would shift abruptly from the grand scale of things, down to the very specific, seeking some relief. It became almost predictable. Let's face it, when you don't have any good answers to the big questions, it's better to just focus on the little victories you can get from life. It's the tangible things that are objective successes, like when one of my friends finally had the strength and willpower to give up drinking—even if he fell off the wagon just a few weeks later.

It's strange, because when I was working in the movie business, everyone envied me. Everyone thought I had the most amazing job ever. People will do anything to break into that world, under the illusion that somehow their lives will be infinitely better if they only had a similar type of job. They thought their lives were shit and mine was some kind of nirvana. The more people project that on you, the more you feel like your life is a lie. And the more theirs is, too. It's a variation on an old theme, along the lines of 'you are what you eat' or 'you are what you wear.' 'You are what you do' is just another version of the same thing. Of course, it isn't true, but people act like it is. They confused what I did with who I was and what the creative people did, what the final product was. What they saw from the outside, rather than the internal reality. It's only during times of crisis when we see clearly and unequivocally who is essential, who the really important people are, and what they do. Who and what we can't live without. I'm talking about the people who really do make a difference in all of our lives on a daily basis but who rarely get any credit or status for it. They do it quietly, with little expectation of extrinsic reward other than getting paid. And *vastly* underpaid. The farmers, food processors, truck drivers, wholesalers, grocers, retailers; the construction, utility and maintenance workers, and waste collectors; the doctors, dentists, nurses, hygienists, physician assistants, therapists, social workers, nutritionists; teachers, childcare workers... The list goes on and on and on. We couldn't survive without this army operating quietly under our noses. Most of us take them for granted while we go about doing our routine business. Some even go out of their way to demean and disrespect them. We need to eat, right? We need water, clothing, shelter. Let's be more appreciative, be aware every day of our life how important these people are. Instead, we lavish our attention on movie stars and rock stars, or worse, the rich and otherwise infamous. On the cult of personality, their leaders. On all sorts of con artists, frauds, charlatans and hypocrites. Does anyone see the irony in rewarding the least essential people the most, and the most essential the least? We'd better wake up really soon, because there's a whole complex of enormous problems coming down the pike, where recognizing the difference between who's important and who's not is essential. It's pretty clear we can barely weather relatively minor disasters without our infrastructure practically collapsing. You think the Cold War and the threat of nuclear annihilation was bad? Just imagine what'll happen when something even more tangible confronts us. It's really tragic, and comically pathetic, how unprepared we are, and how we choose to look the other way, no matter how frightening or grave the evidence is. With all our supposed intelligence!

We don't have the luxury of squandering any more time, or for people to figure it out for themselves anymore. Remember when we didn't have to think about any of this stuff? Life was so much more innocent then. But it really wasn't and shouldn't have been. We were just living on borrowed time and resources. We just weren't so keenly aware of it. But now we know, and we can't continue to be in denial about it. The seeds of our own destruction were sown a very long time ago. But we should start to aspire to a future era when we can recapture that lost sense of innocence, or, at the very least, some imperfect version of it. What a luxury it'd be to appreciate the simple things of life again, to feel free and unencumbered—to watch a movie, or to play the piano; to go outside and throw a baseball around, or have a backyard barbeque with family and friends—without the ominous shadow that's constantly stalking us. We had our time to indulge, and even overindulge. But we're going to have to pay for it now. If we're not careful and aren't willing to adapt, we're not going to be able to enjoy much of anything pretty soon. We're going to be compelled to have to claw our way through life. Hour by hour, day by day. Just to survive. That'll be pretty unpleasant, my friend. To say the least.

Yes, we really are going to have to try to make up for some of the missteps we've made along the way. To correct them and come up with a much better plan going forward. There's not a whole lot of wiggle room left, so it won't be easy, by any means. We'll be lucky if we manage to pull it off, even at full throttle. Even with the collective commitment and brain power that we presumably have. We need to recognize that there's a special class of very clever, conniving people out there, in positions of great influence and power, who have convinced everyone that they're working for the greater good, for the benefit of the general population, but whose actual goal and primary objective is mainly to enrich themselves, whatever the cost. How did that happen? How did we *let* that happen? We're going to need a new kind of leadership—desperately. With a new approach and a different mode of thinking. People who can see the whole picture with a deeper wisdom. There is a profound difference, after all. That much is obvious. Look at what our so-called 'intelligence' has gotten us into. We need to make some clear distinctions and focus on the type of thinking that will lead to better and more sustainable outcomes. But I realize it's difficult for people to tell the difference. Again, like the goldfish in the bowl, except globally.

It's understandable; we've been brainwashed our whole lives, from grade school on. If you boil it all down to the fundamentals, in my mind there are two dominant mentalities that control our culture today: the 'win at all costs' mentality, coupled with the 'you've got to beat the other guy' attitude. Deeply adversarial approaches. Framed as a zero-sum game, in essence. You can't mistake it. Just look at all the mercenaries out there operating in every corner of our society. The functionaries, the smooth operators, the invisible hands that secretly shape our society's norms. It doesn't make any difference whether they wear uniforms or suits, they're all essentially the same. Whether they rule or control with the most powerful weapons, down the barrel of a gun, or wield enormous economic power—usually both—the objective is clear and unadulterated. To dominate with impunity, at the expense of others. To exploit the economy and environment with few limitations. As long as it helps achieve their narrow, self-interested goals. Just look at how the military budgets continue to expand without bound. How elite universities crank out armies of attorneys and MBAs to enable the dirty work. They're rewarded handsomely. They're honored and admired as outstanding citizens, doing supposedly commendable things. But it's all a sham! The last thing we need is more opportunists, or any other type of predator whose sole aim is exploitation for personal gain. Who thumb their noses at any morality or ethical standard. In fact, they openly mock any and all principles that get in their way. They see them as contemptible weaknesses. But, in my view, they've become more essential than ever. Ultimately, they are the *only* things we can count on, the *only* things we can build upon, if we're going to get through this challenge.

Let's get back to the basics. The Ancient Greeks had it figured out a long time ago, at least theoretically. The Ancient Chinese, too. Many of the indigenous cultures of Africa and America. They understood that some attitudes, although advantageous in the short term, were fundamentally destructive and unsustainable in the long run. From one corner of the earth to the other, from one environment to the next, they knew what was most important, even if they fell short and failed to fully express their more grounded, life-sustaining principles. It really hasn't changed much over the centuries, despite our technological advancements. The *only* serious question left, the one that hobbles real progress, is our failure to develop the will to finally follow through with these age-old principles. To date, no civilization or culture has even gotten close to achieving this goal. Not on a global scale, that's for sure. But we'll have to achieve that and sustain it for centuries in order to survive. Are we going to be capable of that? It's like a new world order will have to prevail.

I know, it's ridiculous. It's absurd. I'm off on yet another tirade. You'll have to excuse me if I continue rambling on. But am I crazy? Is it just me? No, I don't think so. It's an emergency, and we have to start acting like it is. Imagine if you were born into one of those obscure tribes in the Amazon, or in New Guinea.

There're reasons the natives don't want people visiting from the outside. First, they don't want anyone to take advantage of them and take their resources away. They've learned from their previous experiences. Secondly, they don't want to be condescended to and 'civilized' by your supposedly superior culture. They've seen what happens and all the problems outsiders typically bring with them. Once they get a foot in, it's only a matter of time before the stealing, pillaging, raping, and killing begins. Not to mention the mass die-offs from the spread of foreign disease. It's not surprising that they don't put out the welcome mat anymore and are perfectly happy with the lives they already lead. They don't want or need your 'help'. They don't choose to be who they are because they're stupid or ignorant. Quite the contrary. They've accepted who they are and have little desire to reach beyond that. They'll take the good, the bad, and the ugly if it means that they'll be left alone. Left in peace. Sure, maybe a few modern conveniences might be helpful. Perhaps even a minor medical intervention. But once Pandora's box opens, it's over. Once outsiders establish a solid foothold, they'll want to take over completely. It's as simple as that. Outsiders use all sorts of novel tools and methods of manipulation to get what they want, but indigenous people shouldn't fall for it. Outsiders always insist others should adjust to them. Shouldn't it be the other way around? Just imagine what we could learn.

I know no culture's perfect, but some seem more holistic than others, without having victimized the rest of the world. We've all got blind spots. But let's embrace what works, do more of it, and leave the rest behind. Let's contribute what we can, without taking more away. Be humble enough to admit that we've gotten things wrong and that we don't know everything. Let's admit our mistakes when we become aware of them, and have the courage and character to correct ourselves for the better. Let's face it: we don't really need all that much to get by, for everyone to have a very fulfilling and satisfying life. The only reason it doesn't happen is because there's a very small minority, with almost all the wealth and power, who are obscenely greedy, and desperately want to hold on to everything they've managed to hoard. Don't let anyone tell you there isn't enough for everybody. I, for one, am not buying it, and you shouldn't either. How are we going to change things? How are we going to make things more equitable? It starts with you and me. But it also requires better leadership. Look who we've had decade after decade. All wolves in sheep's clothing!

I mean, it took some time for me to come to these conclusions. Why so long? Because I had to be deprogrammed. I had to deprogram myself. Nobody's going to do it for you. And it's not immediately obvious how to do it. Thank god there's still some non-conformists out there. Those rare, independent, open-minded, more enlightened voices that stubbornly chip away at the edifice of the perceived truth, the conventional wisdom, the hegemony of thought. Because we're all indoctrinated, in one way or another, from the very beginning. By our families, our schools, our communities, you name it. On just about every level, we're shaped to conform to the interests we're born into, not necessarily to what is true and just. In that sense, the chicken *does* come before the egg. First there are the baptisms, the communions and the confirmations, or the equivalent, according to faith. Then citizenship, pledges of allegiance, marriage, and various other rites of initiation; the conferring of degrees, graduation rituals, professional licensing. Layer upon layer of approval and validation by all sorts of institutions, depending on the particulars of your life. Just take the time to acknowledge how you've been steeping in this thick stew of influences. How these things have shaped your life. Before you even had the capacity to competently and intelligently choose your own path in life. The cliques, the clubs, the associations, the organizations, the institutions. The towns, the cities, the states, the countries. Pledging blind allegiance to all of them. All the infrastructure that's layered on top of you, that seems so natural to you it's like breathing. You barely think about it. You rarely question it. Until some significant, compelling, conflict arises. How do you negotiate it? How do you fight against the forces that have been exerting control over you for all these years? That demand your conformity? Even dominate you? Especially when they all conspire against you?

Well, you're all grown up now, and you've learned an awful lot, haven't you? You can handle it. Well, unfortunately, no! Because the institutions you're up against are the very ones that've already indoctrinated you. They aren't educating you out of the kindness of their hearts. They aren't motivated by civic duty, or in the business of molding an upstanding citizenry. In fact, they're not really interested in your welfare. From pre-school to high school, they're there to take your hand, babysit you, socialize you, train you, and most importantly, demand that you conform. Learning facts, figures, and critical thinking skills only plays a subordinate role. And they're seen as downright dangerous in the wrong hands, especially when brandished by a rebellious adolescent...

Did I tell you already about the experience I had when I worked at a special education high school in the city? Let me know if I'm repeating myself. Sometimes I tell the same story over and over again, and can't remember who I've already spoken to about it. Yes, another one of my temp jobs when I first transitioned in New York. I was tasked with evaluating certain students at the beginning of the school year to ascertain what services might be helpful to them in terms of academic and/or emotional support. To screen for intellectual challenges and mental health issues that might potentially hinder them. Now you would've thought that that would've been a fairly straight-forward operation. Me sitting in a spare office as student after student comes in for a chat and receives the results of various tests, evaluations, et cetera that had been administered. Spending perhaps fifteen minutes with me going over the recommendations I had for them and that would also be communicated to their parents or guardians. After a few weeks of it, it had become routine, and I was certain that I would be finishing up in less than a week when... Well, how can I put this? I was just sitting there in my office one day when I was summoned down to the front office by the vice principal of the school. She claimed she needed help and I assumed that it would have *something* to do with what I was hired for, as a contract worker. Well, no, it turned out to be something entirely different.

As is often the case, there are certain schools in any school district that are perpetually underfunded and poorly managed. This school in particular was already underperforming and reportedly hemorrhaging money for the last several years even though it had been taken over as a 'charter' school on a more or less corporate model. The typical 'charter' school that *appears* as if it's being run by the local community but that's *really* run by a handful of investors who are profiting on Wall Street and, in fact, are sapping resources away from the very neighborhood they purport to serve. At the same time, they claim perpetual instability and always seem one step away from insolvency. Thus, services are reduced to a minimum and staffing consists of a skeleton crew, who are often working two or more jobs for the price of one.

So, on that day, it turned out that there were more than the usual number of absences reported amongst the staff and I was recruited to step in to cover for them. When I met up with the vice principal at the front office, she ushered me into the adjacent conference room where the students first entered the school upon arrival. Now this school was in a pretty rough neighborhood, the kind that has a fairly high crime rate and some gang activity associated with it. Some of the teenagers in the school had associations with various gangs and some had even been killed in past years, victims of the violence these gangs perpetuated in the neighborhood. Some students admitted that they had to carry some kind of weapon, to and from school, to defend themselves from possible ambush. So, if they chose to carry a weapon—either a gun, knife or more makeshift weapon—they would carry them to and from school but hide them somewhere outside the school grounds while they were inside learning. I mean, it's understandable that they'd feel compelled to protect themselves on the outside—it was rare that any of the students would want to bring the weapons inside because the school was a sort of sanctuary for them—where they felt free, if just during the daylight hours, from any fear that they'd be attacked by any rival. So, it wasn't unreasonable, either, for the school to want to keep weapons from entering, too.

Unfortunately, though, instead of setting up metal detectors or some kind of screening system run by security professionals, they went the discount route and asked the staff themselves to screen the students. By screen, I mean, in essence, to pat down and otherwise 'frisk' the students in this conference room in the morning when they arrived. So that was what I was facing as the vice principal ushered me into the room and asked for my cooperation.

I have to say that I was shocked by what I saw, and should've taken a moment to process what was going on. Yet, for whatever reason, after being asked to help, I did—regrettably. I can't offer a good excuse as to why I participated in such an abhorrent, psychically-damaging horror show. Was I caught off guard, not thinking so straight in the early morning hours? Was it pure passiveness and laziness on my part? Or did I feel pressure to be 'part of the team'? Or worse? Honestly, it didn't matter because the deed had already been done—and if I had been called out in *any* way by the students, my reputation would've *deserved* to be

168

tarnished by my actions. I can't tell you how disgusted I felt with myself afterwards. The first two students I patted down didn't seem to mind too much because, after all, they were more or less used to it. At most, I got a little side-eye and snarl from one of them, and quickly got the message that many, if not most of the students, resented this kind of dress-down and humiliation. There were flare-ups happening throughout the room but for the most part it was tolerated and swallowed, if it meant they could move on and start the day that would otherwise be handled with a certain level of respect from the staff toward the students. Yet, the act of touching students, even if they were all the same gender as me, in such intimate ways, seemed wrong to me. Maybe arms and legs are one thing, but edging up against the torso and more sensitive areas, both front and back, seemed downright invasive, at the very least, if not abusive, even if no actual physical contact was made. Of course, no one was authorized to pat down any private areas, but just the suggestion that those areas were being 'searched' was enough to upset me. Especially because no one seemed to have been trained, and no one seemed to care, how these boundary violations worked at extreme cross-purposes to any good rapport the student and the professional may have previously established or might establish in the future. A *classic* example of the pitfalls of maintaining improper dual relationships with clients.

That's what finally shook me up that distressing morning. While the first two young men, as I said, seemed to handle it well overall, it wasn't until I was on to my third student that it hit me in the face, literally. I didn't know the first two young men at all. I hadn't encountered them yet in the course of the legitimate tasks I had been hired to do. But I had had contact with the third young man—not only spending time with him to set him up for supportive services, but putting in extra time having discovered that we had some artistic interests in common. Both he and I had a love for music and the movies that bonded us immediately. We spent perhaps an extra half-hour just chatting casually about our favorite artists, their work and other such things. A truly enjoyable and lovely interaction with a bright young man. I told him a little about my previous professional background and hoped that we could talk more later and keep in touch, in case I could be helpful to him if he decided to pursue a career in the arts. So, with that as the back drop, this young man was next in cue for me to frisk. When his eyes met mine, I offered a weak smile as if to communicate that I didn't find any of what was going on acceptable. But it was clear that even if he weren't necessarily going to hold it against me, I could see the utter disappointment and disillusionment unmistakably written across his face. It was as clear as day. He couldn't even look me in the eye and quickly averted his gaze—more out of embarrassment than anything else, I suspected. As if he were expressing the shame *I* should've been feeling. That was what shattered my obliviousness—what stopped me dead in my tracks. I just couldn't continue to do it anymore— with the mistreatment these students were being victimized by. The whole affair was a complete travesty and farce *from the beginning*; and in retrospect, there were no good excuses for why it had taken me so long to recognize the error of my ways, and make an immediate course-correction *before* sullying my hands. So thankfully, instead of patting this young man down, I squeezed his shoulder with my hand, smiled a remorseful grin, adding 'I'm sorry. This isn't right. I owe you and your fellow students an apology.'

I'm not exactly sure if he understood what I was intimating, but the very next course of action was to locate the two young men I had already frisked to seek some sort of meeting of the minds or reckoning with them. To apologize, of course. But also to have a dialogue about what had just occurred so that, hopefully, we could get back on the right track. And once that was accomplished, to circle back with the vice principal to let her know, in no uncertain terms, how I felt about the events of the morning—and that I would, under no circumstances, participate in anything even remotely like it going forward. I can't say I was surprised that she didn't have much of a reaction to what I said, other than to accept it on face value and move on. I guess she figured she'd just move on to the next willing, ignorant fool. But that was the end of it for me—the only thing left for me was to process what I had done and wear the cloak of shame that I so richly deserved. It was one of those moments you'll never forget. And that, despite the shame, you learn deep lessons from. That's the whole story. But it really shook me, because the whole experience was the living, breathing embodiment of the 'school to prison pipeline' I had heard about— and illustrates just how vigilante one must be every step of the way, if you're going to help protect your clients from getting snared in that net. So, let's just say that my trust in the education system isn't deep. Certainly, at that level, given the incidents I've told you about.

But college isn't much better, to tell you the truth. Yes, it's true that investing in a higher education might lift an occasional young person out of tragic or unfortunate circumstances. Yes, the Ivy Leagues and others will throw a number of very beguiling and seductive scholarships your way, if it's in their overall self-interest. Yet, in the end, it's more than likely that they'll turn you into the very same kind of people whom you've never trusted and have always resented, who profit handsomely off other people's misfortune and suffering. And who've been ruling the world and getting us into *more* and *deeper* trouble, instead of serving one's own community and interests.

But besides all of that, there are other issues that'll pull you off course, in the grand scheme of things… Getting a classic liberal education is all but dead. You don't even get to choose from a full menu. Or have the option of deciding for yourself what you should or would like to learn. In fact, there's hardly anyone left on

171

faculty to teach you anymore. Yes, if you jump through just the right hoops, you'll get your degree, something you can presumably bank on. That is, after you've paid off all your loans, and have freed yourself from a life-long period of indentured servitude. Only to realize that any modest amount of wealth you might've amassed, subsequent to liberation, is only valid at the company store.

Meanwhile, universities compound their massive endowments on Wall Street. These days, educational institutions are mainly in the business of making even more profit off of what they already have. Why shouldn't they live the capitalistic dream like everyone else? They've figured it out pretty well. It's all about research, on the one hand, and entertainment on the other. Patents and sports. That's where the real money is made. Did you ever wonder where all the tuition money went? Where all the government subsidies go? A lot of it goes straight into the pockets of the institution's president, and to the head football coach. And an endless number of their managers and associates. They just can't wait to holler 'Play ball!' at the beginning of every school year. They can't scream 'Show me the money!' after all. That would be exceedingly tactless. Very poor manners. But if you go along with the program, you can certainly count on being rewarded in some way, as long as you continue to play the game and adhere to the fundamental principles. You'll get a firm slap on the back. Your name will be praised from the mountaintops. Even if you feel broken and utterly controlled, you'll still get your championship ring. On the other hand, if you decline membership into this exclusive club, they'll be more than happy to let all of their friends know. You can be sure of that. There is a blacklist, my friend, that much is certain. Safely filed away in their heads. You only need to qualify once. And you're on it forever. So, honestly, you're better off if you pull the emergency chute before you plunge to your death. Or, if you're bold enough to challenge them from within, you'd better be good at fooling people. All of them! All of the time! Good luck with that...

You would've thought that by the time I'd gotten older, I wouldn't've cared as much anymore. Across the board. I've already passed the halfway point for the average lifespan of a male. I probably have more time behind me than in front of me. I don't have any children to worry about, to concern myself with, heading into the future. I could've easily subscribed to a more shrewd, world-weary approach to life after reaching the peak of my profession. I had had a few noteworthy accomplishments—but I still felt chronically frustrated and hemmed in by persistent obstacles that were beyond my control. Losing more battles than winning, and certainly not winning the war. So it sure was tempting to contemplate living a more circumspect life, to achieve a greater number of more qualified successes. The 'tend to your own garden' kind of philosophy advocated by Voltaire. But it didn't seem to be in the cards for me. I've entered into a peculiar stage of quasi-retirement, it's true, but my opinions and motivations only seem to grow stronger. When you're faced with fewer days ahead of you than behind, and the more tangible possibility of imminent death, I guess it inspires, rather than discourages, a sense of uneasiness, no matter what the calculus seems to indicate. The focus has become much more process-oriented than results-orientated. In that respect, the clock never really runs out, does it? It still feels like an emergency is happening, but I tend to frame it more like an urgency, because, certainly, as the end of my life draws near, the greater existential struggle will just be beginning in earnest. Yet, I certainly won't be around to see it through to the end.

Do you ever wonder if anything you do has any real effect in the real world? Well, I guess that's not really the right question, what I seem to be struggling with these days. Because, honestly, what other option is there? It's either sink or swim from now on. I don't think anyone wants to feel, after all is said and done, that they didn't do everything within their power to deal with the overwhelming challenge that lies ahead. Personally, I like to think I left it all out on the court, so to speak, and died having taken all the shots I had in me. Even though the ultimate goal might already be unattainable, I think it all boils down to living the best life possible. To living right. To living fully, with a sense of honor, integrity, and justice, within the constraints that you have. There's immense freedom in that. Yet, after I'd become a psychiatrist, and had settled into private practice with a bountiful slate of dependable clientele, I realized, after just a few years, that there was still something missing. There was still something nagging at me and I didn't quite know what it was. It wasn't going to be broached solely through the world of psychology. There were bigger problems out there, and a greater world, that had to be addressed more urgently. And although I didn't even know how to begin to attend to this dilemma, I knew, ultimately, that I would have to make some changes in the future. That even if it was completely untenable or impossible, my hand would be forced.

It seems ridiculous, doesn't it? Chasing after something you can't even name. And sacrificing something that was so solid and concrete, that I had worked so very hard to attain. I guessed whatever I was striving for—whatever newfound freedom I could potentially have—would necessitate some kind of giant leap forward. A leap of faith, essentially, that I couldn't assess ahead of time, from that vantage point. What I discovered eventually, though, was that it didn't have to be as dramatic as all that. And that there were advantages to undertaking it below the radar, that were inherent in it, without anyone being aware of what was going on. If people didn't catch on, the mission might very well be more likely to succeed and thrive, through dedication and stealth. That's kind of what I'm up to when I'm at Casablanca—confessing, but also trying to gently influence. Like a secret society, affecting things with the force of an invisible sun. If I die before I can influence as much as I can, that would be the real sin of my life. But no matter what happens, no one is likely to perceive what my role was. That's what makes it so tempting, so delicious. It's what gets me out of bed every morning. Besides, the numbers are on my side. You know how it goes: first one, then two, then four. Eight, sixteen, thirty-two… It starts slowly at first. But once it gets going, one person affects others, others affect even more, and so on and so on. Before you know it, it's growing exponentially.

Maybe you think I'm mad. Maybe you think this little universe I dwell in is a farce, and a self-deception. That in the grand scheme of things, I'm wasting my time. How arrogant it is to believe that anyone can affect change, when we're all steeped so deeply in an ocean of apathy and indifference. That may be true, my friend, but I can't seem to help myself. I've still got to try. If we don't try, it's tantamount to death.

We should have to earn our deaths, don't you think? We should keep trying despite the odds, despite the darkness that constantly mocks us. We can use it to our advantage—learn how to harness its energy for the greater good. To take it into account on a daily basis. To help guide us forward. To use it as a measure against our progress. Even if what's accomplished going forward isn't readily perceivable or appreciated, either personally or collectively—for one's own benefit, or the world's—hopefully the ones who have decided to give up can at least strive to avoid inflicting any needless or gratuitous harm at the same time. Even if the difference one makes is minimal, one shouldn't be stingy with praise or enthusiastic reinforcement. We can all use a bit of encouragement, no? A little sharpening of the eye? To be able to see more perceptively and precisely? To get a better perspective, including on how we perceive and evaluate ourselves?

To get to where we need to be, we need to acknowledge where we've been. To be born again, to be baptized anew, we need to understand how the past influenced us and where the future will take us. We certainly need better guidance, and better mentors who can point us in the right direction. Even if those mentors died centuries or millennia ago, they still speak to us from the grave. We can still consult with them. It's not as if their wisdom has a shelf life. If anything, what they tried to teach us has only become more valid and relevant with time. They are just as alive now as they ever were. It's very comforting to me to think that their principles and presence survived far beyond the extent of their biological lives. The same holds true, in general, for the average person, albeit to a lesser degree, presumably. But knowing that makes it easier for me to live more daringly, given the transience of life. I know, without a doubt, that there were people who lived before me who were likeminded. And there will be others after me who will carry it into the future. Whatever influence I have might not amount to much in the real world, during my lifetime. But the same is probably true for everyone else, no matter who's involved, or what the circumstances are. We're mostly equals, as far as that's concerned. But it doesn't mean that there's no continuity, no evolution, no progress happening. Any authentic paradigm shift is going to have a much longer arc across time than any individual lifespan. Yet that shouldn't deter anyone. I know I've committed myself to the end, come what may. What's the alternative? Join me, my friend! Join... us! You won't regret it.

The truth is, you'll come to that conclusion yourself, eventually. I can just tell. You seem to have an inquisitive temperament by nature. Otherwise, you wouldn't continue to engage with me. You're definitely striving for something on a bigger scale. You're headed toward the light, so to speak. It's funny how easy it is to recognize the people who are struggling with things internally, who seem to be constantly resisting the seductive pull in the wrong direction. But they'll do just about anything to avoid hopping on the train all at once. They're thinking about it and processing it every step of the way. There'll be powerful forces that put up all sorts of counterarguments and barriers to contradict you, all the while making your life that much more untenable and impossible. But that's when you've got to start applying some stealth, some sleight of hand, if only to amuse yourself. Pull out your trusted bag of philosophical tricks. Use a little reverse psychology now and again, if the situation's ripe for it. Play the devil's advocate, but exceedingly cautiously, my friend. Employ the Socratic method, too, if necessary. Go ahead and score some points by asking an unending series of challenging, but not *too* irritating, questions. Those'll work pretty well, typically. Slightly more sophisticated techniques may be required, on occasion, to crack the most obstinate nuts out there. You know the type. The most 'educated' people, in the traditional sense of the word. The ones who have the most difficulty seeing the forest for the trees. The professional intellectuals: the scholars and the academics, the exalted professors in their ivory towers. The ones who've conformed all their lives, without ever having experienced life at ground level. The ones who succeed in the upper echelons of society, who were mostly born into it. And bought into it without thinking about it that much. The 'society' people, the 'grown-ups', the 'natural-born leaders', the 'movers and shakers', the ones who have taken on the mantel of responsibility as a right of birth, whether they deserve it or not. The ones who have never had any doubts or questioned themselves, have never been seriously challenged, or have just assumed that *their* way is the right way. They are sometimes the *easiest* people to manipulate!

If you find yourself jousting with these types of people, and really get stuck—if your arguments seem to be going absolutely nowhere—all you have to do to convince them, and get them to finally concede, is to toss out the most outrageous proposition you can think of, and see how they react. They're usually very gullible and pliable, because their ultimate objective is to prove how much smarter they are than everyone else. Just make up some utter nonsense, as long as it's the complete opposite of what you want them to believe, season it with the most nihilistic or anarchistic slant possible, and suddenly your most obstinate antagonist will become your staunchest supporter, with a newfound dedication that will astonish you. But if that *still* doesn't convince them, *still* doesn't point them in the right direction, just sacrifice yourself for a good, old-fashioned witch hunt. Step right up and openly accuse yourself of the most heinous of intellectual crimes, discharged with the most deplorable and vile attitude—the cerebral equivalent of kicking a small child in public. They'll just as suddenly become the most extreme proponents of justice and righteousness you could ever imagine. It's really that simple and easy. You'll have to try it sometime. They might abuse you and call you all sorts of names, but they might just outdo you with their hypocrisy, if you play them well enough. It's kind of pathetic. But a win's a win, and I'll be happy to accept it on everyone's behalf.

It's frightening how many brainwashed people there are out there—how many people there are who've been manipulated by dark forces—who aren't even aware that they've been conditioned and manipulated most of their lives. It's one thing to have beliefs and to live by them. It's quite another to accept a set of beliefs uncritically, and then, in turn, pass them blindly down the line. Or worse: consciously forcing dubious principles onto others, especially if they're meant to exploit. You know who I'm talking about. The ones on the extreme end of the spectrum, whether politically zealous, or devoutly religious. Yes, you've got dogma in the sciences, too, admittedly, but there's usually some kind of demonstrative evidence, one way or another, that helps evaluate the validity of any given claim. There's a fairly robust, rigorous method to science that tends to close in on the truth, especially over the long run. More often than not, it's the undisciplined practitioners in the nonscientific fields—who claim to have the

178

same ironclad discipline and rigor in their area of expertise, who believe that their *arbitrary* principles justify their superiority—who create the most havoc. There's just enough wiggle room for them to be persuasive without having the real evidence to back it up. For example, the dogma these types of people churn out of the Bible, or the Constitution. As if those texts can *never* be questioned or challenged. As if they provide the answer to *every* question, whether ancient or modern, across the sands of time. That they're *perfect* representations of the truth. That they *never* need modification; perhaps only minor amendment, here or there. They *certainly* shouldn't be interpreted flexibly, at any time.

It's all preposterous, but it serves an essential function: to provide for certainty when there is none. To help the weak-minded tolerate a world that doesn't always conform to what they hope for. Of course, there are professionals in these fields who use their knowledge and faith legitimately, but they don't try to manipulate people with it. They're just trying to believe in *something,* anything that helps them bridge the gap and resonate with other people. I have no problem with that. But either way, it's fun to dive into that world and get to know it on a deeper level. To understand where those kinds of people are coming from. Don't get me wrong—every educated citizen *should* have a good grasp of the Bible and the Constitution because they *are* remarkable texts, cultural cornerstones loaded with some real wisdom. But they should never be used as instruments of oppression.

As a layperson, I've certainly spent some time studying them in detail, mulling over their finer points; but more specifically for the purpose of acquiring fluency with them as cultural loadstones—to understand the structure, the vocabulary, the narratives, and the meanings that are embedded in them. Wander around any major city on earth and you'll find proselytizers everywhere, shouting from the street corners, spouting off all sorts of rubbish about this and that. Carrying on about what they believe in, without so much as a shred of evidence; pretending as if what they have to offer is the god-given truth. And if you refuse to accept their wisdom, or them as representatives of that wisdom, you're going to have to pay a horrific price for your resistance.

I just love running into these kinds of people. It's so much fun to engage with them. To joust with them—to tease, to tangle and wrestle with them, like a cat chasing a mouse. The goal isn't to kill. You're never going to change their minds or convince them of anything. They aren't open to it by definition, or to any argument that contradicts their vision. It's been thoroughly internalized. They've swallowed it whole. Once it's stuck in their craw, it's there for good. They can't go back without looking like heretics or fools. Remember, they've been influenced by far more powerful and manipulative people who've been shoving the orthodoxy down their throats for decades. Or, the talking-points version of it. They're just parroting back what they've managed to internalize, as best they can. Meanwhile, their superiors are busy enjoying the ample rewards of their foot soldiers' labor. They just need to make sure they keep winning over more believers and followers, and ever-expanding sources of wealth, without sullying themselves in public. Unfortunately, the general public is naturally the prime focus and recipient of these kinds of influence campaigns and recruitment drives, to cynically win over hearts and minds.

But that's when I jump in—for the rumble! Whenever I run into the foot soldiers, I can't seem to resist engaging with them. But my primary goal isn't to convince anyone of anything, as I said. I'm just trying to run interference, or to amuse myself for a while. Sometimes it's frivolous, sometimes there's a more serious intention to it, depending on my mood at the time. But it's never too difficult to throw the proselytizers off balance and shoot down their inane ideas. To discourage the onlooker from taking them too seriously. Mostly because the foot soldiers—who are shilling for the cult leaders and shysters who pull the strings behind the scenes, getting filthy rich off their clueless marks—are not typically very well-versed in the empty delusions they've bought into to get the job done. They've never done the difficult and exacting work of checking their sources, references, or quotations. If they'd actually absorbed their source material with any kind of sober, critical eye, they would've quickly discovered that for every proposition they sling around to their advantage, there's very often an excellent counterexample in the very same text to contradict it. If not in the exact same section, then in another section of the text, or an ancillary to it. But your average proselytizer is too blind and biased to notice the conundrum they've put themselves in, or admit that there's, at minimum, any complexity involved. Going against the grain is simply not in their character or D.N.A. They're thoroughly committed, nevertheless. But that's exactly when lobbing grenades at their vacuous falsehoods is most effective. It's impossible to resist! It might seem petty, but I can't seem to help myself. I mean, I don't take any of it all that seriously to begin with, because that would make me almost as pathetic as they are. But when you manage to out-quote the holy roller Bible thumpers, and the legal fundamentalists, the strictly constitutional originalists, they absolutely hate it. They become unhinged and get easily flustered. They start flailing around senselessly and you start to feel pity for them. And that has an immediate effect on the average spectator. They see the body language of defeat—and from there, it's over in a split-second. It's so satisfying to get whatever quote you're using *exactly* right! And with the *exact* reference! Whether it's book, chapter, and verse; or article, amendment, or clause. It's particularly gratifying if you can manage to slay them with something really striking or spectacular, like referring to some obscure version or translation of the bible. That'll just finish them off! The crowd will suddenly start to peel off in droves. And the poor sucker left alone at the podium ends up looking like a damn fool.

Yes, it's childish behavior. I freely admit it. But bear with me, there's a method to the madness. If you can't have big-league success on your own terms, mostly because the odds are so stacked against you, the next best thing is an occasional, modest victory, by sabotaging, or at least hobbling, the people you're zealously opposed to. The opposition is already expert at that. In fact, they *thrive* off it. Often, it's their *only* goal. To trip others up. To get in the way. For them, it's so much easier to destroy things than to create something and follow through with the commitment. It's virtually impossible to utilize those strategies ethically in a profession like psychiatry. You're expected to be the 'bigger person', the 'professional' at all times, and act like a responsible adult. You're supposed to play by the rules and adhere to a code of professional ethics and personal morality, no matter the circumstances. But, of course, we're only human, equipped with the same strengths and weaknesses as everyone else, more or less. That's why I decided to drift away from the standards of the psychiatric world. The rules became too restrictive for me. Psychiatrists are disadvantaged because we're only allowed to use certain types of tools, to wield certain types of weapons. Our quiver is only half full. We're hamstrung by the very principles we live by, even if outcomes suffer as a consequence. After honoring those limitations for an extended period of time, I was compelled to reevaluate whether I could keep playing by the rules and thereby stay in the profession. I mean, you're never *really* out of it. You retain the training and the skills. But you cross into a vast new territory.

Eventually, I was forced to strip the mask off. I established a new identity and environment where I could get my message out and earn the sincere respect of a new type of clientele. Not simply as a consequence of my professional status. But as a result of what I can provide for them. Serving a whole range of personalities, spread across the whole spectrum of the population. Not just people who need help getting by. Not just the so-called mentally ill. That became much too confining for me. I was getting a little too comfortable operating in a professional world that likes to congratulate itself for its underwhelming and predominately provisional successes. Meanwhile, your colleagues try everything and anything to keep you in the professional fold—because airing judgments in that vein, in public, strikes a sensitive nerve. Forces them to face their own inadequacies. Most accept it as the price of doing business. They'll even try to promote you or give you a raise, to convince you otherwise. But they simply don't get what's motivating you. It's kind of like dealing with the Mafia—if you inexplicably decide to go legit, they'll tempt you with offers you can't refuse. Even so, you can only stomach holding the mirror up to them for so long, no matter how desperately they try to seduce you. That's when you know you're done, when you have to throw in the towel for good. A point is reached when you can't tell the difference anymore between the average, garden-variety bad-faith practitioner and the villainous ones that covertly and cynically steer institutions in a disastrous direction.

That might sound like a bit of an exaggeration, my friend, but let me provide you with a specific example from my tour of duty at the psychiatric hospital. Most of time I was just minding my own business, trying to take care of the daily concerns that were calling for my immediate attention. But one day, I was pulled into a truly bizarre scenario that forced me to question what the institution was up to, as a whole. The bigger picture revealed an uglier truth, so powerfully that I began to wonder whether the entire institution had been flipped inside-out, whether our usual roles had been switched by some sort of madman. It truly seemed as if, for whatever reason, the sane and the insane had suddenly switched places.

It all began very innocently one blustery winter evening, as a bank of dark storm clouds began to pass through outside. The hospital was just about to close for the day, as far as the official admission hours dictated. Just before the double doors were locked, an African-American gentleman, in his early to mid-thirties, managed to squeeze through security just in time, and quietly took a seat in the otherwise empty lobby. He was of average height and build, wearing appropriate clothes, given the weather: a sturdy pair of blue jeans, a mid-length winter coat, and black waterproof boots with sheepskin linings. Nothing at all out of the ordinary. Nor did he appear or act in any way suspicious. He wasn't wearing a hat, but his hair was well kept and closely cropped, though his hands were thickly callused. He just sat there, minding his own business. But because it was the end of business hours, it was only natural for someone to go out into the lobby and ask what was going on. The receptionist was told, by this gentleman, rather insistently, that he was going to remain in the lobby and wasn't going to leave until he was admitted. That was all he volunteered. That was the only thing he said, in its entirety. Well, you would have thought he had threatened the staff with a bomb or something, because before you knew it, a 'Code Blue' had been called, and all available hands were summoned to the lobby at once, like a dire emergency was in the making. Everyone, and I mean everyone, who could play any role in an extreme emergency arrived on the scene, including security guards, orderlies, clerks of every stripe, social workers, nurses, administrators, all of my colleagues, including the head of the clinical staff, and, of course, myself. Anyone who could do anything was there, including the people who were most qualified to control a potentially volatile situation. Meaning, the people who were the most thoroughly trained and best equipped to intervene by either verbally diffusing tense situations, or as a last resort, by applying physical, hands-on force, preferably the kind that prioritizes the safety of the patient. You know, the 'appropriate' use of disablement and restraint. The soft take-down, no chokeholds allowed.

I was a little confused by what I was seeing because I didn't understand why the man was seen as such a dire threat. Why was it necessary for the entire institution to drop everything, and go into emergency mode, all of a sudden? We seemed to be acting more like a paramilitary police force, rather than an institution that was in the business of caring for people. Suddenly, every standard rule of engagement was thrown out the window. There was a very short period of time when the staff attempted to verbally negotiate with the man, slowly going up the chain of command from admissions clerk, to their supervisor, to a psychiatric nurse, to a psychiatrist, before it all seemed to collapse back to square one. I wasn't able to listen in to the conversation they were having, but the man didn't budge. He didn't change his mind one iota, apparently. But neither did he escalate. It seemed like after about fifteen minutes of interchange they had arrived at a complete stalemate. I assumed the next step was to call the police, to have him removed from the lobby, and forcibly thrown out onto the street.

But suddenly, the C.E.O. of the institution appeared on-scene. She seemed like a no-nonsense type of character who wasn't going to tolerate any bullshit. As an aside, it appeared as if she was having quite a challenging time trying to turn the institution around, in terms of its overall reputation and profitability. She had only been there for less than a year, yet I think the consensus was she wasn't doing such a great job achieving those goals. She also had no clinical experience to speak of, despite the fact that she was the head of a psychiatric hospital. Her background was purely administrative in nature. Neither a doctor, nor a nurse, or any other kind of medical professional. Yet, after the stalemate, and a quick debriefing, she, herself, stepped into the negotiation, as if she were eminently qualified to perform this often sensitive and thorny negotiation work. I think she spent a grand total of about three minutes trying to appeal to the man, before she had had enough.

She had pulled the trigger apparently, and had fully committed us to an entirely different kind of approach, because within a few seconds, a group of orderlies jumped in and cleared a circle around the still-seated man. Everyone else was directed to retreat to the edges of the lobby, to stand by, just in case they could still be of assistance. The orderlies moved in, and asked the man to stand up. He refused. Then, two of the orderlies, who, by the way, were very large, muscular men, one of whom was in charge of training all the rest of us on the finer points of 'responsible' manhandling, grabbed the man's arms on each side, and lifted him slowly out of the chair. The man resisted to some extent, by becoming dead weight. But mostly by hurling some choice expletives their way. Once they held the man in a fully upright position and turned him around, it was only a matter of seconds before they latched onto his arms and collapsed in a heap to the floor.

That's when the man, naturally, began to resist in earnest. The moment he felt like a trapped animal. When they tried to pin his back to the tile floor, he began flailing wildly, with seemingly supernatural strength. It was all very violent and traumatic to witness. Then, two other orderlies jumped in, so that all four of them could pin down each of his appendages. Once he was safely restrained and immobilized, a nurse suddenly appeared from nowhere, and plunged a hypodermic needle deep into his quadricep. He continued to thrash about, like a fish out of water, for another few minutes, until the sedative finally took hold. All of a sudden, he was as docile as could be, but not quite unconscious. Not wholly aware, but certainly immobilized and limp. From there, it was just a simple matter of strapping him onto a gurney and removing him from the lobby.

It turned out, after all that high drama, that he was admitted, after all. But only on the institution's terms, apparently. Why wasn't he just admitted in the first place, the usual way? What was it about this man that seemed to be such a terrific threat? There was never any kind of explanation as to why he posed such a danger. There was no dialogue about it afterwards. There was no debriefing process. There was only speculation based on incomplete information, I assumed, because I didn't hear much more about it later on. I'm sure an incident report must've been filed, as was customary. But none of us ever really had access to it, or got to the bottom of it. It was just going to be one of those disturbing events that happens and then quickly gets suppressed.

It wasn't the first time something like that had happened. Not by a long shot. But this was surely the most alarming, the most extreme, and the most perplexing episode to date. I mean, lots of crazy things go on inside psychiatric hospitals, but most make some kind of sense, even if it requires a bit of warped logic to account for what happens. Nevertheless, for whatever reason, I ruminated on this particular incident for days afterwards. It forced me to ask some very important questions that I hadn't considered before. First, what happened to the process that was presumably in place to safeguard against this kind of treatment, this kind of abuse? Secondly, why did the rest of us just stand there and pretend as if we were helpless to intervene? What ever became of the man? What kind of treatment did he get once he was admitted, and for what? Was he in the position to determine his own fate, and did he have the ability to question what had happened to him? Did *he* consider what had happened abuse? Surely, he wondered whether race had something to do with it. Did he have family members and friends, or other professionals, to confide in? I, for one, wondered if one day we'd discover that he had taken legal action against the hospital, that he had sued. I certainly wouldn't have been surprised to learn that.

But then I began to think even more about the bigger picture. What was I doing working in this kind of institution? What were we accomplishing, for anyone? It seemed to me that we were giving very inadequate care most of the time. That we were

187

pretending to care for the patients. In reality, we were actually just processing them through a never-ending revolving door of poor treatment and lackluster management. Spread throughout the entire social welfare system. I'd have to say that at least three quarters of the beds in our hospital were devoted to a game of psychiatric music chairs, or simply filled with chronic drug abusers, who should've gotten care on an outpatient basis. I'd say the remaining beds were legitimately used to attend to the extreme mental health emergencies of the suicidal or manic. Whatever the case, the treatment was far from adequate and only brief in nature. Mostly a glorified type of babysitting. There was very little *therapy* going on. Unless you believe that group therapy in a room crowded with patients—meaning upwards of thirty-five strung-out addicts—is effective in any way.

Honestly, the primary intervention at the hospital was writing prescriptions, dispensing them, and doling them out to the patients. It was like well-tuned clockwork. Line 'em all up at the appropriate times each day, give them their little plastic cups full of medicine, some water to wash them down, and presto! Let the magic happen! But we all know that in reality, it's just a crapshoot. Though few psychiatrists would admit it. Most hope that those 'magic bullet' pills will cure just about everything. No, deep down, most of us knew that we were barely able to apply the most minimal of care to the majority of our patients. And that the shotgun blasts of life required much, much more than a measly Band-Aid.

Then, I started to have more intense, nagging feelings about the incident. They were truly haunting me, and didn't seem to want to go away. I kept mulling it over in my mind. On the one hand, who authorized the C.E.O. to evaluate psychiatric patients, or even assess safety concerns? She had absolutely no hands-on experience to speak of, as far as I knew. Even so, why didn't she just admit the man in the first place? All the drama could have been avoided. On the other hand, what was she doing to turn the institution around, to address its problems and obvious dysfunction? As I said, it didn't seem as if she were making any progress on the business end of things. There were rumors swirling around that the hospital was a hair's breadth away from bankruptcy, and that her most immediate task was to save it from that fate. *Despite* the precarious financial state of the hospital, though, we heard that she was in the planning stages of opening up a brand-new wing to boost revenues—a facility meant to attend to veterans who had suffered traumatic brain injuries. Well, if it was going to be anything like the last new wing, devoted to people with major neurocognitive disorders—Alzheimer's, dementia, that sort of thing—it *was* going to be a real money maker. What better way to make boatloads of money than to attend to people who *can't* really take care of themselves. Of course, there is a place in the world for those types of comprehensive wrap-around services. But the resources only seem to flow one way in *that* facility. Nothing of any real consequence was ever done for the patients, either medically or in terms of case management. When they got discharged, they very quickly fell back into the void of inadequate care, and would be forgotten about until the next crisis occurred. More of the usual 'slipping between the cracks'. By the time the patients, who were mostly legally incompetent to begin with—or their powers-of-attorney, if they weren't in on the moneymaking scheme—finally managed to figure out it was a complete scam, they either died miserable and penniless, or they were discharged for seemingly arbitrary reasons, as soon as the leger sheet showed dwindling returns on the investment.

In short, both wings were created to temporarily warehouse some of society's most vulnerable individuals, primarily for the benefit of the institution's bottom line. The beds *were* constantly full. The revolving door was less obvious, with fewer eyes to scrutinize the flow. But do you have any idea how inflated the rates are for these beds? How willing and incentivized the government is to pay for them? Problem solved, as far as both parties are concerned. It's the gift that just keeps on giving, cleverly shielded from public awareness. The corruption I found myself getting tangled up in on an everyday basis on the floor of that psychiatric hospital paled in comparison to what they were hiding behind the scenes. Believe me! I'm not sure where all the money ended up, but it was being made and pocketed by someone. It's bad enough that most of the day-to-day staff at the hospital were the equivalent of wolves in sheep's clothing. But the real dogs in all of this mess were the C.E.O. and her cronies at the top of the food chain.

But what could I do about it? What could *anyone* do about it? If your plan of attack lies within the system, as soon as you even question what goes on, you'll either be fired, 'encouraged' to leave, or be marginalized, depending on the severity of your attack, particularly if it damages the institution's reputation publicly. I can't tell you how many times I stuck my neck out, only to have no one else step forward to support my dissent. And if you attempt to change the system from the outside, it'll be a ridiculously lopsided fight that will likely end your career. You'll be ostracized by your peers and frozen out, because the truth is, people either don't care or are too lazy even think about it; or they're already overburdened, and don't have the slightest inclination to take on even a slight bit more. They know from experience, that it'll only lead to more misery for them and no improvement for the patients. Don't get me wrong, many of my colleagues across the spectrum of professions recognized the enormity of the problem and wished they could help. But it was systemic, and, in all likelihood, would have to be handled from the top down, on a political level. So like all the other abuses that occurred at the hospital, this one was forgotten about, too, at least as far as I knew. Hopefully, the victim was able to forget about it and leave it behind. But I doubt it. Can you imagine how it'd feel to be manhandled like that, by anyone? To be traumatized to that extent? Tragically, the lesson learned was never contradict the people in power, especially if you aren't in the 'club', or come from a similar perspective of power.

So I guess I kept asking myself, what to do about it? I guess we can all shuffle around various institutions until we find one that seems to be putting the clients' interests first and profit second. But that's a tall order these days, my friend. The profession seems to be rotten to the core. You think that's a bit extreme, a bit farfetched? It used to be that being a sellout of any kind was one of the worst things that you could be accused of. Today, it's considered a very antiquated idea, and hopelessly naïve, too. That, quite to the contrary, you'll be seen as a pathetic loser and sucker if you don't eventually yield to the status quo. What would *you* have done? It really doesn't matter precisely which profession you happen to be in. The corruption is everywhere. It's inescapable. It got to the point that the only rational option for me professionally was to opt out. To slip free of the suffocating yoke of the entrenched bureaucratic infrastructure. That came with a price, to be sure, but, my goodness, what a relief it was to finally be liberated. And what precious freedom it led to! An imperfect freedom, yes, but a much more satisfying freedom, nonetheless. That's what I decided to do... eventually. After suffering weeks of conflicting feelings and frustration. Because it's especially exasperating and disheartening to vacate your position at one of these institutions knowing that everyone, despite what you might wish to believe, is expendable. That anyone can be easily replaced by some gutless peon who, in all likelihood, is more compromised and unprincipled than...

Oh, my lord! I've lost all track of time, haven't I? I've been babbling away so long... You ought to stop me if I keep going on like *that*. We had better get going. Better get back to Vegas before it gets *too* late. I can sense the day is drawing to an end. The sun has begun its descent. Ha ha!!! Look up there!! It's must be an omen. You couldn't have *cued* the vultures any more perfectly. Look how they're circling above us. They're looking for some choice pickins', sometime soon! Well, it's not going to be *us*, not today. You think they overheard what I was talking about? You think they understood what I was saying? Like most people around here, it probably sounds like gibberish to them, too. No? You don't think what I said was pure rubbish? Oh, thank you. I guess I reached you, to some extent. How, I'm not sure. You seem very careful with your words. You don't volunteer much. But that's good, my friend. You've already developed some good habits. You're already exercising sound practices, I see, to survive in this complicated world! I guess we'll find out exactly where we stand with each other, at some point. But I've still got lots more to tell you about. I think you'll continue to find it interesting. Perhaps even find it a bit disturbing, for all I know! Especially some things that happened when I first arrived in Vegas...

V.

You might've noticed I'm going back a different way. I hope you don't mind. I'd like to show you the more scenic route back, the road less traveled. Most visitors aren't going to travel this way. We took the usual way out, along the highway. But on the way back, I'd like you to see what the landscape used to look like before all the development took hold. I mean, there's development no matter which way you go, but this way is much more intriguing. I love the long stretches of open road, especially when you can see the mirages. Yeah, you see! You can still make them out even when the sun's starting to set. It's *that* hot out. The pavement's been baking in the sun's rays all day long. There probably won't be much to see, but you never know. The animals start coming out at dusk. You have to make sure you don't run over them as you drive by. You're likely to see roadkill, but let's try to avoid that messiness as best we can. It's good not to pick up too much speed, just to be on the safe side. You don't want to miss any animals that might be roaming around the desert. So time may seem to slow down on the way back. That's what the desert does to you. There are fewer reference points along the way. There's the bay, and the lake—but not much more. Before you know it, we'll be on the outskirts of town.

It's so very different here than most of the places I've been. Have you been to Hawaii? Or the Caribbean? Any of the places where people go to get away from it all? I mean, the more lush environments. The places that seem very far away, yet offer a rich abundance. Islands are the best. In the middle of the ocean. In the middle of nowhere. You feel a sense of isolation and calm, like you're living in a dream. And, if you're fortunate, you'll get to enjoy whatever the culture provides. What a joy it is to be in the middle of a lush, tropical forest! Fresh water abounds! Everything grows like weeds! Life literally hums. You might find yourself soaking in a hot spring in the middle of the mountains, only to have nutmeg pods rain down upon you, the scent of cinnamon enticing your nose. Or you might rise before dawn and take a bicycle trip above the clouds, descending through never-ending fields of pineapple, without having to peddle even once. Or come back from a day at the beach just in time to gather the wild mangoes and papayas that have fallen along the roadside, before they've all been collected. It's first-come, first-serve. It's all just lying there for you, even if you're just a visitor. Even better yet, go island hopping on a sailboat in the Caribbean. Listen to the wind through the sails, and the rhythm of the waves. Hang your legs over the bow and feel the splash of saltwater against your feet. Yet you're never more than a hundred miles from landfall. The islands pop up at regular intervals, lined up like buoys marking a passage. Each stop, each locale serves up its unique charms. But time moves along at a faster pace. Compared to here, certainly. You'll want to stretch it out as much as possible. But it always seems to go much more quickly than you'd wish. Well, no worries, because you can always pack a whole lot in, even if it seems to fly by. Oh, the drift of memory! There *is* paradise on Earth, my friend! You better stop me now—interrupt this spellbinding train of thought—or I'm likely to get on a plane tonight and leave you here high and dry. Way before I'm done with you.

It's hard not to reminisce about these moments. I remember one time, sailing into a bay of a remote island in the Caribbean—dropping anchor just a hundred feet or so from a long, mostly uninhabited beach—spending time with a handful of others, who had also found their way there. The beach went on for miles, without interruption, in the shape of a half crescent, both ends terminating at cliffs that faced the open ocean. A lighthouse stood at one end, and a series of salt marshes lay beyond the other.

Most of the people on the other boats and on the beach were locals. During the evening, everyone gravitated toward one section of the beach, to enjoy a last dip in the water before sundown, but also to prepare for the last meal of the evening. I'm not sure if everyone knew one another at first, but over the course of the next few evenings, as we naturally crossed each other's paths, we got to know each other. The ice was broken for us when one couple nearby offered us drinks. After that, we reciprocated, of course, and before long, we were invited into the fold of a larger group of four or five extended families from the area. They were very generous with their hospitality, and we felt an immediate warmth and acceptance that is so rare in this modern world.

There was such a wonderful purity to the experience: sharing a simple meal of freshly-caught, whole fish, grilled over open coals; drinking ice-cold beer from a cooler; chatting and laughing in beach chairs, while the children waded and splashed in the water nearby; watching pelicans dive head-first into the water for their own special meal; and almost complete silence, otherwise, except for a chorus of chirping frogs coming from a dense patch of vegetation lining the back edge of the beach in the evening. We thought they were birds at first, and our hosts laughed when they told us about them.   Hundreds of these tiny, mud-brown amphibious creatures.   Almost impossible to locate, despite the cacophony. No bigger than the size of a quarter.

We felt so at home and relaxed amongst strangers. There was an instant trust and intimacy, where there might have been suspicion or vulnerability, as if shaped by the very environment we found ourselves in. My wife and I sat together holding hands as we watched our new friends interact. They seemed to be free of any kind of self-consciousness.   There was a purity to it, a welcome, spontaneous quality to their actions.   Adult friends weren't shy about walking down the beach hand in hand. Men hugged each other and kissed each other's cheeks unabashedly. Their children had no second thoughts about abruptly perching themselves on our laps. It was all very casual and beautiful. No embarrassment from any quarter.

Can you imagine you and me, my friend, complete strangers, walking down the Strip together, hand in hand? They'd either assume we were gay, or they'd stare at us with gaping mouths. Why is such a simple gesture of affection so taboo? The moment you hit puberty, it's all hands off from then on? Yes sir, apparently in America, and even Vegas, with its liberal and free-wheeling ways. But it's done very differently in Vegas. It has a whole different tone to it. People come here to indulge in sex, and oftentimes prostitution, but we do it all very lustfully, very secretly, as if it's shameful. There's a jaded aspect to it, like it's all very dirty, and that afterwards we're going to have to take a very long, hot shower to wash away all the grit and grime. No, give me that island again! Where couples make love artlessly on the beach, under the stars. Like they're back in some kind of Eden.

Look at the scenery here. Look at the landscape out there. It's an entirely different world we live in here.   More akin to the surface of the moon. It has its own charms, of course, but more as an abstract tableau, don't you think? Hardly a drop of water out there that isn't manmade. Barely a drop of water in the air, either. It's so crystalline clear, but sadly inert, save for the dust swirling around. But it does feel good to get out of town for a while. It also feels good to get back into town, once you've cleansed yourself. It's so easy to get caught up in the 'grass is always greener' mentality. You deceive yourself by thinking that removing yourself from an oppressive environment will somehow magically change everything for the better. I've been guilty of that so often in my own life that I don't care to recall just how many times I've fallen for it. But can you blame people for trying to shake things up? Or for trying to attach themselves to somebody new hoping something good will come of it. Or at least something different. Something you haven't experienced before...

Yes, I changed careers, I changed environments, I changed partners. Changing partners may be the easiest of all, if you're not too picky. Certainly, after my wife's death, and after realizing that my new profession was riddled with so many holes, I did find myself in crisis again. I wanted to find new motivations and new purpose. I guess I could've taken some time off, perhaps to do some travelling or to have an extended rest. But there was something preventing me from choosing that more self-indulgent road. I wanted to escape from the world and its people. Only to find myself indulging in women again. But not in the manner I've already recounted to you previously. After my wife died, I was in such shock and disbelief that the very thought of finding someone else, so soon, seemed almost repulsive to me. I already told you how I decided to focus on my new career, for the most part. But after I moved to New York and settled in professionally, I admit that I had a new desire to find a relationship like the one I had had. I wasn't looking for a substitute, but I was looking for that kind of deeper intimacy. I strongly desired to love and be loved again. The kind of love that is the most precious and difficult to find. The kind of love that feels like a rare commodity. As opposed to the kind that's more superficial—that's a kind of hunger and habit—that focuses mainly on sex.

About a year after I arrived in New York, I met a woman who very much reminded me of my wife, who seemed to spark a feeling within me that it might be possible to fall in love in that way again. The resemblance was so striking that she even looked like my wife physically—all the attributes of her outward appearance matched, from her height, to her build, to the darkness of her features, her sense of style, the sparkle in her eye. But also her personality.   The intelligence, the playfulness, the flirtatiousness, and the sense of surprise you feel when you think you've managed to meet someone out of the ordinary, with attributes that don't typically present themselves.   That instant flutter you feel in your heart when you sense that love is a possibility, the equivalent of limerence before the relationship has even been established. The first time I met her, there seemed to be so much in common, such a meeting of the spirits, that it was only natural to speak with her for hours, only parting by necessity.

Our relationship developed very quickly and seemed to be on track in so many ways, because we bonded easily—there didn't seem to be a lot of previous baggage to work through. When I told her about my past, having been happily married, but widowed, she neither judged nor pitied me. There was no sense of jealousy, and she didn't feel sorry for me. It felt surprisingly liberating and refreshing compared to others I had encountered before her. So, after about a month of what seemed like a normal courtship routine, it was only natural to press forward and become more intimate with her.

But then there seemed to be some hesitancy on her side of things. It felt as if there were some vague feelings of concern associated with going down that path. Whenever people commit themselves and cross that line, there's a superstitious fear that if it doesn't work out on that level, you might just end up ruining the whole thing, friendship included. I didn't have that attitude myself, but I tried to understand and respect what I presumed she was feeling. I made it abundantly clear that I was interested, but at the same time I didn't apply too much pressure. In fact, I had more or less concluded, for whatever reason, that it probably wasn't going to go any further any time soon, despite how it had evolved, and had already gotten myself comfortable with accepting that reality and acting accordingly. But just as I had arrived at that conclusion, and saw myself as unattached again, at least emotionally, was *exactly* when she pressed forward and literally summoned me over to her apartment one night. I had never been there before, and when she answered the door, she didn't seem quite herself. There was something curious about how we were interacting, something off. I wondered if she felt nervous having me in her space for the first time. But within just a few minutes time, I realized that she was nervous for reasons I hadn't anticipated: she had asked me over with an eye toward becoming more intimate. I understood how one could be nervous with a new partner. I wasn't nervous at all, just surprised about her sudden shift in attitude and pleased that I would finally be able to be more intimate with her.

However, when we started to engage, it didn't feel the same as before. She didn't say much of anything. She seemed detached, as if she were a different person playing a role, and seemed to be encouraging me to act similarly. After a few glasses of wine, and a couple of fleeting kisses, we undressed silently. I began taking my clothes off first. She seemed to be prompting me to take her clothes off, too. So, I started to disrobe her as I kissed her body, starting from her lips down. I stripped her down to her underwear and decided to leave it at that to see how she reacted. But then as I started to engage with her again, I discovered that if I initiated anything, she would quickly discourage me from doing it. Again, I took it as a sign of first-time jitters. But then I noticed over the course of an hour that the only things we were doing were the things she wanted to do, and initiated. It was odd because while at first she seemed very passive, she seemed more intent on doing things to me, without getting *any* attention for herself. She also seemed devoid of any kind of passionate feeling: she neither responded vocally to anything, nor did she seem to express much with her body. I felt comfortable receiving attention, and didn't hold back expressing the pleasure I was receiving. But even after she permitted me to turn attention to her, the only thing she wanted from me was to have intercourse with her, in the most basic pedestrian manner. I complied and enjoyed what I was experiencing, but noticed that even after almost two hours of skin-to-skin contact, it still hadn't risen to a level beyond moderate satisfaction—certainly not to climax, for either of us. I held back purposely. I still wasn't exactly sure how she felt about what we were doing. She wasn't willing to verbalize much at all.

After another hour had passed, I became increasingly more distracted and ambivalent about what was going on, and felt myself losing focus. It's almost like I couldn't go on, because I had become so desensitized emotionally—and, honestly, physically. It didn't seem to matter much to her, either way. But she seemed neither happy nor disappointed. We just disengaged and languished around in bed for a time.

By that point, I guess I assumed I would be staying overnight with her. I assumed we would at least sleep together through the night, and perhaps try to engage again, if it seemed right. But after another hour or so, she asked me to leave. I was caught a little off guard—mostly because I had never had such a confusing encounter before. I wasn't aware of anything pressing she had to take care of. Nonetheless, I eventually eased myself out of bed, dressed, and left the apartment, only receiving a limp goodbye.

It was all very strange. I had a few more encounters with her over the next month. More or less the same. I won't bore you with the details, but there was only more frustration and what seemed to be two other significant behaviors going on: some related to fetishes, some related to gender roles. My new partner seemed to have some unorthodox sexual practices. Which were all fine with me. I was game if it meant pleasure for her. But what I discovered was that if I expressed in any way how *I* enjoyed it, she wouldn't do it again. Then, she had this unusually strong curiosity about what it would be like for her to be a man. How it would feel to be a man, particularly in the realm of sex. She wondered what it would be like to penetrate someone, or how it would feel to unbutton your pants and urinate standing up. At first, I thought 'okay, that's a healthy imagination—here's someone who feels liberated and is exploring some things, nothing wrong with that'. As I mentioned before, I've had many patients, and others in my life, who have had a broad range of alternative sexual practices, that run the gamut of creative possibilities. I'd say the greater number of people who wander outside the norm do it for legitimate, healthy reasons. Whether it's to shake things up— whatever it is—they're consciously exploring their sexuality by experimenting, and sometimes breaking taboos. Then there's another sub-section of people. The ones who are appear to be exploring their sexuality, but are actually using it as a vehicle to express some kind of psychological or emotional dysfunction— whether conscious of it or not.

After I confided in one of my colleagues, he related an encounter to me he had experienced some years before. He had had a very similar type of experience with a woman, except in his case, it turned out to be a much more precarious experience—for him, and potentially, this partner. He had gotten past the 'get to know you' stage, too, and onto a more intimate path. Likewise, he and his partner were about to engage sexually for the first time.

He, too, had a strange feeling about what was going on because his partner was also acting very ill-at-ease. He found it absolutely frustrating because whenever he tried to do anything, she would similarly reject him or vocalize 'no'. When he inquired about it, she never wanted to talk about it. Nonetheless, it continued to go that way for him until he gave up and withdrew from the relationship.

Well, it wasn't until months later that he ran into his former partner by chance. It was only then that she let the 'secret' out. They had a brief discussion in passing—and, after an exchange of pleasantries, she brought the subject up, to his astonishment. She explained to him that it had been nothing personal, that what had happened between them was, in fact, no mystery at all. She told him that she was disappointed with him, because when she continued to rebuff him, she actually wanted him to proceed. But that she didn't want to have to explain that to him. And furthermore, that if a guy isn't capable of being more aggressive, of transgressing in that way, he's too weak a personality for her. She couldn't see herself with someone who seemed so timid, from her perspective, and exhibited such a lack of drive and daring.

Of course, you can imagine what my friend thought after hearing that confession. He had to put it into some kind of context, and eventually assumed that there had to be something pathological about how she approached relationships, if not sex. He'd never know for sure. It's true many people have some kind of vague rape fantasy floating around in their heads. But it appeared that this woman more or less required it, and acted on it, as a prerequisite. And the only thing he could guess, because he wasn't privy to her comprehensive past history, was that something had gone very wrong somewhere along the way. He wondered if she had been sexually assaulted sometime in her past. He certainly wouldn't have transgressed the line at the time, for obvious reasons. Nor could he, after she explained it to him. But that certainly got me thinking about my partner again through a similar lens.

Was there something in her past that accounted for her odd behavior? In short, it turned out there was, unsurprisingly. There were quite a few things that had happened to her that, in anyone's book, would've constituted sexual trauma. Foremost amongst them was, I learned when she finally did open up, a full-on sexual assault by her biological brother, when she was a minor. But she didn't interpret it as a trauma she had suffered. She was very much in denial about it. In fact, not only didn't she see it as a sexual assault, or accept that it had had any negative effect on her, she claimed, on the contrary, that it had had a beneficial effect on her! That it had awakened her dormant sexuality, and that she was thankful for it, and furthermore enjoyed it and would've done it all over again, as far as she was concerned. Anyway, to cut a long story even shorter, let's just say she had some serious issues that would've gotten in the way of us having any kind of relationship, even a casual one. Had she not been in such absolute denial, perhaps I would have been willing to work through it with her as a willing partner. But that didn't happen.

I felt bad for her. But I also felt bad for myself, because there certainly wasn't going to be anything remotely equivalent to what I had had with my wife with her. Any naïve or romantic notion about falling in love again had to be completely thrown out the window. It was a bitter pill to swallow, but swallow I did. I actually began to feel a bit sorry for her. And when you start feeling something akin to pity for someone, that's when you know it's the end. It wasn't good enough for me to have feelings of love and tenderness for someone, yet not be intimate with them in the usual way. It might've been fine for her, but regrettably, that was how it had to end. I had to cut it off. If only for my own sanity. It was very unhealthy for both of us, honestly.

Yet, the experience really forced me to think more deeply about how I was going to navigate through the world from that point on, in the romantic domain. It seemed like I was always encountering the extreme end of things. A lot of dysfunctional stuff. So, I guess I reasoned that striving for something like love was going to have to be shelved, for a time. On the other hand, if an opportunity for casual sex presented itself, I'd probably take it. I won't lie. But that's all I had left, as far as expectations were concerned. More or less. At least until I ended up in Vegas. For the most part, I would just go about my business again, without any of the potential drama. Maybe life would be more boring, but that was what I decided, and I stuck to it.

Don't get me wrong—I wasn't exactly one hundred percent disciplined in my approach. There is the call of nature, after all. No matter how withdrawn you wish to be, there's that nagging instinct for sex that pops up no matter how hard you try to suppress it. I certainly felt vulnerable to it. I could only go so long without sex. Of some kind. There were times when I would go out of my way to get a little too drunk, so that my judgement would be purposely impaired. So that I would seek out sex and indulge in it even if it didn't seem right. It made it easy to continue to get what I wanted without having to judge myself, at least in the moment. There is nothing like a little undisciplined debauchery to get your mind off things. You can leave it on the field, so to speak. But then you'll also kick yourself in the morning, until you build up enough desire that it takes over again. Never enough, yet never really satisfying, either. I'm not particularly proud to admit it, but... I'm human, after all. Does that make me any different from anyone else I've told you about? In some ways, yes. But in other ways, no. Aren't they throwing themselves head-first into it, just like me? Doing the best they can, as they see it, given the circumstances?

Yes, there really is no better drug in the world for men than women and alcohol. In the way that they combine to disinhibit, bring pleasure, and allow you to forget the shame of the past, or the anxiety of projecting into the future. If nothing else, it's a great coping mechanism. You might have one or the other crutch at times, but on their own, they pale by comparison. If you can't rely solely on a substance, because your liver has finally rebelled against you, you can just let your hormones do the work. But it can also be frustrating, that's for sure. Because for every woman who's open to an encounter, there's a sea of men who are absolutely willing to dive in. Not so the other way around. Men need to work much harder to get what they want. That's where the psychology tends to come in. The peculiar kind of psychology that men use to convince women that they should have sex with them. Men tend not to think very carefully about how their needs and attitudes will affect the women that they're sleeping with, certainly not in the heat of the moment. They just want it, and want it now, and will do whatever they need to do to get it. A raging blindness, of sorts. I've been guilty of that at times. To a lesser degree, though, I think. I just hope that if I've been guilty of it, nobody was harmed too deeply. I do regret some of my interactions with certain women. But I also hope that if they were hurt by me, they'd be open to accepting an apology, and the possibility of forgiveness. At the very least, in retrospect, I should be profoundly thankful to them, either way, for putting up with my shortcomings.

In any case, when I was living my life according to these questionable principles, I surely understood something was amiss. I was really just flailing around. I was forcing myself to have these kinds of empty experiences without having my heart in it. In short, I compromised, whether or not it made any sense. But I also tried to avoid prejudging what I did, so that I could continue to act unencumbered in this less-than-honorable way. You can make up the stupidest excuses, or use any means to justify the ends. I found myself playing little psychological games inside my own head: maybe if I indulged with older, more mature women, they'd be more experienced and evolved, having worked through a lifetime of various relationships, to varying degrees of success—and not only survived them, but are thriving happily on their own; or perhaps they'd be hopelessly world-weary, yet somehow free of pathology. Or, less likely, I could try to engage with much younger women, who were fresh and unadulterated, who hadn't experienced enough to be wholly damaged or corrupted yet. The rationalizations went on and on, in the interest of finding a suitable sexual outlet, of any variety. Yet in the end, I had to admit defeat. It was inevitable, and, frankly, predictable. As you recall, I wasn't going to be playing the field indefinitely.

And that was fine by me. Once you get out of the game, and no longer worry about having your hopes dashed over and over again, the less pain you feel, the less depressing it is. Some people thrive off the drama of a dysfunctional relationship, even if the negatives completely outweigh whatever positives they're getting out of it. But when one party can't tolerate it anymore, only they can put an end to it for good. In short, the pursuit of sex, not to mention love, was killing me. The drinking alone was catching up to me. It was starting to affect my health, without continuing to provide any of the benefits that enabled me to maintain my state of denial. It was stunting my vitality and exhausting me to the point that I was constantly feeling enervated.

On the other hand, abstaining certainly clarified my thinking concerning the overall nature of relationships between men and women. It became obvious to me, through both my professional and personal experience, that there are vast numbers of women out there who have been traumatized by men, either sexually or otherwise, and that much of it remains unacknowledged. Women, more often than not, carry these wounds around with them silently. The statistics are absolutely clear about that. Yet in our daily lives, we pretend as if none of this is happening. We all go about our business as if everything is fine, until something comes along that forces us to disabuse ourselves of that notion. Women are more willing to talk about it openly, because, naturally, as the offended party, they're more likely to seek out help or support, whether professionally or from loved ones. But it's exceedingly rare to hear any admissions of guilt or culpability from men. Even within the context of psychotherapy, where confidentiality shields them, for the most part, from potential legal consequences. It's equally rare to hear any confessions of that nature from close male friends or relatives, either. That's understandable, I guess. But the facts are the facts, and the numbers simply don't add up.

Of course, most men don't want to admit that they've been abusive, particularly if the abuse is criminal in nature. But what is abundantly clear is that they've been getting away with it for quite a long time, to varying degrees, and are in almost complete denial about it. So, while I might've been confused and frustrated by some of the intimate encounters I've had with women, I have to remind myself, on a daily basis, that it's highly likely that many, if not an overwhelming majority of, women have been abused in some way in the past. And if some of their behavior toward me was off the charts, whether abusive or not, they can hardly be blamed for it. It shouldn't be taken personally.

If I should be upset with anyone, the finger should be pointing toward all the men out there who pretend as if they have nothing to do with any kind of abuse toward women—who claim to be perfectly harmless. Including myself, honestly. To a certain degree. It's a fact—at least as far as I'm concerned—that if you leave women to their own devices, and interact with them on a purely platonic basis, you can be just about sure that things will go well, with a very slight possibility that some conflict or controversy will arise. On the other hand, I came to the exact opposite conclusion regarding men. They're not just responsible

207

for what's going wrong on an interpersonal level—they're responsible, by extension, for all the chaos that's happening on a global scale. Hopefully, men will become more aware, and come to that same conclusion. But it's probably best if we just get out of the way—before it's too late—and help women take the reins from now on.

You might think that's very naïve. And even if women were to take over, they would end up being corrupted just as quickly, and be equally as bad as men. But we haven't tried yet, have we? We don't know for sure whether that's true. Besides, how many women do you know who go around abusing men the way men abuse women? Or get drunk off, for example, the power of owning assault weapons? Whose first instinct is to spar-off, fight or murder? Who are the women who have been responsible for starting wars on a global scale, who have abandoned their children, who are willing to compromise their values solely in the name of self-interest or profit? Where are the women who are capable of destroying the Earth for the sole purpose of enriching themselves? I don't know many of them. I don't see them. In fact, most of what I see runs counter to that. It makes me downright optimistic that roughly half of our species appears to be motivated by better, more constructive values.

Men should try leaving women alone for a change, just to see what can happen. Just like in personal relationships, men shouldn't feel the necessity to be so controlling and possessive. Everyone, regardless of gender, will benefit from a broader freedom, and the unfettered potential of women. That's what I suspect. That's what we should all support. So, speaking for myself, I like to think that I've become the male complement of, and ally to, the women out there who've suddenly found themselves liberated from an abusive marriage, who have finally stumbled upon their true selves, and have chosen to live a happy, but unattached, life.

For me, that meant turning to other things for satisfaction and pleasure. As I've already explained, much of that was channeled into vocation. That had a different focus and that I have a newfound passion for. And, most critically, the unique opportunity for me to embrace an expanded mission that can lead to better things. If I can't control what I can achieve personally, I can at least try to help others get what they wish for. And even though my approach has become more unorthodox, and can still only help from within a significantly compromised system, I nonetheless seem to have had some degree of success.

There's a much more extensive, broken society out there to grapple with, after all, and I often feel overwhelmed by it. There are times when I feel like the best I can do is play the provocateur, when I know in advance that nothing's going to change by my actions alone. I started experimenting with random new strategies, even transgressing the normal boundaries of the helping relationship, to see what might come of them. To shake things up a bit. Desperate times call for desperate measures. Yet, with each successive day, I wondered if I could still imagine working within some approximation of the norms and ethics of my soon-to-be former profession.

At the very same time, it seemed as if the external world was closing in on me. All sorts of things seemed to be happening all at once—chaotically—in quick succession: terrorist attacks, wars, a sudden string of unexpected deaths of personal friends and professional associates; financial collapse, mass shootings almost every month, all on the backdrop of all the other losses I experienced previously. It felt like the sky was falling, or that the world might be coming to an end. Like some great plague was spreading across the Earth that we weren't even remotely prepared for. And that it'd be pointless to try to put up any resistance to it. I was having fears and premonitions that time was running short. And that was exactly when it was time to pull up stakes and leave, to go from the frying pan into the fire, so to speak. To arrive here, to start fresh in this new type of hell…

Whoa! Did you see that? Yeah, it went by in a blur! Oh, I'm so glad I didn't hit it. If we had left just a second earlier or had been going just a little bit faster, it would have wound up road kill. That was a blacktailed jackrabbit you saw. They're everywhere around here. They come out at dusk, and do whatever they do under the cover of darkness. There's probably a coyote on its trail, but thank god they can run faster. Up to thirty-five miles per hour, apparently. They sure do make a good snack for a coyote, if they get caught. But that isn't easy, 'cause they've got these big ol' ears that pick up everything for miles. And they're pretty well camouflaged in this environment. It's funny, though, 'cause when they're threatened and on the run, it's almost impossible to miss them because when they prop up their tails, they have a big, bright white patch under there that warns all their relatives and friends about the danger. Clever, huh? They've even got a bunch of fur on the pads of their feet to cushion and protect them from the desert heat. Just imagine how hot the road is right now, even with the sun going down. Isn't nature remarkable?

Anyway, when I first got here, those dark feelings I was having just before I left New York seemed to linger. But then they started dissipating with time. Of course, that came crashing down dramatically when the shooting occurred. In the meantime, there were other signs and signals that sort of shook me. Remember when I told you about that incident at the casino? You know, the couple who seemed to be cheating at the roulette table, whether they did it deliberately or not? I've told you most of the story. But I left off the part that was the most embarrassing for me.

You might remember that there was another gentleman involved, the one who challenged me, the one who pushed me, and how I struck back instinctively. I ended up felling him. Do you remember? Oh, good! You've been listening after all. Well, after the police arrived, and had gotten several versions of the story, how it had transpired according to varying accounts, they concluded that they would take both me and my adversary down to the station house to hash it all out. My adversary apparently claimed that I had laid hands on him first and that it was only after I had struck him that he had pushed me back. Of course, it was exactly the opposite, and I was quite sure he had pushed me maliciously, with forethought and premeditation. I tried to explain that to the officer in charge, and added that I had only reacted reflexively in response to his attack. I also noted that I had barely grazed him, in fact, before he lost his balance and fell over on his own. It seemed that none of the other witnesses, nor the security cameras, could corroborate our stories, because we were in a thick crowd of people, and it all happened so quickly. In the end, it was a 'he said, he said' situation, and because I had admitted truthfully that I had struck him, technically speaking, I was going to take the lion's share of the blame. My adversary still refused to admit that he shoved me first. So, they ended up giving him a summons, basically a small fine to pay, and sent him on his way.

I, on the other hand, was held overnight in a holding cell until they figured out what they were going to do with me. Of course, that was a very unpleasant environment, to say the least. It wasn't as if there were murderers and rapists being held with me, but there were some very unsavory characters sharing my cell. You had the drunks, the prostitutes, the corner drug dealers, and people who had committed minor assaults, property damage or theft, of course, but also a fair amount of people who were only in jail because they had been swept up around town for petty offenses like loitering, vagrancy or disorderly conduct, and didn't have the means to be processed in a timely manner. Basically, the dregs and outcasts of society, half homeless, half mentally ill, or both. Nobody who could seriously threaten you, but not the most savory of characters. Many of them were destitute, some were physically ill, a few probably capable of violence, but most significantly, from my point of view—half clothed, sweaty, covered with various bodily fluids, reeking of alcohol, cigarette smoke, vomit, and piss and shit from head to toe. Believe me, a most unpleasant experience. And there was nowhere to go to escape from it all. We were packed in the holding cell like sardines. You either had to stand up all night, surrounded by everyone, or find a space on the floor that was the least disgusting to squat over. The best position to take was nearest the entryway, where at least you could take a quick breath every time someone was added to the cell. But then you'd be pushed back farther, naturally.

Anyway, it wasn't until dawn the next day that I was finally taken from the cell and processed. I ended up receiving, more or less, the same punishment as my adversary with a warning that they were going to let me off pretty easily, *this* time. I think part of the penalty had already been paid from my perspective, in terms of the humiliation I received and the contortion my body absorbed. What a joy it was to simply stretch as soon as I got out of there. I felt bad for the people who remained behind, especially the ones who hadn't really committed any crimes or real offenses, but that is the reality of our justice system. I guess we're all seen as guilty, whether we like it or not.

I, for one, saw the distinctions, but I wasn't sure what I could do about it. It was only later on that an idea innocently floated into my head. This was all before I set up shop at Casablanca. Perhaps because of my inward feelings of guilt, and the more motivating notion of lending a hand to those in need, through demonstrable, physical action, I decided it was high time that I make a practical contribution to the world. I was suddenly inspired to learn more about what was happening in my new community, on the street level. I started volunteering at local homeless shelters and soup kitchens, only to discover that even though these institutions supply vital support to those in need, they still have deficits that go beyond a simple lack of resources. I noticed that many of those who needed help were skeptical of receiving help, either because it came with too many strings attached, they felt judged, or because they didn't feel secure enough in those environments. There wasn't much I could do in terms of providing shelter for people, but I could contribute by distributing food when necessary. So, my first plan was to start producing the food myself, and to distribute it on the street. Literally offering it to people as I drove around town looking for takers. And I made the additional effort to provide food that wasn't just adequate in nature. I tried to supply food that would live up to a higher standard, that was truly appetizing and nutritious. So, at first, I started making sandwiches and drinks that met that standard. It didn't cost me too much, and within only a few weeks, word had caught on to look out for my vehicle to get a good meal, with no questions asked, no ulterior motives evident, no judgment, no risk, no hassle. What an operation I had! I would buy the ingredients and make the sandwiches the night before, get up early to load the car, and get on the road by five-thirty in the morning. It was truly a pleasure to go out and serve the community. What a joy it was to get to know people and see how genuinely happy and appreciative they were to receive a simple, quality meal. And to be able to count on it with a clean conscience.

I had gotten into quite a rhythm before... Perhaps you can guess what happened next... Of course, nothing can ever be that easy! One morning, I was out doing my thing, passing a sandwich to one of my clients, when, to my surprise, a police cruiser pulled up beside me. I tried to ignore it at first. But after the client had taken his food, the officers motioned to me to lower my window to be able to speak with them. They wanted to know what I was doing, and if I had a permit to do it. I replied that I didn't, and that I wasn't aware that I needed one. I tried to explain to them that I was acting as a private citizen, and that I was only trying to lend a

213

hand. Well, you would've thought that I had two heads, by the look on their faces! They apparently didn't like the answer I gave. They immediately asked for my driver's license and ran it through the system. And, of course, they found out that I had been arrested just a few months before. And although they had declined to prosecute me, I had still been booked. With that still on my record, it seemed that the net of the criminal justice system would soon be closing in on me.

At that moment, they just issued me another summons, like before. For distributing food to the public without a permit. But then I received a notice in the mail, a couple of weeks later, asking me to show up in court, before a judge. I mean, I can't tell you how infuriating that was! I couldn't believe what was happening to me. You would've thought the city would've thanked me for my services, especially because it was all done pro bono. But, no! I got snagged again by the system. When I went before the judge, he wasn't really interested in hearing about all the do-gooder stuff. I hired an attorney to represent me, but it didn't seem to make any difference at all, really. I think the judge was just dead-set on making an example out of me, particularly because I had just gotten into trouble in the recent past. So, to make a long story short, he sent me to jail for a week, in addition to a larger fine and, believe it or not, two weeks of community service. No, I'm not making this up to entertain you. It really happened! So, I spent a week in that same facility as before, this time, mercifully, in a cell that I only shared with one other person. Luckily, the other person was completely harmless, so the week went by without a glitch.

But that wasn't the worst of it. What was worse was the so-called community service. I was assigned to a small cleanup crew. My job was to sweep the streets for two weeks, each weekday from nine to five sharp. I had a broom and a dustpan, and a rolling garbage bin. I also had to wear the proscribed work clothes supplied at taxpayers' cost. No, it wasn't one of those orange jumpsuits. But it wasn't normal street clothes, either. You know the style, the blue khaki top and bottom, with government insignia on it. I had to supply a good pair of sturdy boots, too, at my own expense. But can you imagine me walking down the streets and sidewalks sweeping up garbage? In public, in broad daylight? Darting in and out between tourists and the very same people I was trying to help in the first place? It was a blow to my ego, I admit. Not that I felt that I was too good for it. But that I had been humiliated in this way, just so the city could make a few bucks off me and save a few dollars at my expense. It was so wrong, so unjust, so...

It's not like this kind of stuff doesn't go on all the time. It's part of the game, and the system. I've witnessed it time and time again. Once you're in the criminal justice system, it's very hard to get out. Unless you have resources and an experienced lawyer. It's a moneymaking machine, regardless of whether justice is being meted out equitably. Imagine what happens to people without any resources to speak of. I guess I never expected it to happen to me. But you can imagine the effect it had on me. I was already feeling so disillusioned. I had just arrived in Las Vegas and the same wretched pattern seemed to be starting all over again. I guess I should've known I couldn't escape it. The feeling lingered, and I had no other option left but to accept the inevitability of my position in life. I knew it wasn't going get any easier. I was just going to have to get used to that nagging, uncomfortable feeling inside me. Why fight it? It's futile to keep resisting. On the other hand, I could move on, certainly, without the denial I had erected around myself in the past. I would continue to live, yet live more authentically. I would persevere, if only to bear witness to the injustices that were happening around me. That, alone, had its value, even if it felt paralyzing at times. At the very least, I could keep score, so to speak. Maybe I'll never really know for sure who's who—who's making things better, who's making things worse, who's just floating along, or even get to understand myself in that regard—but there was surely a growing appeal and allure to distancing myself from the ordinary, day-to-day drudgery of existence.

Yet, the humiliation I suffered seemed to serve a specific purpose, in ways I hadn't anticipated. The scene on the street, as I carried out my punishment, ran over and over in my head, in a continuous loop, like some kind of sick torture being forced on me. It was true that I had little choice but to pay the penalty for my supposed transgressions. And the punishment itself was clearly intended to act as a deterrent. But what I mostly internalized from the experience, sadly, was an intense feeling of shame. It felt unfair and I felt stigmatized. I was angry with myself for falling into that trap, and I couldn't seem to shake it.

In order to feel judged, there's a presumption that there must be others doing the judging. Like the way the courts judge you, or even how people on the street judge you. But what I discovered, eventually, was just how ruthlessly I judged myself. It was difficult to move past it, and I recognized that in order to continue to progress, I had to come to some kind of terms with it. I knew I had to resist it, to some degree. We've all experienced, as we go about our usual, daily lives, how people judge, and how we judge, as a matter of course. It's almost as if there's really no need or reason to have any other system in place to keep people compliant, or to stifle any perceived threat. Yes, we have culture—our religions and governments—but do we really *require* those institutions for *those* purposes? I wonder. It seems like most people, in and of themselves—armed with their own sense of self-righteousness—are perfectly capable of making the most wildly reckless pronouncements, in an openly brazen manner, if it serves their most cherished objectives. The judgment of men, upon others, often shows little mercy or compassion. Just a cursory examination of history demonstrates that. So what I learned, on the flip side, was to avoid judging yourself too harshly or casually. If you get caught up in it, there's no end to it. We can be our own worst enemies, and that's a special kind of curse. There are armies of people out there who'd be more than willing to serve as your judge, jury, *and* firing squad. Even a good proportion who'd be more than happy to take potshots at each other. And still others who'd *love* a circular firing squad. But you don't have to make it easy for them. You certainly shouldn't be shooting yourself in the foot, for their sake.

That's what psychology's for! Yes, it's there to judge, too. It's there to rub your nose in it, in a way, but on your terms. It can also *absolve* you of your sins, right in the here and now. Admittedly, it does a pretty poor job of it. But perhaps that's the best we can expect from it. If we at least try to get it all out in the open, into the clear light of day, there's a chance that we can better ourselves. We can all go about messing things up equally, but let's hope that some of us have the necessary insight to make some good adjustments and manage to self-correct going forward.

God, it's stuffy in here! Do mind if I open the windows? The A.C.'s good at first, after being outside for a while, but then it gets a little oppressive in its own right. In the evening, it's actually not that hot outside of town. Despite global warming. At least for now… You know it's going to get much worse before it gets any better? *If* it gets better. I'm not so confident that we're going to be able to dodge what's coming with climate change, at this late stage. It may already be too late, no matter what we do. That's the thing. I mean, what do you do in that case? We've got hard science. We know what's going on and how to limit the effects. But that's not really the problem, is it? That much is perfectly clear. It's not that we can't fix it, it's that we *refuse* to. The real problem's not something you can solve by appealing *solely* to rational thinking. The last thing people want to admit is that it, in fact, is coming. So they'll do everything and anything they can to deny it. Instead of scrutinizing the situation, accepting it as it is, and doing something about it. We want to believe, and have convinced ourselves, that we can somehow skip most of the steps on our way to recovery, and sidestep all the pain that we're surely going to have to suffer through.

Climate change must seem rather abstract to a lot of people, despite the obvious threat. And while the threat still seems a bit vague and far off into the future, it's no wonder people go into denial. We already have enough trouble just keeping up with the day-to-day as it is, let alone face another major existential crisis. It seems like there's only so much people can take at one time. But that's exactly what makes it so frightening. There doesn't seem to be a lot left in the tank, these days. And because people have been so thoroughly conditioned over the centuries to believe that there should be practically no restrictions on the scope of human activity, they'll rely on all sorts of bogus reasoning that rationalizes an absolute allegiance to limitless economic expansion. To continue living recklessly and unimpeded, no matter the cost.

It's sort of like when people are confronted by the reality of their own deaths—they'll be in denial about their mortality all their lives, but then suddenly go pray to god when they're nearing the end, hoping that god can somehow spare them the fate everyone else has coming. They hope god will swoop in at the last moment and save them. Why *would* god act so impulsively? Why wipe out all the wondrous creatures he so lovingly created, and the very world they depend on for their survival? No, I don't think religion is going to cut it, on the face of it. *Especially* if you don't buy into it in the first place.

So, how do you manage to face the impending doom head-on —the absurdity of the situation? Turn to the great philosophers? No, they don't have very satisfying answers either. They might've had a better angle on it had they been challenged by it. But ultimately, the more they grappled with any number of baffling dilemmas, the more inscrutable the next set of questions seemed to become... Do you ever catch yourself wondering how any of this is possible? How life makes even the remotest kind of sense? I guess after thousands of years of trying, we would have figured it out by now, if we *had* the ability to wrap our heads around it in the first place. I guess we'll never know.

It's understandable that people are terrified by the notion of death. But shouldn't we be more frightened by existence itself? It's clear people are deathly afraid of *not* existing, who wish desperately for immortality. But can you imagine the alternative—how frightening it would be—to live forever? It'd be worse than death itself! Imagine how worn down, how much baggage you'd be carrying, how defeated you'd feel, after a while. Or even bored beyond comprehension! That would be a special kind of hell, no? We should probably be thrilled if any of us are fortunate enough to lead full, prosperous, meaningful lives—and then just drop dead one day from sheer exhaustion, in the literal sense of the word.

So, let's not pretend that we have the answers. We don't even have good answers for the simplest of questions. Let's just live a good life despite it all, and do the best that we can. Even if we all just promised that we'd do our best to do the least amount of harm. A sort of Hippocratic oath for the masses. Wouldn't that be satisfying enough? Despite all of that, there's not a soul on Earth, including Jesus himself, who will escape the law of entropy. You know, dust to dust, ashes to ashes. Maybe going out with a bang isn't such a bad idea... Do you ever wonder what Jesus must've been thinking about, up there on the cross? He was sacrificing a lot for us—he understood that he was dying for a cause that was greater than him alone. For our sins, so the story goes. He understood he was going to have to offer himself up so that we could be forgiven and reconciled to god. It was a necessary evil. But have you ever wondered if *he* was forgiven? It's not as if he accepted god's will without question. Remember when he asked god why he had forsaken him? Jesus didn't exactly seem to accept his fate entirely willingly. Well... it's no different for us now, is it? Every one of us, here on Earth, has a similar, collective cross to bear. If we're smart, we'll all fear for each other, and make the same kind of sacrifice gladly and willingly for the Earth—if we're going to survive, be forgiven, and have a future worth living for.

It's not going to be easy, especially at first. We're going to have to convince ourselves that personal sacrifice for the greater good is an absolute imperative. And we're going to have to follow through with that as a guiding principle no matter how unpopular it might be, or how alienating it might make us feel. Because I think in order to meet the challenge, in order to come out the other end relatively intact, we'll need to approach it with a sense of humility —and without the usual arrogance we've become so accustomed to. The solutions won't emerge from any single, charismatic personality; or some sort of savior—like Jesus—who will rescue us, despite our shortcomings. Only a massive, coordinated, and genuinely collective effort will suffice.

If we have any kind of success, it will certainly be cause for celebration. But I'd caution against taking too much credit for it, even if we're still inclined, regrettably, to heap recognition and praise upon ourselves. It'd be best not to internalize it—because it'll only encourage the kind of bad behavior we worked so hard to liberate ourselves from. It'll distract us, and focus attention away from the ongoing challenge of climate change—while running the risk of getting into a different, but equally harmful, variety of idol worship, as we press forward into the future. We don't want to get back into that kind of mind game, with those kinds of inherent contradictions and vulnerabilities. If there *are* any individual rewards, they should come organically—in and of themselves—as a consequence of one's service to the greater good. Acknowledgement, I learned often enough, leads to unintended consequences. One should be cautious feeding the ego—because it can end up biting you in the ass. There may only be a few fatal, impalpable steps that differentiate and separate praise and acknowledgement from condemnation and punishment. So, if you want to avoid paying too high a price—potentially—you'd be wise to keep everyone off your trail, from the very beginning.

If, in fact, you want to be a *real* hero, to be amongst the *best* of them, the main thing is to carry on bravely and ruthlessly, despite the isolation or loneliness you might feel as a consequence. You have to resist getting off course, or succumbing to hopelessness. Just get behind that big boulder like Sisyphus, and roll it back up again—forever—without too much whining. See it as a challenge, not a burden.

I mean, that's what you're shooting for. If you're so inclined. But, of course, no mere mortal can truly live up to that impossible ideal. That'd be asking *way* too much. But you can, at least, try—surely, you can strive for a reasonable facsimile of the ideal. Even if you'll never triumph, you can be perfectly satisfied stumbling all along the way. There will be obstacles, for sure. But it's not about arriving, as they say, it's about the trip. Yes—another cliché—but it's true. If you must avoid barriers, by all means, do so. If you need to trample all over them, well, don't be too timid to stomp with enthusiasm. Just bear in mind that even if you have absolute, unequivocal justification for your actions, there will always be a significant amount of dissent. There will always be powerful forces that will be more than happy to stick your head in the guillotine when threatened boldly, face-to-face. But beware of the mercenaries and con men, too—the ones who *appear* to be allies but who are only motivated by their own interests. They're the worst of all! They'd stomp on Jesus himself if he were in their way.

Ah, there we are! Look at how transparent the night sky is. You can see the Strip so clearly, even from here. All the twinkling lights. All the colorful neon. What an impressive silhouette the skyline makes. Are you happy to be back? Yes, you've made it back safely, my friend. Do you see the Eiffel Tower over there? Yes, right in the middle of 'Paris'. Ha ha!! I'm not sure if you can make out New York, though. Even with the reproductions of the Empire State Building, the Chrysler Building, and the Statue of Liberty—they don't exactly stick out, do they? Not from this far out. Not like they do in real life.

But I bet you're glad to be back to town. You must be sick and tired of all this blabbering on... stuck in this car, so long, with me. Yet, if I might indulge just a tiny bit more... No, you're very kind. I mean, it's kind of related to what I was talking about... Isn't it odd how insistent we are building these colossal skylines everywhere across the globe, in practically every major city of any significance? We always seem to build up, build as high as possible, whether there is a practical reason for it or not. To make an impression—undoubtedly—to reinforce our own existence and relevance. But there's practically nothing more perverted or artificial than these urban concrete canyons—jam-packed with their countless, secular cathedrals. Monuments to the glory of commerce. Why don't we ever try working *with* the environment, especially here, in the middle of the desert? Why are we always *opposing* nature? Why can't we follow its contours? Capitalize on its beauty and the strength of its character? Act as if we're a *part* of nature—not *apart* from it? Well, you know why. We want to believe that we can control our destiny, and that we are the lords of the universe. That nature should be subservient to man. Ha ha!! What a terrible reckoning and comeuppance we have in store for us!

We've really convinced ourselves that we're going to be able to outsmart nature. We think we're going to be able to solve all our problems by *controlling* nature! What a hideous delusion! A twisted fantasy! A fatal sickness and tragic misunderstanding!! Surely, we know that even if we somehow manage to dodge the catastrophic effects of global warming, these grotesque structures —the very symbols of our arrogance—will still vanish? Yes, even this Babel, this abominable city, will eventually succumb and perish. Will be recalled by nature. Dust to dust, ashes to ashes, once again. What a great image that is! It's going to revert to the lonesome valley it once was—inevitably—complete with rolling tumbleweed.

Don't you find it sad, and terribly ironic, that we hold the seeds of our demise in our very own hands? That we're likely to do *ourselves* in, if we're not careful. We may end up extinguishing *ourselves* out of existence. So deeply tragic! What could be *more* tragic? Nature, as a whole, *will* judge us if we don't start judging ourselves. It'll put a definitive end to our hubris and narcissism— that's for sure—without the slightest vindictiveness, and reclaim us as just another failed terrestrial experiment. Then the world will simply revert to its original state of relative innocence. The beasts of the Earth will undoubtedly celebrate with rapturous joy. The animals, once again, shall be free. The jackal, finally, will have the last laugh.

Will there be a successor to us on the planet? Perhaps it's better that there aren't any. But if any do emerge, let's hope they're a whole lot wiser than us—sage creatures who'll understand the value of living well, within their means. Ones who'll live close to the Earth, who'll work with it, who'll nurture it —knowing that the quality of their lives depend on it—like the life-giving mother the Earth has always been. Ones who *refuse* to rape it and pillage it, and otherwise abuse it. Is it too late already? Even for them? I'm not certain. But, at present, we seem to be caught in the throes of a deathly, collective panic attack while the Earth continues to suffocate and gasp for breath.

I really am insufferable, aren't I? I just can't seem to help myself. I'm like some latter-day John the Baptist, howling into the wind. You probably just came to Vegas to get away from it all.

But look what's happened. I keep blathering on and on about all this misery. I'm probably only making you feel depressed and guilty.

But don't sweat it—ha ha! We're *all* guilty! That should make you feel better. Maybe we should all lock each other up in jail, before we do even more damage. Maybe that's what I should've learned when they threw me into the cell—how to be humble like a monk. How to carve out time to think about things, to really think about them deeply, and stay out of trouble... But no matter how you cut it, it bears repeating—as I've said *many, many* times before, it's pretty clear that we already have all of the knowledge and all of the tools we need to beat this thing. Not just to defeat climate change, but to resolve a whole host of other complicated, chronically intransigent problems that plague us. More than anything else, we need to stop shooting ourselves in the foot. We need to change, to evolve to heights that we've never reached for before. It's hiding in plain sight, staring us straight in the face. All we have to do is have the courage and faith to accept it, and act accordingly.

Well, here we are. It was nice to spend the day with you. I hope you enjoyed the show, so to speak. Ha ha! I do hope you'll be back tomorrow. But I won't hold it against you if you choose to opt out. I do have a way of grating on the nerves. You can't get a word in edgewise, can you? And it wouldn't be the first time I've been accused of being maddeningly loquacious. Sometimes, it gets so bad I even wonder about my own sanity. What really distinguishes me from any of the demented or deranged lunatics you see on the street, right in front of us? I guess, just like with them, you can take it or leave it.

Why listen to anyone? Seriously? There are all sorts of people on the street who claim to be prophets of some kind. I'd say as soon as they try to convince you of that, you might not want to stick around much longer. It'd be best not to buy into it. I mean, how can you trust what they're saying? Even if it's patently obvious they're the real deal, you probably won't realize it. That's the nature of the beast. They'll never disclose who they are, they'll never appear where you expect them to be, and you probably won't want to accept what they have to say anyway. Even if you're smart enough to know better. They do that purposely because they know once they're identified publicly, they'll be labeled a threat, and the people in power will want to neutralize them. Most of what they proclaim is obvious anyway, if it's of any real value. The only difference is they're brave enough and bold enough to say it plainly and clearly, on the street. For the average person, that's just too much to handle. So just listen and bear witness. Share your wisdom, if it helps. But always continue moving toward the light. And the rest will take care of itself, when all is said and done. That's what being a Witness/Confidant is all about!

I'm going to shut up now. No, really... Shall we meet again tomorrow night? I mean, it's up to you. It's your choice. If you feel like it... Oh, you only have two more days left here, huh? You're going back to *New York,* of all places! You're a sly devil... All this time, and not *once* did you mention you're from there. I knew I liked you! You're *so* my kind of guy!

Sadly, I don't think about New York much anymore. But when it does come to mind, I know that I'll never be going back to it again. To live, I mean. That's not to say that I don't have fond memories of it. No, sir. I love to image myself walking down the streets like the flâneur. Just to imagine feeling the sensation of the ground rumbling below my feet, for a minute. Knowing that there's a whole world beneath, below the surface, that keeps things churning twenty-four hours a day. To watch the steam rising from the vents along the streets. What was better or more romantic? There was something strangely comforting about it. Think of the millions of people who are treading the sidewalks of New York right now. Going about their busy lives... Oh, how precious life is, how quickly it passes. But let's not let that trouble us now...

Why don't you come over to my place tomorrow? Let's do something different, for once, if that's not too intimate for you. I don't want to be too presumptuous, but I feel like you haven't quite given up on me yet. I think that's cause for celebration. You really are too kind...

VI.

Please! Please do come in, my friend! The door's open! You can let yourself in. I'm afraid I'm a little laid up today... Not sure what it is. But, every once in a while, my body decides it's going to rebel. Nothing that a little tonic water and lime won't take care of. For whatever reason, the quinine usually does the trick. I've never been able to figure out if it's a real illness, or something else. But it is what it is. Nothing for you to fear. I'm quite confident it's not something that's contagious. That I can assure you of. Full disclosure with me, as usual.

I try my best to tell the truth at all times—or, at least, try to do my best not to consciously deceive anyone about anything. Not that that matters, though. Because even lies end up leading to the truth, eventually. Sometimes even more quickly than just the truth alone. How many times have you had to play the role of the detective in your life, to get to the bottom of things? I know I often have to. Because people lie and deceive all the time—to themselves and others—in a staggering variety of ways, not least of all unconsciously. There are hidden motives, not to mention ulterior ones, that *they* might not even be aware of, let alone go out of their way to tell you about. And what difference would it actually make if you found out that half the stuff I've been telling you are lies? Would it really alter anything? The story's still valid, whether or not it's an accurate representation of the truth, no? The important thing is what you get *out* of the story, whether or not you understand the narrative. Otherwise, I'd be wasting my time and everyone else's.

Anyway, have a seat, my friend. Yes, just pull up that chair and get as close as you wish. Not too far away, or else it'll feel very awkward, indeed. It's already so sparse in here, right? Looks like one of those achingly lonesome Hopper paintings in here, no? If you maintain too much distance, I might begin to feel a tinge of loneliness. Ha ha!! Did you suspect that I lived so modestly? Like a monk, really. Just the bare essentials these days. I never understand why people feel so compelled to fill up every little space. Everything I have, of any value, is stored right up in here, in my head. It's like a library—full of my stories, and all the stories of those I've encountered along the way, during my lifetime. It rivals any real library, but it's all mine. I can enter and borrow anytime I wish, and check out as many books as I want. No limits in here. If only I had a more comfortable bed. This bed is more like a cot. It's fine to sleep on, but lounging on it, for any amount of time, can be a little challenging and uncomfortable. It certainly puts a strain on your body. A stitch in your back or a nagging cramp in your hip can certainly muddle your mind.

Every time I square up with someone this way, in opposing positions, it reminds me of that incident I told you about in the psychiatric hospital. When that man came into the lobby and insisted on being admitted? When they surrounded him, took him down, and restrained him? Pure madness! Something about that physical stand-off, that striking imbalance of power, seems to trigger me these days. I don't mean to suggest that that's the case with you and me presently, but it seems to affect me reflexively. You might think it's silly, but after that calamity in the waiting room, I became much more protective, if not overly protective, of all my patients. And of patients in general, whether they were mine, strictly speaking, or not. Whenever I sensed something going wrong, I'd try to jump in to the extent that I could. More often than not, patients were thrilled to receive whatever support I could offer, because what they typically received was often woefully inadequate.

But then, you'd also typically have a handful of patients who were, understandably, suspicious of your motivations. Who'd rebuff you outright, because they were so determined to get what they so desperately needed, they feared rocking the boat in even the most benign ways. They were so conditioned and accustomed to playing strictly by the rules set out for them that they couldn't even *conceive* of accepting any help, even if it meant breaking through any of the hidden systemic barriers that constrained them. I shouldn't have resented those feelings they so instinctively held. But, I did, truth be told. Every time I got rejected by a patient in that way, I felt a little like that man who had been manhandled and beaten down and humiliated. I took it personally, I admit. Nevertheless, I continued to do everything within my power to help. I can't tell you how much extra work I took on behind the scenes, whether I did so in the open or surreptitiously, with or without the knowledge of the patient or their designated practitioner. It actually amused me how much I got done behind their backs, and absolutely free of charge. In a perfect world, I would've received some kind of reward for all the extra effort I was putting in. I certainly got away with a lot, right under their noses. But I carefully covered up my tracks to avoid detection. Nobody ever discovered what I was up to. Nobody needed to know. That was the whole point. That same covert practice serves me well on many an occasion. I'm sure I'm not the only one who secretly does those kinds of things, with the same devil-may-care attitude and outlook. There must be a secret army of us out there, that's for sure. An invisible hand. Or nothing would ever get done properly.

But then I discovered—much later on, upon deeper reflection —that this sneaky, surreptitious, almost vengeful approach to practice I had stumbled upon, and then wholeheartedly adopted, likely had its origin in the more distant past. From a darker passage in my life. I don't think I ever told you about the circumstances surrounding my wife's death, have I? No, I think I told you, previously, that she had died. But I haven't yet gotten into any of the excruciating and gruesome details of the events from that time. Please bear with me, my friend. It's a long story, but one well worth your attention, if I might presume.

The first shock was the cancer diagnosis itself. For my wife to be diagnosed in her early thirties was bad enough. But to add to the distress, it was discovered during what we assumed would be a standard yearly examination. The gynecologist felt a lump during a routine breast exam that he seemed only mildly concerned about. Nobody was overly concerned, because she had always had dense breast tissue, and some occasional lumpiness wasn't unusual. But, out of an abundance of caution, he suggested she follow up with a radiologist—just to be extra careful. The radiologist was, perhaps, a little more concerned because he ordered a biopsy, but he still implied it was probably nothing—although it would take a few agonizing days to get the results back. Of course, although we couldn't help feeling afraid, I still felt like the statistics would turn out in our favor. It was unnerving to wait those couple days, as anyone can surely imagine. Yet, in hindsight, *that* fear was nothing compared to the devastating news that she had, in fact, a malignant tumor. That it was cancer. That word alone is enough to shake you to the core, but the improbability of it seemed to make it that much worse.

Nonetheless, my wife put on a brave face, and decided there was only one course of action—that we were going to fight it, and prevail. We were relieved to hear from our newly-formed team of doctors that her chances of overcoming the disease and surviving were high. They had caught it early, and the tumor didn't seem overly threatening—diagnostically speaking. Because of her age, the team wanted to treat it very aggressively, so that they would be certain it would be wiped out of her body forever. So, heeding their advice, my wife decided to get—in quick succession—a full mastectomy, followed by aggressive chemotherapy and radiation, and breast reconstruction. She even had fertility treatments to preserve her ova for future use. You can imagine how traumatic it was, every step of the way? Yet the end results were optimal and encouraging, as she entered into a period of 'cancer free' remission. In other words, no evidence of disease. The only treatment left after that was to receive hormone therapy to reduce the odds of reoccurrence, and to get regular diagnostic tests periodically to make sure it hadn't returned.

The hormone treatment was relatively benign, in that there were few side effects. The worst thing about it was that my wife would have to take a pill every morning for the next five years. But if that meant no cancer, that was a small price to pay. On the other hand, the continual diagnostic testing was excruciatingly difficult to endure. The tests themselves were often invasive, and every time one was administered, there would be the inevitable wait time while the results were analyzed by an expert, and subsequently conveyed to us. The wait would rarely exceed a few days, but those few days would pass by very, very slowly. It's was like holding your breath for days—followed by a deep exhalation, if the results came back favorable.

That went on for months, until my wife started experiencing some vague, inexplicable pain in her back that seemed to come and go. That was when the doctors ordered a body scan to try to figure out what was going on. To our shock and dismay, the cancer had metastasized to her spine. And that was, of course, the most devastating news we could've received. Because that development was more or less a death sentence. Whether it took the average of two years to run its dismal course—or twenty—the end result would be the same. Luckily, it hadn't spread anywhere else—to the brain, the lungs, or the liver, the remaining, most potentially lethal areas of concern.

In the meantime—over the course of the next year and a half— more chemotherapy, radiation, and hormone treatments of an increasingly experimental nature. The plan was to draw her life out as long as possible, using all the treatments available at the time, in succession. Yet, each time, the tumors would shrink to some degree, only to rebound with a vengeance—a sure sign that the disease had adapted to the treatment, rendering it useless going forward. But as long as there were new treatments available, we could continue on like that indefinitely.

But then the cancer spread to her lungs. And for the last six months of her life, my wife was tethered to supplemental oxygen, most of the time. That was when the care got much more intensive on a day-to-day basis, and managing pain became another troublesome factor in her overall treatment. Most of the pain medications had limited effectiveness, and, like chemo, they became less efficacious as time passed. Until, thankfully, they started administering morphine. It wiped the pain out dramatically, and also made breathing easier. But it also meant that the end was near, and that she would have to come to peace with her mortality.

It only took a few more months before the cancer spread uncontrollably, thoroughly riddling her upper body—including the liver. By that time, there were no more treatments left to apply.

We got to the point when we ran out of any meaningful medical options. When the oncologist told her there was nothing left for him to do, and that she should consider entering hospice, her reaction was remarkably subdued. I guess she knew the day was coming, and had accepted it a long time ago. She didn't seem to get upset at all. There was no great emotional outburst. She just closed her eyes, folded her hands over each other, and if anything, almost seemed relieved that the struggle would soon be over. She dozed off to sleep. The only thing really left to do was to spend those last precious moments together, and keep her as comfortable as possible.

She required oxygen twenty-four hours a day, and more frequent droppers-full of morphine whenever the pain became more intolerable, or the breathing more labored. It was only the last two-week period before she died that her body seemed to go completely into shutdown. Had that happened seamlessly, I guess our overall experience wouldn't have been any different than anyone else's. Up until that moment, all the doctors, their support staff, and the institutions they worked for, did an outstanding job caring for her, with few exceptions. There was an occasional dust-up with a practitioner here or there—usually with younger ones who hadn't yet honed their bedside manner, or who lacked the social skills to be a graceful bearer of bad news. But the real shocker came from the hospice we hired, with only four weeks left to go.

We had entered hospice just after my wife began having chronic breathing problems. She had to have a continuous flow of oxygen from that time on. We'd go through a multitude of tanks per week, getting regular deliveries and resupply from the same vendor each week, who had been subcontracted through the hospice. The hospice had agreed to provide wrap-around care for as long as six months in exchange for the full hospice benefit payment from my wife's insurance policy. We were closing in on a total of about five months of hospice right around the time my wife had, as it turned out, roughly four weeks left to live. Then, one day, the oxygen delivery didn't come as scheduled. That was alarming enough, but nothing that couldn't be sorted out with a simple phone call to the vendor. They had always been reliable and trustworthy.

So I called them and asked why the delivery hadn't come. To my absolute shock, they informed me that the hospice had discharged us! I could not believe it. At first, I thought it surely must've been some kind of mistake or misunderstanding. But when I called the hospice, they confirmed, in fact, that they had discharged us. I was in complete shock! Why? When? For what reason? I just couldn't wrap my head around it. Surely, it couldn't be true. On what basis? Who would've signed off on it? It was utterly ridiculous and absurd. Anyway, after it had been confirmed, I was understandably distraught and objected vehemently. But what was more pressing, at that moment, was getting the oxygen to my wife, and immediately.

I insisted that they direct the vendor to continue deliveries until we had a chance to clear things up. But they refused! For whatever reason, I had been directed to–and was speaking with–a woman who was in the administrative office, someone who wasn't connected to the medical side of the institution. In fact, I was speaking with the finance officer who had originally offered and signed onto the contract with us. I couldn't understand why she was suddenly handling our case. It made absolutely no sense to me. I explained to her that if we didn't receive the oxygen immediately, my wife was going to have an imminent medical emergency. She desperately needed more oxygen to sustain her. Without it, she'd start gasping for breath, and 9-1-1 would have to be called.

But none of that pleading seemed to matter. The hospice was very firm about their decision, and they weren't going to change their minds. I became indignant and enraged, and started screaming into the phone. My wife began to get upset, the more I lost my self-control. She wanted to get on the phone herself to try to clarify the situation for them. But, sure enough, within a few minutes she was angry, too, and gasping for breath. She began crying and pleading with the woman on the telephone—telling her that if she had any conscience, any at all, she wouldn't have done this to her—and that she would die if she didn't have oxygen soon. She started sobbing uncontrollably, realizing, firsthand and for herself, that more begging, or asking for simple compassion, was a lost cause.

After she handed the phone back to me, I instinctively demanded that they provide the oxygen once more, before I abruptly hung up, frustrated and fuming, over the callous disregard and downright malice directed at us. Then it occurred to me that I could call the oxygen vendor directly and ask *them* to continue while we worked out the details with the hospice later. I told them I would pay for it out-of-pocket, if need be. They apologized to me profusely, after they heard what had happened, and assured me that they would've never cancelled the deliveries had they known how serious the circumstances were; and furthermore, that that was never the kind of policy they would knowingly condone, and that they were just as appalled to hear of it as we were.

They sent the oxygen over immediately, in less than a half an hour. I was very grateful for their quick response. Meanwhile, the hospice called back to explain why we had been discharged. Again, another administrator called, whom I had never had any contact with before. He claimed, like the well-trained bureaucrat he was, that they were discharging my wife because she had received chemotherapy recently that indicated that she wasn't going to be dying imminently, or perhaps even in the next six months. That the type of chemo that had recently been administered indicated that she was going to recover—that it was administered with 'curative' intent. The only chemotherapy she was receiving was palliative in nature, so their claim was patently absurd and, furthermore, medically unfounded. I found out later that they hadn't even called the lead oncologist to consult with him. But it appeared, from what I could tell, that they had begun to see our case as a financial liability, and that they were going to try to discharge us by any means possible, even if it meant bending the facts to their will, beyond comprehension, using some kind of obscure technicality as grounds for discharge.

Then it occurred to me, in hindsight, that they had probably been looking at the financial calculus for a while. I wondered why things had gradually begun to change over the last few months, while still in their care. At first, it was the vague insinuation that we were using too many supplies to treat my wife's skin wounds; then, the not-so-subtle withholding of these materials; then, the demand, and eventual necessity, that we buy our own supplies to make up for it; then, the increasingly limited visits by the nurses, assistants, and other professionals who had been a regular part of the team. I didn't notice at first, but it became more obvious once they started training me to do their work for them. Suddenly, I had to learn how to change dressings myself, and with each passing day I was asked to do more and more, without the necessary skills or training to do it. It all suddenly made sense to me. They were going to cut their losses, no matter what the possible consequences, either legally or morally.

Can you imagine how that felt? To be cut loose at the very hour of your most desperate need? It was a real gut punch, a real existential crisis, the likes of which I had never experienced before. Even our oncologist, with his stellar, international reputation, wasn't able to use his power and influence to have the decision rescinded. Then, when I tried to contact the hospice social worker about the situation, who was supposed to be our advocate, we didn't even get the courtesy of a call back. It was obvious that they had cut us off completely, and that there would be no more communication from them.

Meanwhile, we were left high and dry. Quite literally. The hospice sent some thugs over unannounced, to remove the hospice's property from our home, including the hospital bed that my wife spent most of her time in. It was brutal, my friend. No mercy! No humanity! No nothing! Of course, I thought, momentarily, about refusing them access to the house, so that they couldn't achieve their aims. But then I figured I might as well get it over with and wipe the slate clean. I was concerned that they might end up suing us if we didn't cooperate and comply, or, worse, send the police over so that they could reclaim their equipment forcibly. It wasn't worth the potential risk, so I let it go. But you can be sure I did my damnedest to keep whatever supplies I could…

Nevertheless, I still had to figure out how to replace the equipment they took away, not to mention finding new staff that could help us out. On top of everything, the hospice refused to properly and officially discharge us; in other words, they were legally bound to set us up with another hospice, or to provide an equivalent level of care, before withdrawing their services. But they did nothing. I had to do it all myself, knowing nothing, at that time, about how any of that got done. So, in those last weeks I had with my wife, I was forced to shift into overdrive, and spend my precious time chasing after vendors and medical assistants, to patch together the care that we needed. Instead of sitting by my wife's side, instead of holding her hand, instead of comforting her, loving her to the best of my abilities, having time to attend to her final wishes, to say goodbye, to assure her that I would take care of everything; in short, all the things you should be focusing on, in those final moments with her. It was criminal, my friend! Utterly crooked! But then…

Then... My dear friend, I must say, the world works in mysterious and surprising ways! Just when you're thinking it's all over, that there's no hope left in the world, that you shouldn't trust people... No, there wasn't a miracle recovery, or anything of the sort. In fact, things just got worse. But one night, after a particularly challenging day for my wife—one that included having more pain than usual, and less ability to control it, and furthermore, more acute breathing difficulties—we had to call 9-1-1 to have an ambulance take her to the hospital, so that they could try to get it under control. I wasn't sure if that was the beginning of the end, whether death was imminent, but the staff was able to stabilize her to the extent that she could go home again. I sensed that they were trying to tell me, indirectly implying, that if we wished for her to die at home, then it was imperative to get her home as soon as possible. With that in mind, and because that was, indeed, our wish, the hospital arranged for another ambulance to transport her back home, accompanied by a very competent EMT team who treated her with the utmost dignity and respect.

The real miracle, though, was when the hospital sent a social worker to check up on me as they were preparing for my wife's discharge. The social worker asked a few questions about the care she was receiving at home, and what other kinds of support we were getting. That's when I dropped the whole sleazy story on him, with the aforementioned hospice. I really just needed an ear to hear me out, for the first time. So, I prefaced my narrative with a good dose of exasperation in my voice, and even began my reply with something along the lines of 'You're not going to believe how crazy our story is, but...' before I explained the rest to him. I didn't expect much of a reply, other than the usual 'I'm sorry to hear that, that that's happened to you.' But as I spoke, I sensed a different kind of attitude, reflected in the expression on his face, that contradicted what I assumed would be the usual perfunctory response. His face expressed equal parts shock, disbelief, and indignation—but finally, empathy—before he replied to my loathsome tale of woe. He simply asked, given the current state of the household, whether I needed help of any kind, and whether I would accept some, if offered. He didn't elaborate any further after I answered in the affirmative, except to say that he had to go consult with someone briefly, and that he'd be back in about half an hour.

The social worker returned after about fifteen minutes, and sat across from me with a very earnest look on his face. He explained that he had spoken with the director of the institution, which, incidentally, was operated by the Catholic church. With the C.E.O. himself, the head decision-maker, the administrator who was ultimately responsible for representing the institution and who had the most power to make things happen behind the scenes. It turned out that after having heard my story, they decided that they were going to offer us care through their own hospice—assist us with absolutely everything and anything we needed, at absolutely no cost, and that we should leave everything up to them from that point on, through to the very end, including services provided even *after* her death. A *miracle*, my friend, there's no other word for it! It was as if god himself came down and intervened on our behalf. I sat there in utter disbelief, for a moment, before I burst into a deep, deep, sob—the kind I had seldom experienced before. The social worker embraced me immediately and held me close until I could regain my composure. I remember he was a bear of a man, probably six-six, three hundred pounds; a massive reach, like a former linebacker. It was somehow very fitting for this man to be the one to comfort me at that time, the only type of body that could be able to absorb and contain the depth of my grief. I will never forget that moment for the rest of my life. It's so rare and special to be treated that way, and I felt an instant and enormous sense of relief due to his remarkable and decisive intervention. I couldn't have thanked him any more than I did, or been more grateful, yet his only response was to assure me that we would be in very good hands from that point on. His gracious, humble bearing only heightened the effect. Then, he accompanied me back to my wife's room, where the nursing staff had already started to prepare for her return home.

My wife was still in a bit of a haze, but when I explained to her what had happened, she managed to muster a smile, one that matched the relief I felt, just a few moments before. We *were* in exceptional hands, as it turned out. They honored every single commitment they made to us, without exception. They *did* provide each and every thing that we needed, and then some. Ultimately, my wife died one day peacefully at home, surrounded by her loved ones, in the wee hours of the morning. I was lying right beside her. No one could've asked for anything more. I literally did not have to worry about a single logistical detail the whole time, for almost two weeks after we left the hospital. We had our precious final moments with each other. Meanwhile, the new hospice took care of replacing all the equipment and all the staff. Everything we needed. Total wrap-around services, for absolutely no charge. Not even any paperwork. There could not have been more of a contrast between the two hospices. That much is certain.

Then, following my wife's death, and before her memorial service two months later, I had a lot of time to reflect on the experience, even though my head was clouded by my grief and exhaustion. The first thing that came to mind was just how obscene the dying process was, evidently—I knew that our system was flawed, but I didn't know to what extent. I wondered why it had to be so difficult and fraught with problems. I wondered why such a simple thing, such a natural process, an essential rite of passage, seemed encumbered with such a complex mishmash of countervailing forces. Ideally, I imagine most people would hope to die at home, if they could, in a practical, straightforward manner: just a few adjustments to the home, and a few dedicated professionals on hand, not much else. The active dying phase lasts such a brief time, no more than a couple of weeks at most, for most people. So then why all the layers of infrastructure? Why all the assisted living facilities, all the nursing homes, the hospices? Well, it seems many can't be bothered to give their loved ones a decent send-off in the first place. To fill the gaps, there's a whole industry out there to do it all for you, in a way that buffers you from any of the ugliness or inconvenience that might arise. But at a price, of course. And it's big business, my friend, I assure you.

I know for sure that I don't want to die in the cold, sterile environments that these institutions typify, or, for that matter, any kind of medical or hospital setting. That's my worst nightmare, if given a choice. When, exactly, did we start institutionalizing and industrializing our deaths? How did it happen? I'm sure very gradually and imperceptibly, as things go. But let's try to get back to the good old-fashioned death of the past, my friend. The more humane option.

Then, on the opposite extreme, there's the rather disconcerting, countervailing notion that death needs to occur in the shadows, that we have to be in almost complete denial of it. Of course, death is a frightening thing to face, but let's try to have at least one foot on firm ground when it comes. The goal should be dying with dignity —to have some power or control over your own destiny. And the fact that we have very few options for deaths that are of the premeditated variety, that provides an option for assisted death, by qualified professionals, is abominable. It's enough to drive a significant number of people to unnecessarily complicated and ugly suicides. Ones that don't end well.

The dirty little secret, and hypocrisy, of today's health care system is that the majority of people who choose to die in their institutions die as a direct result of orders that their doctors have written—either carried out by others who are professionally subordinate to them, or by the dying person's family. Nobody seems to want to take responsibility for it. In our case, for example, during my wife's active dying process, I was tasked with administering larger and more frequent doses of morphine to mitigate the pain and breathing difficulties she experienced—and likewise, to suppress the so-called 'death rattle', which, despite its actual medical innocuousness, causes so much dismay to anyone who might witness her apparent suffering. What they won't tell you is that you're essentially killing your loved one at the same time, with their covert and implicit consent. Nobody wants to talk about the reality of the situation, not even the hospice nurse who was coordinating my wife's care, at the very end. I asked her point-blank if my wife was about to die—the only reply I received was a little side-eye, as if to say 'we don't talk about those things'.

Surely, there's a better way to handle death head-on, so that loved ones can plan accordingly, so that they're prepared to do the best they can, no matter how unpredictable the circumstances might be. Given the current state of affairs, it was no wonder I felt so compelled to keep all the medications that were left over, after my wife died. In fact, there was an enormous amount of morphine and painkillers remaining, enough to kill an army. What does that say about the system? It meant that I couldn't and wouldn't trust them going forward, and that if I wanted, ultimately, to have some control over my own destiny and death, having these drugs available to me would give me the flexibility that I wouldn't otherwise likely have. Sad, isn't it? It shouldn't have to be that way. We should have some modicum of control over our own lives. Even if that means partial control, and/or collaboration with well-intentioned, uncuffed medical professionals.

Another thing these institutions don't tell you or prepare you for, despite the fact that they seem to have endless amounts of advice for everyone, is that after your loved one dies, that's just the beginning of a whole other journey that is just as exasperating and puzzling as the one I've just described. Of course, the focus is and should be on the one who is dying. The grief is primarily about the loss of that individual. That goes without saying. But what you learn, as the closest relative or survivor, is that once that person dies, and is presumably no longer suffering, *you* are the one, primarily, who will continue to take on whatever suffering's left. But, in contrast to your loved one, your pain and suffering will often be deliberately overlooked. It's only natural for people to turn away, after the death, so as not to be reminded of the whole unsavory affair. Especially a long, drawn-out death like my wife's. Five years of torture, almost on a daily basis. People need relief, and if they can, they won't be shy about taking it. But there is *no* escape for you. Everything you do for the time being, and into the foreseeable and indefinite future, will have tendrils reaching back over time to your loved one's illness and death. Think about how profoundly it will alter your life. How radically it'll change everything. Well, so be it—you're going to be pretty much on your own, from that point on, on this new, arduous journey.

Nevertheless, I can't tell you how many times I felt obliged to console *other* people throughout the entire process. Ironically, comfort and compassion from the very person who had the least amount to give, whose reservoir had run completely dry... And how little consolation I received. I'm not talking about the usual, polite formalities—or the performative necessities—certainly not the empty gestures. I'm talking about the kind that runs deep, that reaches down into the fathom of your very soul. The kind that can rattle you, even upset you, as a consequence. The kind that challenges you, makes you feel uneasy, but that might lead to something of real significance or value. The kind of interaction that *necessitates* bearing your soul, and all your deepest vulnerabilities. No, my friend, that was, and is, unfortunately, in very short supply, indeed. Even getting a good hug from someone is difficult. More often than not, you get the kind that feels distant, as if by embracing you, death is going to rub off on them.

Anyway. I guess I could go on and on and on. But I should tell you more about what happened with the first hospice—that complete disaster of an experience—the one that completely dumped us at our hour of greatest need. Yes, we had actually managed to arrange a meeting with an official from that hospice before they went ahead with their plans to abandon us. I didn't get into those details with you yet. I had to go on my own as my wife was then too ill to attend. I had insisted upon a discharge meeting, which is required by law, despite their continuing malfeasance. We thought that we might still be able to convince them that what they were doing was not only highly unprofessional and damaging to their institution, but wholly abusive and inappropriate, not to mention unethical and immoral; and if they still refused to manage a smooth transition from their institution to another, replacing their services with others of comparable depth and breath, there would be consequences. I was going to be direct and blunt about our demands and I wasn't going to be pulling any punches.

Strangely enough, at the appointed place and time, I was escorted into one of the hospice's conference rooms by an office assistant who seemed to understand and recognize what was going on—she insisted on meeting me and shaking my hand—going out of her way to acknowledge me in a manner that left no doubt about how badly she felt about our situation, as if to apologize for the institution's abhorrent attitude, without so much as saying so.

Needless to say, though, it was a very uncomfortable meeting as soon as it started, and quickly became heated. It was being chaired by another individual I had never met or heard of before. An administrator who, I discovered—in addition to his role at this meeting—was a psychologist, a former assistant head of a city health department, a grief counselor, and an ordained minister, all rolled into one. Quite the resumé. I learned more later, too. That he was a gay man, who had a partner who was currently very ill with AIDS, who likely only had a few more months to live. I also found out that the woman in the business office who had cancelled our oxygen order—who was conspicuously absent from this meeting—was also an ordained minister! I kid you not, my friend. You couldn't make this stuff up. Whatever the case, none of those professional, and presumably personal, attributes seemed, in any way, to foster an atmosphere of empathetic understanding. Quite the contrary.

The tone from the very beginning was hostile, and the administrator explicitly indicated, from the outset, that we would be discharged no matter what. By the time the meeting was drawing to a close, he repeated their position regarding a proper discharge—insisting that they were not going to follow through with the usual protocol that was required by law—and it would be up to me to arrange for everything in terms of providing for continuity of care. He concluded by accusing *me* of being hostile, and acting in bad faith—an utterly classic projection on his part—and denied that we even had a contract, despite the fact that I brought a signed hard copy with me to the meeting and presented it to him. A more thorough gaslighting couldn't have been carried out, particularly because it was obvious that they had been very careful not to invite any of the other professionals who were involved with my wife's care to the meeting as witnesses. In that moment, honestly, I wondered if I were trapped in some kind of nightmare, in some sort of alternate reality that I would surely wake up from, at any moment. But it was only too real, and the only response I could offer, by then, was to speak the whole, uncensored truth as I saw it—to point out how appalling and abysmal their attitude was, and how blatantly and egregiously they were transgressing the law with their malevolent practices, citing numerous examples from the regulatory code. And that they would be risking serious damage to themselves and their institution by carrying on this way. None of it seemed to matter to them, or made an impression, so I decided my work had concluded, and abruptly left the room, without any of the usual deference to social graces. You can imagine how angry and humiliated I felt! But I also felt stunned and numbed by their monstrous actions and attitudes. A grief counselor *and* an ordained minister! Can you believe that? No, most people wouldn't. But it just goes to show you—job description doesn't mean a thing, sometimes. Often, actually, on second thought.

Well, you would've thought that they might've thought a little more deeply about how they were treating us. If there was any client who they shouldn't have messed with, it was us. The first red flag they would've been wise to notice was that my wife was an attorney. Secondly, my father, as a physician, knew the ins and outs of the medical system, and could be consulted on all the finer points of the greater medical community and its regulations. Thirdly, I was very connected with the media, and my wife knew quite a few people in government who had positions of formidable power. We were very well connected to the professional community in general, with excellent personal and professional reputations.

When the word got out about how we were being treated by the hospice, it was as if a whole army appeared, ready to fight. Of course, there wasn't much to do in the immediate present, because my wife was very ill and dying and only had a couple more weeks to live. We had to concentrate on that and its aftermath first, including following through with the multitude of things you need to do after anyone dies. That alone is enough to keep you busy for months on end. Then there's the planning for the memorial service. Then trying to catch your breath again, before jumping back into the fray.

Yes, my friend, I had no choice but to address what had happened to us. I just couldn't let that kind of blatant abuse go unchallenged. And many of her family members, friends and colleagues felt the same. For a loved one to be unceremoniously dumped on the street and have to fend for themselves, as it were, was just too much. One of my wife's colleagues, her closest mentor, took on the legal aspect of the case pro bono. We made contact and strategized as to how we would put forth our complaint, and present it to the hospice and their attorneys. Negotiations went on for weeks and months, until we finally got a meeting with the C.E.O. of the hospice. A meeting just between her and me, with only my attorney present. No other personnel charged with taking detailed notes or recording the proceedings.

I was surprised to discover that the C.E.O., a woman who seemed more focused on the business side of things, naturally, was by far the most empathetic of all the hospice personnel we had met, up to that point. Just the fact that she invited us for a one-on-one spoke volumes. Her attitude and demeanor only reinforced that. She seemed truly caring and trustworthy, and clearly upset and alarmed hearing about the treatment we had received under her watch. She claimed that she had not been aware of the maltreatment, and wondered how it had been possible in the first place. She was concerned that knowledge of it hadn't managed to make its way up to her. She didn't once question our version of the facts. But then she seemed to veer off course a bit, and seemed more focused on how they could learn from the experience, how her institution could evolve and grow, so that nothing like what we experienced could ever happen to anyone ever again.

My attorney insisted that we all take a moment to acknowledge the human cost of what happened, and suggested I have the opportunity to speak to her about how devastating the experience was to me, and my wife's survivors; specifically, how hurtful and traumatic it was, and how the institution we entrusted with her very life had failed us. Just how much of a cardinal sin it was, in my opinion, for the institution to act like it did. She seemed to be truly moved by my testimony, and responded with sympathy. Then when attention was finally turned back to plausible and potential remedies, she disclosed that after being contacted by our attorneys, she had launched her own in-depth internal investigation—hiring an independent legal team—who discovered that what we had claimed was, indeed, what had appeared to have happened, as far as they could tell. Apparently they did a very thorough job and essentially confirmed that our version of facts was accurate, including the claims regarding multiple violations of the law. So, in the end, from her point of view, the only thing left to decide was how we were going to be compensated for our pain and suffering.

That, oddly enough, was the stickiest part, because in the civil domain, the law focuses mostly on monetary damages as far as any kind of compensation or restitution is concerned. The best you can ask for, truthfully, is some kind of reckoning in purely economic terms. Of course, that was beside the point, as far as we were concerned. That wasn't what we were looking for. But it was how the law saw it, and had to see it. Even though I could've asked for monetary damages, there simply were no provisions for 'pain and suffering', or its equivalent. Which meant that the damages would be limited to a trifling amount of money only. That wouldn't make any real difference, even symbolically, either to us or as a future deterrent to them. I really didn't want to waste more precious time adding up what amounted to pennies, that essentially meant nothing to any of us. That was never the point of the exercise.

What really disturbed me and shook me was the abuse they so casually lobbed at us with seeming impunity. The unethical and immoral treatment that we received at the hands of the two administrators most at fault—individuals who were more than willing to deprive my wife of oxygen, her very lifeblood, who seemed to have no qualms about literally snuffing us out, and kicking us to the curb, just to save a few bucks—was, in my view, unforgivable. The willful callousness and cold maliciousness of both individuals would've sent shivers through the most hardened sociopath. They were evil incarnate, as far as I was concerned.

I'm not joking, my friend. That's how it felt at the time. And it was especially distressing to learn that they hadn't suffered any consequences as a result of the mistreatment we endured. On the contrary, both parties were still employed by the hospice, as if nothing improper had occurred. There was still a massive abyss between how these two staff members were represented to the public—what their professional status and qualifications entitled them to, and whether or not they were still in good standing and privileged to practice—and what we knew of them and had experienced, the glaring hypocrisy with which they conducted themselves. So, it became increasingly clear to us that our main goal, if we decided to keep a dialogue going, was to be certain that nothing even remotely comparable to our experience at the hospice would ever happen to anyone, ever again.

The most obvious way to avoid another calamity like ours, in the long run, would require the hospice to do some serious soul searching—to have them carefully scrutinize the current policies and structure of their institution so that they would understand how such abuses could've happened in the first place—and then to commit to some fundamental changes to staff and structure so that a system of checks and balances would be in place to guard against the possibility of future fiascos. In the short term, however, it would be crucial to remove both of the offending practitioners in our case without delay.

And that, in sum, was what was agreed upon. We were happy, and the hospice was happy. And all the attorneys were happy, on both sides of the aisle. We all agreed that that would be a reasonable approach to the problem at hand, and the controversy would be resolved. A few weeks later, we were informed that all the agreed upon changes had been implemented, and that the individuals had been permanently removed from their positions. They didn't get into the details of what had happened to the staff members, other than to say they were no longer working for the hospice and were, therefore, not going to be causing any more harm. Other than those generalities, they claimed they couldn't disclose any other details due to employment law confidentiality provisions. We would just have to trust that they took decisive action.

Well, maybe you're not as naïve as we were. Can you guess what happened next? Well, we couldn't be sure of the facts, of course. But we did find out that the woman from the business office had, indeed, been dismissed from her position. But she had also moved back to her home state only to take the exact same type of position at an institution there. And as for the man who had led the discharge meeting, it turned out that he had been just a few months shy from a conventional retirement, and merely retired early, without any additional penalties. He retained his full retirement benefits and only had to forfeit a few month's pay. I couldn't believe it! I was mortally offended, to tell you the truth. The so-called punishments seemed almost like rewards, to me. I was very disappointed, to say the least. And angry! But what in heaven's name were we going to do about it?

I suppose we could've tracked the guilty parties down to apply more pressure, to report them to the professional organizations that they belonged to, for ethical violations, or something along those lines. But our attorney advised us against that, on the grounds that it probably wouldn't lead to anything tangible, regrettably. So, the only other option we had was to focus our energy back on the institution they had been employed by—the hospice—to pay a more significant and meaningful penalty. What other options did we have? There *was* no other target. We ended up reporting the whole despicable affair to the appropriate overseers and regulators, both the state health department and the hospice's accreditors.

Each entity opened an investigation, but it took another year until they finally reported the results to us. Guess what? In truly top-notch bureaucratic fashion, both institutions determined that they had 'no finding' to offer from the inquiries! In hindsight, I guess we could've predicted that kind of response. Yet, it was unexpected, because the hospice had *admitted* fault, had admitted that they violated the law. Nonetheless, it appeared as if nothing was going to be done about it.

That's when I lost all hope, in the sense of ever getting any satisfaction from pursuing the matter any further. We had put so much effort into it already, only to be told it meant nothing. When we reported the findings to our circle of allies, nobody could believe it. They were just as astonished and incensed as we were. I was truly touched by their reaction—by the empathy they showed, by their expressions of solidarity, and their willingness to continue to help. To help press forward with any other strategic options that remained open to us, to achieve a meaningful remedy —or at least some kind of closure.

The first suggestion came because of my connections to the media world. An acquaintance of mine was an investigative journalist at a local news station, and our story was exactly the kind that makes for a good, juicy story. It would've been easy to initiate the whole thing, at a minimum of effort. But then I began to wonder what it would accomplish, what it would do for *us*, either my wife or me. It might make a dent in the hospice's bottom line, or damage their reputation, saving others the pain of our miserable experience. The fact was, my wife wouldn't benefit from it, obviously, and it could very well expose me to further litigation if the hospice's legal team felt like pressing the issue. Reporting them to the authorities the first time took them by surprise and caught them off guard, and continuing one more step in that direction was definitely not going to sit well with them.

Then, because of our standing as a couple in the community, many of our supporters suggested we contact some of the powerful political operators they knew, to put more pressure on the hospice, to force them to publicly acknowledge their mistakes and make improvements and amends to the greater community. That also seemed like a great idea, but, again, I wondered how it was going to work for us—how much effort would be involved, and how long it would take to get any results—which, of course, were anything but guaranteed. That's what it came down to in the end. How was whatever was under consideration going to benefit us directly, especially because I was already feeling so exhausted and defeated from my previous experiences. So, I eventually passed on all of it, so that I could focus on doing the necessary grieving and healing and moving on. I think it was the right decision for me at the time. But I really had to swallow my pride to grudgingly step away from it.

There's a certain powerful and exhilarating feeling you get when you go all-in for a righteous political fight. But you should also be cautious and put it into perspective, and weigh it against the rest of the factors that enter into the calculus, in order to feel comfortable diving into that kind of long, drawn-out battle. You never want it to be decided upon based on ego alone. Then you have to consider other people's egos: sometimes they want you to do things because they're going to receive a substantial benefit from it, oftentimes without having to sacrifice much of their own. That was how it was beginning to feel for me. It began to feel like anything I did was going to benefit others inversely proportionately to the potential benefits I would receive. So, I let it go. I let the two individuals at fault go, too. What good would it do, ultimately, to press forward with some kind of action against them? The only real option was to report them to their professional ethics boards. But one was already retired and probably not going to be practicing again, and the other left town and seemed to be keeping a very low profile. There really wasn't that much to grab onto. That, in itself, was enough to discourage me, say what you will.

The only other thing left hanging for me, that really seemed to nag at my conscience, was the uneasy feeling I continued to stomach when I considered how these types of disputes are typically handled, in general. There were such serious violations of ethical and moral principles involved in our case, and I couldn't believe that there was no real mechanism in place, beforehand, to deal with the controversy more equitably. I wasn't so naïve as to think that you could legislate morality, but surely something has to be better than the status quo. I mean, we do legislate morality to a certain extent. There are so-called 'crimes of moral turpitude' that do often lead to real consequences, like taking professional licenses away from offenders. But that was, as far as I understood it, the limit of what you could reasonably do. It may sound overly dramatic to say so, but the kind of treatment my wife got during her final days, seemed just as bad to me as the worst kind of crimes that *can* be committed. It *felt* like murder to me. It *felt* like robbery. It certainly was abuse and malfeasance, at the very least, and a prime example of the kind of extreme and callous disregard for the dignity and integrity of the individual that a professional or an institution can perpetrate behind the scenes, with, apparently, the tacit blessing of even more powerful institutions and cultural forces. So perhaps we *should* consider criminalizing certain extremes of unethical behavior? Or even some types of immoral behavior, in exceptional circumstances. Yes, I can hear the chorus of objections. It *is* dangerous territory. But what'll happen if we don't, when we absolutely must? In our case, it wouldn't have mattered that much, particularly on the grand scale of things. But when you consider other imminent, more global threats to humankind, whether carried out by an individual or a majority population, our ultimate survival might depend on it. But I guess I'll let the politicians and attorneys figure that out. It's over my head, that's for sure. Certainly beyond my area of expertise.

Anyway, enough of that sob story. It's so dispiriting and depressing... Hey! Would you mind doing me a favor? Just go over to the front door and make sure it's shut. Make sure the bolt's in place. I want to show you something before you leave today. Before you go back to New York. Sorry... My head's feeling a little hazy today. If you don't mind, can you double-check the lock before I continue? You never know who's roaming the halls out there. Not that I usually feel at risk—it's just an annoying habit of mine. You needn't worry about it. There's absolutely nothing of value in here. The main thing is that we have adequate control over who's coming and going.

Now see that bureau over there? Yes, head over to it and look up on the top shelf. There's an oval-shaped cardboard box sitting on it. Yes, that's the one. Can you bring it over to me? Thank you. I appreciate how, when you're with me, you're always game for whatever comes your way. That's a rare quality, my friend. People are so guarded, in general, and harbor immediate suspicion, especially these days. Can you blame them? Defensive for good reason, no doubt. But if you can work through that and still maintain a sense of naïveté despite that, I'd say you're doing pretty well, and feeling pretty strong inside.

Well, here it is! I've been saving this for our last day. Not everyone gets this far. But if you do, you get to see the special thing I've been hanging on to for years now. You know what this is? Yes, of course! It's a fedora! Not everyone gets that specific. But it's not just an ordinary hat, my friend. No, sir! Can you guess where it comes from? I'm not talking geographically. I'll give you a hint. It's from a very well-known, classic movie that you've probably seen at some point in your life. There you go again, exceeding my expectations. Yes, you nailed it! And do you remember the glass case down in Casablanca, too? Yes, this is the missing piece from the case. Inside our usual meeting place. And it is *the* original fedora from the movie. The only one left known to exist. Now, I'd better explain what I mean by that. If there is any one iconic object from *Casablanca*, with the possible exception of the piano that Sam plays, it's the fedora that Humphrey Bogart wears in the movie. It's particularly conspicuous in the final scene just before Ingrid Bergman's character Ilsa gets on the plane for Lisbon and ultimate freedom. Remember that scene? When she and Laszlo get on the plane together? And Rick has to practically force her to join Laszlo on it? To escape from the Germans, who are closing in and just about to arrest them? Yes, that's quite an exhilarating scene, don't you think? The very moment Rick finally takes decisive action: he finally takes sides, unequivocally, but loses the absolute love of his life as a consequence, probably forever. That's how the movie ends, and I guess we'll never know what happened after that.

But you might wonder how I, of all people, have possession of this important artifact of American movie history? Well, you can say I'm only its most recent custodian. Before that, it was in the hands of our good friend the barkeeper, from Casablanca! Yes! I think I told you about my past in the movie business. Back in L.A. And the fact that our other friend, the security guard, used to be one of the most notable prop masters in town. Yes, you might not have suspected it, but he probably has more movie credits than most of us combined—certainly more than me. And he had assembled quite the collection of materials over the years, I can assure you. He had quite a few items that were used actively, as part of his business, but also many that he had acquired and compiled over the years. Either retired from his own collection, or obtained through various means, on the open market. Or at least that's how I assume he acquired the fedora. But you can imagine how much it's worth, nowadays? Monetarily, of course, but just take a moment to recognize the cultural value it holds. It should probably be in a museum somewhere, but…

Well, it isn't, obviously. It's right here with me, in my safekeeping. Look, I'm not going to second-guess my friends at Casablanca. He has always been the most consummate professional, and is undoubtedly an honest man. There's no reason to question that. But, the story, apparently, turned out to be a little stickier than I first thought. Though its provenance has never been questioned, there is some ongoing controversy as to whom its rightful owner is. There are rumors that the authorities were looking for it.

As it happens, there were quite a few fedoras associated with the movie, and even with Humphrey Bogart personally. There were at least two or three made for the movie itself, and Bogart was known to own a few himself. Why not? I mean, he does look great in one. And it just fits, somehow. I think people would've been surprised to see him *without* one. So, even going about his usual business, he could often be seen wearing one around town. It wasn't at all unusual. But you know how it goes, after so many years go by... They probably got all mixed up, somehow. Before you knew it, you didn't know which one was which. But I assure you, *this one* has been authenticated. That's the story I've heard, and that's the one I'm sticking to. Of course, if anyone asked me about it, I could just say it's something I inherited from my father, or something prosaic like that. I mean, how could you actually tell? There's nothing in-and-of-itself that could disprove my claim. No special markings or labels or defects. Just an old fedora, nothing more or less.

Well, it was sitting there in the case with everything else they had from the movie—the bow tie, the brooch, the champagne glasses—and that's exactly when we started hearing rumors that the authorities were looking for it. I think it really started to spook my friend, the bartender. And until he could sort it all out, he asked me if I could hang onto it for him, and keep it in a safe place, for the time being. I was flattered that he entrusted it to me. I had no real reason to turn him down. I trusted him, too—implicitly—and assume that whatever he decides to do with it, ultimately, will be the right thing to do. But I've been hanging onto it for far longer than I expected, and as far as I know, nobody's even asking about it anymore. We're in a kind of limbo state with it. We don't want to go volunteering information about it publicly, but we also don't want to put it back in the case, either. So, while I'm keeping it on the down-low for now, I might as well put it to good use. Every once in a while, when the occasion calls for it, I like to take it out for a ride, so to speak. Just perch it on my head, to remember how empowering it feels. It makes me feel like a hero when I'm wearing it, honestly. Particularly if I feel like I've done an especially good job with something, or have had some kind of noteworthy, positive influence on things.

I mean, what else are we supposed to do with it? We don't even know for sure who actually owns it, at this point. Not definitively. It certainly isn't mine, I definitely know that. My friend the bartender can make a decent claim to it, but perhaps he doesn't want to be associated with it anymore. Or any of the go-betweens, including his friend, the security guard, who once had it in his possession... I guess if someone had *really* wanted it, they would've managed to keep it, in the first place. Most people who go by the case in Casablanca probably don't even realize that all the other things in it are actually the *real* articles from the movie, too. I could just as well put a fake fedora in there and it wouldn't make any difference at all to anyone, no matter how one might perceive them. It's become a little bit of a private secret that only the bartender, the security guard, and I are aware of. I have to admit that I'm a little concerned that I might be caught one day, and thrown into jail for it. But will anyone really care by then? It's not like the majority of people care about the movie anymore —any controversy that could've happened in the past, concerning its rightful owner, might just be met with total indifference today, for all I know.

And who would it be returned to, even if we managed to figure out its rightful owner? Everyone associated with the movie is probably dead now. It would have to be returned to an estate of some sort, or whichever entity could make the best case for laying claim to it. Or it could be donated to a museum somewhere. I'm quite sure that determining its ownership, conclusively, is a very murky business by now. So, perhaps the best course is to do nothing. To leave it alone. To keep it here, with me. I think it serves a far more useful purpose here. It inspires me. It motivates me to continue with my work as Witness/Confidant. If I get caught with it, well, so be it. I can make up all sorts of plausible excuses, or claim ignorance. That's probably a pretty good strategy— because why would I, of all people, have it, in the first place? It doesn't seem too likely, does it? I don't know—I just know that I'm in the unenviable, *and* perhaps enviable, position of being stuck with it. Please don't tell anyone about this. Or tell me that you're involved in law enforcement, in some way... Well, even if you are, it's too late now, isn't it?

I may be wearing it now, but even when I'm not, I kind of imagine it on my head. Especially when I'm at Casablanca doing my work. That's not to say that the work isn't being done all the time. The job requires that you live, breathe and eat it, no matter how you feel, or how discouraging it might be. The fedora, whether I'm wearing it or not, symbolizes for me the work that must be done at all times, and that must continue into the indefinite future. I guess I identify with Rick from the movie—but when you really think about it, I wonder if he's really the character I should be associating myself with. If you remember, he was quite the cynic, and even a bit of an opportunist, with a huge chip on his shoulder. Not an entirely savory character. A good fence-straddler, certainly seriously morally-compromised, at least it seems that way to me. Putting in a good deed when it's convenient. Not exactly reaching out for opportunities.

Perhaps a better example, for me, lies with the Victor Laszlo character, the more traditional hero, who not only seems to have his principles and priorities straight, but has managed to live every moment of his life adhering to his noble, self-imposed ideals and goals. Always making the right decisions out in the open, as it were, and having the gumption to pull it off, sometimes against all odds. I think that's the kind of figure everyone would want to live up to, but would, realistically, fall far short of. One would have to be exceptionally courageous and gifted to end up in the same rarified air as Laszlo.

There's even a parallel in the actors' real lives. While Humphrey Bogart was the better known of the two, a bona fide American movie star, with vast influence and power, and by all accounts the typical Hollywood liberal, he seemed to balk when his career was on the line, and would only go so far politically. Paul Henreid, in contrast, was in exile from Nazi-occupied Europe and was deeply opposed to fascism in all its forms, both during World War II and in the McCarthy Era, when he was blacklisted. He certainly suffered the professional consequences of his political actions. Even in terms of personality, they contrasted sharply: Bogart, the driftless, difficult one, early in life, always a bit irascible and inconsistent, a problem drinker and loner by nature, lucky to have found a profession and some key individuals in his life that protected him from an undisciplined, self-destructive life; meanwhile, Henreid, although from a privileged background, was always quick to challenge authority; was steadfastly loyal to his ideals, loved ones and associates; was the kind of guy you'd want on your side in a fight; and by all accounts a solid man, married to his wife for more than fifty years. Those personalities and backgrounds really were reflected in their characters. But there's a very famous scene near the end of *Casablanca* that illustrates perfectly the differences between the reluctant hero and the hero who fully embraces his destiny.

Rick asks Laszlo, point-blank, whether he thinks everything he does to resist the Germans is really worth it, in the end. Laszlo replies, incredulously, that he has no choice, that it's like breathing itself—and just like if we stop breathing, the world will die if they stop fighting. Rick replies with another cynical comment, wondering if we all wouldn't be better off if we just allowed the world go to hell, and that it might be better if we just put it out of its misery. Laszlo replies by calling Rick on his hypocrisy, implying that he sounds like a man who doesn't believe in his own convictions, and that he would be betraying his own heart if he followed through with such a cynical attitude. He asserts that we all have a choice: to either embrace or reject the goodness or evil that each of us has in our own hearts. Rick acknowledges the point, but rather tepidly. That's when Laszlo goes in for the kill. He continues to question Rick's attitude, and asks him if he thinks he can ever truly escape from himself or his ideals, what he feels deep down inside, and how fruitless it would be. Laszlo seems to know Rick better than Rick does himself, and realizes that Rick will eventually be forced to choose one way or the other. And, of course, that's what happens at the end of the movie. Rick sacrifices the love of his life for the greater good. Ironically, the characters have suddenly changed places: Laszlo flees to safety, and will have to continue the fight from a safe distance, while Rick remains in the thick of it. We're not sure what happens after that, but we know for sure that Rick is a changed man. That he will have to fulfill his destiny. You get the feeling that he will carry on where Laszlo leaves off.

Like I said, it doesn't matter so much whether I'm actually wearing the fedora or not. But I guess I told you the *Casablanca* story for a reason. It wasn't just random chatter. I guess, similar to Rick and Laszlo, I'm at a similar juncture in my life. The fact is, we're all at a similar juncture right now. All of us together! But it's not the Germans we're fighting, it's ourselves! It's a fight for our very own survival! How are we going to pull it off? What are you going to do about it? That's not meant as a rhetorical question —but, then again, I won't put you on the spot, and actually ask you to answer it, presently. It's a huge question, and not so easy to answer. I'll give you time to think about it. As for myself, I know that I've fallen far short of what I can do, year after year. I'm certainly not up to Laszlo's standard—that's for sure—even though I've fought the good fight a good number of times, albeit concerning issues on a much smaller scale. I didn't even have much success with relatively minor problems. You might say that I'm more in Rick's league, before his transformation. A man in waiting. I'm going about doing my thing sneakily. Behind the scenes. And with my own brand of pessimism. Or would you say cynicism? I try my best not to be misanthropic. But will I ever be a Laszlo? Will any of us be Laszlos? Or even Ricks, for that matter, before or after the conversion. Still not sure. Not all of us can be cut from that cloth—be that extraordinary. But we all need to do the very best that we're capable of, if we're going to come out the other end intact.

I admit I've had my failures along the way. Maybe it's too late for me to make any sort of meaningful difference. Maybe I just need to get out of the way at this point. But what will it take to finally wake everyone up, to shake people out of their complacency, to force them to take drastic action? Do people have to be literally at death's door before they decide they're ready to throw themselves into the fire? Even then, some will still prefer to perish. But there's no doubt that there are people who *will* rise to the occasion! Look, for example, at those young high school students down in Florida. The survivors of the mass shooting down there. They certainly inspire me! They're not even full-fledged adults yet, yet they aren't going to take it anymore. They rose up, and are making a real difference every day. They've already become heroes, in my book, and on their own terms. Yes, it took a bloodbath, and the tragic deaths of their schoolmates to drive them to action, but look what they've already accomplished in such a short period of time.

Was it only a coincidence they just so happened to go to that particular high school? Was the attack completely random? Carried out by a random, deranged madman from a nearby community? Was it too easy for this young man, who had a hidden hatred in his heart, to have such easy access to such lethal assault weapons? Was it surprising to learn how deeply steeped he was in a subculture that lionized and celebrated virulent forms of racism, homophobia, anti-Semitism—you name it—any variety of bigotry?

Was it an accident he ended up slaughtering completely innocent people, who had absolutely no beef with him whatsoever? No, he was a cold-blooded killer whose heroes were mass murderers, and who made a point of carving swastikas onto the magazines of his guns. No, my friend, the chances were nil that *all of that* was completely random and coincidental. Yet there's a deeper implication, one we might want to pay more attention to. Do you happen to know what the name of the high school is, where the shooting took place? It's named after another hero of mine, who could see things on a much broader scale, earlier on than most. Who had the foresight and gumption to start addressing the ultimate problem facing humanity, which I've really only tangentially alluded to, so far.

Do you know anything about Marjory Stoneman Douglas? No? Well, she was a remarkable woman. She was born in 1890, and needless to say, was subjected to the many limitations that came with the gender roles of the time. But she wasn't the type of person who accepted her fate willingly, when fate meant that she would have to live a compromised life, well within the customary norms of the time. She was born a feminist, and would not limit herself to what society expected of her. She was a precocious, talented child from an unconventional family, whose mother, unfortunately, died prematurely from breast cancer. After receiving a good college education, and after a brief marriage, she struck out on her own, establishing herself as an enterprising journalist in an era when that type of opportunity was mostly closed to women. At the same time, she served with the American Red Cross in Paris during World War I. Subsequently, she had a second career as a creative writer, publishing short stories in popular magazines like *The Saturday Evening Post*. She had also become politically active, taking part in the women's suffragist and civil rights movements, among others. That alone would have secured her reputation as an influential and noteworthy person in anyone's book, but there was still more to come.

In the latter stages of her life, she reinvented herself once again, in 1947, at the age of fifty-seven, publishing a groundbreaking book, *The Everglades: River of Grass*, about the Florida Everglades, which she is most well-known for. It predated Rachel Carson's *Silent Spring* by fifteen years, and although it is a lesser-known work, it's nonetheless considered one of the early classics of the environmental conservation movement. She made a solid case for preserving the Everglades on its own merit, and against any further commercial development that might cause it more harm. If that weren't enough, in 1969, at seventy-nine, she founded 'Friends of the Everglades', a grassroots organization that put her environmental vision into action. These were her crowning achievements, and if it weren't for her dogged and determined activism, the Everglades, as we know it, probably wouldn't exist today. She was able to succeed against all odds and very powerful forces—an absolute warrior, in that respect. Thank god she lived to be so old, and was able to keep on fighting. She eventually succumbed at the ripe old age of one hundred eight. One of her closest friends remarked that death was the only thing that could finally 'shut her up', and that, furthermore, 'the silence was terrible'. Yes, that silence was terrible, and continues to be terrifying—particularly because we haven't seemed willing to fully embrace just how serious the threat is to the Earth, and, therefore, how our very existence is at stake.

Who's going to fill the void? Who's going to take the place of the great activists from the past, the leaders who we so desperately need now? I know there are passionate people out there who are working on it very diligently, on a small scale; but there must be someone, or perhaps a handful of people, with enough influence and power, with access to vast material resources, who can step in and lead us toward earthly salvation. Some person or entity that is charismatic enough to get us all lined up, fully united, so that there's absolutely no question or doubt about where we're headed. So that a resounding majority of us will gladly comply and zealously follow. Our very survival depends on it...

Who's that young Swedish girl? What's her name again? You know, the one who led her classmates on a hunger strike, to call attention to the urgency of facing climate change head on? To bring greater focus to it, to treat it as the emergency that it truly is? She's become a worldwide phenomenon. There are children across the entire globe going on similar such strikes, or equivalent acts of civil disobedience... It's funny how full circle it all is; because it turns out that this young woman's inspiration and drive to become an activist blossomed when she first learned about her spiritual predecessors, and activist counterparts, some of whom were those very same teenagers who had their own profound awakening after the Marjory Stoneman Douglas High School shooting. And she's been awarded the Rachel Carson Prize, an environmental award, for her work. What a strange and wondrous world we live in! How perfectly fitting...

So, here we are, my friend. Just you and me in this little apartment downtown. In our very own version of hell. For better or worse, Vegas is finally where I found my home, both literally and spiritually. Before I got here, I admit I felt a little lost. I was focused on some important things, yes, but not really aware of exactly where I needed to go—what I was chasing after, what I was closing in on, and where I should be concentrating my attention. Admittedly, much of it seemed beyond my control; but some of it was my own fault, simply a consequence of my own shortcomings and shortsightedness. For not comprehending what was missing. I finally realized, after years of flailing about, that my focus was, paradoxically, much too restrictive and modest in scale, despite what my experience was telling me.

What was missing, and what was critical to my new insight and understanding, was the realization that all the problems I had been facing, struggling with and failing to resolve in the past, can be traced back to—in one way, shape, or form—the ultimate questions we're facing now: first, how we're going to manage to save ourselves from escalating global warming and total environmental catastrophe; and second, how we're going to usher in a new world order. One that's guided, first and foremost, by age-old principles that we've always valued and aspire to live by, but so far haven't had the will to put into practice. We've let our reality, our culture and society, slowly go off course. It seems like we've lost our balance—and been hijacked—to serve the interests of an elite, selfish few, who manipulate us with their clever tricks, that only compound the myths, inequity, and division that are tearing us apart. We need to reacquaint ourselves with the basic values of truth, fairness, and cooperation, and break free of our dependence on any sort of religious, economic, or legal system that binds us to carnal or spiritual slavery. Every other major issue depends on achieving these goals, and the greatest obstacle ahead is figuring out how to get there.

Quite the challenge, my friend. It seems completely overwhelming, and perhaps unattainable. But we might not have an alternative. We're going to have to eventually learn how to live *with* nature, not against it. I think the Stoics, for example, had some pretty good ideas, from thousands of years ago, that could apply very well today. Maybe we should adopt some of their practices and strategies? First, they believed that we're a part of nature, not apart from it. They believed that what's good for nature is ultimately good for us. That if we live virtuously—with wisdom, courage, self-restraint, and justly—good things *must* follow. Even if we fail miserably, my friend, the attempt will still have been worth it. But, if we manage to make great strides, just imagine the potential! How transformative it could be.

That might sound crazy and utopian, but why not try? A monumental problem needs a revolutionary solution, after all... Yet, let's bring it back down to the human scale. As far as individuals are concerned, what can we do? What's my role going to be? What's your role going to be? I can't say I've figured it out for myself yet, to be honest. But we'll all need to work on what each of us is going to do. Some will play big roles. Others small. But every individual will have to find their place in the scheme— just the right place—that will be decided by necessity. You'll just need to step into it—try it on, so to speak.

But first, we'll need to cultivate a deeper awareness. We're not even *close* to attaining that goal, my friend. Obviously. Then we're going to have to act with a brand of courage and tenacity that we've never had to muster before in the history of the mankind. Which is clearly the more difficult part of the plan. Yet, in theory, it's really that simple. You'd imagine, presumably, that everybody'd be on board with it. But, no, my friend, human beings are mysterious, complicated, and, most of all, stubborn! Yet, at some point in everyone's life, even in the heart of the most perverted, malevolent soul, there will be a reckoning. Everybody's going to be forced to see the truth, to see what's truly going on, even if you're not actively looking for it, or looking very closely.

Yes, I believe so. I've seen it with my own eyes, in my own experience. At Casablanca. If only it were every day, and every hour! I'm quite certain that I'm going to keep on witnessing it more and more. People can only take so much until it all comes crashing down. Things change constantly—they can't stay the same forever. We're all going to be forced to become foolish idealists, sooner or later, if we're going to prevail. We're going to have to exert every ounce of energy and influence we have left, that hasn't been trampled on and stamped out yet, despite the enormous obstacles that stand in our way.

Are you with me, my friend? Are you ready for the challenge? If you aren't, if you're not capable of rising to the occasion, if you're not able to change, or if you actively resist, you're going to be part of the problem, and the rest of us will have to find clever ways to work around you. But that's okay. Because it's still in our interest to help you out, and we're only too glad to do it, despite your flaws. Ha ha!! No, we won't shame you, or anything so distasteful as that. That would be cruel and counterproductive. But we might ask you, politely, to step aside. I mean, no one, not even the Earth itself, can escape the law of entropy. No one or no thing. We're all contributing, more or less equally, to our own demise—that's certain—but let's try not to encourage it prematurely. Let's try to maintain a certain level of sanity. It just might be the last thing we have to hold onto. Desperation is so unseemly. Let's try to avoid that. But distraction—alone—can be almost as bad. It's possible that while the world dies, we'll all be so very, very busy pretending that it can't happen. But if we wake up in time and keep our eyes on the prize—start to genuinely cherish the Earth, like the living, breathing organism it is, the mother of all mothers—we'll not only care for her, but for ourselves, and everything under the sun, as a natural consequence.

Yes, I know, that all seemed to come out of the blue, to rush out all at once. I understand. Because it came to me like that, too—

culminating after a much longer period of time—when it all finally clicked. It came to me in bits and pieces, after experiencing a number of things that seemed unrelated to each other at first. But if you really look at it, analyze it all beneath the surface, you'll find exactly what I found, in the end.

Why do we suddenly find ourselves in such a precarious position? How did the Earth find itself in the state it's in? Was it the result of natural consequences, the natural course of events, something we had nothing to do with and have no control over? Can we blame it on some outside influence? No, of course not. We can only blame ourselves for getting into this mess. But when we go looking for causes, or for who to blame, we tend to point our fingers away from ourselves, and towards other explanations. Surely it must be *other* people who are responsible for our predicament. Well, the truth is, it's the sum total of all of us, past and present. That's a fact. Some of us have done better than others... If you scrutinize any individual closely, you're likely to find, on average, someone rather innocuous, on the whole. Contributing, yes, but in minor ways. Not to say that all those minor contributions don't add up...

But who are the *real* culprits, the *real* offenders? Who's truly responsible for what's going on on the grand scale of things? You know the saying 'power corrupts, and absolute power corrupts absolutely'? I think there's a lot of truth to that. And what is the one commodity in the world that most easily puts one in a position of power? Yes, my friend, it's obvious! Money, and its earthly counterpart, natural resources. Whoever holds the lion's share of it holds the reins. Government, of course, but also a whole range of other entities who have historically amassed huge sums of capital by investing in private corporations on the stock market. Essentially making more money off the money they already have, without having to work for it. The very same people who have enriched themselves, if you carefully trace it all the way back to

268

the dawn of the Industrial Age, by consuming—that is, burning off —an obscenely massive amount of fossil fuel.   But are these entities beholden or indebted anymore, in any meaningful way, to the general populace and their broader interests?   To the very people who consented to their existence in the first place?   I'm afraid not, my friend. By and large, no.

There was a time when we weren't yet aware of global warming and didn't understand how climate change would affect us.   Remember the carefree, good-old-days of the Industrial Revolution?   Forget about all the filth and grime—the pollution, the disease, the poverty, the child labor—all that nasty stuff. Just try to recall those flush economic times.   The era of unlimited expansion, bull markets, and wealth untold.   Those were exhilarating days, my friend, but they're gone forever.   We've succeeded so spectacularly that we've managed to run ourselves into the ground, and we're well on the way to destroying ourselves. Why? Because our values never caught up with the technology, as I alluded to before.   We were all so busy accumulating riches that we forgot that there were other important aspects of life to consider... It's like an addiction, right?   No matter how much wealth is accumulated, certain people can never seem to have enough. They will always need more, and more, and... They just can't stop! You know, the typical billionaire out there. They just can't stop until they've gotten every last penny. They'll rape and pillage the world, literally destroy it, just to get their fix. Because there's always one more excuse for feeding their sick habits. And they're very skilled at covering their trails—offering up a few crumbs to the masses, every once in a while.

Why anyone would need more than a few million dollars in the bank is beyond me. Once you achieve that milestone, you can live a very full and satisfying life just off the interest alone! Well, you know why. It's the whole damned system that encourages this sort of unsavory obsession.   Our institutions, taken as a whole, have become a giant, runaway bureaucracy—rotten to the core—only concerned, like their corporate counterparts, with narrow self-interest and self-enrichment. In fact, almost every facet of it has become compromised, perhaps beyond repair or reform. That much is obvious to anyone who's still able to see clearly, anyone who's still able to perceive with unfaltering clarity—under the surface and through the cloudy murk—and aren't, likewise, blinded by their own prejudices.

I guess that sounds pretty cynical, but that's what I've experienced and accepted. That's what I saw and what I eventually understood. That's why I gave up everything and drifted out West. I guess, in all honesty, I felt defeated, and gave up. But, somehow, I ended up here in Las Vegas and I don't think it was happentance. No, not at all! We're at the epicenter of all that's wrong with the world, my friend. At least symbolically. Living in a city that's a phony monument to the supposed prosperity of our society—but, in truth, only a garish and vulgar symbol of its utter failures. How many people, do you think, come here with that in mind? Ha ha!! I'm sure you'd agree it's an exceedingly small number. So miniscule as to be insignificant... Well, that's *exactly* why I'm here! Where else might you find such a perfect focus for my mission, my act? You could argue that what I do here is pointless. But you've got to start somewhere. Somehow. You've got to start small... humbly... modestly. And this was just the right place for me, honestly. I might end up somewhere else later on, who knows? But I'm sure I'll be doing exactly the same kind of thing, perhaps in some other manner yet to be determined. That's what I'm trying to tell you, my friend. It's like reincarnation! I'm hoping you'll have a good go at it, too, sooner or later, in your own fashion. Maybe you've *already* gone there? Maybe you've *already* had more success than me. How would I know? But I certainly hope I have better and continuing success in the future. That's what I'm always aiming for.

What I really want to persuade people to do, is do whatever they can, wherever they can, with whatever tools they have, so that we all have a better chance at success. At coming out the other end with something worth living for. Yes, it might get very, very bad, before it gets better. But just *how* bad will depend on how we end up handling it. There's not much time left to get on the path to recovery! Everything we do from this point on will have to be wholeheartedly dedicated to preserving the Earth and its ecosystems, first and foremost. That's not to say that we'll all have to live like hermits, but each and everything thing we do must have *something* to do with these conservation and caretaking efforts. If people don't comply voluntarily, we're going to have to create and empower new institutions that will take on that commitment solemnly, with near-absolute power to enforce. It's not just going to happen magically. I mean, we can't even seem to handle a relatively minor pandemic competently. But if we can manage to achieve some sort of meeting of the minds... Once it's in place, we'd better well be slaves to it. It's the only way forward. To make progress toward a new beginning and a better kind of freedom.

I admit I've fallen short. That much is obvious. We all have. I know I've failed in the past and will continue to flounder, at times, in the future. But I'm still determined to move forward. To try to figure it out. I've already told you about some of what I've done, and how I was up against some exceptionally formidable adversaries. Much-too-powerful opponents for any individual dissenting voice to take on. And unfortunately, while I challenged these antagonistic forces and attempted to effect change from the inside, it was never enough. Now, when I look back on those battles, I realize how utterly naïve and futile my approach was. I threw myself haphazardly into the fight—not once recognizing that the path forward warranted a radical reframing of the problem, *and* a vastly expanded scale of reference. I didn't see the big picture at the time. I was caught up and preoccupied by the opposing mob. You can spend all your time and energy fighting these bureaucratic monsters, on their terms, and on their playing field; but the truth is, it's not in their interest to change—not then, not ever. Whatever I offered or suggested, no matter how reasonable or magnanimous, could *only* fall on deaf ears. That's how bureaucracies work. Look to history for proof. It's a never-ending series of gallant attempts and abject failures. I finally understood, after much agony and heartache, that their interests weren't the slightest bit aligned with mine. Their interests weren't even commensurate with what *they* purported them to be. In fact, as I said before, all they were interested in was... Well, you know... everything else be damned.

Of course, they'll always present a charitable façade to the public. And the public will, more often than not, fall for it. The propaganda is very persuasive, even when the public knows damn well, deep down, that they've been served very poorly by society's institution for decades. At a certain point, out of frustration, I just threw up my hands and shouted 'So be it!' I'd had enough, and decided that I couldn't continue going on that way any longer. I'm not sure whether I adopted this new orientation entirely consciously or not. But I knew for certain that a new course would be all but inevitable. And perhaps the only route left available for me, given the obstacles, was to address the bigger issues—even the most monumental one—at the personal level. That might seem like a contradiction. But I knew, instinctively, that I'd have more success if I connected on an intimate level, face-to-face, with people who seem willing to engage.

Of course, as a psychiatrist, that came naturally to me and dovetailed perfectly with my skills. I'll leave the macro-level politics to the folks who are only too thrilled to throw themselves into the tussle, who've already had success in that arena. Meanwhile, I'll keep working with individuals on the fringe. Hopefully, someday we'll meet somewhere in the middle. We'll squeeze the opposition out, and leave no quarter for the dark and insidious powers that are dead-set on collective self-destruction. Yes, my friend, it's a life-and-death battle right now. Currently, a war in slow motion.

We can continue as we have been... with blinders on. But we'll end up acting too little and too late. What's certain is, if we don't make some serious changes and commitments now, we're going to have absolute hell to pay in the not-too-distant future. Wouldn't you rather avoid that? Wouldn't you rather act responsibly, and proactively, to avoid the worst of it? The alternative is something none of us will hope to experience, I assure you. A very unpleasant potential reality. Yes, it'll take everything we've got. It will be exceedingly challenging and exhausting. We'll have to devote hour upon hour, day after day, week after week, every month of the year, every year upon decade, for as far as the eye can see, to the cause. Don't expect much rest for the weary. Yet the alternative's much more disconcerting. Only failure and death. Starvation and disease. Chaos and anarchy. It'll make the plague look like a casual stroll through the park. 'Quality of life' will only be a quaint, nostalgic notion from a bygone era, if we do manage to scrape by. Only you, and you alone, can decide whether you're willing to join us and actually do something about it—whether you join a picket line, or embody it in some other way in the course of your daily life. Better to have tried and failed, in my book, than to perish because you were too stubborn, and refused to listen. That your own narcissism did you in...

We can't keep going on like this. It's madness! Yet just imagine if we end up pulling it off! It'll be like paradise on Earth, my friend. Compared to today. As close to utopia as we will ever get. Clean air, yes, but also clean living, and the possibility of all of us becoming the best version of ourselves. To live the life of our dreams!

You might think I've gone mad! Even here, in my own home, without as much as a single drop of alcohol, I'm carrying on and on, like the quintessential barfly... A real blowhard! Maybe it's something in the tonic water. Maybe the quinine is poisoning me. Yet...

Well, you might think that the things I've been talking about aren't, in fact, connected. Or that I'm not using sound logic. But just take a minute to try to digest what I'm saying. Take the time to really ruminate on it on a deeper level. Look back on your own history. I'm sure you've had a number of experiences just like mine. Suffered through the same types of hurtful experiences and silently wondered why. Asked yourself why they didn't make much sense at the time—or even with the benefit of hindsight. You've probably been just as frustrated, confused and confounded as I've been. Yet, when you look at the sum total of all those traumatic experiences—the ones that you wish you could forget, the ones that you desperately run away or hide from—you'll discover that all of the suffering and pain, that was so casually dispersed, can ultimately be traced back to, with few exceptions, the solitary issue of extreme consumption—and its ugly stepchild, wealth disparity. Coupled with the need to forcibly maintain that inequity... Surely you've heard of the one percent, by now. You know the types, the ones who are idolized for their extreme wealth, but who should be properly vilified for their monstrous greed. For hoarding all the resources, and for securing their fortunes by means of a meticulously rigged game. The more they enrich themselves, the more it's at your expense. Mine, yours.... your children, the environment, and, ultimately, the Earth.

We're well on the way to driving ourselves—not to mention tens of thousands of other species—into extinction, and should be utterly appalled and ashamed that we alone are wholly responsible for this unique form of mass murder. Something never seen on the planet before, anywhere near this scale. Yet, because we've been

274

so successfully brainwashed and coached over the course of centuries, most of us are effectively blind to the vicious conspiracy that continues to plague us. It's become business as usual to everyone—no matter how persistently severe the abuse.

When are people going to wake up? What's it going to take? Where is the sense of outrage and urgency? It should feel like the greatest crisis we've ever faced. What could be more threatening and frightening? Yet, when facing grave circumstances, people always look for an easy way out when there isn't necessarily one available. No, god isn't going to swoop in at the last moment and save us. Nor will the various gurus or armchair philosophers. There're going to be all sorts of charlatans out there who are going to want to convince you that we can overcome our problems by doing more of the same, or by throwing some lifesaving technology at it. They're going to try to convince us that they'll be able to fix everything—they'll be able to control the weather on the outside, and they'll be able to manipulate our genes from the inside—so that we'll always be able to adapt in time, whatever comes our way. They'll try to convince us that we can find refuge on the Moon or Mars, and that we'll be just as fulfilled and happy there as we are on Earth. Any reputable scientist will tell you that's untenable, if not impossible, for any significant amount of time. Our bodies will not adapt sufficiently in the long run. Yet some are naïve and foolish enough to think that they'll be able to outsmart billions of years of biological evolution—the natural honing of the species—and that natural history, somehow, won't apply to them. Everything we need to solve this most ultimate existential problem is lying right beneath our noses. It's just that those relatively uncomplicated solutions, that could be done right here on Earth, aren't sexy enough, aren't profitable enough, to adequately line the pockets of the obscenely privileged.

No, my friend, just give me some basic, honest-to-god wisdom. We don't need the clever or calculating ones to tell us what to do.

We need an army of citizens who buy into the notion that science and technology work best *with* nature, not against it, starting with the resources we already have here, for the benefit of all. But even more critically, let's start listening to the folks who aren't steeped in denial—who believe in the truth borne by, for example, the fields of evolutionary biology, history, and psychology. Yes, even psychology, if I may say so myself! Ha ha!! Experts and professionals who are invested in disciplines and systems of thought that can be tested against the evidence and reality, that are coherent over time, and have checks and balances built into them —to guard against potential abuse and wholesale fraud.

And last but not least, let's start taking the poets, artists and philosophers seriously—listen to what they have to say—to keep us in touch with our humanity. Let's internalize the best of it, and externalize these values every day of our lives. That's what we should've been doing all along. The ideas've been around for a long time, they've been tested over the ages, and they've been teaching the same damned lessons. Yet, we continue to ignore them, and make the same mistakes, over and over again. Why is it so difficult for us to accept and live by the most fundamental, universally-accepted principles? The ones we all supposedly agree on. Like love, and empathy, and mutual respect. And to reject hate and mendacity, which only lead to failure and misery. If we don't start living by *some* code, very soon, or some sensible combination of well-established values, morals, and ethics—and, not least of all, solid judgement—everything we do will be in vain. You don't need gods or kings to tell you that. You just need to step up and do it. How bad will it have to get before people feel inspired? Do we need to be just a hair's breadth away from death and destruction to do something about it? Have some self-respect, for god's sake. Or at least let your survival instinct take over. Don't collapse and curl into a ball just yet. If you're not going to do it for yourself, do it for others—succeeding generations—like it's your god-given duty. I know that sounds ridiculously old-fashioned and trite, but it may just be the only way to reach the most jaded naysayers. Believe me, we'll try anything, if we're desperate enough! The worst thing, though, would be to let pride and hubris finish us off. That'd be tragic, my friend...

Just bear in mind that there's going to be an army out there that'll try to convince you otherwise. They're going try to make you believe that more of the same will lead us to salvation. There'll be false prophets everywhere, brewing up all sorts of sophisticated arguments and ingenious distractions that are likely to seduce you. All the demons, the wolves in sheep's clothing, the hypocrites, and the bad faith actors—they're already well-established and more than delighted to continue with their dirty work. Their spiritual predecessors have been around since time immemorial, inventing a dizzying array of organized religions and philosophical schools meant to exert power and control over the populace—codifying their self-serving values into a whole host of widely respected sacred texts, scholarly books, and laws. Yet, they're no more legitimate than the most ridiculous cult, and just as responsible as anyone for the mess we find ourselves in. It only stands to reason that most people, given a choice, will choose to align with them. But we must rise up and resist!

We can't continue to give our power away to them—power they don't deserve and shouldn't be trusted with anymore. You know who I'm talking about! They'll try to take your freedom away. They'll punish you if you try to resist. They'll even punish themselves, if it ultimately serves their interests. They'll enact and enforce laws that seem dubious and arbitrary, and only use them when it's to their advantage. They'll apply one set of self-serving principles for themselves, and an opposite set of self-sacrificing principles for everyone else. And above all else, the most potent tool they have for maintaining the status quo is to convince us that we're all sinners—while contending that they're all saints, demigods, and angels. The only way to stand up to it—to defeat it —is to strive to be the most authentic self you can be, whatever your limitations. Love of self, love of others, and love of the Earth. Other than that, all you need is a little grounding in history and psychology. For fighting the good fight and expiring with nothing left in the tank. That's a noble and glorious life!

What's the alternative, my friend? The fact remains, whether or not we're fully culpable for the mess we find ourselves in, we're steeping in it, nonetheless. We've built an elaborate house of cards, spanning the ages, that's teetering precariously under its own weight. It won't be able to sustain itself much longer. It's so ubiquitous, so elaborate—yet so obscured—that most of us still aren't seeing the forest for the trees. Are we going to have the foresight and wherewithal to return to the basics, and acknowledge our runaway obsessions? We've been blinded and shackled for centuries by our very own abilities and success. Let's break free of the chains that bind us—or at least get better at recognizing what works for us from what dooms us. Have more of what'll lead to our survival, and less of what'll lead to our death and destruction. We'll have to reform ourselves and our institutions—and it'll have to become second nature to us. The more we understand, the more educated we become, the more internalized it'll become in our culture and society going forward—and the better off we'll be.

Yes, we all have our faults, vulnerabilities, and weaknesses. But we also have many strengths and positive attributes—that have been acquired every step of the way, through the trials and tribulations of life—that can be leveraged against this menacing threat, this greatest and most ultimate of all possible existential challenges faced at any point in the history of mankind. Let's embrace whatever freedoms and responsibilities we have, and what experience has taught us so far, in the service of achieving this potentially magnificent and miraculous victory over ourselves! Let's live that spirit, every hour and every day! It's everywhere—

all around us—ripe for the taking! All we have to do is reach for it and run! Oh, I know... I can hear the objections and counterarguments already. They'll claim 'but that's not freedom!' Well, no, not in the way that we've become accustomed to. But we all know that every freedom has its price and limitations. We just weren't completely aware of them, and their effects. So, my friend, what I'm saying is... *now* is the time to embark on this most spectacular rebirth...

I guess I don't have to tell you, or anyone else, how poorly we, as a species, have been treating the Earth. That much is self-evident. We've been very selfish and self-centered, my friend. And now the chickens have *certainly* come home to roost. We assumed, very arrogantly, that everything that was good for us was, by definition, good for the Earth. Ha ha!! What a foolish assumption that was! What a fatal blunder! Utter collective narcissism! But that's not to say the converse *isn't* true, as I mentioned briefly before. What's good for the Earth *is* certainly good for us, by definition—and it's high time we make that our guiding principle. To honor the spirit of it, and, thus, ourselves. To approach things with a sense of humility, generosity, and a commitment to service. Maybe I haven't always lived up to that ideal, my friend, but I guess you could make a decent case for me these days, at Casablanca. I'm kind of harmless now, honestly... I guess there's something to be said for the adage 'it's better to give than to receive.' I think if you've truly internalized that principle, you've managed to arrive.

Yes, I know. I can hear the ridicule already. The scornful laughter. The sneering, the sarcasm, and the cynicism. I can envision all the supposedly enlightened and sophisticated people rolling their eyes. They're going to have a great time mocking me. I mean, I'm almost inclined to laugh myself. But go ahead, let 'em indulge. Let 'em have their fun. Because it won't last all that long. The laughter will eventually become more stifled and suppressed, over time. When they *finally* have to acknowledge the truth, deep down inside, in their bones. And feel it in their soul, in its full expression. They still might not accept it outwardly. But they won't even be able to crack a smile anymore. They'll be lucky to feel much of anything, besides the gnashing of their own teeth. They'll become utterly helpless and defeated. Because they're not actually mocking me, but their future selves, and they can't yet fathom how their taunting will come back to haunt them. All of the folks who thought that the rules didn't apply to them will be humbly licking their wounds. The ones who wanted to get 'theirs' no matter what, no matter what the expense. Yes, I know nothing's going to miraculously change overnight. Because so far, the pace has been absolutely glacial. But how else are we going to get to where we need to be? We don't have the luxury of making any more serious blunders, and correcting for them after the fact— if that's even possible.

Undoubtedly, our biggest obstacle is ourselves. Our brains. Our mode of thinking. Remember what Einstein said? What he feared most—during the Cold War, during the era of M.A.D., mutually assured destruction—was that our morals wouldn't keep pace with the destructive power of our technology. Well, my friend, we're living those days right now. The same kind of threat is hanging over our heads, but without a reciprocating, deterring factor. The fear that the world will end in an apocalypse of tens of thousands of nuclear detonations is most likely past. No, sir, our world will most probably end as a result of something much less dramatic: a seemingly infinite number of smaller explosions, combustion of all shapes and sizes, that occur every time we burn, and continue to burn, fossil fuels, with impunity. That would be the final irony, no? Yet so fitting. Mass extinction. A final, dying gasp, at the extreme end of so much hiss and fizzle! Ha ha!!

Well, there's only so much more self-examination we can do. Or so much finger-pointing. Maybe a little 'J'accuse!' *is* in order, but you know how that can go. Remember Zola? The Zola of the Dreyfus Affair? He had his finger on the pulse of the Industrial Age, long before it morphed into our modern-day age of global warming. Before the Dreyfus Affair, he wrote *La Bête humaine,* his most well-known novel. Loosely translated to English as *The Human Beast.* It's set in turn-of-the-century France, during the peak of industrialization—factories were operating at full capacity, and the steam engine was king. Smokestacks and steam locomotives billowed thick, foul clouds into the sky, covering the surrounding landscape with soot and ash. Robber barons were building fortunes on the backs of the common laborer, whose efforts, by and large, went unrewarded, and whose standard of living remained at poverty level, or barely above.

Jacques Lantier, the main protagonist, is one of those laborers. He works for the railroad as an engineer, driving his locomotive back and forth on the commuter line between Paris and Le Havre. He and his fireman, Pecqueux, whose sole task is to shovel coal into the boiler's firebox, spend much of their day on the locomotive as workmates, and spent occasional nights together during layovers. They carouse about town, looking for willing female companionship, though Pecqueux is married. Lantier, as a bachelor, is free to indulge, but has to avoid any temptation, due to a homicidal streak he has presumably inherited genetically and that he has little control over. It seems any time he has sexual feelings for a woman, he feels an equally intense compulsion to kill her. So, he tries to avoid women, despite his longing for them.

To compensate for this blood-curdling aspect of his personality, Lantier channels all his frustration and libidinous energy into his job as an engine driver. He takes a great deal of pride in his competence and professionalism—making sure his locomotive is in perfect running order, that it exceeds every performance expectation, and never fails to arrive to each station on time—to the best of his ability. He is utterly and hopelessly dedicated to the

281

engine—as if it is the only thing he truly loves, with an almost erotic passion. So much so that he gives the locomotive a feminine name, 'La Lison'. He cares for it like a prized, most precious possession—sacrificing himself to it—despite the way it, in turn, 'abuses' him, day in and day out. He leaves work every day covered in sweat, soot and ash, yet is happy that 'La Lison' continues to serve his interests so well.

In the end, however, 'La Lison' isn't enough to save him. After a number of dramatic and complex plot twists, involving intense jealousies between various characters and the execution of a will involving a sizeable estate, Lantier eventually succumbs to his murderous impulses—but only after 'La Lison' is sabotaged and destroyed following a mysterious, catastrophic derailment. He kills a female co-conspirator, just before they are about to murder her husband, but, ironically, gets away with the crime. As fate has it, though, he dies a violent death soon afterwards. While he and his fireman have been reassigned to a new locomotive, Lantier is still despondent over 'La Lison'. He becomes increasingly aimless and ill-tempered—culminating, ultimately, in a vicious brawl with his fireman Pecqueux, who has discovered that Lantier has been having an affair with his wife. They hash it out atop the speeding train—both plunging to their gruesome and untimely deaths.

Meanwhile, the runaway train continues to hurtle down the line carrying a load of unsuspecting passengers. It's overflowing with drunken, blindly patriotic soldiers who are headed for the front—in a recently declared war between France and Prussia—who are oblivious to the bloody disaster that lies ahead of them... You know, Zola couldn't have been more insightful or prophetic! You might not be following the exact line of my reasoning, but I've alluded to *La Bête humaine,* specifically, to illustrate an essential point—that is, we're more or less living our own version of that plot, right now. Personally, and on a societal level. There are millions, if not billions, of Lantiers out there today. Burning fossil fuels with abandon and impunity while vehemently denying the reality of climate change. A perfect recipe for self-destruction. The difference, however, is that Lantier *knew* he was sick. He *knew* what was wrong with him, and what was wrong with society. He was aware of his sinister side, yet resisted it. He knew he was at least partly to blame, but that other societal forces, greater than himself, were also undermining his better self. It's time to admit that most of us are the Lantiers of our time, and quite a few of us are like the soldiers on the runaway train. The fact is, we've all been infected with this illness—we're all sick, our species is sick, and we're living in a very sick society. We'd better stop the train, or at least try to jump off it before it's too late. Yes, my friend, we're on that runaway train whether we like it or not. We've got to stop adding coal to the fire. Got to stop feeding the engine...

I have to admit that I'm not too optimistic about the future. Because there's more to the story regarding Zola's very public political advocacy at the time, that only engenders more pessimism. Do you know much about Zola himself, any of the details of his life? Did you know that Zola had to flee for his life from France at one point? Yes, that's another instructive story that I have for your edification. A true story, but in many ways, stranger than fiction. Do you know how Zola died? The seeds of his demise began with the Dreyfus Affair. Do you remember the specifics of *that* seedy tale?

It took place at the turn of the century, in the wake of the Franco-Prussian War, but before World War I. Decades earlier, the French had suffered a humiliating military defeat, culminating in the loss of the Alsace-Lorraine region to an alliance of German states. Territorial resentments smoldered, and French society was also infected with a particularly virulent strain of antisemitism. There was widespread fear that another conflict was imminent, and the same combination of powers continued to jockey for position, even after a tentative peace had been established. There was spying going on by both sides, including for the purposes of gaining military advantage. The French had developed a new artillery gun, had discovered that some of their technical secrets had been transmitted to the Germans, and were in hot pursuit of the guilty, treasonous party. On the basis of some very shoddy evidence, they arrested Alfred Dreyfus, an unassuming French artillery officer of Jewish descent. Even though they subsequently had very compelling evidence against another French officer, they suppressed that evidence and successfully prosecuted Dreyfus for treason. Not just once, but twice! Dreyfus was stripped of his military status and exiled for life. Both trials were mockeries of justice, clearly biased by the prevailing political, cultural and racial prejudices of the time. The miscarriage of justice became an international scandal. The whole world was talking about it and taking sides.

Because of Zola's esteemed status within French society, his opinions were taken very seriously and held in high regard. He saw the injustice, and was determined to do something about it, to right the wrongs that had been perpetrated. He wrote an open letter to one of the prominent newspapers of the time, entitled 'J'accuse... !', that advocated for Dreyfus' innocence, but also charged the French military courts and government with corruption. It ignited a major scandal, and the figures he accused of misconduct countered by accusing him of libel. Again, the evidence was questionable and the court was similarly suspect. Yet, he was summarily convicted of the charges and sentenced to a year in jail. His friends convinced him to flee to England, until it was safe for him to return.

Then, as time passed, irrefutable exculpatory evidence surfaced, false testimony was exposed—with respect to Dreyfus' case—and more sympathetic political administrations came into power. To make a long story short, both Dreyfus and Zola were eventually able to return to France after their offenses were more or less vacated, after many years of devoted advocacy by numerous parties on their behalf. Oddly, the true culprit was finally charged with the original espionage, but acquitted. Dreyfus returned to the military, eventually rising to the rank of colonel and serving with distinction during World War I. Ironically, during his service on the front lines, he deployed the very same artillery weaponry that was at the center of the original espionage case against him; and, in addition, earned the Legion of Honour, the highest order of merit that can be bestowed by the French military! He died at the ripe old age of seventy-five.

Zola, on the other hand, died at sixty-two, only three years after his return to France. He had long since established himself as one of France's greatest writers, and was buried in Montmartre Cemetery before being reinterred at the Pantheon six years later. Dreyfus was present for both interments, and narrowly escaped an assassination attempt at the second. But the most curious, and least known, aspect of this whole affair were the circumstances surrounding Zola's death. His death was originally attributed to an accidental carbon monoxide poisoning, the result of improper ventilation in his home. The official story held for nearly fifty years, despite evidence that there were many embittered people involved in the Dreyfus affair who still had their sights set on both Dreyfus and Zola, who maintained that they were guilty as charged, and that they should pay dearly for their 'crimes'.

Then one day, in 1953, a physician reported a seemingly routine death to the civil authorities, but with a seriously shocking claim: that his patient had made a deathbed confession, that the deceased had confessed that he was responsible for Zola's death. He claimed he was a chimney sweep in Paris decades before, and that he had purposely sealed the chimney to Zola's apartment to exact ultimate retribution.

Yes, my friend, stranger things have happened. But how's that for closing the circle? The moral of the story is, be very careful pointing fingers, my friend! Ha ha! It might not turn out exactly the way you imagined, or hoped it would! That's the kind of craziness that goes on. That's what we're up against when people aren't willing to see reality for what it is, and aren't willing change, despite the irrefutable facts. Well, anyway... even if you want to twist everything around, there's nowhere left to escape to, anymore! And there's no other way out but to convince people to be their better selves, to be humble enough to change their hearts, minds and actions, when it's most imperative.

Ugh, it's just killing me, thinking about all this stuff! I just keep repeating myself, like a broken record. Do you mind going over to the window and opening it up a bit? I'm still feeling a little unwell. It's so stuffy and stifling in here! Thank you, my friend. You know, every time I get deep into it, into these thoughts that hound me... I think I die a little. I always start feeling a little queasy. Is it too hot in here, or too cold? I'm never quite sure... Poor Zola! The poor guy was just trying to sound the alarm. Not just writing about it, but by leading by example. He really sacrificed himself for the greater good, that's for sure. Is there still such a thing as the greater good, or leading by example anymore? There *is* a certain arrogance to it, don't you think? You know the type, the proselytizers who preach from the bully pulpit? It can be so annoying. Ha ha!! I know, I get the irony! It can be downright *embarrassing*. The pedantry! The sophistry!! Yes, my friend. There's lots of it out there, and a lot of us are guilty of wielding it, to some extent. Yet in certain cases, it might very well be a necessary evil. And our only real hope.

Do you understand how painful it is for me to have to keep going on about this stuff, talking about it this way? It almost disgusts me, honestly. To have to endlessly reiterate all the truisms, platitudes, and tired old cliches. The empty tautologies. The trite, stock phrases. How do you think that makes *me* feel? I wish I didn't have to have anything to do with it, I assure you. But

286

that, my friend, is unfortunately not my lot. There's no escaping it. My hand has been forced by all the deniers and hypocrites out there. They're the ones who should be feeling *double* the shame and disgust... Quite the quandary, don't you think? Not an easy life, by any means. It's like boxing with one hand tied behind your back. You might be able to get a good jab in, but that might make it nearly impossible to block an incoming punch. Thus, the Witness/Confidant role, my friend. I'm just asking questions. Not that different from being a therapist, from how a good therapist should practice. Or a little like our old friend Socrates. The method is as old as time itself. It may be modern times. But what better time to apply ancient technique.

Yes, my friend, the end is near. The end of times, perhaps, but most definitely the end of the road for me. Quite literally. What choice did I have, really? It was so obvious, in my case. It couldn't have happened any other way. When those young children were gunned down, slaughtered, it was the beginning of the end for me. I quickly lost my faith in life, in the world, in myself. I had no direction. But I got in the car, nonetheless. Eventually. Or should I say, my body forced me into the car. I didn't know what I was doing or where I was going or what I was looking for. But I took that leap of faith anyway, that's for sure. I took my time traveling across the country. I didn't have a route planned out at all. I might've ended up back in New York, for all I knew. But something was pulling me West. I assumed it was the pull of the familiar, the pull of where I grew up and spent the formative years of my life. Or just to be far away from where I was at the time. Something about getting west of the Mississippi. Or west of the mountains. The wide-open landscapes and the clean, crisp air. Yes, nature was calling me back, I thought. I lingered in and around the Rockies for some time. I assumed I was looking for some kind of inner peace, to internalize the lush and

287

bountiful environment I was in. Something to lift my spirits, to cleanse me, to carry me along.

Then, suddenly, the impulse to continue into the desert. Those stunning desert vistas seemed to be speaking to me, too. They seemed to be matching the mood I was in. But within a month's time, I felt the urge to move on again. I remember feeling like I had gotten to the end of the road somewhere near the north rim of the Grand Canyon. From there, it made perfect sense for me to decide to head back toward L.A. There were only a little more than 500 miles, or about ten hours, left to go.

I remember approaching Las Vegas on the highway from the northeast, midday. Much of the drive up until that point had been through some rather uninspiring terrain, of the scrub brush variety. Then, eventually, signs of human habitation started popping up on the horizon. And a dramatic backdrop of arid, rugged mountains appeared. Finally, the city itself, in all its gaudy, decadent glory! I was just about to blow by the Strip when I felt compelled to pull off the freeway. Maybe I realized I was going to be hitting some more long stretches of desert soon, after the city, and needed some relief, but I ended up exiting and driving randomly by the New York, New York Casino complex, on Tropicana. It occurred to me, then, how odd it was that I had never been to Las Vegas before. I had never been attracted to it, but because it was right in front of me, I figured it was my chance to take a brief look in.

Well, you might guess what happened next. There actually was something comforting about the ersatz New York motif, especially the replica of the Statue of Liberty outside. But, also something disconcerting, like the feeling you get watching that famous scene in *Planet of the Apes*, when Charlton Heston discovers Lady Liberty half-buried in the sand. That was enough to convince me to stop for the night. Well, the day turned into night, and the following days turned into more than a week's stay, ultimately. Despite my apprehension, I enjoyed my stay tremendously. After so many weeks on the road, it was nice to just sleep in a comfortable bed. To have a good shower and clean linen. I also enjoyed a few good meals, a good number of drinks, sitting by the pool; even a visit to the hotel spa and an evening out. I really let myself go, and indulged in the luxuries that were available and that my body needed so desperately.

Then, one evening, by chance, I discovered Casablanca! To be sure, it was a natural fit, given my previous connection to the film business. That's when I ran into my old friend, who's now the barkeeper, for the first time, and the case with the fedora sitting in it. What a joy it was to just sit there in the bar and catch up with my former colleague, and have a few chats now and again, with random customers. I really did miss the company of people after being off by myself for so long.

That's when the thought of continuing on to L.A. and home seemed to fade from my consciousness. I guess I feared going home for the same reasons I had left it: that I would still feel like a stranger among my friends and family members, and the familiar sites of my youth. Las Vegas seemed much more appealing to me, much to my surprise. In fact, after that first week or so in the hotel, I decided to stay on for another few weeks. It turned out that my friend the bartender had a short-term rental on hand, not too far from Casablanca, and that he was willing to let it to me. I stayed there for a long time—months—going back and forth between Casablanca and my new apartment, on an increasingly regular basis. It was Casablanca, itself, though, that eventually sold me on staying for good. It began quite innocently, but then became the natural setting for my soon-to-be-identified mission. I'm not sure I can pinpoint exactly when I bridged that gulf, but it was inevitable. It was my destiny! I can see things so much more clearly here. Maybe it's the desert air. But where else can you find such an abundance of potential clients? The strategy was, and still is, very simple. So many people passing through, with their guards down.

Stripped down to bare essentials. Pilgrims separated from the comfort of their homes and native environments—from all over the world! Fleeing the humdrum of their mundane lives. Looking and hoping for some kind of temporary refuge. With such a diversity of thoughts and beliefs and motivations and doubts. What could be better? The great masses in search of an escape, any way out! Yes, they're always the most appreciative audiences, and the best pool to cull clients from. That's why I hung up my shingle and jumped right in.

No, this is not therapy. Decidedly not. Not in the usual sense. Otherwise, you'd be paying for it. I wouldn't be doing most of the talking, either, I assure you. And anyone, I mean anyone, can grab a seat across from me and decide if and when they want to engage with me, and whether to continue to engage with me. There are no hard-set rules about that. But what is most crucial is that my guest engages willingly and freely, without too much pressure from me. I'm not here to force anyone to accept what I'm saying. I'm here to allow people to decide for themselves if anything I'm saying makes sense to them. That's it. Let's just pretend we're good friends of a longstanding nature, and we meet regularly at Casablanca to chat. Like an old English pub, the good old 'public house', where people meet to have conversations. I know that's hard in this day and age, with all the distractions around us. But you'll notice that Casablanca doesn't have any TVs. Pretty rare in this town. With all the betting going on, all the sports wagering, especially. Causes such a commotion! No, just me and my guest and a couple of drinks a piece to loosen things up a bit. I'll only insist that you put the cell phone down.

I have to give you a lot of credit for hanging in here today. Coming to visit me in my home is a rare and special distinction. Especially because you've only got one more day before you go home and I've been afflicted with my usual ailment. I'm afraid there wasn't much choice. You needn't worry, though, there's nothing to fear. Nothing I can't handle, and, like I said, the ailment certainly isn't contagious, in the usual sense. But I also want to commend you for holding on for so long. For five straight days! Yes, you're an exceptional specimen! I can never predict how long someone will stay with me, ahead of time. It might be a few minutes, an hour, a half a day; but I really know I've gotten somewhere if it turns out to be multiple days in a row. No one would take *that* much time out of their visit here if they didn't see some greater point to it. No, sir, not likely! There's so much else to do, so many more seductive things to dive into.

On the other hand, I can tell pretty quickly if I'm not going to really click with someone. It'll start out with idol chitchat and end with idol chitchat. After fifteen minutes of that, I'm only too happy to encourage them to go. Of course, they usually can't wait to go, and it's fun to watch how they'll try to back out of the conversation. There's a fixed number of techniques and excuses, my friend. But I certainly won't take it personally. I'm not here to be friends, as you've probably gathered by now. Usually, I just wait for someone to sit down nearby, at one of the surrounding handful of tables, and sit in silence. It's like that silence is a hole that *has* to be filled. People can't stand it until it's resolved in some way. And as soon as they offer up the most innocent gesture, whether verbal or not, you can be sure that I will counter with something, anything to get my hooks in, to see if it will lead in a fruitful direction. It's amazing how skilled I've become at it. It didn't come naturally, if it ever did, because therapists are discouraged and trained *not* to act like that. It's beaten out of them, for the most part. In psychotherapy, the patient leads, ideally. For the patient's ultimate benefit. But we don't really have that kind of time on our hands anymore. I have to jump in like I'm the co-pilot. I don't want to be too obvious about it, because even the most naïve person will quickly sense that. But it's good to get personal right away, because if you divulge, if you expose yourself, if you make yourself vulnerable from the get-go, the ones you hope to engage with will probably go there with you. It's a telltale sign that I'll have a good chance to get through to the end. The more it feels like we're melding into one, the better. When their thoughts and attitudes start reflecting my thoughts and attitudes, and vice versa, we've got a good thing going. Sometimes, you'll even start to attract other people's attention in the room, if the sympathetic vibrations are really potent. That's when I know I'll have another customer, sooner than later. But only one at a time! That's a strict rule for me. I'll have to 'schedule' them in for later. Otherwise, I might lose the original customer, and our train of thought.

You see, it's not too different from any other business. Except the goal isn't necessarily immediately tangible, in the usual sense. But when things are going well, I can always tell. It's almost as if when I'm looking across the table at you, I start seeing myself. I often wonder if the opposite happens, too. Whether they see themselves in me. Certainly, something like that is going on psychologically, at bare minimum. But, sometimes, it's so intense and intimate that I have to look away, for a moment. Then I try to gather the courage to collect my wits again and refocus on the task at hand. Hopefully, when the mission is over, and accomplished, that same sense of unity will return, but with a distinctly different feeling—less intense, more like a warm bath. It's like we're both in the same frame of mind, kind of like a pleasant dream. I imagine myself whispering 'I am you, and you are me' over and over again, under my breath. I hope you're feeling similarly. But no need for any kind of response. No, my friend, that would be going much too far. That would be a little too familiar, even for me. Let's agree to have some amount of separation, my friend. It's only decent to keep some sort of veil between us.

I only say that for your protection. I can take care of myself. But that's not to say that I'm completely confident that I'll be able to keep everyone safe, given what they might bring to the table. We don't want to find ourselves falling into a classic folie à deux, after all. But you can trust me completely with the mystical part. When I sense a merging between myself and the client, I think I understand them better. And I think I understand myself better. I can see things that I don't normally see. If we've done it right, everything seems more transparent. As if you can penetrate deeper, really see inside each other. I can see my whole history in you, and how much effort it took for us to get to where we are. I wonder if people around us can sense it, too. Can see that we've walked down a precarious, but rewarding, path together? And not only survived, but thrived. That we'll both continue on in that spirit, that we'll never feel alone or abandon each other. We might feel exhausted by the experience, but we'll always feel connected. That's when 'I am you, and you are me' turns into 'We are.'

Maybe that sounds a bit creepy, but that's kind of the way it goes. That's kind of the way it feels. I hope that's not too alarming to you. You never know how people are going to react to that revelation, but the ones who hang on until the end never seem to mind. Then again, they're not pushovers, either. You sort of know who's who from the start. I knew I would be able to reach you, but that it wasn't necessarily going to be easy. I always wonder if my counterpart senses that as well. Not everyone is capable of following through all the way. Just because there's a dialogue doesn't mean that we're necessarily going to get there. It's a bit of a Catch-22. You have to take a Zen-like approach. You need to let yourself go, which often means suppressing the overly intellectual part of yourself so that it doesn't interfere with the flow. If you have to explain it step-by-step in excruciating detail, it's likely to fall apart. The more you try *not* to fail, the more likely it is that you will.

Hopefully you've been feeling good vibes all along, and have internalized it the further we go. Have you noticed anything like that? Have you felt it? Yes, I thought so! You did feel it, after all! That's a good sign. If you're ever feeling like it's fading away, you can always come back into town for a refresher. Chances are, I'll still be around, and we can start right where we left off. Isn't it wonderful! It feels so good to be here every day. I finally found my rightful place in the universe. Casablanca has become my rightful home. At this point, everyone *expects* me to be there. They're used to my routine. My presence is predictable. I have the freedom to go about my business on my own terms, with few constraints. Free from the limitations of the past. The shackles have been cast off! That's real freedom! Are you feeling that? The goal is to rediscover yourself and like who you've found.

Yes, ever since I set up shop here, and got the operation going, I strive for more freedom each day. Sometimes I hit the mark. And sometimes I fall short. But I really ended up honing it to the degree that it started filtering into each and every aspect of my life. It felt so gratifying to feel the weight of decades gradually lifting from my shoulders. It seems like I'm spending less and less time ruminating on things that I have no control over, or can't change, and more time focusing on the present. If I feel a strong pull toward acting on something, I do. If I feel uninspired, that's fine, too. I give myself permission to let go. I try to let the spirit of the moment dictate the direction I'm headed in.

Then there are days when I feel more like a tumbleweed blowing in the wind. When I have those moments of doubt, I drive out into the desert and let it cleanse my mind of all the noise and clutter. The isolation and austerity of the landscape cleanses and reorients me. I try to pretend as if I'm a wild animal for a moment, just taking it all in and reacting according to instinct. But inevitably, I feel the pull back to Casablanca, where I'm the king of my modest, but glorious, domain. The pull of my awakening, the calling that began that night I was baptized with blood, is just too strong. I can't help myself. I need to surround myself with people who end up here, who are within reach. I strive to be in communion with them, if they're open to it.

So, don't forget about me after you return home. Like I said, you can always come back for a visit. You can always come back to Casablanca to reconnect. My friend, would you mind bringing me a glass of water? I'm so parched from all this talk. I just keep going on and on about it. It takes a terrible toll. Anyway, if you come back, we can go even further. I can show you how it's done. How this operation works in fine detail. You can start your own thing, too! Wherever you happen to be, you can get into this business, get your own customers, continue with the work that has to be done. Preach the gospel, so to speak. And then you'll attract your own disciples. And so on and so forth.

You know I'll be back at Casablanca tonight, well after you've already taken off and are safely flying through the clouds toward home. I'll be searching again for someone just like you—just like us—at just the right moment of vulnerability. Of course, we'll order a couple shots of very fine tequila from our dependable friend, the bartender. We'll feel that slow-burning sensation down our throats, and I'll know that we're back in the running again. It's so potent and intoxicating, yet exhilarating and exciting at the same time, knowing that there's a real possibility that the next stranger who pulls into port is ready for the journey. I hold court, as you've seen with your own eyes, and hope that that powerful feeling of fellowship wells up in me exactly the way it did with you. I try to act without prejudice and I hope to succeed in convincing our comrades that the journey is worthwhile. It's almost like falling in love, if I might be so bold. It can start as soon as we've committed to sit near each other, with those first furtive gestures. But it's never certain, and there's always a tinge of sadness sprinkled in, knowing that an opportunity can vanish just as quickly as it's appeared. Wondering if the breach will ultimately be bridged or not. With the values and faithfulness that we've been talking about for all these nights. That a new era might slowly be shepherded in by a growing army of true believers.

Yes, I'm getting a little carried away again! But these thoughts keep coming, and they keep me going! They make me want to spring out of bed. I look forward to the early mornings, when the sun is just coming up over the horizon, when most people are still sleeping, all over the world, and only society's outcasts are tucked away on the streets. There are the first rustlings of the day, whether human or animal, all under a dome of pink. I love to get out for a good, long walk before the rest of the world has to get up to prepare for the hustle and bustle of their everyday lives. They long to remain in the comfort and safety of their beds, but dream of a time when they can get away, unwind, and put their minds at ease. When given half the chance, many of them end up here, coming by the planeload, to this city of ours. It makes me happy to think that they're on their way. Yes, they land like eagle feathers floating down from the sky, and it makes me want to soar!

But I better not get too excited, not now. I'm still not ready to get up. I'm already overdoing it. I've got to save my energy for later. My mission never ends. It's good work, but difficult. And it's been such a long, long journey for me already, to get to precisely where I'm meant to be. It's not like everything's going to change overnight, or as if what I'm doing is going change the world, but what choice do you really have? You can only try to make your best contribution. When the goal seems so remote, and potentially unobtainable, process is the only thing left to cling to, ultimately. It will keep you healthy and sane. I finally learned that lesson. I've finally seen the light and will continue to chase after it.

Look! Look out the window! The wind is whipping up now, and the dust is starting to blind our view. A storm has suddenly descended upon us, and the city. Where have all the lights gone? Even the neon has disappeared. The dust is trying to get to us. It's trying to come through the windows. Look at it pile up, like a plague of locusts! Is that what the future holds? Are we going to do what we have to do? How will we stop it? Or is it just going to sweep us away?

Well, you better stay for a little while longer. Now is certainly not the time to go out. But tell me, friend, after spending all this time with me. Do you think I've lost my mind? Am I out of my wits? Is it hopeless? I hope not. I hope everyone proves me wrong. I'm counting on you, and an army of others like you, to pull us through. Please prove me wrong!

Remember *Casablanca*? The film? Who do you think you're more like? Are you more Rick, or more Victor Laszlo? That's a tough call because, I admit, they both have their strengths and weaknesses. Here! Try it on! Let's see how the fedora looks on you! Don't be shy. Oh, it looks nice on you! Either way, it fits. I often feel more like Rick, especially when I'm holding court at Casablanca. The fedora makes me feel safe, as if it shields and protects me. Then again, I often wish I was more like Laszlo. The crucial thing is to avoid becoming the enemy, an opportunist, or, worse yet, a collaborator. Given a real choice, who do you think Ilsa, the object of their affections, would have ended up with? Who do you think Ilsa truly loved? Rick or Laszlo? I don't know. I can never make up my mind. All I know is that I'm just going to continue doing what I've been doing.

Wouldn't it be hilarious if you turned out to be a cop? What if it turned out you were more like Rick and Laszlo's adversary, Captain Renault, the prefect of police? If you had to bust me right now? You're not? No, I didn't think so. I can tell pretty quickly who's who. No, you're kidding! What's the likelihood of that? Oh, I should have known! You've been so patient with me. You've listened so carefully. Of course, you're a *therapist*! It's only *too* fitting. Who else would've sat here all these days and hours and listened so attentively? You're likely *already* on the right course. On the hunt for the truth. Tell me, what do you think you would've done if you'd been here the night of the shooting, the night of the massacre? Would you have had an awakening, like me? Have you had an opportunity like that, to be born again? Would you choose the right path? Have you chosen the right path already? I shouldn't presume you haven't… But, are we one? Can we say 'We are?' I know the waters are cold. But don't worry. Dive right in! It might already be too late to change your mind…

Finita la commedia

GIOVANNI MAC ÍOMHAIR

Descent of Man

Dear Reader,

Lest you think this novel a pure work of fiction—or a mere parody, in the broadest sense of the term—please be advised that nearly all of the clinical scenarios included in this narrative are taken from the real-life case histories of a single mental health practitioner.

G.M.

IVORY
JOVE
PRESS

Made in the USA
Monee, IL
27 October 2021